THE LUCIFER CODE

FORGE BOOKS BY CHARLES BROKAW

The Atlantis Code

THE LUCIFER CODE

CHARLES BROKAW

FORGE®

A TOM DOHERTY ASSOCIATES BOOK

NEW YORK

For my wife, with love.
You make it all possible.

THE LUCIFER CODE

Maps by Rhys Davies

A Forge Book
Published by Tom Doherty Associates, LLC
175 Fifth Avenue
New York, NY 10010

www.tor-forge.com

ISBN 978-0-7653-2093-3

First Edition: August 2010

Printed in the United States of America

0 9 8 7 6 5 4 3 2 1

ACKNOWLEDGMENTS

Thanks to my agent, the excellent Robert Gottlieb at Trident Media, and to my family and students, who are the light of my life.

To the wonderful folks at Tor, including Tom Doherty, Bob Gleason, Linda Quinton, and Ashley Cardiff; I can't thank you enough for your professionalism and enthusiasm.

The Journey of Thomas Lourds
ROMANIA
CROATIA
BOSNIA AND HERZEGOVINA
YUGOSLAVIA
BULGARIA
Black Sea
MONTENEGRO
Rome
ITALY
Istanbul
MACEDONIA
EASTERN MACEDONIA & THRACE
Sea of Marmara
ALBANIA
Tyrrhenian Sea
GREECE
Gulf of Taranto
TURKEY
Ionian Sea
Athens
SICILY
PATMOS
Mediterranean Sea
RHODES
Aegean Sea
CRETE
Rhys Davies 2010

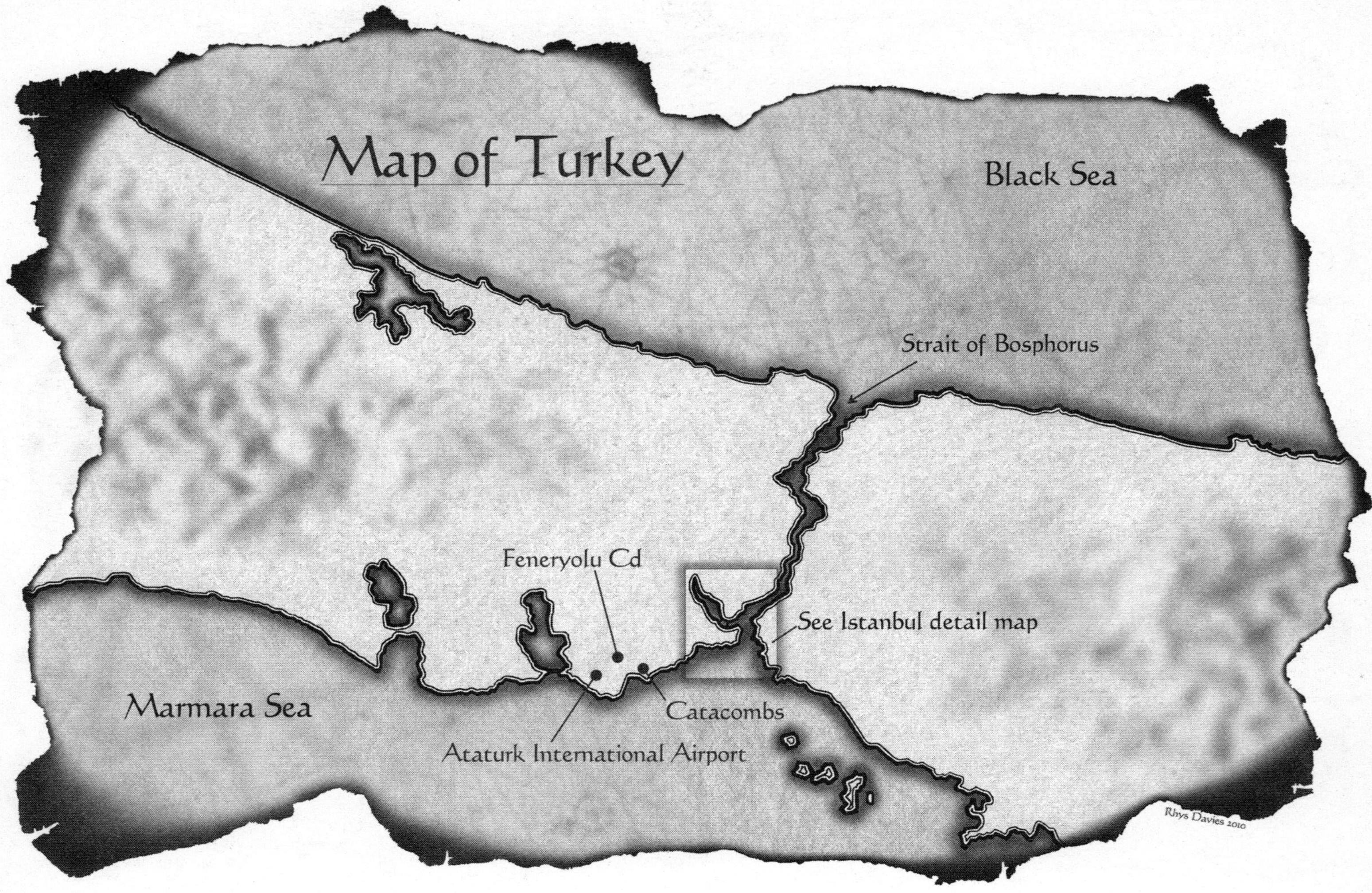
Map of Turkey
Black Sea
Strait of Bosphorus
Feneryolu Cd
See Istanbul detail map
Marmara Sea
Catacombs
Ataturk International Airport
Rhys Davies 2010

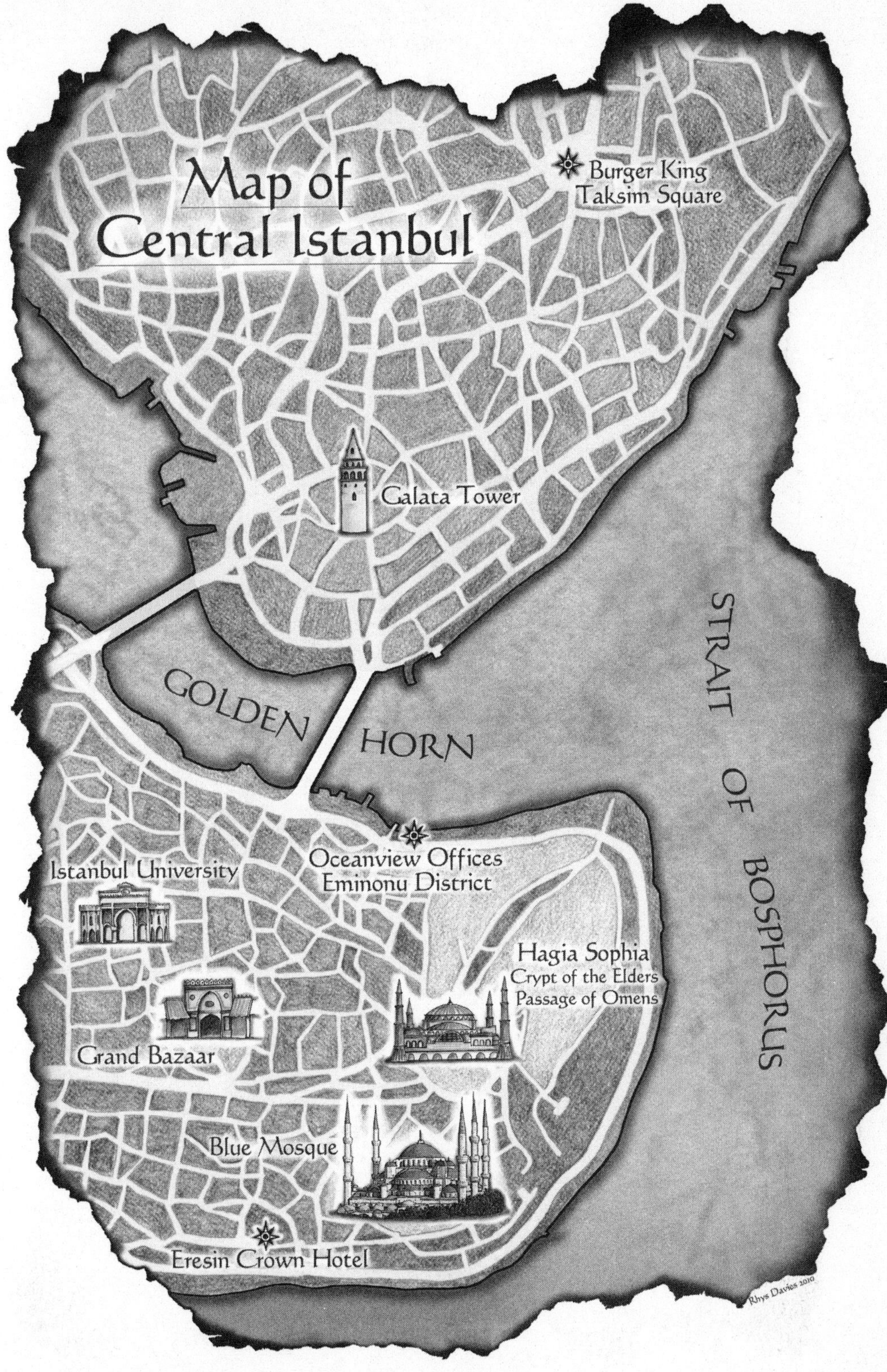
Map of
Central Istanbul
Burger King
Taksim Square
Galata Tower
GOLDEN
HORN
STRAIT OF BOSPHORUS
Oceanview Offices
Eminonu District
Istanbul University
Hagia Sophia
Crypt of the Elders
Passage of Omens
Grand Bazaar
Blue Mosque
Eresin Crown Hotel
Rhys Davies 2010

THE LUCIFER CODE

CHAPTER 1

ATATURK İNTERNATİONAL AİRPORT
YESİLKOY DİSTRİCT
İSTANBUL, TURKEY
MARCH 15, 2010

"Professor Lourds. *Professor Lourds.*"

Dr. Thomas Lourds heard his name being called above the cacophony of languages surrounding him. He wasn't expecting anyone to meet him here inside the crowded passenger terminal of Istanbul's busy international airport. He didn't recognize the voice either—but he could tell it was a young woman's. Thanks to years of teaching college students at Harvard, not to mention a well-earned reputation as a ladies' man, he was rarely wrong when he gauged a woman's age from her voice. Curious, he stepped out of the flow of pedestrian traffic rushing through the airport toward baggage and ground transportation on the lower level.

A pretty redhead waved at him from twenty feet back and fought to get through the crowd between them. A mother leading two small children glared at the young woman. Not every traveler was upset—a young man in his midtwenties wearing a bright French football jersey studied the woman who'd jostled him in open admiration.

There was a lot to like. Tall and lean, she moved with the fluid grace of an athlete or a dancer. Lourds admired the view, too. She was dressed in hip-hugger jeans and a crop top that exposed some impressive cleavage above and a tanned midriff below. A diamond gleamed in her navel, emphasizing toned abs. Her dark red hair curled and glided across her bare freckled shoulders. But try as he might, Lourds couldn't remember meeting her before.

"You *are* Professor Thomas Lourds, right?" The young woman came to an abrupt stop in front of Lourds. Her hazel eyes drank him in. "If you're not, I'm gonna really be embarrassed."

Lourds smiled a little bashfully. It was a look he could pull off when the occasion called for it. He was nearly old enough to be her father, so he figured a little bashfulness on his part might quell the disparaging looks he was receiving from some of the passersby.

"I'm Thomas Lourds." He shifted his cracked leather backpack to his other shoulder and extended his hand. "If we've met, I have to apologize. Your name slips my mind."

"No, we haven't met." She shook hands. Her grip was surprisingly firm, with soft skin toughened at the base of her fingers and the heel of her hand. The young lady must work out a lot.

"You relieve my mind. I didn't think I'd forget meeting such a beautiful young woman. And if I had, someone should shoot me and put me out of my misery."

The redhead smiled at him.

Slow down, Lourds chided himself. *You'll scare her away.*

But the chance meeting perked up his day considerably. He'd spent the last several hours on a British Airways plane from London. The first class seating had been perfect—except for the septuagenarian he'd been stuck with the whole way. She'd regaled him with stories about her life and her digestive tract, and he'd plied himself with wine in self-defense. He still felt some of the aftereffects from the zinfandel and fully intended to lose the card the woman had pressed into his hand at the end of the trip.

Or possibly burn it in effigy.

"You must think I'm crazy," the redhead continued, "calling after you in an airport, but I really wanted to see you."

Lourds released her hand and smiled. "How else were you going to get my attention?"

"True. But I would have liked to be a little more subtle and not so fan girl when I met you."

"Are you an admirer of the study of linguistics?" Lourds had written a few books and several articles in that field.

"Not exactly." She reached into her carry-on bag and brought out a hardback book.

Lourds recognized the lurid red-and-gold foil cover. It featured a languid, barely dressed male lounging in the shadows of a veiled bed. The man looked like he'd just stepped from a Calvin Klein ad. He also, Lourds had been told by women, looked like he would be everything a woman could dream of.

That cover had sold a lot of books, and Lourds had enjoyed cashing the royalty checks. The image had also been a boon to his love life. He'd discovered a long time ago that women loved to talk about sex with him, thanks to that cover. Lourds chose to pursue the subject intimately whenever the appropriate chance presented itself.

And there had been a lot of chances over his career. Even before the publication of the book the redhead held.

"Ah." Lourds grinned. "You're a reader."

"I am." She proffered the book. "I saw you, and I had to try to get your autograph. I figured it was serendipity. So here I am."

"I'd be happy to sign your book for you." Lourds took the copy and rummaged in his pocket for a pen.

"Here." She handed him a ballpoint.

"I gather you enjoyed it?"

"I did," she agreed. "But I prefer the CD. I'm on my second copy of the audio book. I wore the first one out. I love your voice. I turn out the lights and listen to it in my bedroom a lot." She paused, winced, and bit her lip. "Well, that wasn't awkward and embarrassing, was it?"

Lourds waved the comment away. "The audio book publisher insisted that I read the book after she heard me deliver a presentation on the translation."

The publisher had been young and lovely, and had taken a very personal interest in seeing to it that Lourds was treated like royalty.

"The book says everything written in there is true. Is it?"

Lourds couldn't count the number of times he'd been asked that question. The fourth-century scroll containing the narrative published as *Bedroom Pursuits* had made Professor Thomas Lourds a household name. It had also made him something of a white elephant and favorite bastard son at Harvard. The dean of the distinguished university still winced every time he thought of the subject matter of Lourds's bestseller. The original document Lourds had decoded detailed the numerous and various acts of sexual congress of its author in lurid detail. Lourds's translation hadn't skimped on those details.

Personally, Lourds didn't know anything about the author other than what his translation of the scroll had revealed. Given the sexual escapades the man had described himself as having, as well as the natural equipment he'd written about, Lourds figured if the man had been real, he must have been a physical marvel with the stamina of a god.

"Do you think it's true?" Lourds countered.

"God, I hope so."

"Well, I don't know how true the tales are. I just translated them from the original language—"

"And performed the audio presentation."

Lourds nodded. "I did. But the sound studio upgraded the quality of my voice and added background music."

"Kenny G, right?"

"Well, someone that sounds an awfully lot like him."

"I think you have a magnificent voice even without the background music." The redhead gave him a sultry smile.

"Well . . . thank you," Lourds said.

"I am *such* a geek." The young woman looked mortified. "I bet you get this all the time."

"Actually, no. Usually only at book signings. Most people don't recognize me."

"Your picture is right on the back of the book. How can they not know who you are?" She took the volume from Lourds and flipped it over to reveal the color photograph of him on the back.

It was a good picture and Lourds knew it. In it, he stood in front of a dig site in Cádiz, Spain, where Atlantis had been lost, and found, and then lost again. He'd written a book on that discovery and it had become a bestseller as well. But *Bedroom Pursuits* stayed at the top of the lists.

In the picture, Lourds wore khaki pants, hiking boots, an olive drab khaki shirt left open to show the white T-shirt beneath, and his beloved Australian Outback hat. He had that hat on right now. In the picture, his sunglasses hung nonchalantly from his T-shirt collar. He leaned casually on a shovel, and the mouth of a cave yawned in the stone wall behind him. His black hair was longish, a couple weeks overdue for the barber, and hung down slightly in his face. He sported a short-cropped goatee. Except for the outfit, he hadn't changed much since the picture was taken. He knew he looked at least ten years younger than his true age. It had its uses. Especially when he was interested in younger women.

"Believe it or not," Lourds said ruefully, "most people don't even read the author's name on a book. And fewer still remember the author's face. Meetings like this are something that usually only happens to rock stars and actors."

"Well, you are the first author I've chased down."

"I'm glad you did. But you have me at a disadvantage." Lourds held the pen poised over the title page in the book. "Whom should I make this out to?"

"Kristine. Kristine Webber. With a *K*."

" 'For Kristine,' " Lourds said as he wrote, " 'an autograph in exchange for that enchanting smile. I do hope you don't feel cheated.' " He blew on the page to dry the ink, then handed the book and the pen back.

"No way. This is going to be the highlight of my trip to Istanbul." Kristine hugged the book for a moment before putting it back in the bag.

"I sincerely hope that's not true," Lourds said.

"Sad to say, it is."

Lourds shook his head in disbelief. "Istanbul is a fabulous place. Did you know it's the only city in the world that spans two continents?"

"Really?" she said.

"It's an amazing place. I can't imagine being bored here." Lourds glanced at his watch. "Do you have luggage?"

"Oh, my God, I forgot." Panic widened Kristine's eyes. "Where should I go?"

"Since I've been here a few times, maybe I can help you find the baggage carousel. Which airline did you come in on?"

"British Airways. Same as you."

"Good. We can chat on the way." Lourds nodded to the posted signage indicating the direction of the baggage carousel in three languages. He could read them all fluently. He took the lead and they set off.

"What brings you to Istanbul?" Lourds rode the escalator down to the terminal's lower floor. Kristine Webber stood at his side. Her perfume was intoxicating. It, or perhaps the wine he'd consumed on the plane, made his head spin.

"My father's got meetings here," Kristine replied. "He's an international investor." She shrugged. "He's here working some kind of corporate merger and wanted me to spend time with him."

"That sounds nice."

"Usually he spends more time on the phone working at his business than with me. I end up ordering a lot of room service and catching up on movies."

"Sorry to hear it."

At the bottom of the escalator, Lourds got his bearings and walked toward the British Airways carousel. A crowd waited patiently but the warning lights weren't flashing. None of the luggage had yet arrived.

"You should take time to see the city," Lourds said.

"I don't like the idea of wandering around alone."

"You don't know anyone here?"

"Nope. Like I told you, meeting you is going to be the highlight of this trip. I'm going to be stranded at the hotel looking out through the window at a city I've never been to."

Lourds hesitated just a moment, then took the plunge. He and Dr. Olympia Adnan, the woman he'd come here to meet, had once been close, but that was a handful of years ago. The last he'd heard, when she called him back in January, Olympia had mentioned being involved with a Belgian archeologist. So Olympia wouldn't be available to fill all the long evenings he'd be spending here. Perhaps he'd just found a nice diversion.

"I could show you the city," Lourds said. "If you're interested. It's the fourth-largest city in the world, and people have been living here continuously since 6500 B.C.E.—that's nearly nine thousand years. Its first known name, Byzantium, still rings throughout human language. It's a UNESCO World Heritage site. You really shouldn't miss it. "

"Do you offer to *guide* often, Professor Lourds?"

"No." *Often* was such a subjective word.

"Will I be in good hands?" she asked.

"Most definitely." Lourds smiled and felt his anticipation rise. "There's a lot to see in this city, and it would be my pleasure to escort you when you have time."

"I'd like that."

"Good. Now, if you'll just point out your bags, I'd be happy to fetch them for you."

"There's only one. I had the rest of my things sent to the hotel. I refuse to be stripped naked if my luggage gets lost."

That delightful image ricocheted through Lourds's mind and he had to force himself to look for his bags.

"Are you here on vacation?" Kristine asked.

Lourds paced beside the young man wheeling his bags toward the cab and limousine stands. The professor carried his backpack because he never willingly let it leave his side. His work and his computer were in that backpack.

One of his suitcases was crammed with books, and the porter had struggled with it. When it came to research interfaces, Lourds still preferred printed matter he could depend on when electrical outlets weren't plentiful.

"More of a working vacation," Lourds said.

Kristine sighed. "So much for promises of taking me sightseeing through a beautiful city."

"Don't confuse me with your workaholic father," Lourds objected. "I take my playtime just as seriously as I do my work time."

"I'm glad to hear it. What are you going to be working on while you're here?"

"A—" Lourds hesitated over how to address his relationship with Olympia Adnan. "—*colleague* of mine has invited me to speak to her graduate classes at Istanbul University."

"About *Bedroom Pursuits*?"

"No. About more serious matters. There are some items the Rare Masterpieces and Museum Department of the Central Library have that she'd like me to lecture on."

"Will there be a test?"

"God, I hope not." Lourds grinned. "If there is, the students will hate me. Hopefully I'll be able to lead informal discussions that will inspire them." He held up a thumb and forefinger. "A little."

"They're going to want to talk to you about your book."

"Books," Lourds corrected. "You're probably right." Nearly everywhere he went, the topic of *Bedroom Pursuits* invariably came up.

"Are these items you're looking at a big deal?" Kristine asked.

"I hope so. Most of them have never been studied by American scholars," Lourds replied. "I'm going to be the first. I'm really excited about it."

He stopped at the curb and glanced out over the sea of vehicles threading through the terminal streets. His nose and eyes burned from the noxious exhaust.

"Are you going to be in another television special about the artifacts? I saw the ones you did in Egypt and in Spain. The whole *Race to Atlantis* thing."

Memories flooded Lourds's mind. Though he'd seen many things and been part of some wondrous discoveries in his professional career, nothing he'd been through before or since could match the pursuit of Lost Atlantis. It had fascinated, terrified, and very nearly killed him. Now . . . well, now he found he missed being on the hunt.

For the last few months, though he wouldn't have admitted it to anyone, he'd longed for something equally interesting to invade his life again. Living on the knife's edge like that had been an incredible adrenaline rush.

Kristine pointed at the taxi stand. "We can get a cab there. Where are you staying?"

"The Eresin Crown Hotel."

"Really? So am I."

"Well," Lourds said, "isn't that convenient?"

"It is. Maybe we can have breakfast before you go off to your speaking engagement in the morning."

"That would be great."

"In the meantime, want to share a cab to the hotel and get a drink at the bar?" she asked.

"That sounds fantastic," Lourds agreed. "But I'm supposed to have a car waiting for me."

"Someone's coming to pick you up?"

"Yes. A limo service." Lourds reached into his shirt pocket and took out the three-by-five index card his graduate assistant had filled out with his itinerary. Everything was there in neat, precise handwriting. But it was small enough that he had to squint.

"Professor Lourds!" a man's voice sang out. "Over here."

Turning in the direction of the hail, Lourds spotted a sleek dark blue Mercedes and a liveried driver standing beside it with a placard that read: PROFESSOR THOMAS LOURDS. The limousine was parked at the front of the waiting cabs.

Lourds waved his arm to acknowledge the man.

The driver waved back, then walked to the back of the vehicle, opened the trunk, and threw the placard inside the compartment.

"Over there," Lourds told the young porter handling his bags. He turned to Kristine. "Unless I miss my guess, there will be cocktails aboard."

Kristine gazed at the limousine for a moment, then back at Lourds. But she wasn't smiling and her face tightened. "Well, that was somewhat unexpected."

"I beg your pardon," Lourds said. "Maybe offering to share my limo was presumptuous of me. I'd hate to upset you."

"I believe you, Professor Lourds. And that's a shame. You seem like a really nice guy." The flirtatious air she wore dropped away like a costume, revealing a determined young woman on a mission.

Not liking the sudden change in her attitude and unsure what had triggered it, Lourds stepped away from her. But before his back foot touched down, she reached out and caught his hand in hers.

"We're going to be taking my car," Kristine said.

Lourds tried to yank his hand away but wasn't able to pull free. She was stronger than she looked. Something very strange was going on here. He was starting to get spooked. He reached for her wrist with his other hand. He'd never taken martial arts, not even after the trouble he'd gotten into while finding Atlantis. No time, he'd figured, and he wasn't likely to need those skills again. He'd clearly been wrong there. But breaking holds was all about leverage. He was bigger and stronger than this young woman. And, he hoped, faster.

Before he could make his move, she caught his free hand in hers and folded it in toward his wrist in some weird movement. He felt electrifying agony rip up his arm and crash through his brain. The next thing he knew, he'd dropped to his knees on the hard concrete.

What the hell was happening here? One thing he was certain of, this girl was hardly the simple fan she'd told him she was.

"Are you listening to me, Professor Lourds?" Kristine whispered in his ear.

It took Lourds a moment to remember how to work his mouth and voice. "Yes."

"Good. You're going to get up when I tell you to and follow me. You're going to do that without resisting. If you resist, I'm going to break your arm. Do you understand?"

Lourds didn't hesitate. The pain was too strong to resist. "Yes. Of course."

"Then let's go."

CHAPTER 2

Lourds yelped as Kristine pulled him up by his trapped arm, his wrist still bent in the form of a dying swan. A few of the passersby saw what was going on and backed away. Lourds staggered ahead of Kristine—if that was really her name—as she pushed him forward. Black spots danced in his vision and he felt certain that he was going to pass out.

His thoughts raced. It had always been like that for him. No matter what happened to him or around him, his mind worked to ferret out answers to puzzles. And the young woman's stalking and kidnapping of him—he didn't want to think that this might be the prelude to a murder—was certainly something he hadn't expected to face upon his arrival in Istanbul. It was a puzzle, all right, possibly a lethal one. He needed to find a way out.

"Are you positive you have the right person?" Lourds asked.

Kristine twisted his arm and increased the pain for a moment.

Lourds's knees wobbled and very nearly went out from under him. Sweat broke out across his face and he blinked back tears.

"Silence, Professor. We do this quietly and we do this quickly. Talking is not an option."

A bear-sized man wearing a Green Bay Packers football jersey stepped toward Lourds. A large woman and two cub-sized boys trailed in his wake.

"Hey, buddy," the bear-sized man said with an American accent. "You okay? Need some help?" He glanced at Kristine. "Hey, miss, if you need some help with your dad, I'd be happy to do it. I'm an EMT."

Dad? Lourds thought in mortification.

"A lot of guys get sick overseas their first time," the big man said. "They can't handle the local hooch so well."

Damn that wine. Lourds figured he must reek of it if this guy had noticed the smell. But the man wasn't quite the EMT he thought he was if he couldn't tell the difference between someone in pain and someone who was wasted.

"We don't need any help," Kristine replied smoothly, giving Lourds a shove. "My father and I are fine. Thanks for the offer."

"You ask me," the man said, "your dad doesn't look so fine." He took another step toward them and reached for Lourds.

Hope sprang up as Lourds realized they were starting to draw attention. Surely someone would call the police. The police in Turkish tourist areas were abundant and meant business. When they showed up, this whole situation would be resolved. He only hoped his arm wasn't broken in the meantime.

Kristine didn't even bat an eye. She slid her other hand up to join her first on Lourds's wrist. Smooth metal caressed his palm but he had no clue what it was. Then she forced him to lift his arm and point it at the man. A harsh click sounded from under his hand and was followed by an eerie humming noise.

Two thin cords suddenly ran from Lourds's hand to the bear-sized man. It looked a bit, the professor thought vaguely, like Spider-Man shooting his webbing.

The bear-sized man looked down at the wires protruding from his chest and abdomen. "Ow!" he yelled. "What the hell did you just do?"

Lourds wanted to tell the man that he'd done nothing, but he knew

Kristine would damage him for breaking her rules about talking. The bear-shaped man reached for the wires.

Then he started convulsing, twitching, and jerking. His head shook back and forth violently.

"Hey, Mom," one of the cub-shaped kids said. "Dad's break dancing."

"He hasn't even been drinking this time," the other cub put in.

"Harold," the large woman exclaimed. "What do you think you're doing? Get back over here and leave those people alone. *Harold!* Are you even listening to me?"

Harold quit convulsing, twitching, and jerking. He fell like a puppet whose strings had been cut. He tumbled forward and lay spread-eagled on the concrete. A waiting cab braked to a sudden halt only inches from him.

"Harold!" the woman screamed.

"Dad!" the cubs screamed.

Then other people started screaming. The level of general confusion escalated to the point that Lourds was suddenly lost in a sea of upset people. If Kristine hadn't been holding on to his hand with such dogged purpose, Lourds felt positive he could have escaped.

"Oh, my God!" the big woman yelled, pulling at the wires in her husband's chest. "He killed my husband! That man *killed* my husband!" She pointed accusingly at Lourds.

"No," Lourds protested automatically. "No, I didn't! It was—*urfff*!" Pain stole away his breath and he nearly dropped to his knees again. Kristine kept her grip on his hand and grabbed his collar as well.

He tried to struggle, but to no avail. The girl knew what she was doing.

"Move, Professor Lourds," she ordered. "As amusing as it would be to watch you get arrested for Tasering that oaf, I have plans for you."

A million questions flooded Lourds's mind, but he didn't ask any of them. He kept moving, mostly in a straight line, out into the next street.

"Can you see me?" Kristine asked.

Lourds hesitated, remembered the orders not to speak, and looked back over his shoulder at his captor.

"Can you see me?" Kristine repeated.

"No," Lourds answered. "No, not well. It's an awkward angle—"

"Shut up," Kristine said to him. "I wasn't talking to you."

Lourds shut up. He glanced back at the bear-shaped man and saw with relief that the man was starting to stir. He looked incredibly confused. Lourds knew exactly how the man felt.

Behind the downed EMT, three men shoved through the crowd. They pointed at Kristine and Lourds and then reached inside their suits. That wasn't, Lourds decided, a hopeful sign.

Kristine cursed and Lourds couldn't help but think the young woman had quite the mouth on her. "I've got company," she said. "Three men."

Then the men brandished weapons. The flesh-and-blood barrier separating them from Lourds and the young woman evaporated. Pedestrians and cabdrivers screamed in terror. People dived for cover among the cars and kiosks.

Kristine yanked Lourds into motion, pushing him across the street at a run. A car swerved to avoid them, crashing into one of the parked cabs. Lourds's boots crunched over shattered glass that sprayed across the street from the crash. He hoped that none of it had managed to injure anybody—including him.

"No," Kristine retorted angrily, though Lourds hadn't said a word. "I *don't* know who they are. Evidently your little surprise party has a leak somewhere. Where's that car?"

She yanked Lourds to a halt, nearly choking him on his own shirt. He gagged reflexively. To his right, a silver SUV squealed around a corner, barreling straight for them.

Pedestrians tried to get out of the way, but one of them was too slow and the vehicle collided with him, knocking him to the side.

He rolled, then staggered to his feet, clutching his arm.

Lourds cursed in three languages, remembered that he wasn't supposed to talk, then realized he was probably going to get that broken arm, thanks to his lack of control. He braced himself for the excruciating pain. Instead, the SUV skidded to a halt in front of Lourds and Kristine. The rear passenger door swung open and a hulking man reached out and caught Lourds by his shirtfront.

"Get in," Kristine ordered, pushing from behind.

The hulking man yanked Lourds into the SUV as if he were weightless. The professor banged his knees against the transom, but the pain was only an echo of what was being done to his wrist. Unable to catch his balance, Lourds tumbled into the vehicle and sprawled.

Twisting his head to see who his new captor was, Lourds looked at the big man just in time to see the top of his left ear explode in a crimson burst. Blood speckled the window behind his captor, a window that now had a thumb-sized hole punched through it.

"They're shooting at us!" Lourdes screamed. More bullets tore through other windows, and distinct metal taps rang out against the SUV's body.

The big man pulled a machine pistol from under his suit jacket. He pushed Lourds's head into the carpet with one hand while he aimed the machine pistol with the other.

"Smart guy, isn't he?" the hulking man asked. He returned fire as blood streamed down the side of his face and neck.

"He's a university professor," Kristine said. "I don't think he can help himself." She threw herself into the SUV, stepping on Lourds's butt and back in the process. She slapped the SUV's driver on the back of the head. "Go!"

The SUV jerked into motion. Tires squealed in protest and fought for traction. Lourds's face banged against the floor as the vehicle bounded over an obstruction. He hoped it wasn't another pedestrian.

Another fusillade of bullets took out the SUV's rear window. Chunks of safety glass sprayed over Lourds. For the first time in months, he regretted longing for some enterprise as exciting as his search for Atlantis.

Memories of all those near-death experiences that had accompanied the excitement flashed through his head.

What the hell was I thinking?

Now he had kidnappings, bullets, and people screaming again.

What the bloody blazes went wrong?

This isn't supposed to be happening like this!

Dammit, I'm supposed to be having fun!

CENTRAL INTELLIGENCE AGENCY
LANGLEY, VIRGINIA
UNITED STATES OF AMERICA
MARCH 15, 2010

Special Agent In Charge James Dawson stood in front of an immense high-definition wallscreen and glared at the events unfolding at Ataturk

International Airport. Wounded people flopped on the ground and blood streaked the concrete. And every one of them endangered the career he'd built up over the last seventeen years.

This wasn't *supposed to happen like this,* he growled to himself. *This was supposed to be a cakewalk. Easy in, easy out. No muss, no fuss.*

They'd replaced the limousine driver with one of their assets. The three men who'd chased the SUV on foot and shot up the airport couldn't be tied back to the Agency even if they got picked up by the police—whether they were still alive or merely corpses. They'd been hired through a blind. That at least gave him enough room for deniability in case anything came home to roost. But he'd planned on the op being invisible, not merely deniable.

Several technicians hunkered over their computer workstations at the table behind him. Dawson felt them waiting expectantly for his commands. Just as they had on previous operations.

"Give me the best image you have of the woman with Lourds," Dawson ordered.

Immediately, a section of the wallscreen separated from the ongoing live action. A split-second later, the image of the young woman filled the space. Due to their last-minute notice of the assignment, the team had barely managed to remove the chauffeur and hack into the airport's security camera systems.

It would have been much easier to take Professor Thomas Lourds while he'd been in the United States. Exactly why his boss wanted to detain the professor, much less take him out overseas, remained a mystery to Dawson. He didn't plan to ask for answers, though. Dawson's advancement had relied on doing whatever his superior wanted without question.

In the wallscreen image, the woman appeared concerned but not totally surprised.

Was she expecting interference? Dawson wondered. *Or is she just that confident about her skills?* He watched her navigating through the crowd, then shoving Lourds into the SUV.

"If she's that good," Dawson wondered, "why don't we know who she is?"

"We're searching, sir," one of the female techs replied. "If we knew where to search first, we could get the name sooner."

Onscreen, someone inside the SUV fired a machine pistol in controlled bursts. Two of the three pursuers went down, as well as a handful of innocent bystanders.

Dawson cursed again. Whoever had Lourds presently was as determined to get and keep the professor as Dawson was.

"Keep looking," Dawson snapped. "She must have picked up Lourds somewhere along the way to Istanbul." Otherwise the other team would have spirited the professor away earlier. Knowing why everybody wanted the prof would have been useful. "If these people had had a team in place in Boston, the woman wouldn't have been the only person picking Lourds up. Rerun the part where she takes control of Lourds. Where she grabs his hand and forces him to follow her."

Another section opened up on the screen. Footage of the grappling move filled the space.

"Enhance that," Dawson ordered.

The image magnified.

Dawson immediately recognized the hold. "She knows martial arts. Plus she's not looking out for the police, which makes me think she's not wanted in Turkey at least. She's good at close-contact work. She's cool under fire. C'mon, people, we're looking for someone on a short list somewhere. Someone this good, someone female, she can't be that hard to find. She's got to be a pro."

Onscreen, the two pursuers on the ground weren't getting up. Blood soaked the front of their shirts and pants.

Idiots! Dawson thought. *They didn't even wear Kevlar*. Of course, no one'd had any reason to expect what had taken place. It was supposed to be a simple pickup, not a firefight. He focused on the SUV fleeing down the street.

"Can you get that tag number?" Dawson asked.

"Yes, sir."

Another section of the wallscreen opened up and showed an image of the SUV's rear. The magnification increased steadily until the number could be read.

"Who owns that vehicle?" Dawson asked.

"Checking now, sir."

Furious, Dawson paced the floor. He felt for his cell phone inside his jacket just over his heart. He resisted the impulse to see if his supervisor had called. The phone was set to vibrate so only he would know a call was coming through.

He stopped himself from pulling the phone out. He would have known if it had rung. For the last eight years, he'd been aware of the instrument and how closely it tied in to his rapid advancement.

"The SUV's licensed to a messenger and courier service in Istanbul," one of the technicians said. "Strait Messengers. They're located near the Galata Bridge in the Eminonu District."

Dawson didn't know where the Galata Bridge was or how many districts were in Istanbul. All that mattered was that his people could find the location.

He paced the floor some more, weighing his options. He refused to panic. His mentor hadn't chosen him because he froze under pressure.

"Get the address to Red Team," Dawson said. "If this vehicle wasn't stolen and those people kidnapped Lourds, they may take him there. And if they don't, someone there may still know where the professor is. Tell them to find Lourds for me, or find someone who knows where he is."

"Yes, sir."

Angrily, Dawson raked his gaze over the images of the woman, the dead men, and the fleeing SUV. He was behind in the chase, but he wasn't out of it.

His phone vibrated over his heart. He took it out before it could vibrate again and answered. "Yes, sir."

"Jimmy," the smooth, cultured voice said, "I'm in my office watching the news, putting together my notes for the Middle East conference coming up. CNN just came on with a breaking story about Professor Thomas Lourds being involved in a shooting at Ataturk International Airport."

"Yes, sir. We've got eyes on the situation, sir."

"Nowhere in Professor Lourds's background did I see that he had any military training, or connections with the Turkish army. Or any army."

"No, sir, but he was an Eagle Scout."

"I suppose that would be helpful if he needed to start a fire, figure out which way north was, or help someone across the street."

"Some Eagle Scouts are trained to shoot, sir."

"I'm fairly confident that such a background wouldn't enable Professor Lourds to evade the men you sent after him."

Dawson's face grew hot. "No, sir."

"You wouldn't have sent someone who would heavy-handedly take him in a frontal assault. From the looks of things on CNN, there are a lot of wounded and possibly some dead people at that airport." Although the man's words were damning, the flat New Hampshire accent remained even. "In short, this is an international incident. Was this your plan?"

"No, sir. This was not in the plan. It happened in reaction to an outside party we didn't know was in play. Things escalated when that outside party took Lourds before we could get to him. We tried to get him back. Those shooters won't tie back to the Agency or to your office."

"That's good to hear, Jimmy. Really fine. But it appears you've lost Professor Lourds."

Dawson stared at the rear view of the fleeing SUV. "Not yet, sir. We've identified the people who took the professor. We're going after them."

"All right, then. You're showing initiative. That's what I like to hear. You've always been a man I could trust to get results."

Pride swelled Dawson's chest.

"As I've told you earlier, Jimmy, this business is important. Vastly important. I would like very much to speak with Professor Lourds sometime in the near future."

"You will, sir."

"Then I'll leave this in your capable hands, Jimmy. You get back to me when you've got this thing sewn up."

"Yes, sir, Mr. Vice President." The click of the broken connection sounded in Dawson's ear. He punched the phone off and returned it to his pocket.

"Sir," one of the technicians said.

Without turning back to face them, Dawson said, "This had better be good news."

"We've identified the woman, sir."

Dawson stared at the woman's image on the wallscreen. "Tell me."

"She's a member of the Irish Republican Army. Allegedly."

That, Dawson decided, didn't make any sense at all. Why would the IRA be involved in this?

"We've got a helicopter team in the area, right?" he asked.

"Yes."

"Get them in the air. Feed them the information about the SUV and let them find it." Dawson forced himself to let out a breath. Maybe the op was running a little hot, but it was still going to be over in a few more minutes.

FENERYOLU CD
YESILKOY DISTRICT
İSTANBUL, TURKEY
MARCH 15, 2010

Rubber shrieked and the SUV's transmission strained. Lourds could hear the scream of abused metal beneath his position on the vehicle's floor. His stomach twisted sickly as the SUV lurched and seemed to go airborne for a moment. His head slammed into the floor, then into the metal seat anchors ahead of him. He tasted blood from his split lip.

Horns blared all around them.

The man in the front passenger seat swore in Farsi. The driver was asking for divine guidance in the same tongue. The hulking brute with the shot-off ear laughed in a deep rumble.

Unable to see her, Lourds didn't know what Kristine was doing. He lifted his head and wiped blood from his mouth. Crimson stained his fingers.

Someone, and he was fairly certain it was Kristine, kicked him in the head.

"Look out!" one of the men yelled.

"I see it!" the driver yelled back.

The SUV jarred violently, shuddered almost to a stop, then—with a lurch and a whirlwind of screaming metal—the vehicle continued more or less on its way.

The hulking man reloaded his machine pistol with practiced ease. He was either stoned on something or had a death wish, Lourds decided.

"Bleeding wankers," Kristine said in disgust. This time Lourds detected the Irish lilt in her voice. She'd obviously been hiding that, too, while pretending to be the awestruck fan.

Lourds squirmed a little and struggled to move, to bring the woman into view.

Kristine leaned over the backseat for a moment, then returned with a pistol in her fist. She snapped off the safety and worked the pistol with obvious familiarity.

The hulking man stopped laughing.

"Do you know where you're going?" Kristine demanded.

"Of course," the man in the passenger seat said. "Everything is going according to plan."

"Really?" Kristine's voice dripped with sarcasm. This was no kid, Lourds realized. She wasn't at all what he'd thought she was. He wondered how old she really was. She looked about nineteen, but that made him wonder how she could have learned all she'd done today in such a short lifetime.

Lourds guessed she was in her midtwenties at the least. She had a definite taint of the Emerald Isle in her voice right now, but he could tell she hadn't used the accent for some time. Her American accent had been flawless. She must have lived in the States for a while. Either that or she had Oscar-worthy acting skills along with her martial arts training. And lots of target practice. The gun in her hand was rock steady.

Who was she? And how could he escape her?

"Was it in your bloody plans for those men to show up and start shooting?" Kristine demanded.

The two men in the front remained silent. The driver's lack of response was for the obvious reason. It took everything he had to dodge the cars as the van screamed down the roadway. Again and again, the SUV swerved, sped, slowed, and jumped. Only occasionally did the vehicle hit something, and then never more than a glancing impact.

"No," the hulking man said.

"Then why were they there?"

"Our prize is more popular than we anticipated." The hulking man shook his head. Blood droplets from his damaged ear spun into the air. "It doesn't matter. Your part in this is done."

"Not till I get the other half of my fee," Kristine said.

While they sparred, Lourds considered his chances of escape. If he were Harrison Ford in an action picture, he could stand, elbow the hulking man in the face, then open the door and leap out into the roadbed without picking up more than a few scratches from the impact.

Sadly, Lourds knew he was no Harrison Ford. He'd break something if he leaped from a vehicle moving at this speed—possibly even his neck. The impact with the pavement would probably skin him alive. And one of the vehicles they were weaving through might run over him. However, judging from the carnage they'd left behind at the airport, he figured he was a dead man if he didn't do something to change his situation soon.

Nobody was paying him any attention. Maybe it was time to try something.

He'd played soccer since he was a boy. He still played on a university team and joined pickup games wherever he had the opportunity. He was in shape and he was fast. He shoved himself into a crouching position, succeeded in standing on his tangled feet, and slammed his head against the vehicle's rooftop almost with enough force to knock himself out.

Not exactly what he'd planned, but it was something.

"What do you think *you* are doing, pencil neck?" The hulking man reached for Lourds.

Fueled by adrenaline and operating on instinct, Lourds shoved an elbow into the hulking man's face.

He'd hoped to knock the man out.

The blow succeeded only in tearing off another chunk of the man's tattered ear.

Roaring in pain, the hulking man clapped a hand to his head and swung the machine pistol at Lourds. The barrel struck Lourds's forehead with enough force to make him see stars.

Unfortunately, the weapon also fired.

Reeling from the noise and the pain, Lourds staggered back.

The car swerved. He glanced at the driver. The back of the man's head had been ripped away. Blood covered the shattered windshield. As Lourds watched in horror, the dead man fell forward over the steering wheel. The horn blared and the SUV swung wildly out of control.

CHAPTER 3

İSTANBUL CD
YESİLKOY DİSTRİCT
İSTANBUL, TURKEY
MARCH 15, 2010

Lourds lunged for the steering wheel. He met with resistance from the guy in the passenger seat. Lourds slammed his throbbing elbow into the man's head. The guy went down. Dazed, Lourds continued to flail for control and ended up getting soaked in blood from the dead man. His hands slipped on the steering wheel and he watched in growing horror as the SUV sped toward an outside café.

Café patrons scattered, alerted by the SUV's shrill horn, still pressed down by the dead man's head.

A strap whipped over Lourds's head and settled at his throat. When the strap tightened, the pressure choked him. For a moment he thought someone was trying to strangle him.

"Give it up, Professor," Kristine yelled in his ear. "The bloody car is out of control. Let's see if we can survive the impending crash, eh?"

Giving in to the strangling seat belt strap, Lourds fell backwards and landed in the young woman's lap. If circumstances had been different, it would have been a wonderful place to be. For just the briefest moment, he was aware of the feminine curves beneath and behind him as she shifted and dropped the seat belt across his chest.

You're about to die and this is going to be the last thing on your mind?

Lourds couldn't believe himself. Then he had no more time to think because the strap snapped tight around his chest, the woman wrapped her arms around him and buried her face against his back, and the SUV plowed through the abandoned tables and chairs.

Something hard pressed into Lourds's groin. Despite his situation, he couldn't help looking. Kristine's pistol lay in his lap. Before he could grab the gun, the SUV slammed into the side of the café.

The right side of the car crumpled and the bloodstained windshield caved into a glittering haze of shrapnel that ricocheted inside the SUV. Like a dazed boxer, the SUV rebounded from the wall and careened back toward the busy street. Lourds felt the shock of the impact all the way through his body.

But the SUV rolled on.

No sooner had the SUV rolled back into the street than a produce truck collided with it on the left side. More pain.

He was still alive.

The pain made that clear.

The crumpled side of the SUV dropped and Lourds thought he felt the front wheel roll away. With mass and speed on the side of the cargo truck, the SUV sagged and rolled over like a submissive hound before its master.

Lourds braced himself against the ceiling, but he and Kristine were thrown across the vehicle's interior.

Feeling cut in half by the seat belt, Lourds dangled, then watched in horror as the right side of the hulking man's face ground away on the rough street through the broken window as the SUV skidded along the pavement.

The hulking man screamed briefly in agony; then the shrieks stopped.

The SUV continued careening down the street. Lourds fought to stay away from the huge corpse of the hulking man, hideously dead. He feared it would be reduced to scraps and then he'd share the same horrible fate.

Then the SUV and the produce truck stopped.

The sudden lack of movement seemed almost inconceivable after the last few seconds, but the terrible sounds of metal screeching and human screams continued echoing inside Lourds's head.

We're alive! he thought.

Then he looked at the ground-up corpse and the driver missing part of his head.

Well, some of us are still alive.

"Get up," Kristine ordered.

Lourds didn't move. "You've got your pistol in my crotch."

Kristine moved the pistol. "Get up."

Lourds tried, but the strap was too tight with his weight against it. He couldn't pull free. "I can't. The strap's—"

A short combat knife flashed in the young woman's hand. The strap parted like butter before its keen edge.

She has a knife, Lourdes thought. *A very sharp knife . . .*

It terrified him even more than the gun.

The strap's release caught Lourds off guard. He fell onto the hulking man's bleeding body. Before he could recoil from it, Kristine fell on top of him, then swung around, kicked him in the head in her haste, and stood. She pocketed the knife, shoved the pistol into the back of her waistband, then turned her attention to the broken door, currently above her head.

A familiar sickly sweet odor tickled his nostrils.

"Do you smell gasoline?" he asked.

"Yes."

Wetness slid under the hulking man's corpse. Lourds hesitantly touched it and sniffed his finger. It was definitely gasoline. The smell overpowered even the stench of blood and death.

"There's gasoline under us," he said.

"The impact must have ruptured the gas tank. Give me a hand with this door."

"No! All we need is a spark, possibly from messing with that jammed door, and we could be burned alive."

"Do you really think that just sitting here is our best option, Professor? Haven't you realized there's worse out there than fire?"

Lourds didn't say so to his weapon-toting keeper, but he thought waiting for help was an incredibly intelligent idea.

"Get up and help me," Kristine said. "Even if the police arrive to rescue us, I'm not sure I want to answer any of their questions. Turkish jails aren't comfortable. And that's only if the police get here before more of those men from the airport arrive."

"You don't know that there are any more." But she had a point. Even as he said it, Lourds liked his plan less and less.

"They tried to shoot us in public. They mowed down civilians everywhere. Do you really think they would have sent only one team?"

"I defer to your experience." Lourds scrambled out from under her and crouched on top of the corpse. The footing atop the dead man was treacherous.

Several people approached the SUV. Lourds saw them through the smashed front windshield. A few onlookers asked them if help was needed, but others pointed out the dead man to each other and all the blood in the vehicle's interior. It was a nightmare image.

They kept their distance.

Kristine pulled her pistol and brandished it through the broken window. A few of the onlookers gave ground, but that must not have satisfied his kidnapper. She fired two quick rounds into the air. One of the brass casings flipped down the back of Lourds's shirt and burned him until he was able to shake it free. He prayed the gasoline vapor wouldn't explode and kill him.

It didn't.

A mass exodus of spectators began at that point.

"Why did you do that?" Lourds said. "They were only trying to help."

"Because one of those good Samaritans might be standing out there with a pistol or a knife," Kristine answered. "You're a hot item, Professor Lourds. I don't know why these people at the airport wanted you, but I do know some other people paid me a lot of money to bring you to them."

"You were bait?"

"I was told you have a weakness for young women. Judging from the way you threw yourself at me, it appears to be true."

Lourds couldn't believe it. "The way *I* threw myself at you? I did *not* throw myself at *you,* young lady."

"Now you're noticing the differences in our ages? You didn't seem too worried about it earlier, did you?"

Lourds tried to think of something to say, but he couldn't even believe they'd gotten into the argument in the first place. They had more pressing concerns.

"You're standing in gasoline, Professor," the young woman taunted.

"That's right! You could have killed us both by shooting that gun!" Lourds said.

"Both of you, shut up," the man in the passenger seat, conscious again, snarled. He pointed a big pistol at them. "Or I will kill you both."

Kristine turned her cold gaze on the man. For one tense second, Lourds felt certain she was going to kill the man for threatening her.

"You're lucky your boss still owes me money," Kristine said.

The man hesitated, then lowered his pistol and wiped at a cut on his face. "We need to get out of here."

"Agreed."

Kristine turned her attention back to the jammed door. The gasoline stink was stronger now. Not relishing the idea of burning to death, Lourds helped her. This time the door gave way with a heart-stopping shriek of metal against metal.

But they didn't go up in flames.

The young woman grabbed the edges of the door and hauled herself out. Lourds jumped after her.

They both stood on the SUV looking down at the crowd, now hovering a safe distance away. His shirt hung in shreds and his whole body ached. He figured he looked like an extra in a zombie film. His hat was still on his head. He wondered what it looked like after all this.

Several onlookers had cameras, camcorders, and camera-equipped phones pointed in their direction.

"Come on." The man who had been sitting in the passenger seat stood in front of the SUV. He'd crawled through the broken windshield. Blood soaked his clothing and streaked his hands and face. He held a phone to his ear.

"Where?" Kristine asked.

"There." The man pointed to a nearby alley. "There's a car in the next street."

At that moment, Lourds realized he should have been trying to escape his captors instead of looking around in a daze. He shifted his weight and leaped from the SUV, hoping to vanish into the crowd before Kristine or the man could catch him.

Sadly, that wouldn't keep them from shooting him in the back. But maybe they still wanted him alive.

But even as he moved, Kristine shot a hand out and caught his ankle. Rather than landing gracefully, prepared to flee for his life, he crashed inelegantly to the ground onto his already bruised face. His breath left him in a rush, but he struggled to get to his feet again. The crowd was only a few yards away. He could—

Kristine landed in front of him with the grace of an Olympic gymnast. She reached down and caught his hand in that excruciating grip again. "No," she said, addressing him like a canine about to chew on the furniture.

Reluctantly, Lourds got up. And he followed her like a well-trained dog.

The young woman and the man waved their weapons again and the crowd parted before them. Lourds struggled to keep pace with his captors. Running was awkward with his bruised body and his hand held in a death grip. Kristine seemed to be untouched by their adventures. She still moved like a dancer.

Not Lourds. Every bone in his body ached and his face throbbed fiercely.

They ran down the dirty alley. Shop doors thudded closed when people inside saw them covered in blood and waving firearms.

Helicopter rotors screamed overhead when they'd reached the midpoint of the alley. Kristine threw her body into Lourds's. He smashed up against the wall just as the helicopter floated into view overhead.

"Get out of sight!" Kristine yelled at the other man. She pressed her body against Lourds's and held him against the wall. The experience wasn't altogether unpleasant. His body reacted instantly to hers.

He prayed she wouldn't notice.

She cursed. "What do you do? Mainline Viagra?"

"Not hardly. I just like women," Lourds said. "However, I do wish that particular response of mine was a little more selective. I'd prefer someone, say, less lethal and more sane."

"If I hadn't kidnapped you, you would be dead by now."

"As opposed to dead later?"

Her face hardened. "Not my problem. You're just a job to me, Professor. I'm getting paid to deliver you. That's all."

At that moment, a gunner aboard the helicopter opened fire. Large-caliber bullets ripped the other kidnapper to bloody rags and dropped his body to the ground.

Kristine cursed, released Lourds, and shoved him toward the other end of the alley. "Run!"

Lourds did, holding his arms up over his head like they might somehow protect him from bullets. He knew it was a wasted effort but he couldn't seem to pull them down.

The large-caliber rounds chewed into the alley and ripped holes in the stone walls and flagstones. Before he'd gone half a dozen strides, a sedan pulled into the mouth of the alley and sped toward him.

Rescuers? he wondered. *Or more killers?*

He really didn't know.

CENTRAL INTELLIGENCE AGENCY
LANGLEY, VIRGINIA
UNITED STATES OF AMERICA
MARCH 15, 2010

Anxiety shivered through Dawson as he watched the video from the Web camera on the helicopter's nose. Since the camera showed only what was in front of the aircraft, he didn't know what targets the men aboard the helicopter were shooting at. Gunfire rattled in professional bursts.

"Isn't there another camera in the helicopter?" Dawson asked irritably.

"I'm trying to bring it online now, sir," one of the technicians said.

The video coming from the helicopter's nose swung wildly and almost made Dawson sick to his stomach. He crossed his arms, stood still, and forced himself to breathe to keep the vertigo at bay.

The wallscreen split into two different views. The left side continued to show the whirling landscape of rooftops presented by the helicopter cam. The right side of the screen showed local police units driving through the streets crowded with onlookers that were reluctant to give way.

"Where's this feed coming from?" Dawson asked.

"WNN News, sir," technician answered. "The World News Network had a live broadcast in the area. They were covering Brad and Angelina's—"

"Who's the reporter on the ground there?"

"Her name is Davina Wilson."

A small inset appeared on the wallscreen and showed a publicity headshot of a pretty African-American woman in her early twenties.

"Find out everything you can about Davina Wilson," Dawson ordered.

In the street, police officers ran to the wrecked SUV with weapons drawn. Dawson thought they looked well trained and professional. Several onlookers started shouting and pointing into the alley as if the police officers couldn't see the helicopter hanging overhead for themselves. A group of police officers split off and sprinted for the alley.

Dawson cursed. If the gun-happy shooters aboard the helicopter didn't kill Lourds, the local police might. At the very least, they would arrest the professor.

That wouldn't make the vice president happy.

"Get me that pilot," Dawson said.

"Yes, sir."

Out of habit, Dawson shot his cuffs and adjusted his jacket. Sartorial elegance was his preference, the armor that he wore among politicians. It also impressed the little people. The fact that the pilot would never see him didn't matter. If Dawson was going to talk to the man, he was going to know that he looked his best.

Another inset image, this one of a man in his late thirties, showed up on the wallscreen. Close-cropped blond hair stood out against his dark skin. His eyes were too close together and a long knife scar marred his left cheek.

"What's this man's name?" Dawson asked.

"Metternich, sir. Johan Metternich. He's a South African mercenary currently in Istanbul while assigned to a pharmaceutical corporation smuggling blood diamonds out of his native country."

"We've used him before?"

"Yes, sir. Three times on other operations. The Brits and Chinese have used him as well. He's been a solid asset. He doesn't ask questions, doesn't cause problems, and hasn't failed yet."

He's also still alive. Dawson knew that was more telling than anything else in the mercenary's résumé.

"Okay, patch me through to him."

Almost immediately, the up-close-and-personal hammering of the helicopter's main rotor filled Dawson's hearing. The bull roar of the fully automatic weapon punctuated Dawson's presence aboard the helicopter.

"You're risking our package." Dawson kept his voice calm.

"Who is this?" the South African asked.

"I'm the man who cuts your checks. If our package gets damaged in any way," Dawson threatened, "not only will you not get paid, but I'll also put a bounty on your head. Do we understand each other?"

Metternich growled curses. "We're not going to hurt your package. He's still alive and breathing."

The helicopter swung around so the nose cam pointed down into the alley. Lourds and the woman ran for the other end of the alley, where a sedan glided to a quick stop.

Dawson covered the microphone with a hand and looked at the technicians. "Who's in that car?"

"Checking, sir."

Another window opened up on the wallscreen, then zoomed in on the vehicle registration plate at the back of the sedan.

"It's registered in Istanbul, sir."

"Then find out who it's registered to." Dawson cursed vehemently and turned his attention back to the action.

"Who's in the car?" Metternich demanded.

"Doesn't matter," Dawson said. "They're in our way. I want our package."

"If they're not part of the package, that makes it easier." Metternich raised his voice. "Take out the car."

On-screen, Lourds halted as men boiled from the back of the sedan.

Machine gun fire opened up again as the helicopter canted to the right. The heavy-caliber rounds strafed the wall beside the sedan. Two of the men from the ground vehicle raised machine pistols and opened fire.

"I've got access to the second camera now, sir."

"On screen." Dawson shifted his attention to the new image.

The second camera, placed in the helicopter's cargo area, offered a view forward. Metternich occupied the pilot's seat. Two gunmen crowded the cargo door with heavy-caliber machine guns while firing.

Dawson took a deep breath and let it out. He told himself that the op was going to play out just fine. But they hadn't run this hot on one in years. Whoever Lourds was, whatever he represented to the vice president, he'd better be worth the risk they were all taking.

Bullets from the men beside the sedan crashed through the helicopter's Plexiglas shield. Metternich cursed ferociously and struggled to bring the helicopter to safety. The aircraft swung out over one of the rooftops, and the alley was obscured.

"Get on the skids," Metternich ordered. "We'll strafe them on a straight run."

The two gunmen flared out to either side of the cargo area and clambered out onto the skids. They hunkered down into position as Metternich piloted the helicopter around to approach the sedan once more.

"I want that package," Dawson growled. "Unharmed."

"We're going to get it for you," Metternich said. "Just shut up and let us do our job."

Dawson covered the microphone and made a mental note that Metternich was going to get a bullet instead of a paycheck for this one. His insolence, never mind his proximity to the vice president's pet project, rendered him expendable. Dawson took satisfaction in that.

As the helicopter swung back into the alley, Dawson spotted two marked police cars speeding up from the other end. A sinking sensation formed in the pit of his stomach.

One of the men stopped firing, yelled hoarsely, and pointed at the back of the sedan. One of the new arrivals pulled a rocket launcher from the vehicle's trunk. He settled it over his shoulder and aimed even as Metternich tried to pull up from the attack run.

Then the helicopter filled with flames and the cameras went offline.

CHAPTER 4

OFF İSTANBUL CD
YESİLKOY DİSTRİCT
İSTANBUL, TURKEY
MARCH 15, 2010

Stunned, Lourds watched the helicopter go to pieces in the sky above the alley. Flaming wreckage flew in all directions. Some of it dropped onto the rooftops, but a lot of it fell into the alley. The cacophony of explosions and their echoes rolled through the confined space and physically battered Lourds.

Still on his feet, but only because he hadn't thought to throw himself to the ground, Lourds ran his hands over his body. As far as he could tell, he was still in one piece. But he didn't think he was in a good position to know for sure.

At the sedan, the man with the rocket launcher calmly reloaded his weapon. Sirens shrilled behind Lourds. When he turned to look back, he spotted two police cars on the other side of the flaming helicopter debris. The wreckage blocked them from approaching.

Lourds turned and fled back toward the policeman. He raised his hands and shouted, "Don't shoot! Don't shoot!"

The doors on the police car opened and two officers squatted down behind them with guns drawn.

Lourds repeated his entreaty in two different languages

and was on his third when Kristine tackled him. Her arms encircled his knees and he plummeted forward just as the police opened fire. The bullets passed overhead within inches.

Kristine slithered up his body and settled on top of him in a prone position.

"You're going to get yourself killed!" Kristine shouted into his ear. "You must have some kind of death wish." She slapped the back of his head.

The man with the rocket launcher fired again. This time the round streaked for the police car. The police officers had just enough time to abandon their positions before the explosive slammed into the vehicle. The police car flew up from the ground and flipped over backwards. As the vehicle lay rocking like an overturned turtle, flames wreathed it.

Rubber shrilled behind Lourds as the sedan navigated the alley and skidded to a stop beside him. Kristine rolled off him and grabbed him under one arm while one of the men grabbed him under the other.

"This is the professor?" the man asked.

"Yes," Kristine answered.

Together, they unceremoniously shoved him into the sedan's rear seat. Thinking quickly, Lourds grabbed the door handle, yanked, and tried to escape. Another man filled the door and batted Lourds back into the car with a hard elbow to the head. Lourds's hat fell into the alley as he toppled back dazed against the seat. The man stooped long enough to get the hat and push it into Lourds's face, then sat down beside him and slammed the door.

Kristine crowded in on Lourds's other side. The two other men slid into the front seat beside the driver.

"Go! *Go!*" the man in the passenger seat roared, and slapped the dash impatiently.

The driver dropped his foot heavily on the accelerator, swung in a hard U-turn, and they shot out of the alley into the street. They skidded wildly for a moment, losing traction across the pavement; then the driver regained control.

Lourds glanced through the back window and hoped to see a police car there. He didn't know how he was going to explain his current predicamentbut having to explain it rather than survive it had to be an improvement.

A sharp pain bit into the inside of his right thigh. When he looked down, he saw that the man beside him had stabbed a hypodermic into his leg. He grabbed for the hypodermic but the man was already pushing the plunger. More pain invaded Lourds's leg, along with a cool sensation that quickly spread.

"What is that?" Kristine asked.

"Something to knock him out." The man withdrew the hypodermic. "From what we've seen, he is nothing but trouble."

Lourds wanted to object. None of this had been his fault, but a warm lassitude drifted through him and he found he couldn't quite construct his thoughts.

Then the waiting darkness claimed him.

ZOLA
800 F STREET
WASHINGTON, D.C.
UNITED STATES OF AMERICA
MARCH 15, 2010

Dawson grabbed his briefcase, slid out of his Dodge Charger, and tossed the keys to the young female valet.

"Good evening, sir." The valet caught the keys one-handed and held the door for Dawson.

"Somewhere close." He handed her a twenty-dollar bill. "I may be leaving quickly."

"Of course, sir."

The International Spy Museum and the Spy City Café sat adjacent to Zola in the Le Droit Building. The vice president had chosen to meet there for a late dinner. The refurbished restaurant was a favorite of the man's, but wasn't one that the Agency often used. Dawson thought it amusing that the vice president wanted to meet his private spy there.

The Le Droit Building was old, a hangover from past glories in the nation's capital, but it had been recently remodeled and shone like a jewel. Zola was one of the District's chic places to eat and provided private dining rooms.

The maître d' greeted Dawson when he stepped into the foyer. "Do you have a reservation, sir?"

"I'll be joining someone," Dawson replied.

One of the vice president's security people stepped forward. Dawson didn't remember the man's name. They all tended to look alike: young, tough, and emotionless. The earwig in his ear gave him an otherworldly appearance. Most people wouldn't have noticed the device, but Dawson was acutely aware of it.

"He's with us," the security man said.

The maître d' smiled. "Of course."

"Good evening, Special Agent Dawson." The security man nodded to the CIA SAC.

"Good evening." Dawson shot his cuffs. "Is he already here?"

"Yes, sir. He's in the same dining room. Do you know the way?"

Dawson said he did and started off at once. Anxiety knotted his stomach as he strode through the red-and-black decor. The thick carpet muffled his footsteps.

Two security guards stood outside the private dining area. Like the first, both wore black suits and earwigs.

"Good evening, Special Agent Dawson," the older of the two said.

"Good evening, Special Agent Reeves." Dawson remembered this man's name easily. The vice president never went anywhere without him. Without being asked, Dawson gave his briefcase to the younger of the two agents.

Reeves made no apology for their quick search of the briefcase's contents. The vice president was adamant about his personal security. All the briefcase contained was Dawson's encrypted notebook computer and a satellite phone keyed to it.

The younger agent handed Dawson's briefcase back. "Here you go, sir. Everything looks in order."

Dawson accepted the case; then Reeves knocked on the door.

"Yes," the vice president called.

"Special Agent Dawson is here, sir."

"Good," the vice president said. "Show him in."

Elliott Webster, former senator from New Hampshire and party whip and now Vice President of the United States of America, stood at one end of the intimate dining table. He was an inch over six feet tall and maybe twenty pounds overweight but it looked good on him. He was in his late forties but easily looked twenty years younger due to the strong jawline and the dark blond hair that had refused to gray. His cerulean blue eyes invited friendship and promised trustworthiness within a nanosecond of being turned on someone. Many men instinctively trusted him and many women wanted to coddle him.

No matter how imposing the setting in which Dawson saw Webster, the vice president seemed to fill the room. The man oozed charisma.

He'd grown up in a small town in New Hampshire and started his own software company when he was sixteen. By the time he was in college at Harvard, majoring in business, he'd created two dot-com search engines that had boosted him into millionaire status. At about the same time, he'd gotten interested in politics because the oil shortage of the 1970s had impacted his business.

In an interview with Barbara Walters, Webster had admitted that his initial interest in politics had stemmed from corporate affairs.

"You just can't do business in this day and age without knowing something about the national and international political climate," Webster had said. A lot of businessmen had followed his example.

Webster hadn't pawned off the responsibility to lobbyists, though. He'd gotten in and dug into the legislation himself. As he'd learned how to negotiate those murky waters and become even more successful, a groundswell of grassroots support sprang up to put Webster in office as a New Hampshire senator. He'd graciously turned down the offers.

With the advent of stem cell research and his own investments in the field, Webster had again been stymied by legal pressures. That had been the first major stumbling block in his career, but it hadn't lasted long.

Webster's wife, Vanessa Hart Webster, the former Miss America who had won the hearts of a nation with her beauty and glorious voice, had been the perfect foil for her husband. She was glamorous and educated, and loved children and animals. The camera loved her, too. After she'd retired from her year as Miss America, she'd gone to work with Webster. They married soon after. They'd been practically inseparable since.

Vanessa Webster had spent several stints in the Middle East shoring up troop morale. Her husband's gaming companies had donated millions of dollars' worth of products for the young soldiers. The Webplay system and its innovative games had gotten extensive exposure in the media and through the military. Vanessa had organized charitable medical help for the children and soldiers wounded in the war. Her husband had contributed heavily to causes that helped the soldiers and their families back home. The media started talking about "Vanessa's War" as she continued her efforts.

Five years into the marriage, though, Vanessa had become ravaged by pancreatic cancer. She was by that time the hostess of her own nationally syndicated talk show, dedicated to finding charities who would benefit from her husband's money. Even as she fought the disease, she became a spokesperson advocating stem cell research to cure cancer. The nation, and her terrified husband, had watched her wither and die for over a year.

Then the people had grieved with thirty-one-year-old Elliott Webster when he'd buried his beautiful and generous bride. After a year spent out of the eye of the public, Webster had returned and said he was going to run for senator in New Hampshire.

"Since I was a boy," Webster had said with grim resolve, "I have pursued technology and science. I became involved with business only because I needed funding to continue my exploration of emerging technologies. My time with my dear Vanessa has taught me a lot. Her loss, when we have turned away from the very science that might have saved her life as well as the lives of millions of other people, is unconscionable to me. When I'm senator, I'm going to work to free up the roadblocks that an ill-informed Congress has made to science. I'm going to return the future to all people."

That declaration, RETURNING THE FUTURE, had become the rally cry first of New Hampshire, then of the nation. Twelve years later when President Michael Waggoner had selected Webster as his running mate, it surfaced again. They won the election in a landslide victory.

Now, with all the contacts he'd made while helping his wife's efforts in the Middle East, Webster was point man for the Middle East peace talks.

And a whole lot of other things as well.

"Good evening, Jimmy," the vice president said. "It's good to see you."

"It's good to see you, sir." Dawson took Webster's hand and shook briefly. As always, the familiar electric tingle ran through Dawson. Just being near the vice president seemed to inspire well-being and a positive attitude in people, even people who knew him well. The brief contact of flesh almost made Dawson forget the snafu in Istanbul.

"Please have a seat." Webster waved his napkin to the plush chair to his right. The room was small and elegant, set up for an intimate party.

Dawson sat. Whenever he had dinner with the vice president, Webster always had him sit on his right. Dawson liked the feeling of being the vice president's right-hand man. It was the little things, these small details, that Webster was so good at.

"I took the liberty of ordering dinner," Webster said. "I hope you don't mind, but I know we're both pushing the clock here."

"I'm sure whatever you ordered will be fine, sir."

Webster poured two glasses of wine, then handed one to Dawson. "Let's say we get rid of the white elephant in the room, Jimmy," Webster said. "That way we can get on with our dinner."

"Yes, sir." Tension rattled through Dawson.

"I'm not happy with losing Professor Thomas Lourds over in Istanbul."

"No, sir."

"I know you're not happy about it either."

"No, sir. I don't want to make a habit of letting you down."

Webster clapped Dawson on the shoulder and smiled. "I have a short list of people I know I can count on for anything. You're right there near the top."

"Thank you, sir."

Webster took a roll from the covered basket in the middle of the table, then offered the basket to Dawson.

"No, thank you, sir."

"Nonsense. You need to eat. Keep your strength up. We've got a lot to do if we're going to pull a win out of this."

Dawson took a roll and put it on the small saucer in front of him.

The vice president buttered his own roll, then pushed the butter dish toward Dawson. "Indulge. We'll work it off the next time we're on the racquetball court together." Webster smiled.

Dawson buttered his roll.

"How long ago did we lose Professor Lourds, Jimmy?"

Dawson glanced at the PDA he'd deliberately placed on the tabletop within his view. The number in the upper left-hand corner revealed how long ago Lourds had gone missing.

"Five hours and forty-two minutes, sir."

Webster bit into his roll and chewed thoughtfully. "That's a long time."

"I've got people on it, sir. We're using all available intel sources. Including ELINT and HUMINT."

The vice president nodded. "I know you've got good people over there."

"*We've* got good people over there, sir."

"Of course. *We* do." Webster sipped his wine. "This is my fault, actually. I didn't get the information to you about Lourds in time to make all the preparations you needed to. I shot you in the foot on this one."

That was another reason everyone liked Elliott Webster so much: When he made mistakes, he owned up to them and then he worked to correct them.

"I assume that the men killed at the airport were our assets?"

"Yes, sir."

"What about the other men that were killed in the car crash and in the alley? Do you have anything on them yet?"

"Yes, sir." Dawson pointed to his briefcase. "If I may?"

The vice president nodded and reached for another roll.

Dawson took out the encrypted computer and placed on the tabletop. He opened it, powered it up, entered his password, and pressed his right forefinger and left ring finger on the two fingerprint scanners. The password changed hourly and the combination of fingerprints changed twice daily. In the beginning, getting the rhythm of those changes had been difficult.

The screen flared to life and quickly searched for the local Wi-Fi connection. Once the connection had been accessed, a red-and-yellow CIA TOP SECRET screen saver flashed on. But that was just window dressing to scare off normal hackers who might have gotten their hands on the computer.

Dawson entered a series of keystrokes that shut down the main drive and opened up a small partition drive disguised within the computer's OS file registry.

"First of all, we haven't been able to learn anything about the three of Lourds's kidnappers that were killed," Dawson said after all the requisite connections had been made.

"That's disappointing."

"Yes, sir. But the woman is a different story." Dawson brought up a picture of her.

"That's a pretty young woman."

"Yes, sir."

"She intercepted Lourds at the airport."

"Yes, sir. Lourds has an obvious weakness for pretty young women, based on the history we've been able to dig up."

"Young women."

"That's right, sir. Evidently our opposition knows that."

"Who is she?"

Dawson's fingers tapped commands quickly on the keyboard. More pictures of the woman filled the screen. There weren't very many, but there were enough. Some of them showed her on the street talking to people. Others were of her in a bar.

"Her name is Cleena MacKenna."

"Irish?"

Dawson nodded. "Very Irish. Her father, Ryan MacKenna, was part of the Continuity Irish Republican Army. He was responsible for a number of attacks against the British military and Royal Ulster Constabulary. Some reports I've seen put his kills at seven, others at thirteen."

Dawson tapped more keys, and photographs of MacKenna's victims showed.

"A dangerous man," Webster commented. "However, the world seems full of them these days. Is he involved with this?"

"No, sir. Ryan MacKenna was killed six years ago." Dawson brought up the news clippings. "Evidently he got caught up in an arms deal that went south. A Chinese street gang called the Hungry Ghosts intercepted Flynn and his seller. Both of them were murdered."

"If MacKenna's not involved with this, why mention him?"

"Because I think Professor Lourds's weakness may be exploitable for us."

"Explain."

Dawson went back to the pictures of Cleena MacKenna. "When Ryan MacKenna was killed, he left behind two daughters. Years before, his wife was killed in their home, supposedly by police officers seeking revenge for one of their number that MacKenna had slain. No one knows if MacKenna really killed that policeman or even if it was policemen that killed his wife. But, either way, MacKenna moved his girls to Boston."

"That's where Lourds is from."

"Yes, sir. Cleena was twelve when her father moved her to Boston. Her younger sister, Brigid, was six. Evidently, some time in there, Cleena finished high school, started college, and joined her father in the family business."

"Arms dealing?"

"Exactly. The FBI has an open file regarding their business. Ryan MacKenna was good at what he did, a very careful man. Nobody ever got a whiff of evidence against them."

"Until that night with the Chinese gang."

"Yes, sir. It's hard to clean up evidence when you're dead. Cleena was nineteen when her father was killed. According to the FBI files I've seen, Cleena MacKenna spent seven months tracking down those gang members. She killed sixteen of them before they left the city. Not that we can prove it."

"Impressive. Evidently her father taught her all aspects of the family business."

"Yes, sir. After she'd finished dealing with her father's killers, Cleena MacKenna dropped out of college and became a full-time mercenary and arms dealer. She's hired out since then to do retrieval work—assets and people—as well as assassinations."

"Ambitious young woman, isn't she?"

Dawson nodded. "Yes, sir. And very good at what she does. The FBI and Boston Police Department have been on her trail for the last six years. Even Interpol has her marked as a person of interest in some cases they're working. None of those people has made a case yet."

"Obviously a very careful young woman as well," Webster said. "I'm sure the law enforcement authorities haven't been the only threats she's weathered."

"No, sir."

Webster poured more wine and reached for another roll. "What are you thinking, Jimmy?"

"Whoever this group is that has Lourds, they hired Cleena MacKenna to trail him from Boston to Istanbul. She traveled under a forged passport, but we know who she is. We can find her."

"And hire her ourselves?"

"Or at least pay her for any information she might have about the people who hired her to help kidnap Professor Lourds."

"I'd like to know more about these kidnappers," Webster said. "And how they came to be interested in Professor Lourds at the same time we were looking for him."

Dawson didn't point out that he still didn't know why the vice president wanted to bring Lourds in. "Yes, sir."

Webster sipped his wine. "Not to rain on your parade, Jimmy, but Cleena MacKenna might be reluctant to sell out her previous employers. People like that have a reputation they have to live up to."

Dawson hesitated only for a second. A lot of politicians didn't like to risk getting their hands dirty. Vice President Elliott Webster wasn't one of them, but he didn't like getting caught with his hand in the cookie jar.

"If by chance there is some residual moral high ground still lurking inside her mind," Dawson said, "we can just remind her that we know who she is and where her young sister goes to college."

"Do you think you can contact this young woman?"

"Yes, sir. We have assets that she'll need to get out of the country. The cover identity she used to get into Istanbul is blown. The local law enforcement people, and part of the criminal element there, are going to be looking for her. Sooner or later, she'll come to someone we have a relationship with. Then we'll have her."

"That sounds like a good plan, Jimmy. There's only one catch that I see."

"What's that, sir?"

"There is the distinct possibility that her employers won't let her live. They don't appear to be the trusting sort."

"Yes, sir." Dawson had already been thinking along those lines.

"After we're finished with her, Jimmy, I think we should probably limit our exposure as well."

"Of course, sir." And that was the best thing Dawson liked about the vice president: When it came to intelligence work, they thought along the same lines. "I'll take care of it personally." He pressed the keys on the computer and the woman disappeared.

CHAPTER 5

CATACOMBS
YESILKOY DISTRICT
İSTANBUL, TURKEY
MARCH 16, 2010

Lourds struggled to wakefulness.

Then he remembered the helicopter exploding overhead, the flaming pieces of it ringing when they slammed into the alley. And he remembered the hypodermic the man had thrust into his leg. Pain in his thigh suddenly increased.

He forced his eyes open and didn't think he'd succeeded because he still couldn't see. Then he realized that he couldn't see because he was somewhere dark. There was no light anywhere. He felt like he'd been surrounded in black cotton.

Shifting, he tried to sit up, then discovered he was in fact sitting. Not only that, but someone had tied him to a chair. The rope pulled tightly into his flesh. His kidneys also suddenly declared they were losing the war against containment.

He cleared his voice and heard the sound echo for a bit.

Sudden fear spiked through him when he realized that the echoes sounded muffled, like he was in some kind of cave or box. He cleared his throat again and listened more carefully this time.

The echoes, short and repetitive, definitely indicated he was within an enclosed space. He held his fear at bay with difficulty. He wasn't afraid of the dark—he had been in plenty of dark places before while working on transcribing hieroglyphics in Peruvian ruins. He wasn't afraid of enclosed spaces—he had crawled around plenty of those while exploring digs and while dating a couple of aggressive spelunkers.

However, he *was* afraid of what was going to be done to him by whoever had taken him. Stiff patches on his shirt told him he'd been unconscious at least long enough for the blood to dry. He felt more dried blood on his hands and face.

He thought about just sitting there, hoping that whoever had taken him had forgotten about him. But his kidneys were screaming for relief and he thought he'd rather die with some dignity. That meant no wet pants.

Of course, as soon as you see a gun or knife in someone's hand, that's subject to change. Lourds had never been one to fool himself about his personal bravery. He was brave neither by habit nor by choice.

Quietly, he cleared his throat again, then called out politely, "Hello? Is anyone there?"

Cleena MacKenna lounged against the wall of the catacombs her latest employers had brought her down into. She wasn't surprised to find that the city was honeycombed with tunnels. Most port cities and older cities in this part of the world were. In the beginning, the builders had needed places to store water and dump refuse.

Smuggling had also figured into the construction of tunnels in port cities. While growing up in Boston, she had explored several of those tunnels with other kids her age who had gotten into "urban archaeology." They'd called themselves creepers and swore they were uncovering the lost past of the city. Actually, they had just been kids going places they weren't supposed to go.

At first, Cleena's father had been angry with her when he found out where she was. Later, after she'd shown him some places they could use to hide the weapons he bought, sold, and traded, he hadn't been so angry. He just hadn't liked the idea of her crawling around dangerous places in the dark. Cleena had enjoyed it, had relished the excitement of going through those tunnels. It had been like entering another world.

A dozen men occupied the stone room she sat in now. They sat on crates and kegs brought by earlier visitors to the catacombs. Heavy-duty battery-powered lanterns pushed away some of the darkness inside the room, but Cleena still felt like it was a scene from one of those silly horror movies her younger sister liked to watch.

The men were passionate about whatever had brought them together. The tense and strident tones in their voices told her that. They didn't speak in English, which was frustrating because Cleena wished she knew what they were talking about. Several of them kept glancing in her direction, and she was all too aware that she was the only woman among them.

The comfortable weight of the pistol she had picked up during the firefight rested at her back. Her right hand was never far from the weapon. The men knew that. They had the watchful eyes of trained killers.

"Hey," Cleena interrupted.

The men turned and looked at her, but said nothing.

"I don't mean to bust up your little tea party," she said, "but I want my money and I want to get gone from this place. In case you've forgotten, there's a huge dragnet going on throughout the city right now. I need to get out before it closes in on me."

For a moment, the men continued staring at her without speaking. The whole experience was creepy and just a tad threatening.

"Anyone?" Cleena prompted.

One of the men stood and approached her. Cleena's hand slid down slightly to grip the butt of the pistol.

"Please accept my apologies, Miss MacKenna." The man looked like he was in his thirties, dark skinned and dark haired. Lean and handsome, he could've been a ladies' man if he wanted to be. But there was something that burned in his eyes that told Cleena he would never be satisfied with something so trivial as that. "My name is Qayin. Given the circumstances, I must ask you to be a little patient with us. Things did not go as we had planned."

"Things did not go as I had planned either." Cleena put an edge on her words. "You should be grateful that I don't ask you for a bonus on this job."

"I'm sure something can be arranged quite soon," Qayin told her confidently. "You went far beyond what was expected of you."

That gave Cleena a bad feeling. No one in her line of work ever offered a bonus.

"If you'll be patient just a little bit longer," Qayin said, "I'm certain you'll be taken care of."

Cleena made herself nod. She resolved to get out of the catacombs at the first opportunity. Screw the money. It was apparent to her she wasn't going to get the balance of the payment. Either they would simply stiff her or they would try to put a bullet between her eyes. The bullet was looking more and more likely.

A cold light blurred through Qayin's eyes and she wondered if he could read her thoughts. Still, he left her there and went back to the group. Most of the argument amongst them seemed to revolve around a notebook that the men kept passing back and forth. The notebook was obviously handmade. The leather binding was hand-stitched and the paper had a lot of rag content.

Cleena knew about rag content in paper because she had dabbled in counterfeit currency.

Brigid's next year of college at Cambridge was coming up quick and Cleena's nest egg had dwindled over the winter because business had been slow and payments not so good. The recession was causing cutbacks even in crime.

No matter what it took, Cleena was determined that her sister would get the chance to lead a legal and successful life. When she'd gotten the call about the linguistics professor from Harvard, Cleena had just figured the job was a gift. The money was well into six figures. She hadn't gotten many of those lucrative deals lately.

And you didn't get one this time, either. Cleena cursed her luck.

The men had the book open again. They moved one of the lanterns closer to the pages. Even from across the room, Cleena could see the designs that filled the space, but she didn't know what they were or what they signified. However, since she had helped kidnap a noted linguistics scholar, she would have bet Brigid's next year's college tuition that the man expected the professor to read that page.

Qayin sighed in exasperation and ran a long-fingered hand through his hair. His suit coat moved back just enough to briefly reveal the pistol holstered at his hip. He looked up at one of the men, said something, and jerked his head for the doorway.

The man was gone for only a moment before returning. He spoke quickly.

Qayin closed the notebook and turned to face Cleena. "It appears that the professor is awake. Would you care to join us?"

Cleena couldn't help but wonder what the man's response would be if she had said no.

She smiled at Qayin. "I'd love to." Movement was good. As long as she was moving, she had a chance to find a way to escape.

Futilely, Lourds pulled at his bonds and tried to loosen them. The legs of the wooden chair scratched against the stone floor.

He blew out all his breath, then attempted to raise his hands and slither down below the ropes. He remembered reading something about an escape attempt like that in one of the adventure novels he read whenever his studies permitted.

Those people in books were always thinking.

The plan worked a lot better for the character in the novel than it did for Lourds. He just ended up getting more winded and was afraid for a moment that he had trapped himself in a position that would slowly strangle him.

During his frantic efforts to return himself to his previous position, Lourds shoved back against the chair and it fell over with him still attached to it. He landed with a harsh bang and the back of his head struck the stone floor.

Lying on his back, he realized that his new position was much worse than where he had initially been. Now the blood was draining to his head and causing his temples to throb. And it wasn't just his pants he had to worry about wetting, thanks to gravity and angle. He let out a heartfelt sigh.

As an adventure hero, you make a much better linguistics professor.

He wondered if it would be too embarrassing to call out for help again. On the other hand, that course of action might simply hasten his death.

I don't have these kinds of problems in lecture halls.

Footsteps sounded far away and seemed to be coming closer. Given the acoustics in the room, Lourds couldn't figure out where they were coming from. He craned his neck around, but the overturned chair blocked a lot of his view.

Which was of unrelieved darkness.

But only a few minutes later, swaying incandescent light filtered into the room.

Lourds narrowed his eyes against the light because it seemed so bright. At least ten figures approached him and he saw there were multiple lights among them. When they got close enough, he recognized only one of them.

The young redhead peered down at him in disbelief. "You managed to do this to yourself by yourself?"

"It was the chair," Lourds protested. "It wasn't properly set on the floor."

"How do you get out of bed in the morning without breaking your neck?"

Lourds struggled to hang on to his dignity, but lying on his back with a full bladder while tied to a chair made that almost impossible. "I get out of bed just fine. I'm just not much of an escape artist."

The young woman folded her arms and looked at him disparagingly. "You suck as an escape artist."

"Thanks," Lourds said dryly. He looked at the men that circled him. "Who are your friends?"

"Employers."

Lourds tried to shrug, but found he couldn't while tied up this way. "However you wish to designate them."

"You can be a real pain, you know."

"I've been told. But after having been abducted at gunpoint, shot at, and nearly blown up, I think my behavior is perfectly understandable." Lourds kept his fear in check. "So what happens now?"

"Now, Professor Lourds, we'll see if your abilities match your reputation," one of the men said.

Lourds glanced at the man but was certain he had never seen him before in his life. "You know who I am?"

The man regarded Lourds with a cold, penetrating gaze. "I do, but that doesn't mean you're the one I seek."

If I'm not, you've gone to a lot of trouble for nothing. Lourds wanted to say that. It was something a hero in a novel or in a movie would say. But it wouldn't be said while lying on their back tied to a chair. Maybe he should keep his mouth shut.

The man turned away and gestured to Lourds. "Get him up."

Two men grabbed hold of the chair and righted Lourds. The jarring did his kidneys no good at all.

"If I can draw your attention to something important," Lourds said. "I've been tied to this chair for a long time. Is there a lavatory nearby?"

The leader of the group said something to one of the men. Lourds found it strange that he didn't know the dialect or the language. He knew enough of most languages to get along in them.

The man quickly bowed, then departed. He returned promptly and dropped a rusty bucket at Lourds's feet.

Lourds couldn't believe it. "Surely you're jesting."

"You can use the bucket or not," the leader said. "The choice is yours."

"I'm going to need to stand up."

The man nodded. One of the others untied the ropes in a simple movement. Lourds felt even more foolish when the man made it look so easy. His hands and forearms stung as blood rushed back into them.

Lourds looked at the woman. "I would prefer it if you turned your back."

"You're modest?" The woman raised her eyebrows skeptically. "After that moment we shared in the alley?"

Lourds wasn't sure if the young woman was trying to impress him or the men. It didn't matter. He fumbled with his pants and got everything arranged properly.

Gratefully, Lourds let loose and sighed in relief. Unfortunately, his aim wasn't all it could have been. Or that's what he made it look like. The boots of at least two of the men standing near him got soaked. They screamed in protest and jumped back.

"Sorry about that," Lourds said as he fastened his pants again. But he wasn't.

The leader held out a book open to a page. "I want you to read this, Professor Lourds."

Lourds stared at the page and tried to make sense of the symbols across it. The symbols weren't written on the page, not exactly. It was more like the writing had left indentations on the page. Or like a brass rubbing of an old tombstone. The writing was actually white blank spaces in the center of a graphite smear.

"Professor Lourds," the leader repeated impatiently, "can you read this?"

Concentrating on the script, Lourds barely registered the man's question. The symbols were deceptively familiar, yet they stubbornly remained just out of his reach. Excitement filled him and drowned the fear and pain in his mind. In all the years he'd been studying linguistics, all the countries and languages he had learned, there were now few languages that he couldn't fluently decipher in their written form. His professors and later colleagues had insisted his brain had been hardwired with code breakers.

Lourds didn't think that was true. He loved languages, loved the mystery and beauty of them, and—most of all—he loved to read. So much knowledge was lost in the world because cultures had lost their languages over the years, or gradually changed to that of their conquerors.

"Professor Lourds." The leader stepped forward and touched his pistol barrel between Lourds's eyes. "Are you able to read that?"

Lourds glanced at the man and told him the truth. The professor could lie when he needed to, but that generally involved knowing the person he was lying to well enough to lie believably.

"No," he said. "I can't read it."

The man thumbed the hammer back on the pistol and growled in frustration.

Despite the obvious threat to his life and the man's displeasure, Lourds was more afraid that he wouldn't get the chance to puzzle out the document than he was of dying. His death was a given thing. Sooner or later, he would die. But finding a real challenge to his skills and mastery of languages? Those opportunities came few and far between. Even rarer was the puzzle that would not only tax his abilities, but also prove worthy of the effort. The search for Atlantis had taught him that those puzzles were still out there.

And now, perhaps, here was another great mystery to be solved.

He stared into the man's blue eyes. "I can't read it," Lourds said again. "Yet."

The pistol shook against his head because the man was so angry. *"Yet?"* the man repeated.

"Yet," Lourds repeated. "If you give me some time, I can figure this out. This is what I do, and I do it better than anyone else."

Cleena watched the confrontation with a growing unease. Lourds was foolish and didn't know enough to take care of himself. She'd already seen that. In the SUV and in the alley, he'd obviously been in over his head. But as he held the book and stared at the page Qayin had indicated, Lourds changed.

She was certain he still feared for his life, but there was no way to fake the excitement that was in his eyes. The passion she saw there was unmistakable. She wouldn't have believed him capable of it. When she'd read his file and understood how she was to approach him at the airport, she guessed that he was some rich, privileged snob. Exactly the kind of person she wouldn't care about.

Now, seeing him in his element, Cleena understood how young women could find him so attractive. And challenging as well. A woman couldn't ignore passions that ran that strong in a man.

His fascination about the book kept him focused on that instead of on the danger he was in. Cleena actually felt sorry for him. When Lourds was finished decrypting or translating the document Qayin and his followers had brought him, they would kill him. Whatever secrets they were after, they wouldn't want anyone else to know about them.

Cleena realized her situation wasn't much better than the professor's. They had contacted her through one of the drops she used, and offered money. In their world, she was just as disposable as the professor. She didn't understand why they hadn't already tried to kill her. But, unlike the professor, she had a pistol, and she knew how to use it.

Keep your calm, girlie, she heard her father say again. *No one gets out alive that can't keep a cool head. The best weapon you'll ever carry is between your ears.*

"If just anyone could have read this page," Lourds said in a calm, controlled voice, "you would've already had it deciphered. Am I correct?"

The silence stretched in the darkness. Three of Qayin's followers stepped forward menacingly. Two of them grabbed the professor's arms. The third grabbed him by the neck.

"Careful," Lourds said. "Don't hurt the book." Even though the men lifted him from his feet, the professor tried to protect the book.

One of the men slid a knife free and held the keen edge to Lourds's throat. He looked at Qayin and waited expectantly.

Lourds didn't even try to fight back.

Surreptitiously, Cleena slid her hand around the pistol butt. In the darkness, with the men gathered so close together, she liked her chances. At least for a moment, she wouldn't be able to miss her targets. After that, though, things became dicey quickly.

Qayin held up a hand to his followers and peered at Lourds. "Do you think you can translate this document?"

Lourds didn't hesitate and spoke with more confidence under the circumstances than Cleena would have thought possible. "I can. If you give me time, I can translate anything."

Cleena said, "How much time?"

"I don't know. Linguists and archaeologists worked on the Rosetta Stone for years before they made a breakthrough."

Lifting his pistol, Qayin consulted a Rolex on his wrist. "You have twenty minutes to make a believer of me, Professor."

Cleena expected Lourds to protest the time frame. There was no way Qayin could seriously expect the professor to crack whatever was on the page. All he had succeeded in doing was delaying his death for a few minutes.

But he also bought you some more time to think, girlie, so you'd best put your thinking cap on and get to it. You've got a great plan to come up with.

She had twenty minutes.

And the clock was ticking.

CHAPTER 6

CATACOMBS
YESILKOY DISTRICT
İSTANBUL, TURKEY
MARCH 16, 2010

Lourds reached for one of the lanterns the men carried. Before the man could react, the professor had it in hand. He didn't know the man was reaching for a gun until the barrel was pressed up against his cheek.

"What are you doing?" Lourds asked in disbelief. "I need the light if I'm going to be working."

The leader waved the man off, but he clearly wasn't happy about removing the gun. He growled what Lourds believed were curses and walked away.

"My apologies, Professor," the leader said. "Perhaps it would be best if you made no sudden moves. We lead very dangerous lives. There are people out there who would kill us on sight."

As I recall, your people don't have any problem responding in kind. Lourds thought that, but he didn't say it.

"Now that we have reached something of an understanding, allow me to introduce myself." The man bowed his head slightly but never dropped his gaze from Lourds's. "I'm called Qayin. Other than light, is there anything else you need?"

Lourds's mind spun as he looked at the page again. "A desk, perhaps?"

"No, sorry."

Now that he had emptied his bladder, Lourds discovered he was starving.

"I suppose asking for a pizza would be out of the question."

"Absolutely."

"Then do you have my backpack?"

Qayin nodded to another of his followers, and the man quickly sprinted away. He returned momentarily with Lourds's backpack, but when the professor reached for it, the man held it too far away.

"I don't have any weapons in there," Lourds said. "I do have a couple of nutrition bars."

When the man finished searching the backpack, he handed it over.

Lourds hunkered down. All the men in Qayin's gang pointed their lanterns and pistols at him. He could hear safeties click back and pistols cocking. Moving slowly, Lourds reached into the backpack and took out a journal, a pen, two trail bars, and a bottle of water. He displayed his treasures for the rest of the group to see.

"I need something to work with," Lourds said. "And I'm hungry."

The pistols and lanterns slowly drew back.

Lourds stood, hoisted the backpack over one shoulder, and juggled his food, writing utensils, and the book Qayin had given him. He crossed the room and sat with his back against the wall.

"This wasn't written on the page." Lourds traced his fingers over the symbols on the surface. They felt slightly matted, and the texture told him that a fixative had been applied to the page. "This is a rubbing."

"A child could have told me that."

Lourds ignored the sarcasm. "Where did you get this? Where was the rubbing taken?"

"That doesn't matter."

"I beg to differ. Knowing where this rubbing came from and when the original carvings were done might help me isolate this language. Establish the root."

Qayin hesitated, obviously ill at ease when it came to revealing anything about the book.

"It came from here."

Lourds took a bite of his trail bar and chewed quickly. "By here, you mean Istanbul?"

Qayin nodded.

"Or do you mean Constantinople?"

A look of irritation flashed across Qayin's hard features. "This city. That's all you need to know."

"No, that isn't all I need to know. Istanbul began as Constantinople, a city with European history. That's if you discount the Neolithic settlements and choose to begin with the Greek settlers from Megara. Then the Romans took over. After that, the Ottoman Empire arrived under Mehmed the Second. This city has constantly been torn between the East and the West, between Christian and Muslim, and those marks have been left throughout the city on various pieces of architecture." Lourds tapped the paper. "This is a rubbing, and I'm willing to wager that it came from some building within the city. If someone went to the trouble to create a new language, then I need to know if the mind that created that language was European or Eastern or African in origin."

"You think this is an artificial language?" the young woman asked.

Qayin didn't look happy about her asking questions.

"I don't recognize this language," Lourds said. "I know all the languages of this region. But throughout history, a number of people have created artificial languages to keep their secrets."

"Did you think the language that led you to the discovery of Atlantis was artificial?" the woman asked.

"For a time I had to consider that possibility, yes. As it turned out, that language wasn't artificial."

"Then you could be wrong about this one as well."

"You should listen to me here. You're out of your area of expertise." Lourds sighed. "We're not kidnapping anyone here now. This field is where I'm expert."

"The way I hear you, if you don't understand something, you can always cop out and just say, 'This language isn't real.' "

"Even an artificial language is real. *Star Trek* fans insisted that the Klingon language be made real. Tolkien invented languages for his characters, human and nonhuman. People are always creating languages. It's one of the things we do that sets us apart from every other creature on this planet. We communicate via language. Look at cell phones. Only a few short years ago, they didn't exist."

"Maybe at your age they didn't exist."

Lourds ignored her snarky attitude and continued. "People had to come up with a name for telephones that were fully portable. The term *cordless* had already been taken. So people started calling them *cellular telephones* at first. That quickly became bastardized to *cell phones,* and that gave way to just calling them *cells.* Mention *cell* after 9/11 and many people think of terrorism. However, the cell terminology didn't take in Britain. Over there, they call them *mobiles.*"

"I'm aware of that. I'm not a child."

"I have no doubt that you're aware of it. Your accent tells me you are very acquainted with the Ulsterland. I'd go as far as to say that you've been in Ireland often. Probably grew up there."

From the way her face went blank, Lourds knew he had hit close to home.

"But being aware of language and *thinking* about it are two different things," he continued. "Just because you know something doesn't mean you've thought about it. Language was created to express thoughts and ideas, to hand down education and history, to paint pictures of things that could only be imagined. Words have such an ephemeral quality to them because language is so organic that many words quickly pass in and out of usage and disappear. Or the way they are employed changes. Take the word *text.* Until that function was created for cells, it was never used as a verb. Now when people think of a text, they don't think of books. They think of electronic messages they receive on their cell phones."

"Professor," Qayin interrupted sharply. "You don't have time to give a lecture."

"I wanted to make a point. Not only is language geographical, but the time a document was written is also tremendously important."

"You are running out of time."

Lourds fixed the man with his gaze. "Fine. Then tell me where this rubbing came from and when it was made."

Qayin's hot, angry gaze held Lourds. All the fear the professor had been holding at bay returned in a gut-twisting rush.

You've just gotten yourself killed. Lourds tried not to be sick, but his mouth turned dry as cotton.

After a moment, Qayin said, "I'm told that the rubbing was taken from somewhere inside this city. The writing is from early in the second century after the death of Christ."

The magnitude of the statement settled over Lourds. Almost two thousand years had passed since these words were written. He focused on the rubbing.

"This ought to be some form of Greek language, then," he mused out loud. He opened the water bottle and drank as he thought. "We've done a lot of work with Mycenaean Greek, Ancient Greek, and Koine Greek. But we can't rule out the possibility that this is some kind of Proto-Greek."

"It's Greek?" Qayin asked.

Lourds shrugged. "Possibly. Some of the characters look familiar, but they're not quite right. They bear some resemblance to Greek characters, but they're unique at the same time."

"Why Greek?" the woman asked.

"Because Greek was one of the primary languages in this area at that time. The language of the conquerors, of Alexander the Great. At the time, he ruled almost all the known world. When he put his people in place to hold different lands, they were trained to read and write in Greek. Conquerors build buildings. As a result, the Greek language is still scattered throughout Europe and parts of Asia. There was Latin by then as well, but these letters don't look Roman. I'm guessing they're some form of Greek."

Qayin and his followers listened silently.

"When this rubbing was taken, was the inscription new?" Lourds asked.

"I don't know," Qayin answered. "I was told it was taken soon after."

"Soon after what?"

Qayin shook his head. "What I know will not help you."

"I think I'd be the better judge of that."

"You're not going to get to know any more. Now you tell me which Greek language this is."

"This isn't simply any Greek language," Lourds said. "If it were, you would already have had this translated. But it does have its foundation in the Greek language. Of that, I'm sure." He paused. "If we can assume that the date this rubbing was taken was somewhere around A.D. second century, then the root language would most likely be Koine Greek. That was in use from the middle of the fourth century B.C. to the middle of A.D. fourth century."

"Then it is based on this language?" Qayin asked.

"It could also just as easily be based on the Mycenaean and Ancient Greek languages."

"Are those so very different?"

"Of course they're different," Lourds answered. "The Greeks were a culture of traders. They went everywhere across the known world. And they were successful in what they were doing, which made other people want to be like them. The Mycenaean Greek language is the most ancient Greek language we can research. Several clay tablets were found in Knossos and Pylos, and those weren't translated until 1952. It was pretty dry stuff, too. Mostly inventories and lists, accountants' work. That language had seven grammatical cases, including the dative, locative, and instrumental. Both the latter two grammatical cases fell out of favor when Classical Greek was born, and dative has been dropped from modern Greek."

Excitement drummed through Lourds as his mind began grappling with the symbols. He could almost make sense of part of it, not what it said, but how it was put together.

"Ancient Greek was also used heavily in Constantinople. Most of Europe had stopped using it during the Middle Ages, but after Constantinople fell to Mehmed the Second, the language flourished again for brief time because of all the people that fled the city. Both Ancient Greek and Koine Greek were used in Constantinople."

"Was any one favored more than the other?" the woman asked.

"That's an interesting question." For just a moment, Lourds felt a glow of satisfaction. Even here, at gunpoint, he loved being an instructor. *There is something definitely wrong with you, my friend.* "Rome preferred Ancient Greek because they thought it was more pure. Koine Greek was actually a blend of several Greek dialects with Attic, which was the language spoken in Athens. As I've mentioned, that language is spread primarily through Alexander the Great's armies, and it was spoken from Egypt to India. Early Christians adopted the Koine Greek language, possibly to differentiate themselves from the Romans and their gods, which were actually made over from the Greek pantheon. The Apostles preached in it. That language also became known as the Alexandrian dialect, Post-Classical Greek, and New Testament Greek because the Apostles wrote the New Testament in that language."

"The Apostles?" Qayin asked.

Lourds nodded absently, still trying to wrap his thoughts around the language.

"How can you know so much about this and still not be able to read it?" the woman asked.

"Knowing something about the language isn't the same as reading it. As I stated, language evolves, sometimes even from generation to generation. And if you have someone that deliberately tries to disguise information, as I believe was done here, deciphering that language becomes even harder. If you consider the New Testament and its subsequent translations that have fractured churches and religions, you'll get an idea of what I'm talking about." Lourds looked up at her. "Given the religious division between England and Ireland, I'd thought you might have known that."

"Religion is a touchy subject."

"Let me give you another example. Have you ever written down a note, then went back a few days later and saw it without understanding why you had written it?"

"No."

Lourds sighed and rubbed his face tiredly. "Well, I have." *Far more times than I want to remember.* "Just imagine that you have, and you can't figure out why you wrote the note in the first place. Now, instead of a few days, let a hundred years go by. Or even one thousand, just to make things interesting. Do you think that someone a few generations, or several generations, removed from the original writer will understand the context of that message even if they're able to read it?"

Quayin paused visibly before offering, "I will tell you this much, Professor: You are on the right track. I am told that this missive does indeed tie to one of the Apostles."

The excitement inside Lourds grew. He put his water bottle down and held the book in both hands. Desperately, he scanned the lines of writing. More than anything, he wanted to unlock the secrets that lay within the words.

"Now, tell me something about that writing that will save your life." Qayin's tone held deadly menace. The pistol lay naked in his lap.

"It's a warning." Lourds felt certain about that. "Or a command."

"I grow weary of these oblique answers."

Lourds pointed to one of the words. "I believe this is the word *diamarturomai.* That's Koine Greek. It means 'to solemnly charge'. In the New Testament, Second Timothy, Paul instructs Timothy about the danger of false teaching. Timothy was supposed to focus on the truth of God, and to teach that Satan is a liar and the father of lies."

"Church lessons?" the woman asked.

"Religion has always played a major part in the development of language," Lourds replied. "While merchants focused on sums and subtractions, of material things, language had to be developed to express ideals and manifest desired behaviors. In fact, Second Timothy also warns against churches wrangling over words interpreted from the Bible."

"Then this is about God's Truth?" Qayin asked.

Glancing up, Lourds saw that he had the man's full attention. "I didn't say that."

"Then what are you saying?"

In an effort to blunt the naked threat in the other man's eyes, Lourds said, "Of course, since you believe this document came from an Apostle, there is the possibility that this message is about a 'truth.'" He paused. "Or this could be a seal."

"What kind of seal?" The woman took a step closer to look at the page, sliding through Qayin's followers.

"Seals were used on letters. Usually a drop of hot wax marked with an insignia ring or a stamp that was unique. But there were other seals. Sometimes architects placed them on buildings they designed and built. The practice is still continued today, although changed somewhat."

"Cornerstones," Qayin said.

Almost forgetting for a moment that the man held his life in his hands, Lourds nodded eagerly. "Exactly. Cornerstones are laid, and the rest of the building follows."

"You believe this is from a cornerstone?"

Lourds hesitated. "Yes, if I have to guess—and obviously I do, given the time frame—I would say that this rubbing came from a cornerstone."

Qayin smiled, and Lourds decided he didn't like the effect. There was nothing chummy about the expression.

"You suddenly seem to know quite a lot about that inscription," Qayin said.

"On the contrary," Lourds disagreed, "I know next to nothing. This is just guesswork on my part. Under the gun, so to speak. It also stands to reason that the original object bearing this inscription is far too heavy to transport or cannot be moved." He paused. "Or it's been lost."

"Does the message give any indication of location?"

"I don't know. If this is a warning or command, it's most likely that it would've been placed deliberately. There would have been no need to mention the location."

Qayin scowled. "Then this paper is useless."

Lourds nearly choked on his sip of water when he realized what he had done. "I wouldn't say it's useless. There's still a lot that can be learned from it."

"What?"

"With this, I can learn to decipher the language. If there's more writing like this, I'll be able to read it. Given time."

Silence hung heavy in the catacombs and became as oppressive as the darkness.

"There's more writing somewhere," Lourds stated. "I'd bet my life on it."

"Maybe you are betting that life," Qayin said. "But you're right, there is more writing. We're in the process of searching for it now. I think you're going to get to live a little longer, Professor."

Lourds didn't feel happy about his small victory. Living in servitude was no choice he would make.

Still, death was a lot more final.

"Get up." Qayin stood and waved to his followers. "We need to leave this place."

Aches filled Lourds's knees and back as he forced himself up to his feet. He swung his backpack over his shoulder and picked up the book.

One of Qayin's followers slipped up behind the woman. Lourds caught the movement from the corner of his eye. Lantern light gleamed against the thick shiny blade in the man's hand. Lourds began to shout a warning, but he knew he would already be too late.

The woman must have sensed something, though. She moved as quickly as a striking snake and brought up her pistol. She fired point-blank range at the man's head. As the man fell, while everyone else stood stunned, she darted behind Lourds and grabbed him by the shirt collar. Her warm body pressed up against his.

The corpse sprawled to the stone floor in a loose spill of limbs.

The woman was barely tall enough to peer over Lourds's shoulder, but she managed. She also opened fire immediately. Her bullets smashed into flesh, but Qayin and his followers had shaken off their paralysis. They dropped their lanterns and ran for the darkness. Four of them didn't make it. The woman's aim was deadly, and in seconds she had halved the number of opponents they faced.

Certain he was about to get shot, Lourds tried to dive to the ground. The woman held on to him tightly and her forearm was like an iron bar across his Adam's apple. He choked and gagged, and remained on his feet.

"You just be a good boyo," the woman said. "They aren't going to want to shoot you. Not since you can read their precious little book and maybe whatever else they've got tucked away somewhere."

"You could be wrong about that, you know." Lourds blinked against the darkness and waited for bullets to rip into his body.

"No, you have your field of specialty, Professor, and I have mine. They paid a pretty penny—well, half a penny anyway—to get you here. Now that they think you can do what they hoped you could do, they're going to want to keep you alive."

Qayin spoke a harsh command. In response, a brief spate of gunfire rattled through the room. The woman fired back immediately and evidently hit one of her targets based on where she had seen the muzzle flashes. A man toppled into the pool of light created by the abandoned lanterns.

Lourds tried to move again, but the young woman held him firm.

"They didn't hit you, Professor," she whispered into his ear. "See? You're worth something to them. They missed you on purpose. And they've stopped firing."

Despite the fear that gripped him, Lourds knew she was correct. Standing there, highlighted by the lanterns, he knew he was an easy target.

"I guess there's no honor among thieves, is there, Qayin?" she asked. "You needn't bother answering."

"You're not getting out of here alive, Miss MacKenna," Qayin responded.

The woman fired at his voice without hesitation. Ricochets bounced wildly around the stone walls. One of them came uncomfortably close to Lourds's head.

"If you're not careful," he snapped, "you're going to kill us both."

She ignored him. "Are you still there, Qayin?"

Wisely, Lourds thought, Qayin didn't answer.

"Do you want to get out of here?" the woman whispered.

"I'd love to," Lourds whispered back, "but I think you may be getting a little ambitious. All they have to do is wait until you empty your pistol, then they'll jump you before you can reload."

"Okay, Professor, you've been impressing everyone with how knowledgeable you are about languages. Since we're in my field of study now, I'll be giving the lessons. Just make sure you take notes. There'll be a test at the end."

"What are you going to—?"

She rammed the pistol's hot muzzle under Lourds's jaw and declared, "Either you let us leave or I'm going to blow Professor Lourds's head off."

CHAPTER 7

THE EMERALD NIGHTCLUB
TRENTON STREET
BOSTON, MASSACHUSETTS
UNITED STATES OF AMERICA
MARCH 16, 2010

Dawson felt naked without a car, but Boston was a hard city to get around in one. He took a cab from Logan International after deplaning from a private charter. His early dinner with the vice president already felt like yesterday instead of just hours ago.

He pushed his cuff back and checked his Rolex. It was 11:54 P.M.

"Don'chu worry, mon," the Rastafarian cabdriver called from up front. He had long dreads and smelled of ganja. "Dis town, she be *live* at night. T'ings still gonna be happenin'. You have good time. You see."

Dawson ignored the man. The driver had Bob Marley on too loud, but the music seemed to fit in with the neon life tucked into the dark corners of the city.

The .40-caliber pistol on his hip felt good, dependable.

"Dis club," the driver said as he pulled up in front of the address, "she small, but I hear she be rockin'." He pumped his fist in the air and grinned.

"Glad to hear that." Dawson stepped out of the car and peeled bills off a roll.

"You lookin' for college girls, mon? 'Cause I hear this place be tight with 'em."

"Yeah." Dawson handed the man the fare. He wore jeans, a rugby shirt, and a midthigh suede jacket. He was vain enough to know that he could pass for late twenties in the bar light.

The Emerald Nightclub sat between a Chinese laundry and an electronics shop. Residential floors were above it and most of those lights were out. Neon tubing spelled out the bar's name across the curtained windows.

There was no waiting, but there was a big bouncer at the door. He was black, had a shaven head and gold chains, and a club shirt under a Sean John coat.

Dawson turned up his collar against the cold north wind and walked to the bar. The bouncer gave Dawson a cursory glance, then waved him through.

Inside, the club was jumping. Packed wall-to-wall with college students, the noise level was deafening. ESPN filled the large television screens behind the bar. Basketball games were still playing on the West Coast, and *Baseball Tonight* was covering spring training.

Brigid MacKenna filled drink orders behind the bar, moving smoothly and efficiently. At nineteen, she was trim and lean, maybe a couple inches over five feet tall and little more than a hundred pounds soaking wet. She hadn't gotten her sister's statuesque build and height. She wore her long brown hair pulled back in a ponytail and looked younger than nineteen.

A group of young guys, probably athletes judging from the letter jackets, sat at the bar and flirted with her. She seemed to enjoy the attention, but she kept working.

One of the seats near the end was open. Dawson sat and reached for the bowl of nuts on the bar. He shelled them and ate them, building a pile of fibrous hulls in front of him.

"Hey," Brigid greeted him a few minutes later. Her skin glowed from the fast-paced work she'd been doing. Her smile was almost electrifying.

"Hey," Dawson said, and smiled. "You're working too hard." He flattened out his *A*'s to mimic the Boston dialect.

Brigid jerked a thumb over her shoulder to indicate a short, squat man in his forties. The guy had forearms as big as Popeye's.

"Tell that to my boss," she said.

"Real slave driver?"

Brigid nodded, then asked, "What can I get you?"

"Sam Adams."

"Want a glass?"

Dawson waved the offer away.

Brigid reached below the bar and pulled up a bottle of beer. She set it down and opened it, then moved it to a napkin in front of Dawson. He slid a twenty dollar bill across the bar.

"Keep the change," he said.

The kitchen and supply room were directly behind the bar. With the crowd on hand, Dawson felt certain Brigid would have to go back there soon.

He was right.

When she did, he followed her into the short hallway. The kitchen was to his right and the supply room was to the left. Bathroom and the back door exit were in the rear.

Brigid stepped into the supply room and turned on the light. She took down an armload of packages of napkins and two bags of unshelled peanuts. When she turned around to leave, Dawson blocked the way.

She tried the smile first. Girls her age always did. But she caught on quick that approach wasn't going to fly. So she tried authority.

"You're not supposed to be back here."

Dawson kept his face expressionless. "Do you know where your sister is?"

That caught her attention, but she tried to bluff her way through it. "I don't have a sister. I have two brothers."

"You have zero brothers," Dawson told her. "You have one sister. Cleena MacKenna."

"You need to get out of here." She took a step forward as though she were going to bull her way past him. But he didn't move and she stopped short of touching him. All her bravery evaporated.

"I know where your sister is," Dawson said in a flat tone. "But I don't have a way of getting in touch with her."

"If you don't leave, I'm going to scream."

Dawson slapped her face with his open hand, hard enough to knock her back on her heels. She dropped the packages she'd been holding.

"You need to shut up," he stated, "and listen to me. If you scream, you'll never see your sister again. I promise you that." He moved his jacket enough to show her the pistol holstered at his hip.

Brigid held her face in her hands. Tears streamed down her cheeks. She shivered in fear.

"You've got a way to contact your sister when she's out of town," Dawson said. "Just nod your head. If you try to play me, I'm going to put you in the hospital."

She closed her eyes fearfully and nodded.

"Good." Dawson reached into his shirt pocket and took out a business card that had only a phone number handwritten on it. The writing wasn't his. "I need you to call her now."

Trembling, Brigid wiped blood from her face and nodded.

Dawson smiled to show there were no hard feelings. "If she's not there, leave her a message. I want her to call me back at this number." He stuck the card on top of a box of bottled beer. "Tell her if I don't hear from her in the next couple hours, she's never going to see you again."

Brigid shook as she silently cried, but she nodded in understanding.

"Hey, Brigid," a deep voice said. "What's taking so long? Those bums are outta nuts and they're startin' to get rowdy."

The man with the Popeye arms came around the corner and looked at Dawson and Brigid. Dawson turned to face him.

"Hey, what's goin' on here?" he demanded.

Dawson hit the man in the throat with the *Y* of his hand, then drew his pistol and whipped the man down to the floor with three blows. The man didn't even have a chance to cry out before he was an unconscious heap.

Breathing hard from the exertion, Dawson wiped blood from his face and turned back to Brigid. She finally found her voice.

"Help! Someone help!"

Dawson grinned at her, flipped the safety off his pistol, and raised it into position beside her head. "You shouldn't have done that."

The young men in letter jackets that had been flirting with Brigid ran to the doorway.

Dawson met them with the pistol in his fist. "Get back," he ordered coldly. "Get back or I'll kill you."

The would-be heroes griped and cursed, but they backed away before the pistol.

"Your sister," Dawson said as he eased out of the supply room and forced the young men backwards. "Have her call me as soon as she gets your message. Understand?"

"Yes."

Casually, Dawson stepped over the unconscious man, held the would-be heroes at bay with the pistol, and went through the security door at the back of the bar. The alarm blatted loudly and the sound rolled through the alley.

He stepped his pace up to a jog. A full run would have inspired some of the young guys to chase after him. Young guys were wired like that. But a lope told them he wasn't afraid. He also kept the pistol in his hand.

Luck was with him at the other end of the alley. A cab coasted up the street. At this time of night, a driver could make good money running people between bars and homes.

He changed cabs three more times before he headed back to the airport. By that time, with all the walking and changing cars, he was certain investigators wouldn't be able to pick up his trail.

Back aboard the private jet, Dawson settled into the comfortable seat and poured himself a glass of expensive bourbon. His heart rate was back to normal, but he kept thinking of how frightened Brigid MacKenna had been of him. A dark part of him liked that a lot. He sipped the bourbon as they waited tower clearance, then called the vice president.

"It's done, sir."

"Good, Jimmy. I take it you're all right?"

"Right as rain, sir. Couldn't be better. There are times like this when I really regret leaving the field."

Webster chuckled. "I'm glad you're all right. And I understand completely. When something needs doing, there's nothing like getting your hands dirty to make sure it's done properly."

"Yes, sir."

"You're certain Miss MacKenna will be calling?"

"Absolutely, sir." Dawson saw the young woman's face etched with fear in his mind again. "I'd say once she gets the message, calling that number will be the first thing on her mind."

"Now, then, we need to talk about what we next have on tap for Professor Lourds. We're going to need to expose him as an enemy of our great country."

Dawson took in a breath. "Sir?"

"It's true, Jimmy. There are some things that I haven't yet told you, and I'm going to tell you some of them now. We're going to need a team in Istanbul to pick the professor up as soon as he surfaces. This is a dangerous thing we're working on, Jimmy. A lot is riding on our success. We have to be slicker than we've ever been before. But you and I can do this."

CATACOMBS
YESİLKOY DİSTRİCT
İSTANBUL, TURKEY
MARCH 17, 2010

"You're going to kill me? If they don't kill me, you're going to kill me? *That's* your plan?"

Cleena thought she heard anger in Lourds's words, but it might only have been hysteria. Though either emotion would have been understandable.

"Shut up," she whispered as she held tightly to Lourds. "I'm trying to save your life."

"*My* life?" Lourds sounded as though he couldn't believe it. "They didn't start shooting until you grabbed me. I'd already saved my life."

"No, you just postponed the execution."

"It was working for me."

"Look," Cleena snarled through gritted teeth, "they were going to kill us no matter what. And truthfully, it would be easier for me to get out of here without you."

"Oh, really? And if you didn't have me to hold hostage, whom would you use as a human shield?"

Cleena knew Qayin and his men were moving in the darkness. They wouldn't stay down much longer, and reloading her weapon wasn't an option. She couldn't do it before they'd be on her.

"Here's how this works," Cleena whispered. "Either you come with me, or I shoot you. I won't shoot you to kill you, but I will wound you. Qayin and his lackeys will be concerned about you now that they've seen that you can read their mysterious little book. They'll busy themselves trying to save you. I'll take my chances in the confusion, but you'll still remain in their clutches." She shook him by the collar. "So, Professor, this is your last invitation. Do you want to come with me, or do you want me to leave you here?"

"Is there an option number three?"

She shook him again.

Lourds gave a brief nod. "Let's do this while my legs are still under me."

Slowly, Cleena backed out of the room. Instead of reaching the door, she bumped into the wall.

"What's wrong?" Lourds asked.

"The bloody door isn't where I left it." Cleena sidled down the wall.

"Are you lost?"

"No. Perhaps a little distracted and disoriented."

Lourds sighed. "Some rescue."

"Still thinking about the option of shooting you. It's getting more attractive."

The professor shifted, juggling the book in his arms and clapping his hat on his head. He pulled a Zippo lighter from his pocket and flicked it to life. The yellow-and-blue flame shimmered in the darkness and chased back the shadows.

"Do you see the door now?" Lourds asked. He focused on watching Qayin and his followers. The men slunk back into the shadows like cockroaches.

Cleena glanced over her shoulder. The light from the flame exposed a rectangle of blackness.

"Yes," she answered.

Qayin called out of the darkness left in big room. "Professor Lourds, I would advise you not to trust this woman."

"I don't trust her any farther than I could throw my left eyeball. However, trust appears to be a capricious thing down here at the moment. I already know I can't trust you. She's still a question mark."

Cleena backed through the door and glanced over her shoulder to make sure no one was behind her. The next room was as big as the last, and just as empty.

"Do you know where we are?" Lourds whispered.

"They weren't handing out maps when they brought us down here, and I didn't get the chance to leave a trail of bread crumbs."

"So you're just as lost now as you were a few minutes ago? Only in a bigger room? And these catacombs go on for miles beneath the city."

Catacombs were one of the most necessary engineering feats for thriving ancient cities. In centuries past, they'd served to contain water, store food, and house the dead. The thought of graves lodged somewhere in the dark walls left Cleena chilled.

"You are very irritating. And for your information, stating the problem doesn't solve it."

"Recognizing the problem provides focus."

"Do you have to have an answer for everything?"

"I'm a professor. It's my job."

"Professor," Qayin called.

"He's closer," Lourds whispered.

"I can hear that. I'm just lost, not deaf. And now that we're out of that room, they'll creep up to the doorway." It was what Cleena would do in their situation.

"Professor, are you listening?" Qayin called.

"I'm listening."

"Don't listen to him," Cleena snapped.

"I'm buying us time," Lourds said.

"Leave the book," Qayin urged. "Leave the book and we'll let you go free. Unharmed."

"I don't believe him," Lourds whispered. "Do you?"

"No." Cleena kept backing up, dividing her attention among the doorway, the professor, and the area behind them.

"We can find someone else to read the book, Professor," Qayin called.

"Right," Lourds whispered. "As if they haven't already been trying. I bet I've been the only one they've found."

"Kind of high on yourself, aren't you? You seemed to be struggling with that translation."

"I read part of it. In twenty minutes, I might add. Under pressure. And without my resource material."

"You're really modest, too."

"I'm good at what I do."

"They'll put that on your tombstone," Cleena whispered.

"I thought the objective was to get out of here alive."

"Ah, so you *are* listening."

Lourds cursed.

"Professor," Qayin called. "Do we have an agreement?"

Cleena thought desperately, then seized on an idea. She glanced at Lourds and the Zippo he held in his hand. The lighter had to be getting hot.

"Set fire to the book," she said.

Lourds balked and looked startled. "What?"

"Set fire to the book. If they care about it as much as they seem to, they'll be more interested in saving it than in pursuing us."

Lourds wrapped his arm tightly around the book and held it to his chest. "I'm not going to burn this book."

"It's not your book."

"It's not *their* book."

A fresh wave of irritation swept through Cleena. "You don't know if that book is even a real artifact. It could be a fake."

"I don't think someone went to all the trouble to fake an artificial language based on outdated Greek for an April Fool's joke. We don't know what we have here."

"Is that book worth our lives?" Cleena asked.

"I don't know. Maybe."

Qayin spoke again. "Professor, if I'm prepared to try to have another linguist decipher that book, then you have to know that I'm also prepared to shoot you and the woman at this point. I'll take my chances with finding another translator, but I won't lose that book."

"Set fire to the book," Cleena commanded again.

"No. I have a responsibility as a scientist to protect this book."

"So you can get your name on an article in some dusty science magazine."

"That's not what this is about."

Cleena cursed. "Are you really this stupid?"

Lourds suddenly yelped in pain and dropped the Zippo. The lighter hit the ground and the flame went out. Darkness immediately surrounded them.

"Oops."

Unbelievably, Lourds bent down as if to search for the dropped lighter. Cleena jerked on his shirt collar to get him moving.

"Come on!" she yelled, then threw a hip into him and knocked him to one side.

Lourds staggered and almost fell. He gagged as she kept hold on his shirt collar and guided him toward the door she'd seen on the other side of the room.

"I can't see," Lourds protested, and struggled to slow their headlong pace.

"Neither can they. Keep moving."

"We're going to hit a wall."

Qayin and his men opened fire behind them. Bullets ricocheted from the stone walls, trailing sparks in their wake.

"Okay. I see your point." Lourds stepped up his pace fast enough that he was dragging her after him.

Behind them, Qayin's followers retrieved their lanterns. Streams of fluorescent lights bounced over the wall ahead of them in time for them to correct their direction before they smashed into stone. Cleena and Lourds sprinted into the next room and took advantage of the partial lighting from the lanterns of their pursuers.

The gunshots echoed inside the chamber and the sound was enough to let Cleena know that the area was immense. Several stone pillars stood out in the darkness ahead of them and created a maze of obstacles. She pulled on Lourds's collar to slow his breakneck pace.

"To the left," Cleena ordered.

Immediately, Lourds veered to the left. He rounded a thick pillar and halted when she pulled him against it. She fell into hiding beside him and took time to reload her pistol with a fresh magazine. She had only one left after that. The odds weren't in their favor.

"What are you doing?" Lourds asked. "Shouldn't we be running?"

Cleena peered around the pillar and took a two-handed grip on her pistol. "Running sounds fantastic to me. Do you know *where* to run?"

"Haven't you been here before?"

"This is my first time."

"At least you were conscious when you were brought in."

"I was somewhat distracted getting to know all my new friends and trying to figure out if they were going to double-cross me. Which they did."

"You obviously stink at measuring character . . ."

Cleena lost the rest of what he was saying when one of Qayin's followers exploded through the doorway. The swinging lantern he carried made him a perfect target. She aimed for the center of the man's body and squeezed the trigger three times in quick succession.

At least two of the bullets caught the man and staggered him backwards. He sat down hard and his lantern rolled away. Thankfully, the light played over the doorway so Cleena could see if anyone else approached. Just as she realized the light was going to play in her favor, Qayin or one of his followers realized the same thing.

A burst of gunfire shattered and extinguished the lantern. Cleena waited a moment and fired at where she remembered the doorway was just to keep their opponents honest.

Almost immediately, a hailstorm of bullets struck the pillar they were hiding behind. Stone chips stung her face as she ducked to safety.

"Well, that's narrowed the odds to four to two," Lourds whispered. "Those odds are a lot better."

"Really?" Cleena responded. "Which two did you want to take?"

The professor sighed. "Okay, four to one."

"Now, be quiet. I've got to listen. I'd suggest that you do the same before they creep up on us in the dark."

"They're going to be just as hampered by the darkness as we are."

"Not if you keep talking. *Shut up!*" Cleena turned slightly away from the direction of the door to better use her peripheral vision. She held the pistol ready in her hands and tried not to think of Brigid alone in the world.

Beside her, Lourds suddenly started.

Angry with him even though that noise was not enough to alert Qayin and his followers to their position, Cleena said, "Be still."

Before she could say anything else, someone clapped a rough, callused hand over her mouth. She twisted and tried to bring the pistol up, but even as she did, someone grabbed her wrists. Instinctively, she fired at the shadow that stood out in the darkness around her.

Her body and the body of the man who held her trapped the muzzle flash between them. The hard white-yellow light illuminated the man who held her. A dark robe swaddled his body, and his face was a pallid oval within a peaked cowl.

CHAPTER 8

CATACOMBS
YESİLKOY DİSTRİCT
İSTANBUL, TURKEY
MARCH 17, 2010

"Please, Professor Lourds, don't be afraid."

After what he had been through since arriving in Istanbul, Lourds couldn't believe anyone would actually say that. The echo of the woman's shot still rang through the large chamber. Now his imagination was in overdrive as he confronted the cowled man.

Many of the documents Lourds had translated over the years involved myths and legends of monsters in places like the catacombs under Istanbul. In fact, some of the work he had done involved stories of horrors during the Ottoman invasion and the fall of Constantinople.

Lourds was prepared to fight for his life, but then something happened that he didn't expect: The man holding him spoke the same plea—except this time he spoke in Ancient Greek. The dialect was a little off, but it was easy to distinguish the root.

"What did you say?" Lourds asked in that same language.

"My friends and I are here to help you," the man said.

"We have been looking for you since you disappeared this morning. I apologize that it has taken so long to locate you."

"Who are you?"

"For now, all that I can tell you is that we're friends. We're here to get you out of this place. Please instruct the woman to stop fighting."

Lourds was suddenly aware that the woman continued to battle at least one and possibly two men. He turned to her but could not see her in the darkness. "Stop struggling," he said. "These are friends."

The woman stopped fighting and leaned into him. Tension tightened her body like a bow string. "How do you know they're friends?" she demanded.

"One of them just told me."

Derision dripped from her. "*How* have you managed to stay alive for so long?"

"I happen to believe him," Lourds said defensively. "He spoke to me in Ancient Greek."

"Now there's a reason to trust someone."

"He says he and his friends can get us out of here. Interested now?"

"We're doing fine on our own."

"Qayin has reinforcements coming," the man beside Lourds said.

"You're just saying that," the woman responded.

"Actually, we followed them in here."

"Then where are they? They could be making that up."

Lourds wasn't inclined to be so skeptical, but before he could say anything to that effect, the noise of people trying to move quietly at the other end of the catacombs reached them. As he was about to ask if anyone else had heard the noise, someone from that end of the catacombs opened fire.

Acting quickly, Lourds dropped to the ground. The woman did the same. They were face-to-face in the darkness, their features intermittently lit up by the muzzle flashes as bullets crunched against the pillar overhead.

"Convinced?" Lourds asked dryly.

The woman made no reply.

"Professor Lourds?" the man closest to Lourds asked.

"We're coming, but they have us boxed at both ends."

"There is another way out. Follow me."

Running footsteps echoed through the catacombs. The woman rose briefly to her knees, held her pistol, and fired. Lourds didn't wait to see the results of her handiwork. He had seen how devastating she could be with her weapon. The mortal screams behind him let him know she had been just as accurate again.

Rising to his feet, Lourds remained crouched as he followed the robed man through the darkness. Several of their opponents turned their lanterns in their direction. The bright lights spilled across Lourds just as he saw the narrow opening in the wall ahead of him.

He followed the man through the opening and into a tunnel. The woman was on his heels, closely trailed by two more men in robes. Once they were inside, one of the men shoved a recessed section of the wall into place and sealed the opening.

One of the robed men took out a flashlight and switched it on. The bright light hurt Lourds's eyes and filled the narrow tunnel with illumination. He studied the faces of the five men in the tunnel but recognized none of them.

"It's safe in here, Professor Lourds," one of the men said. He was young, no older than his late twenties, surely. A carefully trimmed goatee framed his chin. His eyes were lost in the shadows of his cowl.

The woman reloaded her pistol. "Can they get through that door?"

The man shook his head. "Not now. We've locked them out."

Satisfied with her weapon's readiness, the woman studied the five men. "Who are you?"

"As I have stated, we are friends." The young man spoke patiently.

Lourds noticed that the woman had turned so her pistol hand was kept clear of the five men. She could quickly bring it into play. It seemed a habit as ingrained as breathing.

"I know all my friends," the woman insisted.

"Perhaps I should have said we are friends of the professor," the young man amended.

"That true, Professor?" she asked without taking her eyes off the strangers. "Do you know them?"

"Not yet," Lourds said. "But I'm always open to meeting new friends." He looked at her. "Especially ones who don't kidnap me when they first see me. That's a first impression that's hard to recover from."

She shot him a hard glance. "We can save the meet-and-greet for later. This tunnel has to go somewhere. Maybe Qayin and his little friends might not be able to get through this door, but they can come at us from the other end of this passageway."

"Actually, they don't know all the secrets of these catacombs. We know more about them than they do," the young man assured her.

"That's terrific," the woman said sarcastically. "You win. But I'd still prefer to be elsewhere."

"Of course." The young man nodded to the man with a flashlight.

Immediately, the man with the flashlight headed down the dark throat of the tunnel. Lourds followed the light.

Lourds guessed that several minutes passed as they made their way along the passage. He thought he detected an upward grade, but wasn't sure. It was too dark to tell and he was more interested in listening for sounds of pursuit.

"I see you're carrying Qayin's book," the young man said.

"I had the impression that this book didn't actually belong to Qayin," Lourds replied. "He couldn't read it anyway."

"My bad," the man said, sounding for a moment like one of Lourds's Harvard students. "I didn't mean to infer that the book belonged to Qayin. It doesn't."

Unable to control his curiosity, Lourds asked, "Whose book is it?"

"I'm not at liberty to say at this moment."

"Well, isn't that delightfully mysterious?" the woman asked.

"Were you so curious about the people who hired you to kidnap Professor Lourds?" the man countered.

The woman didn't say anything, though Lourds couldn't tell whether that was because of shame or anger.

"What makes this book so special?" Lourds asked.

"Were you able to read it?" the man asked.

"I had barely gotten started, but, yes, I believe I can read it. Given time."

Behind him, the woman cursed softly. Lourds suddenly realized that the admission might endanger him with their newfound friends.

"Watch your head here." The young man reached up to touch a low-hanging section of the passageway ceiling.

Lourds ducked and followed the man through. The passageway came to a *T* only a short distance farther on. They bore to the left.

"What did you find out from reading the book?" the young man asked.

"Not enough," Lourds responded.

"But you think you can decipher the book?"

Lourds hesitated only a moment. *If I say I can, are you going to take me captive? Or if I say I can't, are you going to kill me?* Neither of those options appealed to him. He had a mystery on his hands, a true enigma of the sort that he loved to unravel. He wasn't prepared to let this go without a fight.

"Yes," he answered.

"That's good." The young man halted behind the man with a flashlight. He held the flashlight while the leader worked on the wall ahead of them.

"Do you know what the book is about?" Lourds asked.

The young man looked at Lourds with deep sincerity. "Something has been lost, Professor Lourds. Something very valuable and very important. This thing must be found. Much depends on that."

"What has been lost?"

Sadly, the young man shook his head. "That isn't for me to say. I apologize. I know you've had a difficult day. But anything I may tell you could interfere with your translation of that book. The impressions you form regarding the material you'll find there must be your own. Many people over the years have tried to decipher the book. If you fail, it must be your own unique failure."

Up ahead, a section of the passageway wall opened up to reveal a small space. Iron rungs climbed the opposing wall.

The young man with the light shone the flashlight up into the vertical passageway. "All clear," he said.

Lourds was third in line and grabbed one of the rusting iron rungs above his head. He settled his backpack, with the book inside, across his shoulders and hoisted himself up. The corroded metal bit into his palms and flaked off as he climbed. A brief glance revealed that the vertical passageway went up some distance. He couldn't keep watching, because rust flakes spilled into his eyes. As he climbed, he felt the steady burn of his abused muscles and longed for bed. And a meal of some kind.

But the mystery of the book chafed at his mind as surely as the rotten iron dug into his hands.

Just when Lourds was about to let the others know he couldn't go any farther, the lead man called a halt to the procession. Metal rasped overhead; then sunlight poured down into the shaft.

Morning? Lourds couldn't believe what he was seeing. But he had no frame of reference for how long he had been rendered unconscious by the drugs he was given.

The first man climbed slowly and peered around for a moment, then climbed out from the tunnel. The young man who had done all the talking followed him. Then in short order, he and the girl followed. Lourds stood in a narrow alley that could have been a twin of the one where the helicopter had crashed.

The woman trailed Lourds from the passageway and stood with her pistol naked in her fist. Somehow she'd made the long climb with the weapon in hand.

The five men watched her uneasily.

"So how do we handle this?" the woman asked.

"We're escorting Professor Lourds to his hotel," the young man with a goatee said.

"What about me?"

"You're free to go."

The woman looked at the five men suspiciously and took a fresh grip on her weapon. "What? Just like that?"

"Yes."

She smiled. "And if I preferred to take the professor with me?"

"That wouldn't be acceptable."

"I've always been told the person with the gun makes the rules."

Uneasily, Lourds shifted and took a step back from the woman.

The young man spoke calmly. "I assure you, you're not the only one with weapons here. You were allowed to come with us because we don't like to kill, nor would we allow Qayin and his followers to murder you. But our people have fought and died for centuries for the secrets contained within that book."

Lourds didn't know if the robed men were armed. He could see no weapons, but the robes concealed a lot. He suddenly felt like a choice meat bone being growled over by two dogs.

The thing that most captured his attention was the statement about how long people had been searching for the secret he presently had his hands on. He snugged the backpack's straps a little tighter.

Then he remembered the other men at the airport. "By chance, you didn't try to contact me at the airport yesterday morning, did you?"

"No, Professor," the young man answered.

So there is a third party after me, Lourds realized.

"Professor?" the woman asked. "The decision is yours. Do you want to stay with them?"

"They've said that they're taking me to my hotel room," Lourds replied.

"And you trust them?"

Lourds shrugged. "They haven't kidnapped me."

An insouciant smile quirked the young woman's lips. "Yet." She paused. "I wish you well, Professor. It's been . . . interesting, but I hope you don't take offense when I tell you I hope never to see you again."

"No offense taken. And I hope you don't mind that the feeling is mutual."

Gun in hand, the young woman backed down the alley for one hundred paces. Then she turned and fled, rounding the corner at the end of the alley and disappearing.

"Professor Lourds," the young man prompted. "Are you ready to go to your hotel now?"

"Of course. Give me just a second." Lourds rummaged in his backpack and took out the pen and paper he'd worked with earlier. He already knew the avenues he wanted to follow with the translation. As he made notes, his fascination grew.

Returning to the hotel proved less clandestine than Lourds would have believed. The group had doffed their robes, thrown them into a trash bin, then escorted him to the other end of the alley and hailed a cab. Only the young man with the goatee accompanied Lourds.

No longer dressed in the robe, the young man looked like anyone. Like a student, actually, Lourds thought. The man wore khaki slacks, loafers, and a soccer jersey. He would have been perfectly at home on the greens at Harvard.

Around them, Istanbul had come to life. Pedestrians and tourists filled the crosswalks. Others window-shopped or sat at tables in outdoor cafés. He'd always loved the city. Istanbul, as Constantinople before it, had a long and exciting history.

The initial settlement there had been in 6500 B.C. on the Anatolian side of the area. The Fikirtepe mound had revealed artifacts dating from 5500 to 3500 B.C., during the Copper Age. One of the ports, Kadikoy, also known as Chalcedon, had been active during the time of the Phoenicians.

The Bosphorus River held the record for the narrowest strait used for international travel. According to ancient Greek myth, the river had been named after Io, one of Zeus's lovers after the god turned her into an ox to protect her from his jealous wife.

Usually Lourds found himself soothed by the presence of so much history around him. Despite the modern additions to the area, it wasn't hard to imagine the seaport city as it had been during its heyday. The salty sea air wouldn't have had the taint of diesel, but otherwise it would have smelled much the same.

But Lourds couldn't relax. He kept expecting an assault from any front.

"You didn't mention your name," Lourds said.

The young man smiled and shook his head. "I cannot. Please forgive me this social inadequacy. I have very strict orders."

"Regarding me? Or the book?"

"They are the same."

"Seeing as how I've been under the threat of death since I arrived in the city, isn't there something you can tell me?"

"Only that many things are coming to a head and danger is loose in the world."

"Kind of oblique, don't you think?" Lourds asked.

"In your field of study, you've covered a lot of history. Have you ever known a prophecy that was not oblique?"

"This is about a prophecy?"

"No. I don't want you to get the wrong idea." The young man trailed his fingers through his goatee and looked pained. "Honestly, Professor, I wish that I could tell you more."

"Besides you and Qayin's people, who else knows about this?"

"Several people know something of the background regarding the book, and the secret it protects. Qayin's people have had it for a very long time."

"How long?"

"The last three hundred and thirty-seven years."

"In this city?"

"That book," the young man said, "has *never* left this city."

"Why?"

"It isn't permitted."

Lourds shook his head. "I don't understand. Anyone could leave this city with the book."

"Could you?" The young man smiled with bright interest. "I wonder if you could."

"Is that a challenge?"

"The challenge, Professor, is whether you can decipher the book and find what it hides."

"I could do that at Harvard," Lourds said. "In fact, it might be far easier to do it there." He paused. "Or would you stop me?"

"Yes. As would Qayin. There are others who seek the book as well. If you stay here, we can protect you to some degree."

"Like you did yesterday?"

"We didn't know you were in jeopardy until yesterday," the young man said.

"You didn't know Qayin would kidnap me?"

"No. It wasn't until his lackeys were recognized that we knew of Qayin's involvement."

"Qayin thought I might be able to decipher the book and your people didn't?"

"Sorry, but no, we didn't."

Lourds emitted a displeased grunt.

"Please don't take that as a slight against your ability, Professor," the young man said. "We've had people working on that book for generations. Over those years, my superiors had come to the conclusion that we weren't waiting on an individual to translate that text. We were waiting for a time."

Somewhat mollified, Lourds nodded. "You think now is the time?"

"We are prepared to wait and see. And to allow you your chance with the book. When we found Qayin's hiding place and discovered that you were able to translate portions of the book, it was decided that perhaps the time might be now." The young man glanced out the window but Lourds knew he wasn't seeing anything out there. The young man's mind was elsewhere.

"Qayin must have had a higher estimation of my abilities than you," Lourds said.

"Perhaps." The young man glanced at Lourds again. "Or perhaps he was merely more desperate."

"I suppose there's no slight intended in that observation either."

"No. I apologize. I'm used to being very blunt in matters concerning that book."

The cab slowed, then pulled into the entrance lane of the Eresin Crown Hotel. A liveried expediter stepped up to the side of the cab and opened the door for Lourds. The man was professional enough that he looked at the professor's disheveled appearance askance for only a moment.

"Good morning, sir," the expediter greeted. "Welcome to the Eresin Crown Hotel."

"Good morning," Lourds responded. "Thank you."

"Do you have any bags?"

Lourds almost laughed. Had the situation been funny, he might have. "No, I suppose I don't." That was going to be a problem. He turned back to the young man in the cab. "Will I see you again?"

"That remains to be seen." He extended a hand. "Good luck, Professor. I hope you're successful in your endeavor. In any event, we will be in touch."

Lourds didn't know if he was supposed to feel threatened, but he did. Having nothing else to say, he closed the cab's door and stepped back.

The cabdriver cruised sedately into the lane of traffic. The young man glanced back through the window and waved in a purely innocent gesture.

Lourds waved back and felt immediately stupid. He turned to the expediter. "I suppose the hotel has good security?"

"Of course, sir. Only the very best."

"And someone on-site?"

The expediter looked at Lourds curiously. "Yes, sir."

"Very good." Lourds allowed the man to open the door for him and stepped into an elegant foyer. Guests and staff stared at him as though he were a street person. He had to admit that, with torn clothing and covered in dirt and blood, he would easily have passed muster as one of those.

Gathering his dignity, Lourds approached the check-in desk. A beautiful young woman in a business suit looked up at him and politely said hello.

Lourds gave his name to the clerk.

The young woman's face brightened immediately, but it was clearly a struggle. Lourds was certain she was probably downwind of him.

"Ah, of course. Professor Lourds," the young woman said brightly. "We had expected you yesterday."

"I take it you haven't been watching the news."

The young woman gazed at him blankly. "Excuse me?"

"I was delayed," Lourds replied. "It was in the news."

"Sorry. I must have missed it." She made quick entries into the computer and asked for a credit card against room expenses. "Would you need one key or two?"

"One, thank you." Lourds took the proffered key and headed for the elevator bank.

"Oh, Professor Lourds," the desk clerk called.

"Yes?"

"You'll find your bags are already in your room."

"Really? Who delivered them?"

The clerk shrugged and looked at her computer. "The screen doesn't say. Only that the bags were delivered yesterday afternoon."

Lourds thanked her and took the elevator up to his room. *You really shouldn't be doing this,* he thought. *If you had any sense, you'd take a taxi to the airport and board the first flight back to Boston that you could get.*

But he knew he wasn't going to do that. The mystery of the book was calling out to him.

Outside his room door, Lourds hesitated with the electronic keycard in hand. Cold fear shivered through him and nausea twisted through his stomach. He really wasn't prepared for anything like this.

Despite his efforts to find lost Atlantis, and all the dangers he'd faced then, he wasn't mentally or physically suited for the rigors of getting shot at and beaten. Those were experiences he much preferred to read about in the thrillers he relished. He was a simple man, really.

With his hands shaking the way they were, it took three attempts to get the keycard through the reader. The lock clicked and the light flashed green, indicating the door was open.

Lourds eased into the room slowly and carefully, listening for the slightest noise. He spotted his luggage at the foot of the king-size bed. The sight of the bed alone enticed him into the darkened room. He stripped out of the backpack and dropped it on to the room's desk.

A mirror hung over the desk. When Lourds flipped on the nearby light and sought to check the damage done to his face, he saw the reflection of the man sitting comfortably in a chair beside the bed. In that corner, Lourds hadn't been able to see the man until it was too late.

Lourds spun and headed for the exit, pausing only long enough to snag the backpack. Before he reached the door, it opened and a large man filled the doorway. The man stepped into the room and Lourds backed up.

"Ah, Professor Lourds, I presume." The man in the chair beside the bed smiled apologetically. "I beg your indulgence. That's what Stanley actually told Livingston when he located him."

Lourds stood his ground when the big man stopped advancing. The room was on the fourth floor. Even if he were able to crash through the reinforced glass of the window, when that shattered, he wouldn't survive the fall.

"I understood the reference," Lourds said.

The man smiled. "I knew you would. I don't often get to talk to people so well educated in my line of work."

"Maybe you should tell me what your line of work is. Other than breaking and entering into hotel rooms."

"Oh, I didn't break and enter, Professor. I had an invitation." The man reached under his jacket, and the brief movement revealed the pistol residing in the shoulder holster tucked neatly under his arm. "I have a legal document that allowed me to enter. I assume your Turkish is good?"

"My Turkish is fantastic." Lourds took the document the man held out and glanced at it.

"I assure you, Professor, you'll find everything is in order."

Lourds looked over the top of the document at the man. "You're a policeman?"

The man spread his hands and smiled. "A detective, actually. Detective Dilek Ersoz at your service." He inclined his head slightly. "And I'm a fan. I enjoyed your Atlantis book and some of your other analytical treatises. And my wife continues to sing praises of *Bedroom Pursuits.*"

"Can't ever have too many fans, according to my publishers." Lourds handed the document back. "I assume you're not here about an autograph. The last one I signed didn't turn out so well."

"An autograph would be most excellent at some point," Ersoz replied. "Sadly, this is not that point."

"What do you want, Detective Ersoz?"

Ersoz held his thumb and forefinger about a quarter inch apart. "Only a short amount of your time, Professor."

"I suppose I have no choice?"

"Of course you have a choice." Ersoz smiled. "You can come of your own free will, or we can arrest you and take you out of here in handcuffs."

"I suppose a shower is out of the question."

"I must express my apologies for the hurry. My superior did ask me to bring you in the moment you showed up."

Lourds sighed. "Of course he did."

"People died yesterday morning, Professor. There always has to be an accounting for something like this." Ersoz stood and fastidiously shot his cuffs. "Let's go."

Without another word, Lourds clapped his hat on his head once more and grabbed his backpack. He followed the big man out of the room.

CHAPTER 9

OLİVİUM OUTLET CENTER
ZEYTİNBURNU DİSTRİCT
İSTANBUL, TURKEY
MARCH 17, 2010

When you have to disappear, the best place to disappear is inside a crowd.

Cleena's father had taught her that when she was twelve and she'd started carrying guns for him to sell on the streets. That had been back when Ryan MacKenna had been working hand-to-mouth on the street in Boston's Combat Zone. He'd sold weapons by the piece in those days, and often Cleena had carried them for him.

She'd learned how to run and hide during those days, and she'd become one of the best at it. No one had ever caught her, not the police and not other street gangs. She'd had a mental map of all the alleys and rooftops that afforded some measure of concealment and paths to safety. She'd ducked through tight places slick as a rat, and flown from rooftop to rooftop like one of the pigeons.

As soon as she quit Lourds and the robed strangers, she'd headed into the Zeytinburnu District. She'd been to Istanbul before, procuring weapons, and knew the area well enough. The neighborhood was hard and hungry.

During the day, quick-footed boys stole purses and wallets from tourists adventurous enough or ill-informed enough to come into the neighborhood in search of vice. At night, the prostitutes and street-corner hustlers came out to ply their trades in the shadows.

In the beginning, Zeytinburnu had been home to the leather industry in Turkey. That coastal area had been called Kazlicesme, after a famous stone fountain featuring a carved goose. These days, the goose was gone and so was the leather industry, but a mixed stew of Greeks, Bulgarians, Jews, Turks, and Armenians still eked out a living there.

Despite the difference in culture and dialect, Cleena knew she spoke the same language as the rough men and women who worked the streets. And she knew a lot about the struggling middle class that lived the straight life. Every metropolitan city had an underbelly like this one.

She'd bought clothing from a secondhand store and was now dressed in American jeans that mostly fit her, a pastel gray pullover that looked new, work boots, and a quilted jacket. Wraparound sunglasses hid her eyes and she'd tucked her flaming red hair up under a black watch cap.

She carried a Czech 9 mm pistol at the back of her waistband where she could quickly get to it if she needed to. A quick visit to a gun dealer she knew netted her a clean pistol, with the understanding that the one she'd used as part of the payment was too hot to sell as it was.

Now you just make your arrangements and blow this pop stand, Cleena told herself as she strode through the Olivium Outlet Center. Throngs of people surrounded her as she walked through the shopping mall.

Four stories tall, and huge, the mall housed well over one hundred shops these days. Many of them carried name brands from the United States and Great Britain. There were theaters, a supermarket, and several fast food restaurants.

Cleena found a cybercafé and purchased time on a card. She gave a false name and false identification to secure the computer.

Selecting one of the computers near the window that looked out over the wall, Cleena logged on and brought up the phone server her sister used. Brigid was forever texting her friends. Cleena had learned how to text, but she didn't except rarely. She'd preferred since childhood not to leave trails.

At the server, she checked the text log of the prepaid cell phone she'd purchased in the airport. She'd ditched that phone when she'd dumped her clothes, and bought another phone in the mall.

Normally there were only occasional messages from Brigid. This time there were fourteen messages. All of them said the same thing.

CALL ME.

Cleena could almost hear the panic in her sister's voice. She canceled the session, dumped the access card in the basket, and left the shop.

Returning to the ground floor, Cleena took up a post near an escalator bank that allowed her an escape route in both directions. She watched the crowd, looking through the individuals to spot independent predatory approaches. She kept her jacket loose so she could easily reach the pistol. There were too many people looking for Professor Lourds, or the manuscript that he'd taken.

She took the cell phone out and dialed the number of the clean phone she'd given Brigid before leaving Boston. Cleena made herself breathe.

The phone rang once, twice, then three times.

Answer! Cleena almost cried out. Her mind filled with images of horrible things that could have happened to her sister. Memory of her father's torn and bloody body still haunted her dreams.

The phone rang a fourth time.

People went about their business all around Cleena with maddeningly carefree attitudes. She wanted to move, to pace, to be in motion and not stand there waiting for no news.

Then Brigid answered the phone. "Hello?"

From that single word, Cleena knew how frightened her sister was. Brigid was always happy-go-lucky. And if she wasn't, she was whiny and sarcastic and near insufferable. It was what younger sisters were, after all.

"Hello." Cleena heard the tight scratchiness of her voice.

"Are you all right?"

Cleena kept her eyes moving. Now that she'd made contact with her sister, it was possible that someone could already be tracking the connection through a GPS satellite.

"I'm fine. How's the bird?" The question was a code Cleena had established to ensure that Brigid was alone.

"Forget about the code," Brigid angrily. "Something has happened that you need to know. I've been waiting for hours to get in contact with you."

"I haven't been able to get to the phone. Tell me about the bird."

"There isn't time to—"

"To what?" Cleena snapped. "Be careful? If you're freaked, then this sounds like the perfect time to be careful."

Brigid cursed at the other end of the connection. She never did that.

Cleena forced herself to remain calm and focused. They had safety procedures built in for a purpose. She and their father had lived by them.

"Jughead," Brigid said. "There. Are you happy?"

They'd had a bird, a dove, and they'd named it after a popular comic book character they'd liked. They'd loved the bird, but one day Brigid had brought a stray cat home. When they'd come back to the apartment from school, the cat had knocked Jughead's cage into the floor and killed the bird. Only its head and feet were left.

Brigid had cried for days, but she'd never forgotten that Jughead was safer alone. When a stranger was in the house, or near, all of them were at risk.

"What's wrong?"

"Someone came to the bar last night. He threatened me. And then he *hurt* me."

Swiftly, Cleena bottled the rage that swelled within her. *A hot mind is only a danger to itself, girlie,* her father had told her over and over. *You save that mad for when you need it. But before you use it, you make sure it's gone cold and hard. That's when it'll be dangerous to someone else, not you.*

"Are you all right?" Cleena asked.

"No, I'm not all right. I don't know who this guy was. He came into the bar, waited till I was alone, then he slapped me."

"He slapped you? Nothing more?"

"Yes."

"Nothing broken?"

"No, nothing's broken. But he did break Liam's nose when Liam tried to stop the guy from hitting me."

Cleena tried to remember who Liam was. Brigid was always talking about friends and coworkers and young men. It was hard to keep them all straight.

"My boss," Brigid said.

"Right," Cleena said. "Got him now. Remember: no names."

"This guy already knows your name."

"Someone else might not. Take a breath and calm down."

Brigid sucked in a ragged breath.

"Do you know who this guy is?" Cleena asked.

"No."

"Ever seen him before?"

"I don't think so."

"You need to be sure," Cleena said.

"I don't know! A lot of people come to the bar."

"So he looked like a regular?"

Brigid was quiet for a moment. "No. He was a little too clean. Too straight. Except for when he started whaling away on me."

"What did he want?"

"You."

"Why?" Cleena asked.

"He didn't say."

Cleena forced herself to be calm. "What did this guy say?"

"He told me he wanted you to call him. He left a number."

"Give it to me." Cleena quickly copied the number on the receipt from the secondhand store. "Don't go back to the apartment."

"I didn't. I'm not going to. If this guy knows I'm your sister and where I work, he probably knows where we live, too."

"That's right. Keep thinking clearly like that and we're going to be all right. Are you somewhere safe?"

"Yes. I'm at—"

Cleena interrupted. "Don't tell me. It might be a good idea for you to stay away from work for a while. You're too vulnerable there."

"I can't miss work. I like that job."

"I know."

"And I know money is tight," Brigid went on. "The only time you ever go out of town like this is when money is tight. And tuition is coming up soon."

"There'll be enough money," Cleena said. Even if she had to rip off a few drug dealers in the Combat Zone, she'd make it. "I promise. In the meantime, I want you to be safe."

"What about you?"

Cleena felt the weight of the Czech pistol at her back and scanned the mall crowd. "I'm safe enough, girlie."

"You sound like Dad when you call me that."

"Sorry."

Brigid's voice grew softer. "It's okay. I don't really mind. It's just that when you do that I know you're thinking about him, and you never think about him unless there's serious trouble."

"I'd say a man coming to your work and slapping you is pretty serious," Cleena said. *And if it wasn't serious before, it is now.* She tamped down the rage inside her, cooled it, and held it tight.

"There's something else," Brigid stated more quietly.

"What?"

"This guy, he said if you didn't call him, he was going to kill me."

Cleena made herself count to ten. The anger and fear had almost gotten away from her.

"Are you still there?" Brigid asked.

"I am. Don't worry. I'm going to call him."

"Okay, but then I'm going to have to worry about you."

"It'll be all right," Cleena made herself say in a light, almost worry-free tone. "It's probably just a client that got a little overzealous."

"If that's the case, it might be better if you never dealt with him again."

"I won't. I can promise you that." Cleena focused on the task at hand. "For now, you need to get rid of that phone. I'm getting rid of this one as well, so this number will no longer work."

"We go to backup?"

"Yes." Backup was computer contact only through ads placed on popular exchange lists.

"Are you sure?" Brigid asked in a much smaller voice that betrayed a lot of the fear she was undoubtedly feeling.

"That everything's going to be all right?"

"Yes."

Cleena answered instantly and smoothly. "I'm perfectly sure." But her heart was beating much faster than it should have been.

"Love you," Brigid said.

"Love you, too, kiddo." Cleena made herself break the connection. Tears misted her eyes but she didn't let them fall. She checked the crowd again, saw nothing suspicious, and walked to the nearest trash bin. She dropped the phone into the container and kept walking.

Just keep breathing, she told herself. *Keep breathing and keep focused. Whoever hurt Brigid, whoever threatened her, you're going to make them pay.*

After buying another pre-paid cell phone inside the mall, Cleena dialed the number Brigid had provided. The exchange was in Istanbul, which didn't make much sense. Why would anyone go to Boston to threaten Brigid if they were already in Istanbul?

The phone rang only once.

"Ah, Ms. MacKenna, I knew you'd be calling, but I really expected you to call me much earlier."

"I've been busy," Cleena retorted. "And if you mention names again, I'm hanging up."

That seemed to catch the man at the other end of the connection by surprise. Cleena took advantage of the pause to listen for noises at the other end. The voice sounded American, and much too full of himself to be anyone's peon. Whoever the man was, he was used to having and using power.

"Listen," the man said in a much harsher voice, "this is going to be done my way—"

"No," Cleena replied. She gazed up at the sky through the foyer windows and tried to pretend this was a day like any other.

"Did your sister tell you what I promised I'd do to her if—?"

"Spare me." Cleena checked her watch. "You have another minute and twenty-three seconds till I hang up."

"If I wanted to track this call, it would already be done."

"You work with a United States intelligence agency then? You have to in order to make that claim and not even feign false modesty."

The man didn't speak.

"Not only that," Cleena said, "you're a desk jockey. A paper pusher.

You're a mouse playing at being a lion." She knew that pushing his buttons was dangerous, but it was also the only way she knew to find out more about him.

He cursed at her.

"See how easy this is to play?" Cleena asked. "The more you talk, the more I'm going to learn about you. And the more you can be sure that one day—when you least expect it—I'm going to walk in behind you and slit your throat for threatening my sister."

"You don't call the shots here," the man said.

"I do. Otherwise you wouldn't be sitting there waiting on me to call. And you've got twenty-nine seconds to bring this to a close."

"Your sister—"

"Already couldn't be in any more danger, so don't even bother trying to up that particular ante." Cleena made herself sound cold. She was good at that. Even her father had been impressed. "Seventeen seconds."

"You cost me a team," the man snarled.

"Those oafs at the airport? Please." Cleena waited for the man to deny the charge. If he didn't, she could try tracing those dead men back to their master. She was already certain she was looking at an American intelligence agency, so she felt sure the task wouldn't take too long.

"So you're going to be my team now."

Bingo, Cleena thought triumphantly. *There* is *a connection I can exploit.*

"Eight seconds," she said.

"I want you to shadow the man you kidnapped and let me know what he's up to. You can call me at this number any time of the day or night."

"You're too late. I already lost him."

"The Istanbul police department has him currently. I suggest you get over there and pick him up."

"If you know so much, why do you need me?"

"Go. Play nice. If you do, your kid sister gets to see her next birthday."

But you won't, Cleena promised herself. *Not unless it's coming up really soon.*

"It would help me if I knew what makes him so important," she said.

"They say curiosity killed the cat. In this case, it could get your sister killed. Pay attention to your assignment. Call me the minute you have news, and call me at least every twelve hours. I know you won't be keeping this phone, so I won't try calling you."

The man hung up. Silence echoed in Cleena's ear. She squeezed the telephone so hard that it broke in her grip. She forced herself to breathe out, then took the escalator down to the first floor. She never broke stride as she walked to the front of the mall. Her mind was fully engaged. If she was going to be staying in Istanbul for a while longer, she needed more supplies.

But most of all she needed information. And she knew where to get it.

STONE GOOSE APARTMENTS
ZEYTİNBURNU DİSTRİCT
İSTANBUL, TURKEY
MARCH 17, 2010

"Sevki, open up." Cleena banged again on the weathered door with her fist. It was only 10:37 A.M., much too early for the man she had come to see.

The apartment was deep in the heart of the Zeytinburnu District, on the sixth floor of a building that had seen much better times long ago. Rickety metal stairs zigzagged along the side of the building. Cleena thought they shivered much worse than they had the last time she'd come calling. Even then she'd been worried that the stairs might completely fall off the building while she ascended them. The bottom floor of the building had once been a textiles factory but now served as a way station for homeless people.

No identifying markings existed on the door. Cleena knew that Sevki hadn't moved, though. Although the other renters didn't know it, Sevki owned the building. That fact was hidden through a small series of shell holding companies.

"You better off come back," a screeching voice said.

Turning slightly, her hand already dropping under her coat to grip the Czech pistol, Cleena looked across the alley to a neighboring apartment building. There in the shadows, a little old woman sat on a narrow windowsill with her feet on the landing and smoked a cigarette. Her dress was faded and looked brittle, but it was clean.

"That one," the old woman continued, "he no get up in morning. Sleep all day, that one."

"Thank you," Cleena said. "But I think I'm going to try anyway." She waved, then turned back to the door. This time she kicked the door, hard.

A harsh flurry of curse words in a mixture of languages approached the door. A moment later, a brown eye peered through the peephole.

"Oh my God," a male voice groaned. "Go away. Come back at a more decent hour."

"Sevki, let me in before I break the door down." Cleena kicked the door again, harder.

"God, have you no decency, woman?"

"None, nor shame either. Let me in, Sevki, or you'll think the three little pigs got off easily."

"As I recall, the three little pigs won that one."

"Not in my world."

Sevki shot the bolts, seven of them, and opened the door. It was heavy and swung on well-oiled hinges. Beneath the aged wooden veneer was a metal core thick enough to withstand bullets and low-yield grenades. Sevki believed in security.

"Is anyone with you?" he asked. He stuck his head out and glanced along the walk.

Cleena slapped him on the back of the head. "It's stupid to stick your head out like that. Someone will shoot it off."

"No, no, no, no one will shoot my head off. I knew you were here, and I knew you were alone. I took your advice and put in a precautionary measure." Sevki pointed at the building across the alley. "Look under the eaves along the rooftop."

When Cleena did, she spotted the small camera mounted there.

"Wireless feed," Sevki explained. "I see what it sees on my computer."

"Very well done."

Sevki grinned like a kid. He stood a little taller than Cleena and was lanky. His black hair was thick and in obvious disarray. Blue highlights showed on the ends. He wore olive cargo khakis and a black flannel shirt under a green shirt sporting a costumed superhero with a glowing ring. Round-lensed glasses softened his narrow face.

"It's been a while since I've seen you," he said.

"A few months," Cleena agreed.

"Five months, three weeks, and two days."

Cleena wasn't surprised that he knew that. Sevki had a phenomenal mind, which was what had brought her to him now as well as before on other business.

"You look well," he said. "Life has been good?"

"I'm in trouble."

Some of the carefree attitude slid from Sevki's face. "What kind of trouble?"

"The bad kind. The kind that you don't know how bad you've really got it until it's on you."

"And it's on you?"

"Yes."

"Has any of this bad kind of trouble followed you here?"

"No. I'm sure of that."

Sevki stepped back and opened the door wider. "Come in."

CHAPTER

10

STONE GOOSE APARTMENTS
ZEYTİNBURNU DİSTRİCT
İSTANBUL, TURKEY
MARCH 17, 2010

"I'm surprised you don't know where the police department is." Sevki sat in a comfortable chair in front of a desk that had six computer monitors spread across it. His fingers clacked across the keyboard with practiced ease. Images changed on the monitors with astonishing regularity. Cleena didn't know how he kept up with everything, but she knew he did.

"I've made a habit of never getting arrested." Cleena lounged on the couch with accustomed familiarity. When she was in Istanbul, she and Sevki spent time together, as friends and as lovers. Neither of them could afford to have someone else permanent in their lives. And neither of them was willing to give up the world they felt safe in to live together. Besides, though the friendship and fringe benefits were good, both preferred independence.

Sevki shrugged. "Getting arrested isn't so bad."

"I'll take your word for it."

"It's when they try to keep you that things become less fun."

"I'm going to try never to put jail and fun in the same sentence again."

The apartment was a mix of adult and child, of technician and dreamer. Everything in the kitchen was neatly in its place. Sevki liked to cook, which was one of the things Cleena appreciated about him. The computer area was immaculate, neatly organized and carefully arranged. That was where he did his work.

One wall held shelves filled with boxed American comic books and graphic novels. Each box was carefully coded. Posters of scantily clad women carrying magic swords and impossibly large handguns cluttered the walls. Cleena recognized Lara Croft and Wonder Woman, but none of the others. A few were even alien, but unmistakably female.

"Have you eaten?" he asked.

"I'm famished," she admitted.

"There is some arabasi soup in the refrigerator."

"Sounds delicious." Cleena got up from the couch. "Want some?"

"Yes, please."

"Is there enough for two?"

Sevki turned and grinned at her. "Yes, even when one of the two is you. I also baked some *ekmek* a couple of days ago. Warm that up in the oven—"

"I know how to fix leftovers," Cleena interrupted. "I'm not exactly helpless."

"You're right. Not exactly helpless."

A warm feeling spread throughout Cleena as she set about preparing the simple meal. It felt good to be in the kitchen again, doing something domestic with someone who knew all her secrets. She located the arabasi, poured it into a pan, and warmed it on the stove. She unwrapped the small loaves of *ekmek* and placed them on the tray inside the oven. Within minutes, the delightful smell of chicken broth and bread filled the apartment.

She took down a couple of big bowls from the shelves, filled them with soup, and cut the *ekmek* loaves into manageable chunks. She put a couple of pieces of bread into each bowl, then added slices of Havarti cheese.

After she handed Sevki his bowl, Cleena returned to the couch and peered over his shoulder at the monitors while she ate. The soup was good, just spicy enough with the red pepper, and the *ekmek* sourdough complemented the taste.

"According to what I'm able to find here," Sevki said, "your Professor Lourds—"

"He's not my Professor Lourds."

Sevki glanced at her and smiled. "Struck a nerve, did I?"

"The man is an idiot. He nearly got us both killed. Several times."

"Anyway, he's here in Istanbul to deliver a series of lectures to classes a colleague teaches."

"What colleague?" Cleena blew on her soup to cool it, then soaked a chunk of bread and ate it.

Sevki rattled the keyboard with his lightning-fast strikes. "A professor at Istanbul University."

"What's his name?"

"*Her* name, actually. Professor Olympia Adnan." Sevki brought up an image from the university on one of the monitors.

The woman in the picture had dark hair styled to fit the shape of her head, dark eyes, and a smooth olive complexion. Cleena put her age at her late thirties, but most of that aging was done out of spite. The woman looked too beautiful to be a university professor. She wore square-rimmed glasses.

"Hey, she's quite the babe," Sevki commented.

"If you like older women," Cleena retorted.

"Uh, yeah." Sevki turned his attention to his soup. "It might help if I knew what I was looking for."

"I need everything you can find out about the professor, and what he's doing here. Beyond what you see in the news."

"So I'm supposed to be a mind reader?"

"Think outside the box on this one, Sevki. I need you to use those brilliant instincts of yours."

Sevki smiled. "Now you seek to play on my ego." He nodded and tapped his forehead. "Very good strategy. You must really be in trouble."

"Yes." Cleena's appetite nearly soured at that thought but she forced herself to keep eating. That was one of the things her father drilled into her from the beginning: when she was tired, she slept, and when there was time, she ate. Someone malnourished and overly tired couldn't function in survival mode. And she was certainly there.

"I'm not the only one in trouble," Cleena said. "I have a younger sister. Last night, someone got to her and threatened her. The professor isn't my job. He's someone else's."

Sevki remained still, taking in everything she said and showing no emotion.

For the briefest instant, Cleena wished she could take it all back. But she couldn't. Brigid needed Sevki at his best, and Sevki needed to know what he was up against.

"This guy who threatened my sister, Sevki, he's not a commonplace thug. He's connected somehow. A major player on the international scene." Cleena told him about the phone call she'd gotten and the visit Brigid had received at her work.

"You think he belongs to an espionage agency," Sevki asked when she'd finished the summation.

Cleena nodded.

"Not my government?"

"If it had been the Turkish government, why travel all the way to the United States to threaten my sister?"

"What do they want you to do with Professor Lourds?"

"Just to watch him," Cleena answered.

"Why? What is he supposed to do?"

"That's why I came to you. I want you to dig around and see what you can find out."

"Without bumping into these American spies that are threatening you."

"They may not be spies. They could be corporate interests. Someone like Blackwater. The espionage threats aren't just political these days. Economies are uncertain, and religious fervor ignites everywhere."

Sevki nodded. "I know. The Middle East has been increasingly restless of late. The disruption of the balance of power, of the uprising in Iran and of the Americans' insistence that the Shia followers outnumbered the Sunni followers in Iraq, still hasn't settled. I've been tracking that."

Cleena hadn't. She didn't care for politics. Her father had been swayed by them, and been murdered because of a man who'd waved the flag of the Irish Republic under Ryan MacKenna's nose. Her father would never have tried to make that weapons deal if he hadn't been chasing politics. He'd known how Cleena felt about it. That was why he hadn't taken her with him that morning.

"I'm telling you this because you need to be careful," she said. "For yourself. And for my sister."

He nodded.

"And if you choose to back away from this thing, I'll understand."

"But you will still do it."

"I have no choice."

Sevki licked his spoon thoughtfully. "What you're asking, this is a very dangerous thing, Cleena."

"I know."

"But it's for family. I understand family."

Before she knew it, tears trickled down Cleena's face. She wiped them away.

"I will do this thing for you. Carefully, as you say. But only so far. I myself have family."

"Thank you. Do you know about the kidnapping at Ataturk International Airport?"

"Of course. It was in the news. I keep up with the news."

"Three of those men there were killed or wounded. I need to know who they are, or at least who they worked for. If possible."

Sevki tapped on the keyboard for a moment. Pages of archives flashed up on the screens; then one of those on the right suddenly showed the airport.

He grinned. "Isn't technology marvelous?"

A chill ghosted through Cleena as she watched the scene again. She'd known she and Lourds had been close to death, but she hadn't known the eye of the storm had been so near.

"The camera work is sloppy," Sevki said. "Taken by a tourist." He froze a screen that showed her and Lourds together. "If I'd been looking, I might have identified you."

Cleena stared at her own red hair and thought a change might be in order.

"If you do anything to your hair, make sure it's temporary," Sevki told her.

Cleena looked at him. "Maybe you do read minds."

"That one was easy. But if you are caught, if you are questioned, dyeing your hair with something permanent might be suspicious. If you punk it out—" Sevki halted and made spraying motions with his hands.

"Highlight it with effects."

Sevki snapped his fingers. "Yes. No one would look for a redhead wearing outrageous hair. And you look young enough to look like you're going for that kind of style."

"I *am* young enough."

"Pardon me." Sevki pulled out a flat device and drew on it with a computer pencil. On the screen, bright yellow circles appeared around the three men. "These men, yes?"

"Yes. There are also men who were killed in a vehicular accident only minutes later."

"And the exploding helicopter? That was *you*?" Sevki looked surprised.

"I didn't shoot the helicopter."

Sevki cursed and turned his attention to his computer. "There are bodies all around the city."

"There are also some in the catacombs beneath it," Cleena said. "They'll be connected to the men in the vehicle accident."

"But not the men at the airport?"

Cleena took a deep breath. "I hope not. If they are, this is getting too twisted to follow."

"And this is just getting started."

"Oh, one other thing. These other people, the ones in the catacombs, they gave Lourds a book."

"A book?"

"Yes."

"Finding bodies, I can do. But do you know how many books there are?"

"Not like this one." Cleena described the book and what Lourds had explained about the Greek language code.

Sevki folded his hands together and cracked his knuckles. "Ah, now that is something I can work with."

Cleena took his empty soup bowl and put it with hers. She returned to the kitchen and placed them in the sink.

"I've got to get going," she said.

"Why?"

"I've got to catch up to Lourds. I've already stayed here longer than I should have."

Sevki shrugged. "At the moment, Lourds is not going anywhere. The police have him."

"They could let him go at any time."

"They don't appear to be in any hurry to do that." Sevki performed a short rhythm of keystrokes. A moment later, two screens changed images and showed a picture of Lourds seated inside a sterile room and another scene of a hallway.

"Is this coming from inside the police station?" Cleena whispered.

"Of course." Sevki grinned. "I am very good at what I do. I am not the only one who does this, but I am one of the few who hasn't been caught spying on the police. This is very expensive. *Very* expensive. But I pass those expenses on to others. And I find it good to know things the police don't know I know."

"They haven't found you out?"

Sevki shrugged. "Every now and again, yes. But I cover my tracks most carefully. When I get discovered, I wait a few months, then I hack their systems again. They are not so impregnable as the police would have you think. For now, I am undiscovered once again. The addition Cisco Systems made of the Mobile Electronic Systems Integration has tied together a lot of information from all around the city. The infrastructure is complicated, but I like a challenge."

"This is pretty unbelievable."

"Not so much. I am Webmaster of some of the porn sites here in Istanbul." Sevki smiled. "I make sure some of the police get free pass codes to the sites. When they log on at work, I creep in. It's a very good system." He paused. "I often get a look inside government buildings that way as well. But you have to be very good at this."

Cleena stared at Lourds. His head lay on his crossed arms on the table and he looked like he was asleep. Despite the time that had passed, she felt she had fared better. At least she'd gotten a change of clothes.

"Do you know what I think you should do?" Sevki asked.

"What?"

"You should rest. I can keep watch over your Professor Lourds—"

"He's not my—"

Sevki held his hands up defensively. "I will watch him. You should try to get some sleep. Hanging around the police station will only get you spotted by the police or someone else watching the professor."

Cleena thought about it. What he said made sense.

"All right," she acquiesced. "But only if I can borrow your shower first."

İSTANBUL EMNİYET MUDURLUGU
VATAN CAD./FATİH
İSTANBUL, TURKEY
MARCH 17, 2010

Someone gently shook Lourds by the shoulder. With great regret, he climbed out of the dream he was having of the young skin diver who had shown him the reefs around Haiti. Her skin had been the color of warm chocolate and her kisses as sweet as—

"Professor Lourds," a stern voice called.

This time the shake was not so gentle. Irritated as well as tired now, Lourds swung an elbow to bat the offending hand back. Someone caught his elbow and pushed it back down to his side.

"Are you awake, Professor Lourds?"

Reluctantly, Lourds raised himself from the tabletop and rubbed at his eyes. "I am now. As far as how awake, that remains to be seen."

"It's all right. We're almost finished here."

Lourds smiled a little. "I can't say that I haven't been waiting for you to tell me that."

Ersoz returned the smile as he took a seat across the conference table from Lourds. He emptied packets of sugar into the thick Turkish coffee he'd brought in with him. The strong aroma of the brew tantalized Lourds's appetite and made his stomach growl.

"There is still coffee if you'd like," the detective offered.

"No, thank you. When I leave this place, I'm going to the hotel—" Lourds looked at Ersoz. "I *am* going to the hotel, right?"

"You are."

"Thank God." Lourds ran a hand through his hair. "When I get there, I'm going to sleep for a week." He stretched in the chair.

"We went to the catacombs where you said you had your confrontation with Qayin and his men."

Lourds nodded. He'd provided a close approximation of where he and the woman had come up on street level. His memory gave him the twists and turns they'd taken.

"We didn't find any corpses," Ersoz said.

"I'm certain she killed them. At least some of them. Although I've never wanted to be, I've been around enough of these things to know when someone is dead."

"I understand this. I was surprised to discover how factual your Atlantis book was."

There was a lot left out of that, too, Lourds couldn't help thinking. Not every part of that story had been something he could tell. The Catholic Church took care of their own, and the hidden book of the first flood had been locked away, physically by them and forever in Lourds's memory. But there had been a lot of death and killing along the way.

"Are you certain you found the right place?" Lourds asked.

"We did find the area where you said the encounter took place," the detective went on. "There was a lot of blood. The crime scene people say it is human blood. And some tissue, also human, has been recovered. All of it is fresh."

"But no bodies?"

"None."

"Then they took them with them," Lourds said. "That's easy to explain."

"Is it?" Ersoz leaned back in his chair.

Over the last several hours of being questioned by the man and his partner, Lourds had learned that Ersoz was intelligent and good at his job.

"Do you know of another way six or seven dead men could have gone missing?" Lourds asked. "Outside of a stage magician's routine?"

"No. Of course not."

"Then they carried them away."

Ersoz nodded. "The crime scene techs assured me they found much evidence of this. Footprints in the blood. Drag marks. Many things."

"Then what is the problem?"

"My superior is very uncomfortable with the idea of a group of people that would go to such lengths to keep from being identified."

"Me, too," Lourds confessed. "And let me assure you—and your superior—that it's even more uncomfortable knowing that group of people is looking for me."

"I imagine that it would be." Ersoz paused. "Even more mysterious, we've not been able to identify the two men found in the wreckage of the vehicle you were transported in."

"In a city this size, you'd have to expect that," Lourds said.

"But the kind of men who kidnap people off the street in broad daylight? Who kill other people with no compunction?" Ersoz shook his head. "No, those kinds of men aren't often without records of some kind, not even in Istanbul."

A tingle of dread shot through Lourds as he contemplated that.

"Have you given any thought to abandoning Istanbul at this point, Professor?" Ersoz asked.

"I have." The only problem was the manuscript. If he left, maybe he couldn't take it with him.

"And will you?"

Lourds hesitated. "I don't think so."

"Why?"

"I don't understand." But Lourds was afraid he was starting to.

"A rational man," Ersoz explained patiently, as if to a child, "would already be throwing himself at the State Department and Embassy to get out of this country after such an ordeal. At the very least he would seek asylum there. Yet you have done none of these things."

"No."

"Why?"

Lourds thought quickly. He wasn't going to tell them about the manuscript. He'd already made up his mind about that. If he told them of it, he might as well surrender it and reconcile himself to the fact he'd never see it again.

"What's to say I'd be safer anywhere else?" Lourds said finally.

"I've reviewed your records, at my superior's insistence," Ersoz said. "When there was trouble in Jerusalem, you decided to forgo your trip. When the team you were part of in Iran was attacked, you also chose discretion as the better part of valor. In all your endeavors, Professor, you've always chosen the path of the wise and careful man."

It pained Lourds to hear a note of contempt in Ersoz's voice.

In those instances, nothing important had been at stake. In none of them had he any real reason to stay and fight. This felt different. The book felt different. . . .

It felt like history in the making. And he had it in his control.

"In this instance," Ersoz said, "you choose to foolishly risk your neck. I don't understand your decision."

"Is there any reason to think those men would come after me again?" Lourds's pulse beat at his throat and temples. If he had been in Ersoz's shoes, he would be suspicious, too. The last thing he needed was eyes upon him while he was trying to be secretive. Stealth wasn't his greatest skill.

"I don't know, Professor. Is there any reason to think these men would continue their interest in you?"

Lourds didn't say anything.

Ersoz crossed his legs and bored into Lourds with his steady gaze. "Those men had you for some time, Professor. It's hard to believe they didn't talk about what they hoped to gain from taking you captive."

"As I told you, I was unconscious most of that time. They drugged me. I thought they were going to kill me." Thankfully, that was the truth.

"At some point, though, you became conscious enough to run for your life."

Lourds nodded and felt his throat drying as he felt the detective closing in on him. He wondered how many people were on the other side of the one-way glass watching him answer Ersoz's questions.

"I don't think you have to be very conscious to know to run for your life when you're being held against your will by people who might kill you," Lourds objected.

"Yet they didn't kill you, did they? In fact, they went to great lengths to keep you alive. Killing you would have been much easier."

Lourds couldn't argue that point.

"They must have wanted something from you," Ersoz insisted softly.

"I would agree."

"But you never found out."

Lourds tried to keep his face neutral. He didn't want to be caught lying to the Turkish police, and he didn't want to tell them the truth. He hated when his life got this difficult.

"The woman interfered with whatever plans they had," Lourds said. "I told you that."

Ersoz nodded. "You did. But that's even more troublesome. Why was she there?"

"She was working with them."

"And then she wasn't."

"So I said. But she got into an argument with them over money."

"Her fee. Yes. You said they weren't going to pay her the rest of the agreed-upon amount. They were going to kill her."

"Yes. They admitted this." Lourds nodded. "These people didn't bother to hide that fact."

"She was foolish to work for them."

"I would think so."

"But not so foolish as to get herself killed."

"She was lucky."

"It wasn't luck that made her take you as a bargaining point. She knew those men wouldn't risk killing you."

Too late, Lourds saw the box he'd put himself in.

"My question to you is, how did this woman—whose identity you don't know and whom you say you've never seen before—know those men wouldn't kill you both?"

Lourds tried to think of what one of his celluloid or print spy heroes would do in this case. He came up with nothing.

"I suppose she knew," he replied lamely.

"Everyone knows but you?"

"Well, you don't know either."

Ersoz smiled and leaned back in his chair. "No, we don't. And that troubles my supervisor greatly. Everything you've told us would lead someone to believe this is some kind of conspiracy."

Lourds didn't know what to say to that, but the mention of everything being a conspiracy said out in the open like that made the ordeal somehow even more chilling.

"My supervisor wants to deport you," Ersoz said. "He has made this very clear."

Fear rattled through Lourds and he sought desperately for some argument that might allow him to stay in Istanbul. Somehow the fact that he was scheduled to do presentations at the local university didn't seem compelling enough.

"However," Ersoz went on, "your government has interceded in your behalf."

Lourds was stunned. "They have?"

"Yes. Your State Department has been very persuasive in this matter." Ersoz held his hands palm up. "So, in the interest of good political relations, you're going to be allowed to stay in Istanbul."

Relieved, Lourds let out a pent-up breath. He didn't know what he'd have done if they'd handcuffed him and thrown him on the nearest plane out of the city.

"Personally," Ersoz went on, "I like you very much." He smiled. "My wife would like to meet you. But—"

Lourds waited, torn between dread and elation.

"—but," Ersoz went on, "I fear for your safety within this city, Professor Lourds. I should hate to see anything untoward happen to you."

So would I. Lourds nodded. "I appreciate those sentiments, Detective Ersoz."

The policeman dipped his head in acknowledgment. "I understand that you don't know who the men were that kidnapped you. We're working on identifying them. But we have managed to identify two of the men who sought to apprehend you at the airport."

"Who were they?" Lourds didn't want to know, not really, but he knew Ersoz would expect him to be curious.

"Terrorists," Ersoz said. "Political extremists of the Shia faith." The policeman's gaze bored into Lourds's. "Do you know why men like that would choose to apprehend you?"

Religious extremists . . . He knew too much about what religious extremists were capable of. But why whould they want him? Lourds swallowed the thick lump at the back of his throat. "No. I don't."

"Well, that is something you may wish to find out." Ersoz stood. "If you choose to stay in Istanbul."

Lourds nodded and wished he could leave the city. With the manuscript. That was the only way he was going. Unless, of course, he knew for certain that staying would only get him killed.

"Am I free to go, then?" he asked.

"You are. A man from your State Department is here to collect you and take you to your hotel. I told him that we could take you, but he insisted."

Ersoz led the way out into the hall.

An intense dark-haired man in his early thirties, dressed in a suit, sat in a chair in the hallway. Lourds recognized his backpack on the floor beside the man.

The man held the manuscript in his manicured hands. A gun butt showed at his belt line. He lifted the manuscript out to show Lourds.

"Heavy reading, Professor Lourds?" the man asked. "Or are you smuggling documents out of the country?"

CHAPTER 11

İSTANBUL EMNİYET MUDURLUGU
VATAN CAD./FATİH
İSTANBUL, TURKEY
MARCH 17, 2010

Lourds made himself smile instead of throw up as his stomach lurched with sudden sickness. "Heavy reading, I'm afraid. Please be careful with that. It's very old."

The man thumped the book and it sounded hollow in the hallway. "Actually, I kind of got that already."

Without thinking, Lourds stepped up and took the book from the man. His hands shook as he put it away.

"Sorry. I knew it was old. Didn't know it was important. And it obviously is."

"To me," Lourds said.

"I glanced through it. Couldn't read it."

"Unless you know Ancient Greek, I wouldn't expect you to."

"Nope. The drawings look interesting. Some of them are kind of creepy."

"I would agree with you."

"What's the book about?"

Lourds hesitated only a moment. "Architecture."

"I thought so. Early stuff?"

"I haven't ascertained that yet." Lourds held the book carefully at his side. "I'm still translating it."

With a casual wave, the man indicated the backpack. "I see you travel with a lot of books."

"I do. Hopefully they have the rest of the books I brought on this trip at the hotel."

"I think everything was found. May have a bullet or two in them, from what I understand. I guess you take a lot of work with you wherever you go."

"I do."

"Ever worry about any of it going missing?"

"Not really," Lourds said, "no. Most of the documents I work on while traveling aren't original. Usually I bring photographs or scanned copies."

The man smiled. "I guess it would be hard to bring in a boulder covered in hieroglyphics."

"It would be. Or a wall covered in cuneiform."

The man's glance cut back to the book in Lourds's possession. "I guess that's an exception."

"Yes." Lourds left it at that.

The man reached into his suit jacket and the pistol was revealed briefly. He unfolded his State Department identification and showed Lourds the photograph and card. "My name's Hayden Mullins. I'm an attaché with the United States State Department here in Turkey."

"Are all State Department attachés armed in Istanbul?"

"No. But after the events of your arrival, they decided to make special rules for you." Mullins leaned down and caught hold of Lourds's backpack. "If you'll follow me, I've got a car waiting outside."

Lourds nodded.

Ersoz extended a business card. "This has my contact information on it, Professor Lourds. I took the liberty of writing my personal mobile number on the back." He flipped the card over to show his neat handwriting. "In case you should decide you need something I can provide."

"Thank you." Lourds took the card. "I hope you find the men you're looking for."

"We will, Professor. Istanbul is an old city filled with many old secrets, but rarely do the new secrets go unnoticed. These men, whoever they are, don't seem to be the type to go away empty-handed." Ersoz shrugged. "This could be a bad thing for you, but it will give me and the police department another chance to catch them. We will do so successfully. But our timing, let us say, is in the hands of Allah. . . . Do take care of yourself, Professor."

Not knowing what else to do, Lourds nodded and went to join Mullins.

"He's not exactly a Pollyanna, is he?" Mullins asked when they were well away from Ersoz. "He thinks you're a walking dead man."

"I guess he's got reason to," Lourds responded. "My trip has been too eventful for his taste. And mine."

"A word of advice, Professor?" Mullins glanced at Lourds.

"Sure."

Mullins flicked his gaze to the card in Lourds's hand. "I wouldn't trust the locals too much, if you know what I mean."

"Why?"

"Everybody in the city has their own personal axe to grind. It would be a pity to see you get ground up as well."

"Believe me," Lourds said, "the last thing I intend to do is get ground up."

"So you really don't know what those jokers wanted?"

Lourds lied without hesitation. "No."

"Weird, huh?" Mullins grinned at him. "I got to hand it to you, Professor. You have a pair of stones. Most men would be ducking and running for cover after what you've been through. But here you are—ready to go deliver those speeches to college students."

"Believe me, bravery isn't why I'm staying here."

"Oh, so it's a sense of duty? A promise to a friend?"

"Something like that." *More like a sense of curiosity.*

Lourds stopped beside the sedan Mullins indicated in the parking area. As he waited for the man to open the door locks, he stared at the street. No one appeared interested in him. The gentle breeze carried a chill bite and the scent of spicy food. He didn't know if he wanted food or a bed first. And he needed a shower and clean clothes.

Mullins must have caught him gazing around. "Paranoid, Professor?"

"Maybe a little," Lourds admitted.

"Will it help to know that we're going to be keeping an eye on you for a while?"

"Yes," Lourds lied. He was still suspicious of the way the State Department had come to his rescue, and of the fact that they hadn't had a bevy of questions of their own for him. That didn't sound reasonable to him. And all the pros he had encountered here in Istanbul had made a point to tell him to be reasonable.

He slipped into the car seat and fastened his seat belt.

CENTRAL INTELLIGENCE AGENCY
LANGLEY, VIRGINIA
UNITED STATES OF AMERICA
MARCH 17, 2010

"You're telling me no one we know can read this book?" Dawson demanded.

On the left section of the wallscreen in the command center, Josiah Hedges looked like he was beside himself with worry. He was in his early fifties and not used to coming up as empty as he was. He wore a white dress shirt with the sleeves rolled to midforearm. His tie hung at half-staff. A fringe of cottony white hair surrounded his bald pate.

"No one that we've found, sir."

"And we have no idea what this book is even about?"

Hedges hesitated. "Architecture, sir?"

"As our subject suggested?"

The analyst cringed just a little.

Dawson shook his head angrily. He'd slept on the flight back from Boston and caught a couple hours in his office while the Turkish police had grilled Lourds, but he didn't feel rested. In fact, the news from the chief cryptology analyst made the fatigue even worse.

"We're the CIA," Dawson said. "Nobody is supposed to be better than us at cracking codes."

"Sir," Hedges said, "in our defense, this isn't just a code. This is a language—"

"We have linguists. *You* have linguists."

"Yes, sir. We do. We've even got people who can read and write Ancient Greek like nobody's business. But we all feel this isn't just Ancient Greek. We think this is a coded version of Ancient Greek."

"Then break the code."

"We're trying, sir. With a little more time—"

Dawson glared at the other half of the wallscreen. The "State Department" representative Mullins was actually a CIA agent. While Lourds had been detained, Mullins had captured digital images of the old book the professor had tucked away in his backpack and uploaded them to Langley. The book was the only possible lead among the other things the backpack had contained.

"Do you know who I report to, Hedges?" Dawson asked.

Hedges swallowed with difficulty. "Yes, sir."

"Believe me when I say the pressure on this one rolls down from on high. If you don't get this thing cracked—and soon—your next assignment is going to be in Antarctica. Am I making myself clear?"

"Positively crystal, sir. But there is one upside, sir."

"Waiting to hear it," Dawson snarled.

"If we've been unable to crack this code with all the software and manpower at our disposal here, sir, it's most doubtful that anyone else will be able to."

"That's not good enough. Get me that translation."

"Yes, sir."

Dawson tapped one of the buttons on his headset and severed the communications link to Hedges. The section of the wallscreen showing the analyst blanked and the images of Lourds's mysterious book filled the space.

He picked up an air mouse and clicked through the digitized pages. Looking at the symbols for the past hour had given him a headache. Then he cut to the wireless camera mounted in the sedan Lourds was presently riding in.

Lourds sat in the passenger seat and massaged his temples. The man didn't look like a threat to national security. He didn't even resemble an erudite Harvard scholar. He looked like a bum. He was disheveled, unkempt, and dirty.

But there was something about Lourds's gray eyes that spoke of the intellect lying inside. He had translated documents and writing no one else in the world had translated.

Dawson tried to imagine what made the man so good at what he did, and couldn't.

He's lucky, Dawson thought. *Everything's that's gone on since he arrived at Istanbul has proved that. He could have—maybe even should have—been dead a dozen times over.*

Except, in that case, they would never have gotten their hands on the book. Dawson muttered a curse and wished that he knew what this chase was all about. He had the sense that Vice President Webster knew, but the man wasn't giving him a clue. Normally the vice president kept him in the loop, but that wasn't always the case.

Unable to stand still any longer, Dawson paced in front of the wallscreen. "Have we got audio and video inside Lourds's hotel room?"

"It's going in now," one of the techs behind him answered.

"Bring it online."

The wallscreen shimmered and the view changed. In the blink of an eye, the book pages dissolved into a view of the inside of a hotel suite. Two men and a woman dressed in motel staff uniforms worked quickly and efficiently inside the rooms.

"Sequencing video," one of the techs said.

A series of perspectives cycled across the wallscreen. Dawson counted nine camera angles that provided differing and overlapping views of the suite's living room, bedroom, and bathroom.

"All video is online," the tech reported. "Beginning audio check."

On-screen, the three techs walked through the suite conversing in normal voices. A few small adjustments were made to the audio gain before the system was declared satisfactory.

"We have the hotel phone?" Dawson asked.

"First thing we did," the tech answered.

"What about Lourds's sat phone?"

"A clone application was installed before the phone was returned to him. We'll be privy to all his incoming and outgoing calls, as well as to his answering service."

Dawson relaxed a little. At least they had eyes-on. No matter what he did, Professor Thomas Lourds couldn't make a move without them knowing it. Dawson just wished he knew why the vice president was so interested in the man.

"Where is Lourds?" Dawson asked.

The upper right corner of the wallscreen scrolled into a street map. Two locations marked *1* and *2* lit up. The number *2* was stationary while the number *1* was in motion. The car Mullins drove was equipped with GPS tracking.

"Three minutes out, sir," one of the techs said.

"We're going to need about ten minutes to clean up in here," one of the hotel staff said. "Can you delay the arrival?"

"Call Mullins and let him know," Dawson directed.

A moment later, the *1* changed directions, taking a left onto a side street away from the hotel. Dawson watched Lourds on-screen and saw the professor sit up a little straighter.

"Lourds knows Mullins is deviating from the hotel route," Dawson said. "Let Mullins know."

In the car, Mullins turned to the professor and said, "I've got a quick stop to make, if you don't mind."

"Of course," Lourds replied.

Two blocks farther on, Mullins parked the car at the side of the street and got out. "You mind staying put, Professor?"

"Not at all."

Mullins nodded happily and walked into a small jewelry store. Lourds immediately reached into his backpack and brought out the mysterious book. He perused the pages, took out a small notebook, and began taking notes. He worked quickly and confidently.

Dawson paced anxiously. "Can we get an angle on what he's writing?"

The camera views offered inside the car cycled through, but to no avail. Whatever Lourds worked on remained hidden.

A few minutes later, the team on-site in the hotel suite radioed that they were cleared from the scene. Mullins confirmed the information, then came out of the shop carrying a small bag.

"Looks like the Professor's working away," Mullins said on the way back to the car. "We could take what he's got."

Dawson thought about that. Whatever Lourds had seen was definitely more useful than anything the cryptology department had put together at the agency. He had to wonder if the few crumbs the professor had assembled would be enough to leverage the answers the book would give.

"Well, how do you want to handle this?" Mullins asked as he reached for the car door.

Lourds only then noticed Mullins at the door. Quietly, feigning disinterest and boredom, the professor put the book away and tucked his notebook into his shirt pocket.

Mullins slid in behind steering wheel.

Dawson took in a big breath and let it out. Guys like the professor liked to play things smart. He'd already stonewalled the Istanbul police.

Playing things smart would also mean that Lourds had created a code of his own to keep his notes in. They had already seen evidence of that in the notes Mullins had found in the backpack. Since the guy was so good with languages, there might be more than one code.

"No," Dawson answered. "Leave him room to run. We know where he is. We can pick him up anytime we're ready." As he watched, Mullins started the car and eased out into traffic.

ERESİN CROWN HOTEL
SULTANAHMET DISTRICT
İSTANBUL, TURKEY
MARCH 17, 2010

At the door to his suite, Lourds swiped the keycard through the slot, turned the handle, then eased into the dark room. He halted before he was halfway through the door.

Someone was inside. Or had only just left. The smell of expensive perfume lingered in the air.

As interesting as that scent was, and perhaps familiar, he didn't feel like trying his luck. The trip to Istanbul—except for the interesting manuscript—was turning out to be something of a surprise.

He eased back out of the room, contemplating getting a berth in another hotel. One that wasn't quite so heavily traveled. Before he could clear the door, someone tapped him on the shoulder.

Lourds started violently and almost yelled in fright. He raised his empty arm up defensively before him, clutching his backpack to his chest with the other.

"Thomas?" Olympia Adnan yelped as she dodged backwards. "What do you think you're doing? You could hurt someone flailing around like that."

"Olympia!" Embarrassed, Lourds stood a little straighter. "You shouldn't go around sneaking up on people like that."

Still somewhat confused, Olympia shook her head and looked rather cross. "I had hoped you'd be glad to see me. After all, we haven't seen each other in almost three years."

High cheekbones and wide-set brown eyes made her beautiful. Her thick black hair lay in shimmering waves of ebony past her shoulders. Her clear olive-tinted complexion gave her an exotic aura. She stood only an inch or two above Lourds's shoulder. The teal skirt suit she wore emphasized her lush figure to its best advantage. Spiked strappy heels, which also explained how she came up to Lourds's shoulder, showed off her trim calves. A ruby pendant on a white gold chain was held just above the hint of cleavage Lourds could see in the *V* of the jacket.

"Has it really been three years?" Lourds asked, wishing he wasn't grinning so foolishly.

"It has."

"You look amazing."

"Thank you. I work at it." Some of the old playfulness flickered in her brown eyes. She reached out and pulled at his shirt collar. "Perhaps it's something you should work at."

"The last couple of days haven't been anything like what you promised when you invited me here," Lourds countered.

Olympia wrinkled her nose. "I know. The news programs have been full of that. I'm sorry about it. But you have to admit, most of this has been far beyond my control."

That reminded Lourds of the perfume he'd smelled inside the suite. He put a finger to his lips.

Intrigued, Olympia narrowed her eyes and leaned in closer to him. "What?" she whispered.

"Someone's in my room."

"Nonsense!" Olympia looked affronted. "This is a very good hotel,

I'll have you know. I've stayed here myself. And I arranged for your booking."

"The security isn't what it could be," Lourds replied quietly.

"The security is good here."

"They let the police in earlier."

Olympia put her fists on her generous hips. "They were the police, Thomas. Of course the hotel had to let them in."

"They could have mentioned it at the desk."

"Mentioned what? That they let the police into your room?"

"Yes."

"Maybe the police told them not to tell you. Have you thought about that?"

"Of course I have. And of course they probably did. I'm beginning to strongly dislike surprises."

Olympia rolled her eyes. "I rather gathered that when I tapped you on the shoulder and you nearly wet yourself."

"No, I was preparing to defend myself."

"Well, in case no one has mentioned it before, as an expert in self-defense, you're a great linguist."

Lourds frowned in response. "Maybe you have changed. I really don't remember you being this unkind three years ago."

"Nonsense. Any time you got overly pompous, I was always there to prick you."

"I've told you before that I really think that should be my line."

She smiled at him disarmingly. "Then you should really concentrate on getting it in sooner."

While Lourds was engaged with the latest bit of double entendre, Olympia slipped past him. She plucked the keycard from his hand and before he knew it, she was going for it.

Lourds put his hand against the door as if to stop it from opening. "Don't go in there."

Olympia arched an eyebrow at him. "Really? That's supposed to stop me?"

"Seriously, Olympia. Someone is in there."

"How do you know?"

"I smelled her perfume."

"Well, you've got a fabulous nose for perfumes. But maybe it's something left by another woman who's been in your room."

"If there's been a woman in my room, I don't know about it." Even as he said that, Lourds was more than a little intrigued by the suggestive nature of their conversation as well as the flirting and hint of jealousy. "How's your love life?"

Olympia grimaced at him. "What love life?"

"I thought you were involved with the Belgian archeologist."

"I was. Sadly, he and I both discovered that he's a lot like you."

"Me?"

"Yes. Too involved in your own pursuits to let any woman slow you down for long."

"Ouch."

Olympia patted his cheek. "You never hurt me, pet. You made it very clear from the beginning that what we had was fun. And it was." She caught him by the shirt collar and pulled him down for a lingering kiss.

Lourds's head swam at the intoxicating feel of her lips pressed against his. *Definitely looks like it can be fun again.*

"Thomas," she whispered raggedly as she pulled away.

"Yes?"

"The door, pet, opens *inward.*" Olympia slid the keycard, turned the handle, and pulled the door inside.

For a moment, Lourds was caught flatfooted between sensory overload from the kiss and surprise at seeing how quickly she'd outmaneuvered him. Despite every instinct in him screaming to flee the premises, he trailed her inside the room.

CHAPTER 12

THE OVAL OFFICE
THE WHITE HOUSE
WASHINGTON, D.C.
UNITED STATES OF AMERICA
MARCH 17, 2010

Vice President of the United States Elliot Webster walked along the carpeted hallway to the president's sanctum. Excitement vibrated through him because he knew everything he had planned for so long was coming to a head. He'd actually thought that this time might be as much as two or three years away. He had had a handful of plans in mind to trigger the coming events, but Professor Thomas Lourds's arrival in Istanbul had been too good to pass up.

He knew the reemergence of the lost book was a sign of successes to come.

Two young Secret Service agents, one male and one female, stood in front of the Oval Office door. Both of them nodded as he approached.

"Good morning, Mr. Vice President," one of them greeted.

"Good morning, Vincent. How did your mother do with her hip surgery?" Webster's mind was like a steel trap. He remembered everything he learned, and every person he ever met. All of them were little people who wanted some kind of recognition from those in power. He utilized his talents to make them feel appreciated. It bought him loyalty at no cost to himself. He'd cultivated that trait since he had gone into business.

Vincent smiled eagerly. "She's doing much better, Mr. Vice President. She's up and around these days, and talking about going dancing."

Webster chuckled. "As an incentive to your mother, tell her that when she's able to dance again I'll take her out one night and we'll paint the town red."

Vincent reddened slightly. "I'll tell her, sir. And she said to tell you thank you very much for the flowers."

"She's very welcome, Vincent. After everything you do for the president, it's the least that I can do." Webster turned his attention to the female Secret Service agent. "How are you this fine morning, Mildred?"

"Fine, sir. Thank you."

"How is the new Little Sister coming along?"

"She's good, sir. A bit of a handful at times, but I enjoy taking her places." The young agent had recently signed up to be a Big Sister. Webster had provided the letter of recommendation that sealed her sponsorship.

"Excellent, Mildred. I'm glad it's working out for you." Webster rubbed his hands together briskly. "Well, I guess I should find out why the president called me out of my meeting this morning."

Vincent nodded, then turned and knocked on the door of the Oval Office.

"Yes," a deep voice answered from within.

Vincent opened the door and said, "Mr. President, Vice President Webster is here to see you."

On the other side of the room, President Michael Waggoner rose from behind his paper-strewn desk. He was a tall, gaunt man with dark hair that had gone gray at the temples while he'd been in office. In college, he had been a basketball player—had, in fact, almost gone pro—before enlisting in the marines and putting in twenty years.

Some people believed Waggoner had joined the military to avoid his father's political dynasty. Senator Kendall Waggoner had been in politics his whole life, and had died while still in office. On his deathbed, he asked his son to finish out his term. Everyone had known about the illness that eventually killed him, and his death came as no surprise.

What was a surprise to most people was how well the son had served the senator's last two years. That service also changed Michael Waggoner's view of politics. It had gotten into his blood and he made a career of it. Another term and a half later, he'd gotten the Democratic nod to run for president, and had swept the nation. Especially after he'd added Elliott Webster as his running mate.

Waggoner's popularity remained high in the polls and everyone agreed that he was one of the best presidents who'd ever served. But it had taken its toll on him.

"Good morning, Elliott," Waggoner said as he walked around the desk. He wore slacks and a shirt, but his tie lay in a wad on one of the two chairs in front of the desk.

"I'd say 'good morning,' Mike, but this looks more like a long night." Webster took the offered hand and shook. Then he sat in the unoccupied chair in front of the desk.

"It has been a long night," Waggoner agreed as he crossed the room to the coffee service.

"You could have called, you know."

"I did. The minute I was sure I needed you on this. You've got a host of duties to perform, too. Don't think I don't know that. I knew I was going to be working late on this, and I wanted one of us with a clear head."

"Me?"

"Yours is usually the clearest in the room at any given time anyway," Waggoner said with a smile. "But, yes, you. Coffee?"

"Please."

The president poured and served out. He didn't bother sitting, though. He blew on his coffee and sipped, but Webster didn't think Waggoner even tasted it.

"What's the problem, Mike?"

"We've got an unconfirmed report from Riyadh that someone assassinated King Yousef bin Abdul Aziz and Crown Prince Muhammad bin Abdul Aziz last night."

Webster placed his coffee on the president's desk and sat back as he contemplated what that meant. "Is anyone taking the credit for this?"

Waggoner ran a hand through his hair and sighed. "We haven't got anything solid yet. It's still too early, but this looks like the real deal."

"What happened?"

"Things have gone crazy over there. Despite the amount of oil Saudi Arabia has and how much it's able to produce, those oil fields can't keep up with the demands put on them by the Western world, India, and China. Everybody wants a piece of the petroleum pie, and they're willing to do whatever it takes to make sure they get their share. More, if they can get it." Waggoner folded his arms across his chest. "We're just as guilty as anyone else in this, Elliott. We've wooed the royal family for generations. At that time, we were the only ones with economic and military means to protect them. With China, India, Pakistan all emerging this century with strong economies as well as strong military forces, we've lost ground. Our economy is shaky and our protracted military engagement in the Middle East bleeds us dry. Iraq was just the beginning there."

"Where did you get the report?" Webster asked.

"From the CIA units working on the ground in Saudi. They got the information from one of their assets near the royal family."

"What happened?" Webster's excitement and anticipation grew but he didn't let it show. He had known that the Middle East would be the ignition point for the conflagration that would sweep the world. He counted on it.

"What we're getting is that the king and crown prince were having a meeting off the books in King Abdullah Economic City."

"A meeting with whom?"

"We're not sure of that, either. Possibly a coterie from the Indian government."

"Renegotiating deliveries?"

Waggoner shrugged. "Possibly brokering a deal for a pipeline across their country."

"That's supposedly been in the works for some time."

"I know. And if they do that, it'll change the economic model we've been working from over here. A lot of people I talk to are nervous about this."

"I know. I've been talking to them, too." Webster thought for a moment. "You know, Mike, as a businessman, I can't blame the royal family for wanting to negotiate this deal. No one knows for sure how much oil they've got in their reserves. No one outside the ruling family knows. Maybe they're reaching a point where they're going to have to cut production. They may be afraid that the United States will take their business to South America or Africa."

"Or that we'll finally be motivated enough to find an alternate fuel source since our economy has flatlined for a while. A viable alternate fuel source would change the United States, but it would really change the entire face of the Middle East. That possibility has to be on their minds."

"It is," Webster acknowledged. "The way the Middle East is set up now, in order to be successful, they've got to export oil. They don't have a lot of other options—no manufacturing base, limited water, limited other resources. If another fuel source becomes viable, the distance we have to go for oil and the price we have to pay is counterproductive to us as an economy and a military force. We can afford to have our Middle Eastern fuel lines cut if push comes to shove."

"I know. But we're not there yet. Someday soon, maybe, but not yet. We're still dependent on these people. The problem is, they don't want to be dependent on us any more than we are on them."

"Right now, though, we still need each other."

"Not so much, these days." Waggoner shook his head. "We need them more than they need us. They have other buyers lining up. Right now we've invested so heavily in the Middle East that we can't think about pulling out for years. Or losing their resources."

"Yousef and Muhammad are—were—both actively seeking some kind of alliance regarding increased oil production for India and China. They haven't been chasing Pakistan, to my knowledge at least, because of all the terrorist concerns in that country." Webster was silent for a moment. "Have you given any consideration to the possibility that maybe *we* were the ones who killed—or at least tried to kill—the king and crown prince?"

"I have. It might just be possible. I don't like the idea that some mercenary force employed by an American citizen or an American corporation would do something like this." Waggoner shook his head. "But these are desperate times, and this country isn't so well liked overseas as she has been in the past. I'm betting it's somebody else. Somebody who doesn't like us. We're still coming out of the recession, and we're overextended militarily. We're vulnerable. Other countries are going to throw that possibility around."

Webster let the silence in the room stretch out for a time before he said anything. "You know I'm there for you, Mike. Anything you need, anything at all, and I'll do my best."

Waggoner stared out the window, put his cup on the desk, and shoved his hands into his pockets. "I know you will, Elliott. That's why I'm telling you this now. You've got friends over in Riyadh, and it may be time for us to call in a few favors from those people."

Webster waited for the president to cut to the chase. It sometimes took the man a while to get to it, but he never flinched when it came to making hard decisions. Part of it was because of the military training he'd had, but part of it was due to the fact that Waggoner was a man who believed in good and evil. His weakness, as far as Webster was concerned, was that he still believed good always triumphed over evil.

"What do you want me to do?" Webster asked.

"I want you on the ground over there in Saudi. I want to know what's going on there. And I want to know it as soon as you can find out."

Webster stood. "All right, Mike. Is there anything else?"

Waggoner shook his head wearily. "Just be careful, Elliott. I watched the sun come up this morning and I felt that somehow the whole world had changed overnight." He paused. "Isn't that a strange thought?"

Smiling confidently, Webster dropped a hand on the president's shoulder. "You just need some sleep. That's all. You get some sleep and you'll feel better. Me and you, we're keeping the faith. That's what we promised the American people we would do when they put us into office."

"I know, I know. I keep telling myself that. You just keep your head down over there until you figure out what's what."

"Will do." Webster shook hands a final time, then turned and left the room. He said good-bye to both Secret Service agents and took out his phone to start making arrangements. Between figuring out what to do with Professor Thomas Lourds and the coming unrest in the Middle East, it was going to be a busy day.

BURGER KING
TAKSIM SQUARE
İSTANBUL, TURKEY
MARCH 17, 2010

Cleena sat at a booth in the back of the restaurant and tried not to feel like a voyeur on the laptop Sevki had given her before she left his apartment after Lourds's release from the police department.

Of course, a voyeur was what she was. There was no getting around that. She was watching Lourds and his lady friend—the older college professor, whatever her name was—in the hotel room.

The problem was Cleena wasn't the only voyeur.

"Your professor—," Sevki started.

"*So* not my professor," Cleena interrupted.

"Sorry. One of us was working while you were sleeping and may be a little fatigued at the moment."

"Spare me. I went three days without sleep working on something for you."

"And you were paid quite handsomely for it, as I recall."

Cleena glanced from the laptop monitor to the restaurant's clientele around here. It was late afternoon, before the early evening rush would start. Most of the clientele would be American tourists looking for a familiar meal, or Istanbul college and high school students wanting to sample food from an American chain restaurant.

She had chosen the place as a base of operations because Taksim Square was only four kilometers from the professor's hotel. If he went somewhere, she felt certain she could intercept him on the motorcycle she'd purchased from a black market contact. She also hoped that the men from the catacombs, if they could find the professor, would stand out in a place like Burger King.

Sevki had given her an earwig tied into an encrypted sat phone that also functioned, like now, through Wi-Fi hot spots. The device felt bulky in her ear, but she had been surprised at how small it was. Unless someone looked closely, no one would know she was wearing it. *Except for the way I apparently keep talking to myself.*

"Anyway," Sevki went on, "as I was saying, the professor isn't alone in there."

"I can see the woman."

"I know, and I must say she's even better looking than her photograph."

"Focus."

"The room is bugged," Sevki said. "That's why you're getting video feed from inside the room instead of just the hallway."

Cleena was so used to Sevki producing technological marvels that she hadn't even realized she was peering inside the hotel room when he had told her he wouldn't be able to provide that.

"Who bugged the room?" she asked.

"Judging from the frequencies and the hardware, I'd say it was the United States Central Intelligence Agency. Or a similarly equipped corporate security team. It's getting hard to know whose toys are whose these days. Corporate espionage has cutting-edge stuff, some of it even better than the CIA's"

"The CIA?" Cleena pushed back from the laptop a little. "That doesn't make sense."

"As in, if the CIA has already got someone watching the professor, why do they need you? I started wondering the same thing when I locked into these feeds. I played with the idea that this might be the work of some corporation, but no likely suspects spring to mind. Why would anyone, including the CIA, suddenly develop an interest in the professor?"

Cleena didn't like the route her mind automatically took.

"If this is the CIA's handiwork, the only thing I can figure you for is a fall guy if things get sticky."

"Can they catch you spying on them?" The idea that the CIA might even now be spying on them while they spied on Lourds was unsettling, to say the least.

"Doubtful. But look at our professor. Looks like he's got his hands full."

On screen, Lourds and the college professor were more amorously engaged than previously. Cleena wasn't mortified, but she wasn't interested in watching either.

"Lech," she growled at Sevki.

"Sticks and stones and all that rot."

"I was talking about the CIA catching you."

"Oh." Sevki sounded distracted, and Cleena had to admit that what she was watching was distracting, and a little more intriguing than she'd thought it would be. Lourds was evidently a man of considerable skills.

"The CIA," she reminded.

"Them. No. I don't think they'll find us. I've masked all the work I've done to break in there. If they even find out we're in there, it'll be a miracle."

"Can you trace their video and audio feeds back?"

"Already done that. The trail leads back to the United States Embassy offices here in the city."

"And . . . *the professor* has no idea he's being watched right now?"

"Would you be doing what he's doing right now if you knew someone was watching you?"

Mild irritation swept through Cleena. "You really shouldn't be watching this."

"Then who's going to watch the professor and makes sure he stays put?" Sevki's tone was mocking.

"You said you have access to the video in the hallway."

"I do."

"Then you can use that to keep tabs on the professor."

"And miss the show? I'll make you a deal. You turn your computer off—and I'll know when you do—I'll do the same for mine. Up the ante, so to speak. Do we have a deal?"

Cleena didn't answer, and she didn't cut the video feed either.

"Are you using the audio feed?" Sevki asked.

"I'm in a public place."

"There's a pair of earbuds tucked into the computer case."

Cleena hesitated only a moment, then opened the computer case and took out the earbuds. She attached them to the computer and adjusted the volume. The sound was good. It was like she was in the room with Lourds and his professor lady friend. The idea was faintly embarrassing but more erotic than she would have thought.

While on the flight over to Istanbul, she had listened to the audio book version of *Bedroom Pursuits.* The narrative was more compelling than she had imagined. And that type of entertainment definitely wasn't her usual venue.

"Ah," Sevki chuckled. "Aren't you the dirty girl?"

"Shut up."

ERESİN CROWN HOTEL
SULTANAHMET DİSTRİCT
İSTANBUL, TURKEY
MARCH 17, 2010

Lourds kissed Olympia as he unbuttoned her jacket. They stood just inside the room. No one else was there, but the scent of the strange perfume he'd noticed still lingered on the air.

Breaking free of the passionate kiss they shared, Lourds gazed into Olympia's wide-set brown eyes. "Do you smell the perfume?"

"Yes." Olympia's hand curled around the back of his neck and played with his hair. The sensation was incredibly delightful and Lourds knew she was aware of that. They'd been good lovers who explored each other's bodies well enough to know what worked and what didn't.

"Doesn't that worry you?" Lourds ran his hands under her jacket and the matching teal chemise she wore to unfasten her bra. He managed the feat with one hand, which brought a smile to Olympia's beautiful face.

"You've still got your touch, I see," she whispered.

"The perfume?" Lourds reminded.

"And you still have a one-track mind."

"I wouldn't say that." Lourds closed his hands over the tender flesh of her breasts and gently tweaked her nipples. "I'm quite capable of multitasking when there's a need."

A quiet moan escaped Olympia as she tilted her head back. "Oh, there's a need. A definite need."

Lourds grinned and kissed her again. He slid his hands across her back and pulled her close to him. He felt the heat of her melding into his.

"The perfume could have been from a maid stopping by to turn down the bed," Olympia suggested. She pushed free of Lourds and gazed up at him. "There is a bed, isn't there? I specifically asked for one when I reserved this room."

"There must be one in here somewhere. I just haven't seen it yet."

Olympia looked around the room. "If it were me, I'd guess it was behind that door."

"Well, then we'll try that one. You do have a doctorate degree, after all."

"Three, actually."

"You're obviously overcompensating for something." Lourds bent down and lifted her into his arms, then started for the bedroom door. Once inside he fumbled for and found the light switch. He turned it on and a soft glow filled the room.

The bedroom was spacious and adorned in pastel-colored curtains and bedding. The king-size bed dominated the room. Lourds carried Olympia toward it and gently laid her on it.

When he tried to crawl in after her, she pushed him away. "You're dirty," she said.

Lourds stood at the side of the bed, only then remembering his current state. "You weren't objecting a moment ago."

"A moment ago, we were in the living room, not in the bed where I expect to be happily entertained for the next ten or twelve hours."

Lourds cocked an eyebrow in mock surprise. "You do have grand designs, don't you?"

"A large appetite, thank you. And it's already been kept waiting for two days while you've been off gallivanting around."

"I'd hardly call nearly getting killed—on more than one occasion—and getting interviewed by the local constabulary 'gallivanting around.' "

"An imposition, then."

"Most impositions I've had don't included getting shot at."

Olympia sat on the edge of the bed and unbuttoned his shirt. She ran her hands across the flat planes of his chest and stomach. Years of playing soccer had kept him taut and lean. He ran his fingers through the shimmering waves of her hair, then bent down to kiss her.

As they kissed, her fingers busied themselves with his belt buckle and pants. A moment later they slid down his slim hips. He'd already been erect, and getting freed only promoted that. Her fingers closed around his erection and he shivered in anticipation. He cupped her breasts again and squeezed just enough to elicit a moan.

She broke free of his lips then trailed kisses down his chest and stomach. She made him wait, his hands knotted in her hair, before she slowly, delicately took him into her mouth.

Lourds's knees almost buckled at the sensation. His breath came in ragged gasps and he teetered on the edge of control. He was aware that she knew that, and doubtless enjoyed being in a position of power.

Olympia had always been a generous lover, but she'd also been an incredible tease.

Just before he begged for mercy or permission, Olympia drew back and smiled wickedly up at him. "Go," she said sternly. "Shower. We'll continue the frivolity after you're clean."

"Of course, my lady." Lourds took her hand and kissed her fingers. "I won't be but just a moment."

"You'd better take longer than that. You reek."

Lourds turned to walk away and very nearly tripped over his own pants, which were down around his ankles, forgotten during the distraction. He unlaced his boots and stepped out of them, then the pants. He glanced back at Olympia, who sat on the bed half-undone with one sleek leg tucked under her.

CHAPTER 13

WASHINGTON DULLES INTERNATIONAL AIRPORT
WASHINGTON, D.C.
UNITED STATES OF AMERICA
MARCH 17, 2010

Vice President Elliott Webster's cell phone rang as his private limousine glided out onto the tarmac to the waiting military jet scheduled to fly him to Saudi Arabia. When he checked the caller ID, he answered and said, "One moment, please."

The limo driver parked the vehicle in the shade of the jet. Webster raised the soundproof glass that separated the rear of the luxury vehicle from the chauffeur. Then he nodded at the three Secret Service men that were part of his personal detachment.

"If you'll excuse me, gentlemen, I need to take this call alone."

The three Secret Service agents opened the doors and stepped outside the limousine. They stood watch while Webster relaxed in the backseat.

"We're alone, Colonel, and on a secure line. You may speak freely."

"Very good, sir," Colonel Anthony Eckart said. In his early forties, the colonel had been a marine officer for twenty-one years before taking retirement. The retirement hadn't entirely been his idea. His outspoken "America first" policy as he'd pursued it hadn't set well with the marines. The media had loved him for his volatile diatribes on who he believed America's enemies truly were. His list included all of the Middle East, to start with.

After separating from the marines, Eckart had gone to work for Webster as part of his clandestine security group that was still secret from the press and the president. He'd served in that capacity for the last three years.

"I assume you've heard about the deaths in Saudi?" Eckart asked.

Webster's gaze flicked to the plasma television hanging from the limo's ceiling. WNN News had been covering the story since early that morning. The footage of the flaming building in King Abdullah Economic City had been taken by a ship out in the harbor. Black smoke hung above the city.

Currently, it was evening in Saudi Arabia. Arranging the trip had taken hours.

"I have," Webster replied. "I've been expecting your call."

"Things here have gotten little crazy," Eckart said. "After the attack, the whole city was blacked out—all ordinary communications are down. I didn't want to use the sat phone till after the media people had descended into the metro area en masse. Otherwise the Saudis might have tracked our signal."

"Understood. I take it you and your men survived?"

"Yes, sir. We got lucky on this one. Both targets ended up at the same twenty. They were at the king's grandson's birthday party."

"I'd heard they might be negotiating oil disbursements with the Indian government."

"Those people were at the party as well. The hardest part was managing to take out the two primary targets without killing Khalid, the younger prince."

"That was done?"

"Absolutely."

"So how is our young prince?"

"Khalid was wounded, but sustained no permanent damage."

"I take it the prince—now king—is talking of retribution."

"From what I've heard, he's positively foaming at the mouth, sir."

Webster smiled. "Khalid was always hotheaded and looking for a fight."

"He's going to turn that country into a hornet's nest."

"As we'd planned."

"If our enemies destroy each other, sir, it saves a lot of our soldiers."

Webster knew the coming military conflagration would do more than that. He was counting on it.

"There was some collateral damage," Eckart went on. "Some of the king's servants and personal bodyguards, a few of the wives and children, were also killed, but no one we're going to lose any sleep over."

"That's all perfectly acceptable, Colonel. You and your men did a good job."

"Thank you, sir. I'll mention it to them."

"There's been a change in plans," Webster said. "I want you and your team in Istanbul as soon as you can get there."

Eckart transitioned smoothly. He always did. "It'll be a few hours before we're able to move from here without alerting suspicion."

"That's fine. For the moment I've got someone sitting on your target."

"May I ask who the target is, sir?"

"A Harvard professor named Thomas Lourds. You've probably heard of him. He's the man who was involved in the hunt for lost Atlantis."

"I have, sir. That story was all over the news."

"I don't want Lourds terminated at present," Webster said. "I just want to talk to him."

"Yes, sir. I'll let you know when we're en route."

"Very good. I expect to see you soon, Colonel. Until then, best of luck." Webster broke the connection and pocketed the cell phone. Then he unmuted the television to listen to the news anchor.

"The Saudi Arabian government hasn't confirmed who died in last night's fiery attack in King Abdullah Economic City," the anchor said with sterling confidence. "But it's clear several injured and several dead were removed from the rubble of the building that was struck by a missile weapon."

The television cut away from the anchor to the night scene of the attack. For a few seconds, the three-story building stood overlooking the harbor; then in the next moment an explosion blossomed in the center of the building. At first, the building held and smoke poured from some of the windows near the blast site. Several people in the street had run for cover, but some of them started trickling back toward the stricken structure. They were caught flatfooted when the building shivered a final time and collapsed in a way that made Webster sit back in the limo's plush seats.

"We have unconfirmed reports that King Yousef and Crown Prince Muhammad were among those injured and possibly killed in the attack."

Images of the king and crown prince formed on-screen, overlying the destruction.

"If those two men are casualties," the anchor continued, "many political analysts fear the changes that may take place in the Middle East. Here for a special look at the situation is Jane Keller."

Webster listened to the special report with zeal, for it agreed exactly with his assessment of what would happen.

Georgetown University Professor Clarence Doolan looked grim and foreboding in the television studio. In his seventies, tan and withered, Doolan looked like a hanging judge about to pass sentence. Jane Keller, the young television reporter, looked like she'd stepped straight from a Victoria's Secret commercial.

"Khalid isn't like his father or brother," Doolan said to the perky young reporter. "If he takes the throne, that whole region may be in jeopardy."

That was precisely the reason Webster hadn't had him killed.

"What makes you say that, Professor?" the reporter asked.

"Saudi Arabia occupies a singular niche within the Middle East," the professor explained. "It's a powerful country, and its impact on oil production is immense. However, the United States has depended on Saudi Arabia to maintain a nonaggressive presence within that community. Sometimes the U.S. has had to be heavily persuasive to manage that feat."

"Why is that nonaggressive presence so necessary?" the reporter asked.

"You have to understand the fundamental differences in the Muslim world. There are two distinct religions within Islam, the Sunni and the

Shia. They have differing interpretations of the line of succession regarding the prophet Muhammad, and they're willing to kill each other over those differences when they come into conflict. Saudi Arabia has sometimes prevailed to cool the fires of war in the Middle East, but I'm afraid that Prince—now, possibly, King—Khalid doesn't have a stable temperament."

"Why?"

"From the beginning, Khalid has chosen a much less generous path than his father and brother. His mother, one of King Yousef's many wives, was killed during an alleged Shia attack when he was only seven. She died in his arms."

Webster remembered seeing the video footage of that attack twelve years ago. It had been most compelling and had, briefly, captured the attention of the world.

"If this attack on his father and brother also turns out to be Shia initiated," Doolan said, "the young prince may choose to retaliate."

"Against the people who killed his father and brother?"

"No. He won't settle for a handful when he's got a whole people to punish. He's been very vocal about wanting the Shia driven from Saudi Arabia. That attitude has already fomented political and economic repercussions for the country and the royal family. He's also not been a big supporter of the United States policies in those areas."

"Are we talking about the country possibly being torn in half as a result of Khalid's ascendancy? If that is indeed the case?"

"Not Saudi Arabia, no. That country is primarily Sunni. However, you have to remember that country is bracketed by Iran, Azerbaijan, Bahrain, and Iraq, all of which are primarily Shia. Lebanon and Kuwait are almost equally divided between the two Islams. But there are many Shia in Afghanistan, India, and Pakistan."

As the professor spoke, a map appeared on the wall behind him, quickly marking the mentioned countries as Shia or Sunni.

"What you're talking about," Doolan said, "is the distinct possibility that the Middle East might draw battle lines that we haven't seen before. The continued American presence in Iraq, on the ground militarily and lurking in the political background, is a constant red flag to the Islamic world."

"Looking at the map, I see that Iraq is marked as a Shia region."

"Yes, though there are many who disagree, myself among them, with that designation."

"You don't agree that Iraq is primarily a Shia nation?"

"I don't. I think those numbers were inflated at the beginning of our second Iraqi conflict."

Another limousine pulled up in front of Webster's location. As he watched, the driver helped a beautiful woman from the backseat. Her blond hair, neatly coifed, shone in the afternoon sun. A black leather coat hung to her sculpted calves. Her burgundy red Manolo Blahniks were anything but sensible. Webster wouldn't have expected anything less.

He knocked on the window and the Secret Service agent nearest the door let him out.

"Thank you, Brandon," Webster acknowledged.

"My pleasure, sir."

Webster approached the woman and he watched her head swivel to face him. She smiled, and the effect was dazzling.

"Mr. Vice President," she greeted.

Smiling, Webster waved a hand. "Vicky, please, if I've told you once, I told you a thousand times. Call me Elliott."

ERESİN CROWN HOTEL
SULTANAHMET DİSTRİCT
İSTANBUL, TURKEY
MARCH 17, 2010

Inside the bathroom, Lourds set the shower for a hot, invigorating spray, lathered quickly—twice, and shampooed. Despite the promise of the lovely woman waiting on him in his bedroom, his mind kept wandering back to the book in his backpack. When it came to his relationships, the women in his life could only be mistresses that pulled him away from his love of his work.

Or, in Olympia Adnan's case, he could share that work. Unfortunately, they were both tied to different fields of expertise and to different geographical locations. Neither of them would give up their university environment. Those were their retreats as well as recharge centers.

When he returned to the room, Olympia still sat in a state of near undress while perching cross-legged on the bed. The book Lourds had stolen from the men in the catacombs lay in her lap and consumed her attention so much that, for a time, she didn't know he was there.

"Find anything interesting?" he asked.

Olympia started, then swept the hair from her eyes and smiled. "My apologies. I thought I'd set up your workstation." She waved to the nearby desk where she'd spread out his books, computer, map tools, cameras, and digital recorder. "Then I found this. Something new you're working on?"

"It is. Does it look familiar to you?"

She shook her head. "It's written in Greek, but not any kind of Greek I was ever trained to read."

"I think very few people could read that."

"Why?"

"Because I believe that's an artificial language."

"Hundreds—I'm assuming here, of course—of years old?"

"More like two thousand, unless I miss my guess."

"I would trust your instincts on something like that."

"Good." Lourds sat on the bed beside her.

"But what makes you think this is so old?"

"A test?" Lourds grinned.

"As I recall, you always did well with tests."

Lourds flipped through the pages of the book. "The paper is old, probably hundreds of years. Handmade. Not purchased off a rack at a department store."

"The size gives that away immediately."

"Very good." Lourds dipped his head in appreciation. "But that only covers the handmade part. The age I'm going to guess at because of the stylized lettering and because of the rag content in the paper rather than wood. Charles Fenerty and F. G. Keller invented a papermaking machine and technique that used pulped wood instead of rags in 1844." He tapped the book. "These sheets were made out of a rag fiber slurry and calendered to improve the writing surface."

"Impressive."

Lourds shrugged, but he was pleased with himself. "Even if this turns out to be a copy of something else, which I think it could well be, its age alone makes it a worthwhile artifact."

"So what's this about?"

"I'm not sure yet."

"You?" Olympia smiled in disbelief. "The incredible Professor Thomas Lourds is stumped?"

"Only a minor setback, I assure you." Lourds ran his fingers over the textured pages. "I'm already starting to make some headway, I think."

"All this while dodging terrorists at the airport?"

"Multitasker, remember?" Lourds gazed longingly at the flowing script, then reached out and flipped through the pages.

Olympia closed the book. "Nope. Not at this moment, Professor. You're tired, and you know you're not at your best when you're overly fatigued. All you'll do is stare at those pages while your brain spins helplessly."

"Really?" Lourds loved the way she knew him so well.

"Yes, really." Olympia ran her fingers through his hair and massaged his scalp. "After you get a few hours' sleep, you'll perform much better."

"At solving the riddle of the book, I assume you mean."

She tweaked his nose playfully and grinned. "That. And certain other distractions."

"Any clue as to what those distractions might entail?"

Without a word, Olympia set the book aside, then put a hand on his chest and pressed him back on the bed. When Lourds lay supine, she shimmied out of the skirt suit and straddled him wearing only her teal panties. The gauzy material didn't leave much to the imagination.

She leaned forward and kissed him, and her hips naturally pressed against his hips. His erection was trapped against her sheer panties and her warm excitement soon allowed her to glide up and down against him. They continued kissing, and Lourds's tongue parried hers again and again. Her breath came in shorter gasps and she inadvertently shivered as she stroked against him harder and harder.

Lourds thrust up against her and held in check his own impulse to flip her over and rip the thin material away. Within the next moment, though, she shivered and convulsed, then collapsed against his chest. He luxuriated in the warm feel of her flesh pressing against his. He stroked her back, running his fingers from her shoulder blades to her buttocks.

Minutes passed. Lourds was beginning to think she'd fallen asleep.

"That," she said groggily, "was better than I'd expected."

"I'm only here to please."

Olympia pushed her head and shoulders up and rolled her hips against his erection. "I don't totally believe you, Professor."

"Well, please you, please me."

After a quick kiss, Olympia rolled onto her back. Lourds gently followed her over, grateful for the spacious bed. He watched as she hooked her panties and slid them off. Then she took a condom from her purse. She'd come prepared for this. She put it on him slowly. He nearly lost it as her hands caressed him.

"Come on," she urged, opening her legs to receive him.

Lourds moved above her, supporting his own weight, then he teased her, rubbing his slick length against her desire-thickened center without penetrating her. She squirmed against him in an attempt to find the proper angle to capture him within her.

"You . . . you really aren't playing . . . nice," Olympia protested.

"As nice as you were earlier." Lourds leaned down and nuzzled her neck, licking right below her ear and sending her into a paroxysm of jangled nerves. He knew she loved and hated the sensation equally. Before she could admonish him, though, he adjusted and sheathed himself in her hot flesh. Whatever complaint she might have intended to lodge died when she gasped in pleasure.

Lourds moved against her, amazed at how familiar and how different everything seemed. He had missed her over those years, and he knew he would miss her again in the near future. But for now he gave himself to her and took what she had to offer.

It was over far quicker than he thought it should be. For a time, he lay atop her and stroked her and held her, basking in their shared delight. Then, politely, she nudged him off her and he lay beside her.

"Wow," Olympia said quietly as she snuggled into the crook of his arm.

"Likewise," Lourds gasped.

She ran a forefinger over his lips. "Why don't you sleep for a little while and later, when you wake up, we'll go to dinner."

"I may sleep through dinner." Lourds felt himself already fading.

"I won't let you. You'll need to eat. You're going to need your strength."

"Is that a threat?" Lourds grinned.

"It's a promise."

He closed his eyes and let his senses go away, but in the back of his mind, that part of him that never slept, the lizard brain that kept heart and respiration cycling, still worked on the book's contents.

WASHINGTON DULLES INTERNATIONAL AIRPORT
WASHINGTON, D.C.
UNITED STATES OF AMERICA
MARCH 17, 2010

Vicky DeAngelo was from old money, earned the old-fashioned way. Her great-great-grandfather had been infamous, the head of an organized crime family that got rich during the Prohibition era. Francis DeAngelo had dreamed of being a respectable man, though. While his contemporaries continued to toil in illegal industries, DeAngelo went legit. Not only that, he'd been smart about it, and ruthless. He had battled and blackmailed his way into the ranks of the major capitalists who hung with the Rockefellers and other captains of industry.

Francis DeAngelo had been inventive about making his money. He sank his criminal profits into Hollywood, radio, and television.

Those risky investments had proved themselves, and he managed to leverage other businesses in the health and electronics industries. Today, the DeAngelo television network maintained a prominent presence in news and entertainment. Vicky had been friends with Webster even before his wife's death, and it had been Vicky who had produced Vanessa Webster's show.

The DeAngelo communications empire had also been a major player in President Waggoner's campaigns, publicly and behind the scenes.

Vicky smoothed Webster's coat lapel into place.

"If my great-great-grandfather could see me now, hobnobbing with the Vice President of United States, I know he'd be pleased," she said. "Not everyone gets to hang with the veep."

"Trust me, my dear, not everyone would want to." Webster took her hands in his and squeezed.

She kissed him lightly on the cheek. "Then they'd be fools and I don't want to talk about them."

Webster chuckled. "I'm so glad you could join me on this trip."

Vicky gave him a knowing look. "The king of Saudi Arabia has just been assassinated, possibly by religious rivals, the oil trade may hang in the balance because the successor to the throne isn't a big United States fan, and you think I would pass up a chance for a front row seat to the coming Apocalypse?"

The choice of words surprised Webster. His eyes narrowed. "Well, I hoped you wouldn't."

She smiled. "And here I am." Vicky pulled her coat a little more tightly around her.

"Come on," Webster said. "Let's get you out of this weather." He held out his arm and she took it, automatically falling into stride with him as he walked toward the jet.

Two more luxury vehicles sped along the tarmac for the jet as well. Overhead, an executive Bell helicopter dropped in for a landing nearby.

Vicky shaded her eyes with a hand as she looked at the new arrivals. "Stephen Napier and Tristan Hamilton?"

Webster nodded. Stephen Napier was CEO of Prometheus Experimental Energy Research, one of the leading alternative energy developers. Tristan Hamilton was son of the legendary oil wildcatter Wesley "Dusty" Hamilton, the latest mogul in one of the biggest oil families in Texas.

"Bringing in the big guns, aren't you?" Vicky asked.

"The president wants me to make an impression over there," Webster said. "I aim to do that."

The helicopter touched down effortlessly. The door opened and a young man with dreadlocks, skin the color of good coffee with cream, a soul patch, and a copper colored Armani suit got out. Wraparound sunglasses hid his eyes. He carried a slim valise and walked with innate rhythm. Bright turquoise iPod earbuds nestled in his ears.

"Who is Mr. Cool?" Vicky asked.

"My secret weapon," Webster answered.

Vicky lifted an eyebrow. "After all these years, you still find ways to surprise me. I felt certain I knew everyone you knew that was worth knowing."

"Not all my friends want to be known."

Stephen Napier was a solid block of a man in his late forties with black hair. He worked out religiously and had a chiseled jawline. The weight lifter's physique camouflaged the gifted scientific mind. Napier had graduated college at fifteen and earned dual doctorates in physical science and chemistry by the age of seventeen. He had taken out his first three million-dollar patents between graduating college and earning his Ph.D.s.

Tristan Hamilton wore jeans, cowboy boots, a dark brown leather duster, and a chocolate Stetson complete with a turquoise-and-silver hat band. In his late twenties, he had practically grown up dividing his time between the family ranch and the family offshore oil wells in the Gulf of Mexico.

Both Napier and Hamilton watched the newcomer with cool gazes. The young man ignored them and walked straight to Vicky DeAngelo. He took her hand delicately and pressed his lips to the back of it as he peered over the sunglasses. "Ms. DeAngelo. It's a pleasure to meet you."

"Thank you, Mr.—"

He released her hand and stood straight. Up close, he was taller than he looked, six-three at least.

"Call me Spider. All my friends do." His voice was musical. A hint of Jamaican Reggae ran through it, though Webster knew the man wasn't a Jamaican by birth or upbringing.

"And what is it you do, Spider?" Vicky asked.

"These days, I do whatever it is I wish to do. And I like it like that."

"So you like playing mysterious?"

"I don't *play* at being mysterious." He grinned good-naturedly. "If Vice President Webster had wanted you to know who I am, you'd know by now. So I guess you'll know when he gets ready for you to know." He shrugged. "Or maybe not."

Napier and Hamilton joined them. The Texan towered above them, standing six feet six barefooted. The boots and the hat pushed him up over seven feet tall. He tipped that hat to Vicky.

"Good to see you again, ma'am," he said.

"Call me 'ma'am' again and I'll punch you in the eye," she threatened.

Hamilton gave her a slow smile. "Honestly, I don't think you could reach that high. You're just a little bit of nothin'."

Vicky smiled sweetly. "How would you like to be the center of an exposé, cowboy? Maybe we'd get a few of those skeletons in your closet to rattle around."

The easygoing grin held firm. "Vicky it is."

"Thought you'd see it my way." Vicky turned to Webster. "Are we expecting anyone else?"

"No," Webster answered. "Not on this flight, at least. There will be others who show up in Saudi. People that have vested interests in the Middle East. But I expect you four to be the key players in this enterprise."

Spider glanced around the group. "I guess this promises to be some shindig."

That, Webster knew, was an understatement. If everything happened the way he hoped and planned, the meeting in Saudi Arabia was going to be world-changing.

The only obstacle in his way was the book in the hands of Professor Thomas Lourds. But that would be taken care of soon.

CHAPTER 14

BEYAZİT TOWER
İSTANBUL UNİVERSİTY
BEYAZİT SQUARE
İSTANBUL, TURKEY
MARCH 19, 2010

A cool breeze blew in from the Golden Horn, the inlet of the Bosphorus River. Lourds stood with his face in the breeze and smelled the salt of the sea.

From his vantage point at the top of Beyazit Tower, he could see all of the Old City, both banks of the Golden Horn, and the mouth of the Sea of Marmara. If he squinted, he could even see the Princes' Islands where he had once taken Olympia Adnan to picnic. Travel there was by horse and cart, and the pace was a lot slower than on the mainland. Many of the cottages and dwellings dated back to Victorian times when the island became a vacation resort for the wealthy.

Throughout the history of the islands, royalty had been banished there. European kings and princes had been followed by Empire sultans as Constantinople fell again and again, to be reborn as Istanbul. As a seaport and as a tie between the East and the West, the city had never had a peer.

The tower had been constructed of wood in 1749, then

burned during the Great Fire of Cibali seven years later. Due to its importance as a fire watch station, the tower had been rebuilt almost immediately, but it had been once more made of wood. It wasn't until after the tower's destruction again in 1826 that the existing stone tower had been built in 1828. The Ottoman baroque architecture made it look like something out of a fantasy story.

Three more floors were added in 1849 so the watchman could signal the approach of unfriendly ships and the danger of fire, as well as where the fire was located in the city. During the day, baskets of different numbers were lowered to indicate where the fire was. At night, colored lamps were lit to replace the basket system.

Lourds easily imagined what it had been like during those early years. The watchman stationed there would have found work and hobbies to fritter away the long boring hours between fires and excitement. No matter how the years passed, there were things in human experience that never changed.

"You're smiling."

Lourds turned to face Olympia. "Of course I'm smiling. I'm standing at the top of the Beyazit Tower. All the times I've visited here, I've never gotten to climb the tower."

"You have to have special permission to climb the tower."

"I know. I was told. On every occasion I asked."

Olympia smiled. "And if you wanted to climb the tower so badly, why didn't you ask me?"

"I didn't want to embarrass you in case you couldn't make it happen."

Olympia arched her brows. "Did you doubt I could make it happen?"

"Never. Your connections have surprised me."

"So were you just smiling? Or is there somebody else?"

Lourds reached for her and pulled her into his embrace. "Actually, I was thinking about the picnic on Princes' Islands."

Olympia snuggled into him and held his hands. She felt warm against him and smelled like lavender.

"When we missed the ferry and ended up stranded for the night?"

"In the rain, as I recall."

"Obviously I remember it more romantically than you do."

"No, you remember it because it was the one and only time I submitted to sex outdoors."

"See?" Lourds nipped her neck with his teeth. "Romantic."

"I remember being cold and wet."

"We couldn't be romantic all night. Besides, the rain was refreshing."

"Maybe to you, but I stay at the university and do research. I'm fond of my creature comforts. You like a little hardship. That's why I don't go chasing after artifacts while being shot at, and you do."

"You really don't know what you're missing."

Olympia broke free of his arms and turned to face him. Her smile held the hint of sadness. "I beg to differ." She stroked his face softly. "I have a very good idea of what I'm missing."

Lourds stood frozen for a moment, not knowing what to say.

Olympia laughed at him.

"You were quite brilliant in class today. The students loved you, but I knew that they would."

"You've got a good group," Lourds told her.

"I know. So how are you doing on your secret project? With all this attention aimed at me, I know you can't be doing very well. You use sex as a distraction when you're stymied."

Lourds feigned displeasure. "I am also quite capable of being distracted by a beautiful woman, I'll have you know."

"I'll take that as the sincerest form of flattery, in the spirit in which it was intended, but I do know the truth. You've hit a wall."

"Not true."

Olympia's eyes widened in surprise. "You translated the piece?"

"I did."

"That's incredible. Why didn't you tell me?"

"Because we were both agreeing that you're very distracting."

"You could have come to me earlier and told me the good news."

Lourds shook his head, feeling the excitement inside him build anew. The last two days had been a marathon of nearly exhausting sleeplessness. Despite the fact that Olympia had come back to the hotel with him every night, sex had only drugged him into unconscious for a few hours at a stretch.

"There was no good news until I visited this tower," he said. "The final pieces of the encryption finally tumbled into my head while I was climbing the stairs. Two hundred and eighty-six steps, I believe."

"Is it an artificial language?"

"Actually, that was partly where I was wrong. There's not one artificial language involved in that writing. There are three. And there's a complicated substitution system for the three languages that must have depended on some kind of random generator."

"A random generator?"

"Imagine the game Twister. You have played Twister, haven't you?"

"Of course. When I was a girl."

"Remember the spinner?"

Olympia nodded. "It gave the directions on where to put your hands and feet."

"Exactly. Left foot, green. Right hand, red. That kind of thing. That's actually two languages in a sense."

"I'm not following. I'm only seeing one language: the directions."

"That's because you're processing both languages at the same time," Lourds said. "The spinner actually translates into a physical movement language and a visual acuity language, if you follow me. The spinner is divided into quadrants—"

"For the hands and feet," Olympia interrupted. "And the colors for the vision. Two languages."

Lourds smiled. "Now you've got it."

"So what is your mysterious book about?"

"It deals with the location of something called the Scroll of Joy."

All of the animation seemed to drain from Olympia's face at once.

Concerned, Lourds put his hand on her shoulder to steady her. "Are you all right?"

"I am. But this is just so unexpected." Olympia seemed flustered. "I mean not really unexpected, of course. I hoped for something like this, but I didn't know if you'd be able to manage a translation. Hundreds of people for the last two thousand years have tried to do what you have just done. And not one of them has been successful."

Lourds realized something. "You knew about this book?"

Olympia struggled to collect her thoughts. "I *knew* about the book, but I'd never seen it before. No one I know has ever seen it before. Several of us had begun to think it was just a legend. Or, if it had existed, that it had been destroyed."

Lourds seized her by the shoulders. "Olympia. Olympia, look at me."

She did, but he could tell she still wasn't completely with him. Suddenly, the uneasiness he'd experienced down in the catacombs swept through him again.

"Olympia, what are you talking about? How did you know about this book? What is the Scroll of Joy?"

She took his hand and looked up at him. "Do you trust me?"

Lourds didn't know how to answer.

"Please, Thomas, we've been friends—more than friends—for years. In all that time, I've never asked you for anything big. I'm asking you now, to please trust me."

"All right," he answered, and hoped he didn't live—or die—to regret it.

CENTRAL BUSINESS DISTRICT
KING ABDULLAH ECONOMIC CITY, SAUDI ARABIA
MARCH 19, 2010

Standing at the window of the luxury office building's top floor, Elliott Webster looked out over the shimmering green waves of the Red Sea. His thoughts were of the past, of the empires that had risen and fallen along the coast. All of them were dust now, except for a few buildings and structures here and there.

The new empire King Abdullah bin Abdul Aziz Al Saud had given his life to took shape all around Webster. Construction crews and earth-moving machines pieced together the steel bones of the tall buildings and carved foundations and streets from the baked sand. Noise filled the area and even the soundproofing of the room couldn't eliminate it. The muted throbbing vibrated the window.

One of the most impressive areas of the new city lay out in the harbor only a short distance from the coast. Several tall buildings jutted up from the outer perimeter of the island. Sunlight splintered on the steel frameworks where men walked narrow beams and continued building for the sky. The center of the island held more buildings as well as a gridwork of streets and elevated highways.

To the right, the designers had used the natural harbor to echo the island's shape. The large sickle-shaped marina held a flotilla of ships, yachts, and boats. Most of those vessels were pleasure craft but some of them were barges that carried materials and equipment to the construction crews.

"What are they calling the island?" Stephen Napier asked. He stood at Webster's side.

"Financial Island," Webster answered.

"Catchy," Napier said sarcastically.

"Maybe it sounds better in Arabic," Tristan Hamilton drawled. He stood only a short distance away and leaned with one arm on the window.

"You gotta admit, naming the place that, they're hanging it right out there for everybody to see. Ain't trying to hide what it is." Spider sat in one of the plush chairs and worked on his laptop.

Vicky DeAngelo stood on the other side of the spacious room, one hip cocked against a credenza. She talked rapidly on her sat phone, outlining the agenda she wanted her film crews to follow throughout the city. While on the flight over to Saudi Arabia, she had put together plans for a television special on the city.

Webster appreciated her business acumen and drive. It was those qualities that made him seek her out. She had also made tentative agreements with Saudi Arabian advertisers to underwrite the cost of the special's production.

"It's gonna be a pretty city when they finish up," Hamilton stated, "but it looks a mite underdefended, if you ask me."

"The Saudi Royal Navy is out there," Webster said.

"So are American navy ships," Napier said. "I'm willing to bet that the American navy is going to keep more troublemakers out of the area than the Saudis."

Webster nodded. That was one of the selling points he hoped to push to the young king. Instead of persuading him to listen, though, Webster was certain Prince Khalid would take the suggestion as a personal affront. In fact, the vice president was counting on that fact. Khalid's youthfulness and inexperience, as well as his burning desire to drive the Shia people from his homeland, should be enough to tip the scales toward war.

And if that wasn't enough, the intel that Dawson had only that morning passed along through informants he had access to within the country would. Webster was waiting for it all to hit the fan.

In the meantime, he would look like a hero, the man trying to put a lid on the seething cauldron that was the Middle East. When everything was said and done, Webster knew he would be seen as a savior. Even when his initial efforts rendered no success. That thought caused him to smile.

"What's on your mind?" Hamilton asked. "You look like the cat that ate the canary."

"Building confidence," Webster replied. "Stockpiling positive energy."

"That's good, because me, I'm feeling like the canary about now."

"It's going to work out," Webster said. "Believe me, once the dust settles on this thing, we're all going to be in a lot better places."

At that moment, Hamal, Prince Khalid's representative, entered the room. He had met them at the airport and been with them ever since. The representative was a burly man in his early forties with swarthy skin and a fierce forked beard. His scarred, callused hands testified to harsh years and a hard life. As a counterpoint, his white thawb and ghutra were immaculate.

A lot of people might overlook and underestimate the man, Webster realized. He wasn't among them.

"Mr. Vice President Webster," Hamal said politely, his black eyes roving over the group. "Prince Khalid will see you and your guests now. If you will follow me."

"Of course," Webster said, and did.

The opulent offices showcased wealth, privilege, and power. All of them were stocked with expensive furniture, rugs, and computer images of the proposed look of KAEC—what the locals called King Abdullah Economic City—when it was finished hung on the walls.

"Ostentatious much?" Vicky whispered.

"Presentation is everything," Webster whispered back.

"Not when it's overkill."

Six guards armed with machine pistols stood in front of a heavy security door that bore the palm tree over crossed swords coat of arms of Saudi Arabia. One of the guards stepped forward and motioned the others to work. In short order, Webster was frisked and checked with a wand metal detector.

One of the men held out a straw basket. "Please put your phones and PDAs into the basket. They will be returned to you once you are out of His Excellency's office."

Webster led the way by putting his BlackBerry into the basket first. The others followed suit. Then the door was opened.

Prince Khalid, dressed in a flowing thawb and ghutra, stood facing a wall of polarized glass that held the bright afternoon sun at bay. Six feet tall and slim, he didn't look imposing in any way. But his manner compensated. Rigid defiance molded his stance. He held his hands behind his back as he looked down on the city like a predatory raptor. He wore two large pistols holstered at his waist and a curved sword was sheathed down his back. Wearing weapons in public was something his father would never have allowed, but this prince looked like a warrior born.

Webster noted the young prince's reflection in the polarized glass. Khalid had his father's long hooked nose and sharp hawk's eyes that gave his handsome features a dangerous edge. His beard was short and patchy, not quite filled in, and it gave him the appearance of a young man trying to appear much more mature than his tender years allowed.

If he hadn't been who he was, Webster might have been inclined to feel sorry for the young prince suddenly plunged in over his head.

Khalid flicked his gaze to Webster, held his eyes full measure for a moment, then roved across the others. His lips pursed in disdain, as if they had failed to come up to his standards.

"Prince Khalid," Hamal said, "I present to you the Vice President of the United States, Elliott Webster."

Knowing that the next move needed to be the young prince's, Webster stood his ground. "Good afternoon, Prince Khalid. On behalf of the United States, President Waggoner, and myself, I'd like to express our condolences at the recent losses you've suffered. Your father was a good man and a great friend to my country. He'll be missed by us all."

"Thank you, Mr. Webster. You are most kind." Khalid's voice was almost a monotone, and Webster could hear the sharp edge of anger underlying his words. "However, you're not here entirely to offer your support in my time of grief, are you?"

"No," Webster said. "That's the price a head of state must pay. Your personal life is forever wound throughout the things you do as a leader."

"So my advisers tell me." Khalid knotted his left fist and placed it against the window. "I also did not wish to see you today, but they told me I must."

"Perhaps it might be better if we came back at a later time," Webster suggested.

Khalid turned to face them and fury tightened his face. "That wouldn't do, would it? As soon as it was found out, and it would be found out because you have brought Ms. DeAngelo with you, that I refused to meet with you, my choice would be seen as weakness. Isn't that true?"

"Your Excellency, I mean no disrespect, but these are trying times for us all. The world has grown more tightly knit over the past few decades. Your father's death—"

"It was *murder,*" Khalid snapped. "Call it what it was or don't speak of it at all."

Stung, Webster had to remind himself that this was the attitude he needed from the young prince. Still, it was hard to take. He nodded. "Your father's murder is going to impact the world."

"Strange, isn't it? That no one thought to tell him that his life impacted the world."

"I enjoyed a good friendship with your father."

"He talked of you a lot," Khalid agreed. "If not for your diplomacy in this area, your country might not have had the oil agreements they currently enjoy."

"What's been good for my country has also been good for your country."

"I'm afraid that that's where we're going to have to disagree." Khalid paused. "With all due respect intended, of course." He waved to the city on the other side of the polarized glass. "It has taken time for my people to realize that our future lies here, not with the United States or the Western world."

"What do you mean?" Vicky asked. "Many of your people love the United States and the Western world."

"That is because your country and others have seduced my people for generations," Khalid said. "Outsiders have shown my people a way of life that can never be theirs. We live under Allah and the teachings of his Prophet Muhammad, not the god of excess and extravagance as you people live."

"Your father never felt—"

Khalid's voice rose in anger. "My father and many of his advisers were just as seduced as those fools who follow your ways. He harbored vipers to his breast, and in the end they murdered him."

"I don't remember anyone saying they knew who murdered your father," Webster said.

"It was the Shia. I have no doubt of this. They have grown more emboldened since your country invaded Iraq and put those godless people into power." Khalid's dark eyes blazed. "You were warned about what you did, yet your government chose to do it anyway."

"Forgive me, Your Excellency, but I didn't come here to argue over the war in that country. That war doesn't have anything to do with this."

"If you think that, you're a fool. That war is part of the war that has gone on between the Sunni and the Shia since those unworthies chose to name prophets of their own and reject the will of Allah and his prophet Muhammad."

"Saddam Hussein was a sadistic dictator who menaced the world," Hamilton snarled, taking a step forward. "If we'd let him keep on, he might have eventually put his boot on the back of your neck. Brave American servicemen put their lives on the line to preserve the peace in the Middle East. I won't have you talking ill of them."

One of Khalid's personal guards took a step forward, but Webster threw out a hand to stop Hamilton, and Khalid gestured to his men to stay back. The prince's right hand wrapped around the butt of one of his pistols.

"No man will put his boot on my neck," Khalid said in a low, threatening voice. "I promise you that."

"Perhaps we could all take a step back," Webster suggested. The situation was getting out of control faster than he'd thought it would. Part of him was glad to see that, but he knew he had to at least appear to keep control of things now.

"What your government did was mask its villainy and greed as patriotism," Khalid growled. "China's economy has been steadily rising, and they've been able to match your dwindling American dollars for oil. My country—in fact, all the Middle East—would be better served to sell oil to China and India than to the United States. Our profits will be greater and the risk will be less."

"Until the Chinese decide to annex the Middle East," Napier said evenly. "It's been a habit with them for millennia, you know."

"Ah, Mr. Napier, I was wondering when you would have something to say. To counter your supposition, the United States never managed to *annex* the Middle East, although they certainly succeeded in making their presence felt, so what makes you think the Chinese would be any more fortunate?"

"Americans aren't inclined to pursue war unilaterally—"

The prince snorted in derision.

"—with a very few exceptions," Napier continued smoothly. "And our recent experiences in that arena have confirmed our reluctance to do so as good policy."

"The Chinese can roll an army right into your country," Hamilton said. "Do you really think you've got soldiers and hardware that will stand up to them? Or even be willing to stand up to them?"

"I would sooner choose to believe that than that the United States would stay to protect us. Your country doesn't have a good record of defending other nations when the price gets too high." Khalid said. "And your people, your soldiers, wouldn't be fighting for my people. They would be fighting for the oil."

"Common interests," Hamilton said. "That's what makes brothers of people."

Khalid lifted his eyebrows. "So now we're brothers? Then I suppose it was your father and brother who were murdered also?"

Hamilton cursed beneath his breath.

"Familial relationships notwithstanding," Webster said, "we do have common interests."

"We sell; you buy," Khalid said. "We could have that relationship with anyone. The United States, however, can't. Your people depend on us for oil, but now we find ourselves surrounded by people that could depend on us for the same thing. Without having any of them meddle in our business and seek to impose restrictions on how we handle our relations with other nations in this area."

"We have domestic oil wells that can pony up and deliver more oil if we need to," Hamilton threatened.

"So you say. Yet, when oil prices soared, your country paid and didn't aggressively seek to increase domestic production." Khalid shook his head. "No, your government worries about the domestic supply of oil and they hoard what they possess like a fearful widow."

Hamilton turned to Webster. "It ain't worth it to talk to this joker."

"Your country," Khalid went on, "has made a habit of becoming friends with an oil-producing country, forcing economic treaties on them through bribery and coercion, rewarding the handful that hold the most power in that country while ignoring the struggling masses, then siphoning the oil away until there's nothing left. When the oil is gone, so is the goodwill. My country is not some roadkill waiting for carrion birds to pick her bones clean."

"Your Excellency," Webster said, "that's not what we're here to do."

"Nonsense," Khalid said. "That's exactly what you've been doing for years. Let's fantasize for a moment. Let's say that China does indeed decide to take advantage of us and invade because we insist on trading with the United States and our output cannot meet the demands of both countries. Let's fantasize further and say that the United States even chooses to enter a land war against the Chinese." He turned his attention to Napier. "And let's say Mr. Napier's corporation became successful in finding an alternative fuel energy source that is competitive in price—maybe even slightly higher than the cost of oil." The prince's voice became even quieter but had a harder edge to it. "How long do you think it would take America to withdraw its armies?"

"Those things you worry about are a long way off," Webster said. "It would take an enormous amount of time to turn a country like ours around from petroleum-based products to something else."

"Perhaps in your vision." Khalid looked out at the city again. "Not in mine. That future lies just around the corner. I have seen this future in my dreams. My father would never recognize that it exists."

"Maybe it would be better if we could talk again in a few days," Webster replied. "When your mind is more settled."

Khalid faced him. "My mind is settled. I have not had myself crowned king today because I choose to wait for that honor until after my father's and family's murders are resolved. Then I will take my crown, and I will take my people. I will initiate a cleansing of my country. All those who live within our borders who do not live according to the rules of the Prophet will be driven out or killed. I will not be merciful or foolish as my father was. I know who my enemies are, and I will not suffer them to live in my kingdom."

"My God," Vicky whispered.

Webster noted the fear that had settled into his companions.

He rejoiced.

They would return to their hotel rooms and they would spread that fear to others among them that had money and investments in the Middle East. Panic would ensue. And it wouldn't just end with the collapse of confidence in the economic sectors in America and the Western world. It would also affect the military, as the Pentagon realized how many of its soldiers and materials might be at risk.

It looked like his timetable for the Middle East meltdown had just escalated.

"How are you going to resolve your father's murder?" Webster asked.

"I will find the Shia assassins responsible, and I will have them executed. I have military teams that are already closing in on the men behind that cowardly attack."

Webster knew that was only because Colonel Anthony Eckart had left a false trail behind him leading to known Shia dissidents within Saudi Arabia. The frame would be believable. And in the end, who knew? Those Shia dissidents might even claim credit for killing the king and his family members.

Khalid focused on Webster. "There is another matter I would speak to you about. Perhaps you could help."

"Of course, if I can."

Khalid nodded to one of his personal guards, who walked to another door and opened it. The guard led another man into the room.

The second man was in his twenties. White gauze covered his left cheek and his right forearm. Scabs clung to recent lacerations all over his body. He walked with a limp.

"Do you know this man?" Khalid asked.

Webster made a show of looking at the man, but didn't recognize him. "No. Am I supposed to?"

The man stood trembling, sucking in air and looking at the floor as if afraid to look anywhere else.

"His name is Farok," Khalid said. "He came to me seeking asylum. He claims to have worked for your CIA."

"I wouldn't know anything about that."

Khalid smiled, but the expression was frosty and distant. "I suppose if it were true or false, you would deny it all the same."

Webster didn't bother to reply.

"He insists that the CIA hired him and his friends to abduct a man from Ataturk International Airport only a few days ago. A man named Professor Thomas Lourds. Do you know that man?"

"I know who he is, of course. That story of the attack on him has been in the news. The last I heard, Professor Lourds had been allowed to stay in Istanbul to pursue his studies."

"He has," Khalid commented. "This one managed to elude the police, but he brought back an interesting story. Would you like to hear it?"

Webster made himself remain calm. This wasn't at all expected. "Of course, Your Excellency. If you think it's of interest."

"This story is of interest." Khalid walked behind the trembling man and put a reassuring hand on his shoulder. "This man went on to tell me that not only was he supposed to take this professor captive, but he was also supposed to find out if the professor was in possession of a document."

"A document?"

"Yes, evidently something of historical significance regarding Istanbul's religious history. Do you know anything about that?"

"No," Webster lied. He throttled back his anger that somewhere there had been a leak. It had been ill-timed luck after all that the Scroll of Joy had turned up at the same time he was making his move on the Middle East. And Dawson should never have told anyone they were looking for a religious manuscript.

"Perhaps," Khalid suggested in a neutral tone, "you could make inquiries when you have the time."

"Of course."

"Istanbul is an important city to my people's history."

"And to mine."

"Muslims and Christians have warred there for centuries," Khalid acknowledged. "That city contains the histories of both our cultures, and any religious documentation would be of great interest to me."

"I understand."

"I have sent a contingent of warriors to Istanbul in hopes of securing that document."

"If it exists," Webster countered.

Khalid stepped back from the handcuffed man. "It is no secret to me that there are spies among my people. I know some of them belong to you. This man feared for his life, and he came to my father seeking absolution for his sins against us. Is this not true, Farok?"

"Yes, my king."

"My father would have forgiven him and perhaps sought to find a way to use Farok to find out more of what the CIA wishes to know about my country."

Vicky suddenly closed her hand over Webster's. Her nails bit into his palm. "My God," she whispered, and turned her head away.

Evidently sensing what was about to come, the handcuffed man tried to turn around and duck away at the same time. He raised his hands to defend himself.

With a quick movement, Khalid whipped the sword from his back. He cut sideways at the man standing in front of him. The blade slashed through the prisoner's hands and caught the man just under his jawline. The keen edge passed cleanly through flesh and bone.

Blood sprayed over Khalid and the polarized window as severed fingers rained to the floor and wriggled. Crimson stained the prince's thawb, ghutra, and face. He stood without flinching.

The decapitated man dropped to the floor and sprawled as he jerked through the final moments of his life.

Khalid knelt and cleaned his sword on the dead man's clothing before returning the weapon to the sheath across his back. Then he stood and addressed Webster.

"I am not my father," the prince said as blood trickled down his grim features. "I will not be betrayed. And this country will become strong in its faith in God. My enemies will not be forgiven or ignored." He stepped over the corpse. "Do you understand, Vice President Webster?"

"Of course." Webster had to work to sound shocked. He was surprised by Khalid's personal bloodthirstiness, but that trait would only make his plans work out better.

However, the prince's knowledge of the events in Istanbul could pose a problem there. But Webster reconciled himself with knowing Eckart and his men should be on the ground there now.

The prince would be too late.

Thomas Lourds would be in Webster's custody again soon.

CHAPTER

15

İSTANBUL UNİVERSİTY
BEYAZİT SQUARE
İSTANBUL, TURKEY
MARCH 19, 2010

Do you know who the author of that book is?"

Despite his longer legs, Lourds struggled to keep pace with Olympia as she strode down the halls of the college of history where she taught. Several students remained on campus for afternoon and evening classes. Conversations buzzed all around and bright laughter seemed counterpoint to the dark, anxious mood that had infected Olympia so suddenly and mysteriously.

"No name was given."

"Any other names?"

"No. None." Exasperated, Lourds reached out and caught her wrist. He brought her to a halt beside one of the glass display cases that held Roman weapons. "What's going on? What has you so concerned?"

Her liquid eyes held his. "Just trust me, Thomas. And you'll have to wait just a moment longer." She took a breath. "Before I try to explain any of this to you, I need to show you some files. The thing you deciphered has a long history and we don't know all the answers."

" 'We'?"

"I can't talk about that yet. You don't know what you're dealing with. Or how important it is."

"There was just a message," Lourds said. "I'm not convinced that is anything important yet."

Olympia placed her slim hand over his mouth. "Don't tell me about it yet. I need to wait. I want to think about this as clearly as I can and be as prepared as I'm able. Understand?"

Having no other choice, physically as well as logically, Lourds nodded.

She grabbed him by the hand and pulled him into motion again. They almost barreled up two flights of stairs at an embarrassing speed. Olympia was small enough and slim enough to slip between the students without a problem. Lourds wasn't so aerodynamically built, being taller and broader. The backpack made stealth moves even more difficult. He inadvertently bumped into a few students while trying to remain on his feet. He excused himself as best he could.

Mild cursing and a few snickers as well as comments about why Professor Adnan and the visiting professor were in such a hurry chased them up the steps.

Finally, Olympia deserted the stairwell and headed for her office. She pulled her keys from her purse before she reached the door. The frosted glass pane held precise black lettering in English and Arabic that read:

PROFESSOR OLYMPIA ADNAN
DEPARTMENT OF HISTORY

The key rasped in the lock and finally turned. Olympia took a final wary glance over her shoulder and headed inside. After Lourds followed her, she locked the door behind them.

The office was clean and tidy, the books neatly organized on the shelves, and the desk immaculate. Artifacts from the Roman and Ottoman empires that had helped build the ancient city were artfully arranged throughout the room in shadow boxes. Lourds had been through

Olympia's collection before and found nothing unique. She had gathered most of the items during her grad school years when she occasionally went out into the field on digs with archaeologists. She had proudly shown Lourds photographs of those days, but she had never pined to return to them.

One of her favorites was a vase depicting an image of a young woman kneeling before a young man. Carbon dating had verified that it had come from the Mycenean Period, probably around 1600 B.C. It had belonged to a believer in the Eleusinian Mysteries, which had been based on the mythology of Demeter and Persephone.

Persephone had been the daughter of Zeus and Demeter, brother and sister gods, and she'd been seized by Hades, her uncle. Hades had taken her to the underworld to live after he'd fallen in love with her. Zeus had given his permission for the kidnapping, but Demeter had brought eternal winter to the world of mortals in her grief.

At length, Demeter had freed her daughter from the underworld for nine months out of the year, providing an explanation for the winter months to those that wondered about such things. The Eleusinian Mysteries, one of the so-called Mysteries practiced in the Greco-Roman culture at the time because they continued without benefit of doctrine or written support, had been instituted to define some men and women as more godlike than others.

Which, Lourds reflected wryly, was often the case with religion.

The other piece on her desk was from the Ottoman Empire at the time the Roman empire entered its decline. Olympia had found a sizable trove of artifacts on a local dig and had received a plate depicting Osman's Dream.

Osman I had been the nickname of the charismatic and idealistic king of the empire during its glory days. Although even during the days of its telling, the idea of Osman's Dream was never accepted as a real event, it was nonetheless attributed to him.

In his "dream," Osman was driven to conquer the lands around the empire by a vision of a big tree with roots spreading through three continents. The branches had woven throughout the sky. As a result, he'd formed the Ottoman government that changed the lives of everyone living within the empire, and those that became subjugated.

"Sit down." Olympia waved him to a chair while she knelt down in front of her bookshelf. "If you're going to keep anything secret in your office, where should you keep it?"

"On the lowest shelf," Lourds replied immediately. "All the other professors will probably be too old and fat to get at it. And the young ones will be too proud to search."

Despite her tense mood, Olympia laughed. "And if that isn't the case, most of them aren't athletically inclined enough to get up quickly. So if they're snooping, you'll catch them."

Lourds placed his backpack between the chair and the wall out of the way, then sat.

"Do you have the book with you?"

"Yes."

"But you haven't written down the translation?"

"No."

"Don't write down any translation. I don't want that translation to fall in the wrong hands."

"And whose hands would be wrong?"

"For starters, the men you ran into down in the catacombs."

"They know about the Scroll of Joy?" Lourds asked.

"Of course they know about the Scroll of Joy. Why do you think they tried to kidnap you?"

"Actually, they did kidnap me."

Olympia found what she was looking for, then stood and returned to her desk.

"That's not a book," Lourds observed.

"It's a thumb drive. It's better than a book."

Lourds groaned in disgust.

That earned him a sharp look of reproach. She wagged the thumb drive under his nose. "I can carry more books on this one device than you can pack into this room."

Lourds held his hand up in mock surrender. He preferred books, enjoying the smell and the heft of them, as well as the solid link to the past they presented. And a book was more informal than an electronic document. A book was a personal experience for the reader.

Olympia plugged the thumb drive into the USB port on her computer and booted it up. She turned the widescreen monitor so Lourds could easily see. Then she looked at Lourds.

"You're familiar with John of Patmos?" she asked.

That sharpened Lourds's attention immediately. He didn't know what he'd been expecting, but that name was certainly not one of them.

"John the Divine?" he asked.

"Exactly." Olympia gazed at him. "As I said, Thomas, this is huge and it's important."

"Tell me we didn't lose our subject," Colonel Anthony Eckart snarled as he walked through the college hallways. Students quickly got out of his way. He was used to that kind of reaction. Head on, he looked like trouble.

In his early forties, he kept himself in shape with a strict diet and physical regimen. Whenever he could, even in the field, he ran ten miles daily and did solid PT. Off-duty, he hit the gym and dojo wherever he lived in whatever country he happened to stay.

He stood six feet three inches tall in his stocking feet and wore a size 48 jacket. These days he kept his head shaved skin smooth. Scars showed there and on his features, giving him a hard look that frightened people away.

To blend in with the college crowd, he wore black Dockers, a black turtleneck, and a sports coat cut to hide the longslide Colt .45 semiautomatic pistol holstered under his arm. In a pinch, he didn't need a weapon. He knew over a hundred ways to kill a man with his bare hands.

"We didn't lose him," Jude Mayfield replied over the earwig Eckhart wore. "Guy went into the building there. We've got all the entrances covered. He hasn't come back out."

Eckart walked as quickly as he could without missing an opportunity to peer into the various rooms along the hall. Occasionally students and faculty would meet his gaze, but they quickly looked away.

"Are we connected with the college security net yet?" Eckart asked.

"That's affirmative," Beale replied. He was running com for the team. "If they get a squeal, we'll know about it."

The next door was closed. Eckart approached it and turned the knob, but found it locked. Cursing beneath his breath, he reached into his jacket pocket for a pneumatic driver. No longer than a screwdriver, the device held pneumatic charges that drove a bolt through the end.

Eckart pressed the driver's barrel against the lock and pressed the button. He muffled the solid *ca-chunk* of the device operating with his body and felt his hand jump. But the expended force blew the locking mechanism into the room. He opened the door and peered inside in case Lourds was hiding inside.

The room was empty.

Cursing again, Eckart once more took up the hunt.

"Has anyone figured out why the subject rabbited from the tower?" Eckart demanded.

No one answered for a moment.

"Whatever it was," Mayfield said, "it wasn't us. We had him under surveillance, but he didn't know we were there."

"Maybe we aren't as alone here as we think we are." Eckart hated the way they had veered from their game plan. Trying to find someone on the move through unknown territory wasn't easy. They didn't have the home court advantage, and they couldn't operate with impunity.

He wished he could've stayed in Saudi Arabia and seen the fallout from the assassinations he and his team had put together. That had to have spooked Prince Khalid. Judging from the television footage coming out of King Abdullah Economic City, Khalid was gearing up and preparing for war. Or, better yet, retribution. That was what Webster had wanted.

As a result, other Middle Eastern states as well as India, Pakistan, and China were all on high alert. The moment someone made a wrong move there, those nations would be at each other's throats.

That was fine by Eckart. He felt the United States had worked way too long trying to keep those people from killing each other. It would be better, just as Webster said, to let them go at each other hammer and tong, wait till the fires died down, then go in and take over the whole area. No more being under OPEC's thumb. America could go back to being great.

He could hardly wait.

He found the stairwell and started up to the second floor.

Lourds's thoughts spun as he took in what Olympia had just told him. John of Patmos, also known as John the Divine and John the Theologian, was the man believed to have authored the Book of Revelation in the New Testament.

"You're saying you believe John of Patmos wrote the book that I translated?" he asked.

Olympia shook her head. "No. But that book you translated is about John of Patmos. He's the one that wrote the Scroll of Joy, which that translation talks about."

"Then why haven't I ever heard of it? Something like that, you'd think the whole world would know."

"Because the scroll was hidden and kept secret."

"Why?"

"The Scroll of Joy is dangerous, Thomas," Olympia said. "Possibly the most dangerous document in the world."

"Why?"

"The Scroll of Joy talks about the end of the world."

"So does the Book of Revelation. John of Patmos is believed—by some scholars and theologians—to have written the Revelation while in exile in Greece. And there are some that believe he was also John the Apostle and that he wrote the Gospel of John."

"Those are the same man," Olympia said. "One individual. And he did have those visions and write about them while on the island of Patmos."

"Scholars and church leaders disagree with the possibility of all those men being the same. In fact, some of them believe there were three separate Johns. The Apostle, the author of the Gospel, and the author of the Book of Revelation. Historicists and critical readers of the Bible have strong arguments for that."

"How many times have you seen people, nonbelievers and doubters, prove some aspect of the Bible false? How long did scientists and historians doubt the veracity of the Flood, only to finally—scientifically—prove that the Mediterranean world was once flooded."

"They also make the case that the flood was from geological events, not divine intervention. And that not one but several floods took place around the world at different times."

"They *believe* it was a geological event, but they can't agree on what that event was."

Lourds didn't argue, because he knew she wasn't listening. She was tied into her own beliefs and wasn't about to be swayed.

"Don't look at me like that," she said.

"I'm not looking at you any way."

"Yes, you are." Olympia turned to her computer and began opening files.

Increasingly amazed, Lourds watched digitized images of scrolls fill the monitor. Most of them were written in Ancient Greek, but a few appeared to be more modern in origin.

"What are these?" Lourds leaned closer.

"All three Johns were one, Thomas. I have proof. These are documents—letters and journal entries—from the men that worked with him."

"Who?"

"The acolytes provided by Peter and Paul. This first one details John's passing. The others all talk about John's final days and how he dictated the book of the Apocalypse to them. As well as the Scroll of Joy."

"I can see that these are journal entries." Lourds translated the script easily. Whoever had done the digitization of the original source material had reproduced them meticulously.

"You see this and you still doubt what I'm saying?" Frustration edged Olympia's words.

"I would prefer to see the original documents before I passed judgment on the authenticity of this replication." Lourds was diplomatic.

Olympia's cheeks turned red and her eyes narrowed. "Thomas Lourds, if you think I would bring you all this way for a wild goose chase, you don't know me as well as you should."

"If you think I'm going to simply accept this without questioning it, you're mistaken. And you don't know me as well as you should. Maybe you want to believe in this so much that you've lost perspective."

Taking a breath, Olympia leaned back in her chair and crossed her arms. "This is ridiculous."

"All right, for the sake of argument, let's say those documents are legitimate." Lourds ignored her glare. Unable to calmly sit, he stood. "If you've had this kind of information, why haven't you come forward with it before? Or why hasn't anyone who's had it before you?"

Olympia paused a moment before answering. "It's complicated. You need to know more of the story. You're making a judgment without all the facts."

"These documents have been around nearly two thousand years and scholars haven't been allowed access to them?" He shook his head. "Nothing's that complicated."

"Really? Not even the end of the world?"

"John of Patmos wrote about the end of the world as he saw it. His words are in the Bible. This isn't news."

"He wrote about the end of the world as it would be when God comes back for those that survive the Tribulation," Olympia said. "This is another end."

"According to what I've studied, while he was living on Patmos, John had two visions of how the world would end. He wrote a long letter, which became the Book of Revelation, to the seven Christian churches in Asia, all of which were here in Turkey. In one of the visions, John saw seven candlesticks which represented the seven churches: Ephesus, Laodicea, Pergamum, Philadelphia, Sardis, Smyma, and Thyatira. None of those communities exist now. They were ousted under the Treaty of Lausanne in 1923. That document also recognized the country as the Republic of Turkey and it succeeded the Ottoman Empire."

"The churches weren't actual physical buildings. I mean, there were structures there, but the reference was inclusive of the Christian communities that lived in those cities."

"After the Treaty, the Christians were ousted and forced to live elsewhere." Lourds paused for a moment to gather his thoughts. "In the middle of the candlesticks was the Son of Man. He held seven stars that were supposed to signify the seven angels that protected each of those communities. At the command of Jesus Christ, John wrote to each of those angels, citing what was wrong with them and what they needed to do. And what would happen to them if they didn't do those things."

"Exactly." Olympia seemed mollified.

"In the second vision John saw a door opening up in the sky, which he interpreted as the end of the world and the final destruction of Satan here on earth."

"That's all here." Olympia tapped the keyboard and an image of a snarling dragon filled the screen. "This is how John saw Satan, not as the horned and tailed visage made popular later."

"You have the original journals the acolytes wrote?"

"Yes."

"And you know they're authentic?"

"There's not a doubt." Olympia pointed at the computer. "Everything I'm showing you today exists. It's all real. We have them."

Lourds stared at her. "I guess my next question is, who's 'we'?"

Cleena stared at the scar-faced man as he started up the stairwell to the second floor. His dead gaze had raked her with brutal intensity then moved on as if she were nothing.

Now there goes a nasty guy who's looking for someone. She thought she knew who that someone was.

She turned and rushed for the other stairwell leading up to the second floor. Lourds and his lady friend were at this end of the building on the third floor. Evidently the dead-eyed man didn't know that.

"Sevki," she called as she caught the railing and hurled herself up the steps. Her motion caught the eye of another man coming down the hallway from the other end than the dead-eyed man.

"I see him." Sevki had hacked into the college security camera system. "You should get out of there."

Cleena was of the same opinion. Over the last couple of days she had managed to get Brigid out of Boston with the aid of some of her business contacts. They had also agreed to keep her little sister at a safe house until Cleena told them everything was finished. Brigid hadn't been happy about that, but she had been scared enough to go without making too much of a fuss.

The man who had contacted Cleena had called on a regular basis, usually every four hours or so, to check in. She had given him reports about Lourds and he had seemed satisfied. The man hadn't mentioned Brigid's disappearance and Cleena felt certain he hadn't noticed.

Despite Sevki's advice, Cleena flew up the stairs.

"What are you doing?" Sevki demanded.

Cleena saved her breath for running.

Sevki cursed vehemently. "Come on. Be sensible. It's time for you to get out of there. That man looks dangerous. So does the one following you."

The one following me? Cleena spared a glance over her shoulder and saw that the other man she had spotted was indeed following her.

"Both of those guys look like Americans," Sevki said. "They also look like the type of guy the CIA would send in to hit someone."

Cleena knew that. That was why she was running. "They're after Lourds."

"That doesn't take a rocket scientist to figure out."

"If they kill him or take him, I'm not going to be able to find out who hurt Brigid and threatened us. I'm not going to let whoever that was escape without getting a chance to even the score."

"Having that guy forget about you would be the best-case scenario."

Holding tightly to the railing, Cleena powered herself around into the third-floor hallway. She had familiarized herself with the layout while Lourds was lecturing Olympia Adnan's class.

"I'm not going to forget about him," Cleena said.

"You're going to get yourself killed."

"I am if you continue to insist on distracting me. And all the negativity is killing my confidence." Cleena stepped to the first open doorway and entered. The lights were off and the room was in semidarkness. She stepped behind the door as she heard the man's foot scuff on the top step.

For the moment, she left her pistol holstered at the back of her waistband. She reached into her coat pocket and pulled out a lead-filled leather blackjack. Her father had taught her how to use one when she was ten years old.

"He knows you're there," Sevki told her.

Cleena didn't reply. If the man hadn't known where she was, he would have been a fool. Even so, he couldn't expect what she was about to do. He would count on his gun and his size and dismiss any possibility of her overpowering him. That was going to be a mistake.

She heard him outside the doorway. He barely made any noise, but shoe leather scraped the floor, and she heard him let out his breath. In the hallway, the student conversations outside the door abruptly quieted.

The man leaned through the door cautiously. Once his body was inside, Cleena swung the door with all her strength. The door banged against his boot where he had jammed it to keep from getting battered by the door.

Quickly as she could, Cleena slammed the blackjack into the frosted glass and shattered the pane. Razor-sharp shards poured over the man. Instinctively, he raised his arms to protect his face from the flying glass. Before he realized what was happening, Cleena reached through the empty doorframe and was on him with the blackjack.

She swung viciously, holding nothing back, striking as quickly as she could with enough strength to damage but not kill. Her first blow broke the man's wrist and sent his pistol spinning from his numbed fingers. She hit him four more times, aiming for his face and head. Blood covered his features as he went down. She hit him once more at the back of the skull to knock him unconscious.

Breathing raggedly, more from the adrenaline rush than physical exertion, Cleena stood over her opponent.

"Are you all right?" Sevki asked. The security cameras he had taken over weren't in all the rooms.

"I'm fine." Cleena dropped the blackjack into her pocket and wiped the man's blood from her face. She knelt quickly and went through his pockets. "Where's the other guy?"

"Covering the second floor. Are you robbing that guy?"

Cleena found the man's wallet and passport, then dropped both into her jacket pocket. "Getting his ID. It might be helpful to know who these people are."

"It might be helpful for you to get out of there."

Moving again, Cleena headed for the lady professor's office at the end of the hallway.

"You shouldn't be planning on making this a hobby," Sevki said.

"They came after me. Do any of those security cameras you've hacked into allow you to see the grounds around this building?"

"Yes."

"Check to see how many men out there might match up with the men in here. The guys in here didn't come alone."

Sevki cursed. "I'd have to be a fly to keep an eye on everything you want me to keep an eye on."

Cleena halted outside the lady professor's office. Voices came from inside but they were too low and indistinct to understand. She got the definite impression that Lourds and the lady professor were trying to hide something.

"One other thing," Cleena whispered.

"Yeah?" Sevki sounded both distracted and worried, a dangerous combination.

"If we can't get out of the building through the exits, see if you can find another way for us to escape."

"And why would you try to escape with the professor?"

"Because he's got answers to some of what's wrecked my world. I want to know those answers."

"Want some advice?"

"No." Cleena reached behind her and freed the pistol.

"It sounds to me like whatever hole you stepped into over here, you're only digging yourself in deeper."

"You're really harshing my mellow, Sevki."

At that moment, the scar-faced man reached the top of the stairs at the other end of the hallway. He swept the hallway at once and locked eyes with Cleena. She cursed and reached for the doorknob only to find it locked.

"There's an organization," Olympia told Lourds, "a society pledged to secrecy, that protects these documents. That book that you stole from those men in the catacombs was part of those documents."

"But Qayin and his people aren't part of this protective organization?"

"No." Olympia shook her head emphatically. "Qayin and his followers are something else. They want the Scroll of Joy for their own purposes."

"What purposes?"

"They want the power presented by the Scroll of Joy."

"What power would that be?"

"We don't know for sure. John of Patmos was in ill health when he returned from seeing the visions. He was already an old man. Seeing those visions, and dictating what he had seen to the acolytes, exhausted him. He never again climbed from his bed."

"So this protective group, I assume, came from the acolytes?"

Olympia nodded. "They call themselves the Brotherhood of the Scroll of John."

"I suppose they had to call themselves something, but that's not going to easily fit on stationery."

"This isn't humorous. There's a lot riding on this."

"The fate of the world," Lourds said, and couldn't help feeling completely ridiculous when he said it.

"I asked for permission to bring you here," Olympia said softly. "There was a lot of resistance to my suggestion, but after you found Atlantis, the Elders were more open to the idea."

"If there was a translation involved, I should've been your first choice. In fact, you should have told me this years ago."

"The choice was not mine to make. If it weren't for my brother, they wouldn't have listened to me at all."

"Your brother? Joachim?" Lourds had never met Olympia's younger brother. She rarely talked of him and he thought some kind of family rift had existed.

"Yes."

"From the way you've never talked about him, I didn't think the two of you were close."

"I couldn't talk about him."

"Because what he was doing was a secret."

"This isn't a joke, Thomas."

Lourds looked back at the image of the snarling dragon on the computer monitor. For the moment, he struggled to set aside his doubts. After all, he hadn't been certain about Atlantis either.

"You choose to believe that books from the Library of Alexandria still exist." Olympia gazed into his eyes. "I've never said anything to dissuade you from your hope of finding those books. But that's all you have: hope. I have these documents. And you have whatever you found out from that book."

"All right. But if all this is so secret and the Brotherhood is tight-lipped, how did Qayin and his people find out about the Scroll of Joy?"

"Just as there are those who worship God, there are also those who worship Satan."

"That's going too far."

"Is it? Think about the name of the man who kidnapped you."

"Qayin?"

"Yes. Did you stop to think where that name came from?"

"I suspected a mother and father." Lourds's sarcasm deserted him when he realized what she was getting at. "Qayin is different in other languages."

Olympia nodded. "In English it can be translated into Cain."

"As in, 'And while they were in the field, Cain attacked his brother Abel and killed him'? That Cain?"

"Yes."

"You believe that the descendants of Cain are pursuing the Scroll of Joy?" Lourds couldn't hold back his incredulity.

"God banished Cain after he murdered his brother," Olympia said. "And he marked him. Perhaps Cain's descendants feared the legacy of that mark and chose to follow a path other than one of righteousness because they were already doomed."

"Different religions disagree about that mark. Judaism speaks of the mark as one of mercy. God let it be known that anyone who harmed Cain would be punished seven times as much as Cain was. That can be viewed as a preventative measure."

"Either way, we believe that name was deliberately chosen."

"Why?"

"Because as long as the Brotherhood has existed, there has also been a Qayin."

"Surely you don't believe it's been the same individual." Although Lourds couldn't bring himself to believe that might be true, the thought still chilled him.

"It doesn't matter. What matters is that we get the Scroll of Joy translated."

"Why now? What has made now any different than, say, a few years ago when you and I first met?"

"Because the Brotherhood doesn't trust anyone outside its own ranks," Olympia told him. "It has taken years to persuade them that you are the right person for this. Even then they didn't want to listen to me. If you hadn't been abducted by Qayin, if you hadn't gotten that book—and been able to translate it, you would've been tested."

"And if I'd failed?"

"You would never have gotten to learn about the Scroll of Joy, much less been offered a chance to translate it."

"What if, after being abducted and shot at, I decided I wanted no part of translating that scroll?"

Olympia grinned at him. "I know you enjoy my companionship, but no matter how good we are together, I don't flatter myself into thinking that I'm the reason you stayed in Istanbul. If you could have found a way to take that book with you out of the country, I think you would have left. If you had felt that you could've learned enough from a copy of that book, you would have copied it and then gotten the first jet out of here."

Lourds knew she had him.

"All your protests aside? I knew all I had to do was mention I had a manuscript no one else could read. Your vanity alone would have hooked you."

Lourds resettled his hat on his head. "I refuse to believe I'm that predictable."

"When it comes to translation conundrums, *everyone* can predict how you will act."

"Surely I'm not that transparent."

"Yes, you are. It's just one of the reasons I care for you so much, and one of the reasons I know better than to try to hang on to you."

Lourds fixed his gaze on the image of the dragon. "I'll want to see the original documents."

"Once you prove to the Brotherhood that you translated that book, that won't be a problem."

"What about the Scroll of Joy?"

Olympia frowned. "That's a bit more problematic, but I promise that it will depend on your abilities more than on our decision."

Before Lourds could ask her how that was problematic, the frosted glass door pane shattered and fell into the room. The redhead from the airport stood on the other side of the door with a pistol her hand.

CHAPTER

16

İSTANBUL UNİVERSİTY
BEYAZİT SQUARE
İSTANBUL, TURKEY
MARCH 19, 2010

"Get up." The redhead waved her pistol at Lourds.

Calmly, Lourds stood and blocked Olympia from the woman's field of fire. The move wasn't out of bravery as much as it was feeling responsible for endangering Olympia. *Obviously she's still intent on collecting her bounty*, Lourds thought sourly.

As clearly and calmly as he could, hoping his voice didn't crack and the woman wouldn't shoot him, he said, "Olympia, phone the police. Tell them what's going on."

"Thomas, who is this woman?" Olympia demanded.

Lourds couldn't believe it. A woman had shown up in the office with a *weapon,* and Olympia wanted to know who she was in a tone that suggested jealousy.

"This is the woman that kidnapped me from the airport. *Call* the police."

The redhead glanced down the hallway. "We don't have time for the police. They're coming."

"Who?" Lourds asked automatically. "The police?"

"Not the police. If I knew who these people were,

I'd have given you names. They're big, scary guys. And they have guns."

"Everybody you know seems to have guns," Lourds said.

"Don't blame me. They're after you. I could have ducked out and not risked my neck. And you want to blame *me* for this?"

"How did you find me?" he asked.

An exasperated look filled the woman's face. "You're kidding, right? You're here to speak at the university. It's been in all the papers. Especially after the scene at the airport. All of Istanbul, those that would care, knows you're here."

Without warning, the woman cursed and ducked into the room just as bullets shattered the doorframe. Lourds stepped back and nearly fell on top of the desk. Olympia's frightened scream echoed in his ears and galvanized him into action. He reached down for his backpack and slung it on.

The redhead ducked back around the door and fired several quick shots. Then she pulled back inside and took cover.

She glared at Lourds. "At gunpoint, do you always have to ask so many questions?"

Lourds glared back. "I'm not up on all the protocol for getting abducted."

"I'm not abducting you. I'm protecting you."

"By bringing these men here?" Olympia still had the phone pressed against her ear.

"I didn't bring those men here." The woman sounded really put out.

"I'd have seen someone following us," Olympia insisted.

"You haven't seen me for the last few days," the woman snapped. "You've been busy tearing up the sheets at the hotel. I've been expecting footage on YouTube. Now let's get moving. They want the professor. I don't think they care if either one of us are alive."

"I'm on the line with the police." Olympia spoke rapidly in Turkish.

Another fusillade of bullets slammed into the open door and tore gouges in the wood.

"The police won't get here fast enough." The redhead changed magazines in her pistol and released the slide. "By the time they get here, you'll either be in the custody of those men—or you'll be dead. It's a cell phone. Take it with you. You can talk to the police on the way. Just try to keep up. And dodge the bullets."

The woman grabbed Lourds by the elbow, but he resisted. He trusted her not to shoot him. She *had,* in a way, saved his life down in the catacombs. And she hadn't shot him. Yet.

The woman cursed again and tried to push him into motion.

"Cleena MacKenna," a man's voice boomed.

Lourds immediately recognized the accent as American, probably by way of Philadelphia. He looked at the woman as she returned to the door.

"Cleena? That's your name?" Lourds asked.

"So not the time for introductions," she growled.

"Cleena MacKenna," the man called again. "You don't have to die today. You can just walk away from this. We're just here for the professor. Back away and you can go."

Cleena looked at Lourds. "Do you believe him?"

Lourds started to answer, but wasn't sure what he was going to say.

"I don't believe him," Cleena went on before he could say anything. She looked around. "There's a back door to this room?"

"I don't know," Lourds replied.

Cleena shot a scathing glance at Olympia. "You could have mentioned there's a back door to this office."

Olympia crossed her arms and looked defiant. "The police are on their way. I have them on speaker phone."

"I don't think the speaker phone function is going to stop those guys."

Olympia raised her voice. "I have called the police. They are on their way." She said that for the men outside in the hallway.

Cleena ignored her and raced to the back of the room. "Where's the door?" she asked. A second later, she swiveled her head to the left and looked at the bookshelf covering one of the walls. "Shelving and books cover that wall."

Lourds realized she was talking to someone else, not him. Then he saw the glint of metal in her ear.

"Okay, okay. I'll look." Cleena raked a shelf clear of books. The heavy volumes toppled to the floor, along with a snow globe containing a statue of the Greek god, Poseidon.

"Hey!" Olympia protested. "What do you think you're doing?"

Abruptly, out in the hallway the fire alarm rang, strident and harsh. Lourds guessed that someone, a student or a professor, had pulled the fire alarm. That had been good. At least all the students would get clear of the situation.

"Ma'am," a man's voice called from the phone in Turkish, "is something wrong? Is everything all right?"

Undeterred, Cleena moved on to the second shelf and began clearing those as well. In the shadowy recesses, the door was hard to see, but Lourds spotted the straight lines. Impulsively, he went to help the woman, wading over and through the books.

"Thomas?" Olympia called.

"Ma'am?" the Istanbul policeman inquired loudly. "Please stay on the line."

"There's a door back here." Lourds pulled at the higher shelving.

"Olympia, you don't think those men are really here after me, do you? I don't make enemies like this. They have to be after the book I got down in the catacombs. And if they find out you know something about it, they're not going to stop with just questioning me."

Cleena swung around with a shelf and nearly caught Lourds in the face with it. She locked eyes with Olympia. "Get over here!"

"Don't tell me—"

Out in the hallway, something metallic struck the floor and skidded to a stop near the door. Lourds took in the spherical shape, then redoubled his efforts to get to the door.

"They've got a grenade!"

"It opens inward!" Cleena yelled.

Understanding, Lourds reached for the doorknob but found it lacking. Someone had taken it off. As he started to turn around to Cleena, she shoved him aside with her free hand and fired the pistol three times at the locking mechanism. The bullets cored through the cheap metal and splintered the wood.

Before the echoes of the shots died away, Olympia joined them and the grenade blew up. The tremendous noise deafened Lourds and vibrated through his body. He expected shrapnel to rip through him, but it didn't. Bright lights and gas followed the explosion.

Flash-bang, he realized. He'd read about those in the novels he consumed during long plane flights and dead time at sites. Those grenades were used to confuse and disorient people.

Cleena grabbed his arm and shoved him toward the door, which still hadn't opened. Lourds saw her mouth moving but heard nothing. Knowing what she wanted, he set his shoulder to the door and threw his weight against it. The door shivered and sprang open, revealing that it had been covered over by Sheetrock on the other side. Evidently some alterations had been done to increase office space.

The other room was thankfully empty. Lourds didn't want anyone else in danger or joining their little group. His attempt to open the door ripped it from its hinges and it smashed into someone's painstaking model reproduction of the Ottoman Siege of Constantinople in 1453. Ships and warriors went flying, followed by the blue waters of the Golden Horn and the fabricated brown coastline.

Olympia followed, almost running over Lourds in her haste. She held the cell phone to her ear, but if anyone was on the other end of the connection, apparently she couldn't hear any better than Lourds.

He looked around the room, trying to figure out what he was supposed to do next. They were still on the third floor, too high to risk jumping and breaking a leg.

Olympia grabbed his arm and, when he turned to face her, spoke to him anxiously. He read her lips, missing it the first time because she was speaking her native tongue, not English. *Where do we go?*

I don't know, he replied. *Up? Down?* He used his hands in case she couldn't read his lips. His mouth, eyes, and nose all stung from the gas contained in the flash-bang. Tears blurred his vision as he swept his gaze around the room.

Two sharp cracks pierced his deafness and he recognized the sounds as gunshots. Anxiously, he peered back into the opening, wondering if the woman—Cleena—had made it out of Olympia's office alive.

She barreled through and hit him full on. Lourds wrapped his arms around her and they went to the floor on his back.

Cleena glared at him as if he were a bumbling moron, which—Lourds reflected irritably—was unfair. He'd been concerned about her.

She forced herself up and partially kneed him in the crotch while doing so. Lourds was certain he'd cried out and was glad no one had been able to hear him. Then his thoughts focused on survival again.

Smoke rolled into the room from the grenade. It got harder to breathe. As he glanced around, he didn't know how they were going to get out of the office. They were still in a death trap.

Eckart stood his ground in the hallway with his pistol up. His left hand wrapped tightly around his right so the semiautomatic pistol's recoil would respond perfectly and not jam. He peered through the smoke, expecting Lourds and the two women to emerge at any second. The flash-bang held pepper gas as well as the pyrotechnics.

No one came out.

"Humboldt," Eckart called over the com. Three of his men had set up behind him. Three others held the stairwell at the other end of the hallway. There was no way their target could escape. "Set up outside that office."

"Yes, sir." The man ran forward without hesitation. He wore a mask against the effects of the pepper gas. He waited a moment, then peered around the door.

Two shots rang out in quick sequence. Humboldt jerked, then stumbled back. He turned around and clutched at his face, but blood already poured from one of the shattered lenses of his mask.

Eckart cursed. For a homegrown terrorist, the woman was good.

Humboldt staggered twice more, then turned boneless and dropped to the ground. His head rebounded from the floor and Eckart knew the man was dead.

"Are you sure there's no other way out of the office?" Eckart demanded.

"No, sir," Mayfield replied over the com. "Two elevators. The stairwells at each end of the building. That covers everything."

Eckart tried to put himself in that office and figure out what he would do if he was trapped in there. *You wouldn't have gotten trapped in there,* he told himself.

"What about the windows?"

"The grenade blew the glass out of the one in the office, sir, but the people inside haven't left."

"Can you see inside?"

"No, sir. The smoke's too thick."

"Keep watch." Eckart kept his eyes on the door. "How much time has elapsed since the first shots?"

"Two minutes thirty-seven seconds, sir. We're coming up on the threshold for this mission."

Eckart knew they couldn't stay much longer. The local police would arrive shortly, and the college security armed response teams had to be en route as well. If they didn't leave soon, things were going to get messier. He willed himself to be patient. Whatever threat Lourds presented against the United States was about to end. Eckart fully intended to take the professor into custody.

Or kill him.

"Sevki?" Cleena cupped a hand over her ear and struggled to hear Sevki at the other end of the earwig connection. "I can't hear. A grenade deafened me."

"—other wall—elevator shaft—emergency." Sevki sounded like he was breaking up as he shouted, and she could still barely hear him. But she understood what he was talking about. They'd managed something like this before.

Approaching the wall on the other side of the new office, Cleena bent down and took her knife free of her boot. When she reached the wall, she fisted the hilt and drove the broad blade into the Sheetrock. The material gave way easily. Two strokes made an *X*.

She stepped back and drove her boot through the Sheetrock. Big pieces of the material dropped to the floor but others vanished in the space beyond. In seconds, she'd stripped the Sheetrock away to reveal the two-by-four studs beneath. She used the knife again to score the wall on the other side. When she kicked this time, her foot went through.

"—you see—it there?" Sevki asked. "Cleena—you—now?"

Cleena shoved Sheetrock out of the way and peered into the empty space. Darkness filled the area on the other side of the broken wall, but the light that filtered in around her exposed the greasy network of cables.

"I found the elevator shaft," Cleena said. She checked the wall studs again and hoped that Lourds could squeeze through. If anything, it would be the professor's big head that got him stuck. She almost smiled at that, but the thought of the men waiting out in the hallway with guns took the fun out of that possibility.

The elevator sat at the first floor. When the fire alarm had been pulled, the cages had all automatically settled to the ground floor.

She pulled her head back out and addressed Lourds and the woman. "Elevator shaft. We can use it to get downstairs." This time she could hear herself a little.

Lourds nodded, then picked up a leg from the broken table that had held the miniature war pieces. He swung it experimentally, then went to work on the Sheetrock still barring the door.

Cleena had to admit that once the professor decided on a course of action, not much deterred him. When he was satisfied, he reached into his backpack and took out a mini-flashlight. The fact that he seemed to be prepared for everything except being kidnapped irked Cleena. But it was probably more because she hadn't thought to bring a flashlight herself.

"The elevator cage is downstairs," he said. "We can't get through."

"We go to the second floor," Cleena said. "Then to the stairwell."

"They've got to have men outside," Lourds told her.

Cleena nodded. "They do. We'll have to get around them."

"No," Olympia said. "We go downstairs. To the basement. There are tunnels that connect this building to other buildings on the campus."

"Sevki?" Cleena asked.

"It's true," Sevki said. He sounded tinny and far away. "There's an infrastructure throughout the colleges there. The maintenance people use the tunnels to move large pieces of equipment and check on the utilities."

"All right." Cleena gestured to Olympia. "You know the way."

Olympia peered through the hole, then back at Cleena. "You expect me to jump?"

"I'll go first," Lourds volunteered. He took off his backpack and handed it to Olympia. "That way I can help you down." He shined the flashlight around, then put it in his mouth and eased down into the elevator shaft.

Tension wound Cleena almost to the breaking point. Images of the scar-faced man and others like him kept bouncing through her mind. The effects of the pepper gas made her eyes and nose run as she scanned the hole in the wall and the office door, and she knew she couldn't rely on her damaged hearing to hear anyone approaching.

When he was below, thankfully without breaking his neck, Lourds talked Olympia into descending, guiding her feet with his hands. Cleena followed at the other woman's heels in case they decided to bolt and attempt to get away from her.

"Sir, we're about to enter the red zone on our time line," Mayfield stated calmly.

"I know. Everyone outside be prepared to exfiltrate instantly. There should be confusion enough on the campus to cover some of our retreat." Eckart didn't like giving those orders. It was too near admitting failure, and he wasn't prepared to do that yet. "Let me know when the police are on-site."

"Affirmative."

Too much time had elapsed for Lourds and the women to emerge from the office. If they hadn't come out by now, they'd either been overcome by the gas—or they'd found another way out.

He took a fresh grip on his pistol and stepped forward in a combat crouch. He wore Kevlar under his shirt, but his head was unprotected.

He reached the door, took a breath to steady himself, then ripped away his gas mask to clear his vision. The gas stung his eyes but he'd been exposed to it on close-quarter battlefields numerous times. Whipping around the doorframe, he dropped to his knees with the pistol gripped in both hands before him.

No one was inside the room. It took him a moment to spot the hole in the wall through all the lingering gas. He slipped his gas mask up from his neck and back over his face.

"They're not inside the room," Eckart growled. He coughed as vestiges of the gas raked through his lungs.

"There's not another way out."

"They found one. It looks like a door."

"It *was* a door. Evidently it had been sealed off sometime in the past."

"Where does it lead?"

"To the adjoining office. If you've got that office door covered, then you're covering the office next door as well."

Eckart looked down the hallway and saw the office next to the elevator.

"They can't get out of there," Mayfield said.

"They couldn't get out of the last room they were in." Eckart swung back to the doorway and fired a half-dozen rounds into the hole in the wall.

There was no response.

A bad feeling ripped through Eckart's stomach as he gazed back at the elevator next to the other office. The woman was a street rat. She was clever and dangerous.

"Open the elevator doors," Eckart ordered. "Check the shaft." As his men ran to do that, he ducked into the office and crossed over to the hole in the wall. The door lay inside the room, torn from its hinges. He cursed as he scanned the room over his pistol sights and saw no one.

Then he spotted the hole in the opposite wall.

"They're in the elevator shaft. Check the cameras on the second floor."

Mayfield took a moment to reply. "Negative. They haven't exited either set of elevator doors."

"All right." Eckart stepped across ships and soldiers and paused at the second hole. "They're still inside the shaft. Kill the two women but I want our target alive."

He took a mini-Maglite from his pants pocket, flicked it on, then crossed his wrists so the flashlight beam and the pistol pointed in the same direction. He leaned into the hole and spotted movement below.

"Let's go." Olympia spoke in Turkish and yanked at Lourds's arm.

Lourds looked up at the hole. The air inside the shaft seemed to burn his lungs and nasal membranes even more. The logical side of his brain that wasn't hunkered down in fear realized that the gas was heavy enough to hug the ground and now it was settling into the elevator shaft.

"Come on, Thomas. Let's go before she gets down here." Olympia pulled at the elevator doors in front of her. Standing on the elevator cage, the second floor exit was almost at her chin. "Help me."

"We're not leaving her," Lourds said as he joined Olympia.

"What?"

"We're not leaving her."

"You've got to be kidding."

Lourds hooked his fingers into the seam between the door and yanked. The doors gapped open a few inches, then slid back into place.

"We're not leaving her," Lourds repeated. "She's part of this. We need to know what she knows."

"As if she's going to tell you."

"You don't know where the Scroll of Joy is, do you?"

Olympia hesitated. "No."

"I thought so. Otherwise you wouldn't have needed the book."

"We have a copy of the book. We couldn't translate it. That was why—that *is* why we need you."

That stopped Lourds in his tracks. "Qayin didn't have the only copy?"

"No."

"How many copies are there?"

"We don't know. There can't have been many."

Lourds tried the door again. "I would hope not. And we're not going to leave her. She has a gun."

"Do you think she's going to shoot us?"

"No, but she's been doing fantastically well shooting the people chasing us."

Cleena dropped into the elevator shaft and looked at them.

"Too late," Olympia grumbled in Turkish.

"Did I miss the lovers' quarrel?" Cleena asked.

Lourds ignored her and bent his attention and strength to prizing the doors open. This time when the doors opened he kept pushing till he reached the breakover point. The doors slid back into the wall on either side. He turned and hooked his hands together in front of him.

"Okay, Olympia, up you go."

Olympia placed his backpack on the elevator cage beside him, then stepped into Lourds's hands and he boosted her up over the second floor edge. He handed his backpack to her and turned to face Cleena, who was shorter than Olympia.

"I don't think your girlfriend much cares for me," Cleena said.

"She's not my girlfriend." Lourds didn't know why he felt the need to clarify that, especially in the heat of a pitched gunbattle. He thought it was more out of reflex than anything. "We're just good friends."

"*Very* good friends." Cleena ignored his clasped hands and lithely jumped to the second floor under her own power, then rolled to her feet.

Lourds leaped up after her. As he managed the final frantic scramble, darkness filled the elevator shaft and he knew someone had stepped into the hole in the wall on the third floor. He renewed his efforts to get clear. Olympia grabbed his arms and yanked. Cleena dropped to one knee and fired up into the shaft.

A brief flurry of bullets ricocheted off the elevator cage then stopped.

"Let's go." Cleena swapped magazines in her pistol and stood. "They know where we are now. We're going to have company." She looked at Olympia. "Maybe you could lead the way."

Shooting her a scathing glance, Olympia quickly took the lead and headed toward the stairwell just ahead of them. Lourds grabbed his backpack and slid it over one shoulder.

"You'd be faster if you left that," Cleena advised him.

"That's not going to happen," Lourds assured her.

Lourds fell into a jog on Olympia's heels. Gunfire blasted in the elevator shaft again.

Eckart touched the burning area on his neck. His fingertips came away wet with crimson. He cursed the woman and hoped he got the chance to kill her up close and personal. Homegrown terrorists were always the worst, and she was beginning to seriously tick him off.

Echoes of full-auto fire filled the room and boomed out of the elevator shaft.

"Do you have the elevator shaft?" he asked.

"Affirmative, sir, but they're gone."

"Gone?" During the brief encounter, Eckart's eyes hadn't adjusted well enough to pierce the fog of white gas in the elevator chamber. He peered again, and this time he spotted the open doors on the second floor landing. He cursed as his mind raced.

"Do you have them on the cameras?" he demanded.

Mayfield answered at once. "Yes, sir. Second floor. Headed for the stairwell."

"Do we have anyone there?" Eckhart jumped down into the elevator shaft. His boots thudded against the cage but he kept his feet.

Two of his men dropped in after him. Together, they headed into the hallway.

"Negative," Mayfield said. "They'd closed on the office with you."

The second floor was empty. The door was closed at the end of the hallway. Eckart increased his pace.

Lourds followed Olympia and was in turn followed by Cleena. The sound of shots fired above echoed around them. He wanted to talk, a thousand questions zipped through his mind, but his breath was ragged from the pepper gas and from exertion. His feet pounded against the concrete steps.

They passed the first floor landing and headed into the basement. Footsteps struck the steps behind them.

"Hurry," Cleena urged, and Lourds didn't know how she found the breath to speak.

Olympia never broke stride, reaching the basement level and shoving through the door. Out in the underground area, she turned right immediately. Security lights burned weakly in the darkness. Olympia fumbled in her pocket, then produced a key ring.

She halted at a large steel security door and tried keys.

"Don't you know which key it is?" Cleena stood nearby with the pistol clenched in her hands as she faced the door they'd just run through.

Olympia ignored her and concentrated on the keys. Lourds knew the history department would have needed to move exhibits or research materials through the tunnels beneath the university because it would have been much simpler and more possible even during inclement days.

The locking mechanism clicked and Olympia pulled the door open. She reached for a light switch and turned it on. A row of low-wattage bulbs flared to yellow incandescence down the length of the tunnel.

"Let's go." Cleena ushered them inside as the basement door flew open. She held her fire and Lourds knew that she had because she didn't want to mark their positions. His confidence in her abilities grew. She was a remarkable young woman.

Lourds entered the tunnel after Olympia.

"Which way does the tunnel go?" Cleena asked as she closed the door behind them. She took a moment to manually lock it.

"A short distance ahead," Olympia said, "it splits in three directions. All of them lead to different buildings."

"That's a strong door," Cleena said. "It should slow them."

Olympia nodded. "We'll reach the intersection before they can open that door."

"Unless they brought a rocket launcher," Cleena said.

That, Lourds thought sourly, was entirely possible given past history.

Eckart glared at the security door in front of them. Two of his men worked on the locking mechanism, but it was going slowly.

"Where did they go?" he asked.

"Service tunnel infrastructure beneath the university," Mayfield answered. "I found a map. The tunnel they're in branches off into three hallways a short distance from that point."

"Are there cameras in the tunnels?"

"No. I'm blind there."

A one-in-three chance didn't sound appealing to Eckart. Not with the local police and the university security people closing in.

"All right," Eckart growled. "Pack it up and let's hit the wind."

Without a word, his men pulled their gear together and fell in behind him. "We need a route out of here."

"Yes, sir."

"And we've left dead behind." That was something Eckart wouldn't have done when he'd been back in uniform. Now there was no helping it.

"I'll take care of it, sir."

Eckart called off the names of the men the woman had killed. Within minutes, Mayfield would have plugged fake IDs into Interpol's intelligence center. He'd also activate the false identification they had at the

Pentagon. Eckart and his team operated off the books, but Vice President Webster made certain they had access to all the resources they needed.

Professor Lourds may have gotten lucky in this first encounter, but Eckart intended to write a much different ending the next time.

CHAPTER 17

GALATA TOWER
NORTH OF THE GOLDEN HORN
İSTANBUL, TURKEY
MARCH 19, 2010

"You'd better be worth all this trouble."

Lourds looked up from his notebook at Cleena. "As far as I'm concerned, you started all this."

Currently, they sat in the café near the top of the Galata Tower. Several European and Asian tourists occupied the tables near the windows overlooking the Golden Horn and other historic parts of the city. He couldn't help but think about the microcosm of East and West meeting inside the café being a reflection of what went on in the city on the other side of the three-foot-thick walls. And those meetings had been going on for generations. Some things never changed.

Well, didn't change much, actually. The Galata Tower had also been known as the Christea Turris, which translated into the Tower of Christ, by the Genoese. The Byzantines had named it Megalos Pyrgos, the Great Tower, because the cone-shaped stone capping had been—and remained—one of the most recognizable landmarks in the city.

The Genoese had built the tower in 1348 when they'd

been expanding their holdings within the city. It had been originally planned as a defensive enhancement, then served as housing for the Janissaries, the elite Turkish Army corps, and later as a jail for war prisoners.

Over the years, the tower had needed reconstruction a number of times. Partially destroyed by fires and storms, the tower had lost its cone-shaped top in 1875 and that hadn't been replaced until a restoration in 1967.

Hezarfen Ahmet Celebi, an early aviator, glided from the tower out over the Bosphorus to the Uskudar foothills on the Anatolian half of the city. That had happened sometime around 1632.

Lourds couldn't imagine launching himself with a pair of wings from the tower. Of course, he couldn't imagine himself running from gun thugs, either. But throwing oneself from the tower was a conscious decision. Running in the face of death was more of an instinct. As always, he thought about the ancient aviator and respected the man's drive to discover flight.

The view was wonderful, overlooking the harbor as well as most of the historic old city and several of the most worshipped—literally—sites. Lourds had enjoyed it on several occasions. At the moment, he was more concerned about police intervention. Given a second running gun battle, he felt certain the Turkish authorities would kick him out of the country as an undesirable. *Politely*, of course.

Until everything got sorted.

Lourds hoped to have the mystery of the book—*Books,* he amended, feeling the time crunch of others working on the transcription as well—in hand before the authorities caught up with him. Olympia was on the phone with someone she thought could hide them out for a few days but hadn't seen fit to mention who it was. Matters weren't helped by the fact that Professor Olympia Adnan was also being sought by the police at present.

Several enterprising students at the university had gotten video of the raid on the university on their phones and PDAs. Many of those clips had shown up on YouTube and the local television networks were broadcasting the story.

Cleena sat on the other side of the table and gazed up at the television behind the bar. "It's you everyone is after."

Lourds tried to turn his attention back to his work, but Cleena sat across from him and he was too aware of her gender to ignore her. He looked back at her and watched as she calmly ate a piece of *kabak mucveri,* Turkish zucchini fritters, and sipped her bottled water.

"All right." Turning his attention back to the manuscript, Lourds focused on his transcription once more. Sulking he could deal with. Sulking meant silence. Silence meant—

"I can't see how you don't want to talk about this." Exasperation tightened Cleena's voice.

Lourds glanced at her in bewilderment. "You said you *didn't* want to talk about this," he pointed out.

"I don't."

"All right."

"But we have to. That doesn't mean I'm going to enjoy it."

Sighing, knowing he wasn't going to be allowed any peace if he didn't listen to her and take whatever misery she wished to dole out, Lourds leaned back in his chair and took a sip of his beer. He'd opted for Efes Pilsen, a local lager brewed in Izmir that he'd found particularly pleasing.

"Do you realize the trouble you're in?" she asked.

"You mean with the local police?" Lourds countered. "Or the United States State Department, whom I suspect is working with the local CIA? Or Qayin and his troops? Or the paramilitary unit that tried to kill us at the university a few minutes ago, all for whom I can't guess at? That trouble?"

Cleena hesitated. "Yes. That trouble."

Lourds studied her. "You've already known about this trouble. There's something you're not telling me."

Cleena leaned back and broke eye contact then. "No, there's not."

"Why were you at the university today?"

"I told you. I was tailing you."

"For whom?"

"No one."

"I don't believe you were there on your own."

"Why?" Fire glinted in Cleena's eyes. "Don't you think I'm smart enough to figure out there's a payday involved in this?" She flicked her gaze at the book. "I'm just here for a share in the profits."

Lourds placed a hand on the book. “You haven’t tried to take this.”

Cleena looked sullen but didn’t say anything.

“My guess is that you haven’t a clue about whom to take this to in order to sell it. Or even what it’s worth.”

“I could sell it to Qayin.”

Lourds smiled. “And he proved so trustworthy the first time.”

She said a particularly bad word only loud enough for Lourds to hear her.

“And I don’t think the men back at the university are looking for more partners,” Lourds said. “Not to mention the fact that you’ve pretty much burned that bridge by shooting a few of them.”

“There are other collectors.”

“A collector wouldn’t be interested in this manuscript unless he—”

“Or she.”

Lourds acknowledged the response with a nod, but he knew she only delivered it to be more annoying. “Or *she* knew the story behind the book. Which you also don’t know.”

Cleena grimaced at him. “Enjoying your little secrets, Professor?”

“I think we all are.” He took another sip of his beer and leaned across the table. “And then there is the matter of the little friend in your ear. Want to tell me about him? Or her?”

She drained her water bottle and stood. “I’m going to get a refill. Want one?”

“Please. If you think you can refrain from spitting in it.”

“Actually, I hadn’t thought about it. Until now.” She headed for the bar.

Lourds watched her go and admired the twitch of her lean hips. The motion was definitely hypnotic and intriguing.

Olympia slid into the chair next to him and shook her head. “My God, Thomas. You haven’t changed a whit. Here we are running for our lives, not to mention that you’ve been keeping me company in bed the last few days, and you’re ogling a young girl like this was your last day on earth.”

“Sorry.” Lourds felt his face flush with heat. “Ogling is one of those male traits that I’m afraid is hardwired into every cell of my being. I didn’t mean to be disrespectful.”

She smiled at him. “No disrespect taken. I’ve known what you were about from the day I met you. That's been part of the attraction, actually."

Lourds lifted an inquiring eyebrow.

"A red-blooded male who doesn't feel the need to take over or change your life is the dream of many professional women," Olympia explained. "The fact that you're a tender and caring lover is a bonus."

"Well, I'm glad you feel that way."

"What I *don't* understand is how you can let some lovely little girl twist your head around when you should be concentrating on keeping it firmly on your shoulders. After all, there seems to be no shortage of people willing to remove it for you."

"Not all of my interest is in ogling," Lourds said. "I'm concentrating fully—well, almost fully—on the task of surviving this debacle. That young lady presents mysteries—and perhaps dangers—of her own."

Olympia sipped her wine and gazed at Cleena. "Like for whom she works?"

"Exactly."

"She was working for Qayin. But that's obviously over. Isn't it?"

"Qayin didn't want to see her survive their first joint venture," Lourds replied. "I don't see a future version of that partnership in the offing."

"Then do you suspect she's here on her own at this juncture?"

Lourds shook his head. "She's working *with* someone, but I don't think it's who she's working *for.* She's a professional. A professional wouldn't have an investment in this. There's too much she doesn't know."

"She'd be better off getting clear of the city. And us."

"I agree."

"Then why isn't she?"

"Because," Lourds said, "for whatever reason, she doesn't have a choice. An investment is there and she's not happy about it." He smiled at Olympia. "I really think that's one of the reasons she doesn't like me."

Olympia chuckled. "Why, Professor Lourds, I do think that you're upset by that."

"No. She's already made it quite clear that she isn't interested."

*Tsk*ing with feigned sympathy, Olympia trailed her fingers through his hair. "Oh, you poor dear. That must have hurt deeply."

"I'll live. But the question remains, what do we do with her?"

Olympia drew her hand back and raised her eyebrows in surprise. "You're actually thinking of letting her accompany us?"

"Unless I can figure out everything involved with this book, *us* isn't going to be going anywhere."

"Nonsense. You'll figure this out. I have faith in you. That's why I asked you to come."

Lourds gestured at the television hanging over the bar. Scenes from the university played again, followed by still photographs of Olympia and Lourds.

"We're running out of clock," he said.

"Personally, I think we need to ditch her. I know the kind of woman she is. She'll only bring you—*us*—trouble."

Lourds pierced her with his gaze and he spoke in a low, friendly tone. "I suppose it doesn't strike you that the same could be said about you? You did bring me here and immerse me in this whole fiasco, and very nearly got me killed. Without giving me a choice in the matter."

Olympia's features softened and looked guilty. She smoothed a stray lock of hair from Lourds's forehead. "I really didn't intend for this to happen, Thomas. I thought your part in this would already be done. And I had no idea anyone else knew you were coming."

Lourds captured her hand and tenderly kissed her palm. "I don't doubt that for a moment, Olympia. And I have to admit, I find this quite exhilarating. This is the kind of work I'm meant to do."

"Like with the Atlantis search?"

Lourds smiled. "I rather hope this doesn't turn out to be that dangerous."

"The fate of the world," she reminded him.

"I cling to the belief the case is rather overstated. After all, nearly two thousand years have passed. Surely the stakes have been exaggerated by the passage of time."

Olympia glanced back at the bar. "Either way, that young woman's going to complicate matters if she stays around."

At the bar, Lourds saw Cleena watching their reflections in the mirror. She was talking, but he knew she wasn't talking to herself.

"She stays," he declared.

"That may not be your decision to make," Olympia replied.

Lourds waited a beat. "If you want me working with you, Olympia, this is how we'll do it."

His sudden resoluteness about the subject caused her to cock her head in surprise. "And if I say no?"

"Then I'll take what I already know and continue working on my own. I'm quite hooked on this project. As you doubtless counted on."

"What if I turn you over to the authorities and you get deported?"

"Then," Lourds said, "I'll find out if news agencies are in interested in this book and the story behind it. 'The fate of the world,' and all that."

"You wouldn't." Olympia looked shocked and pulled her hand free of his.

"You know me. You know I would. If I talk loudly enough long enough, especially about an artifact written by John of Patmos, the Turkish government may see fit to invite me back in and give me whatever resources I need to see this project through to completion."

"You've never been a blackmailer."

"With you, no. And I do hope it doesn't come to that. But there is the matter of me getting shot at and taken captive. And all the curiosity you've built up. Without quite ever telling me everything you know." Lourds paused. "At this point, I'll do what I have to."

"You can't."

"Because the fate of the world depends on finding the Scroll of Joy?"

Olympia didn't answer.

"You can't have it both ways, love. Either this document needs to be found quickly, and I'm the right man to do the job, or neither of those things is true. Which is it?"

Obviously angry, Olympia folded her arms. "Bringing her along is going to be dangerous."

"Having her dogging our trail would be dangerous as well. For her, and for us. If she's with us, we can at least keep an eye on her. And maybe find out who she's working for. That could prove important to know while we put the rest of this puzzle together. This isn't just you and the people you represent, or Qayin. Someone else knows about the Scroll of Joy and we need to know who that is." He paused to sip his beer. "Besides that, she's handy with weapons in a fight."

At the bar, Cleena paid for the drinks, then turned and came back to the table. As she sat down, she looked at Lourds and Olympia. The tension between them was palpable and showed in the woman's tense posture. Evidently things hadn't gone as the lady professor had planned. That pleased Cleena to no end.

"Lovers' quarrel while I was gone?" Cleena asked.

"Not hardly." Lourds accepted his new beer and surreptitiously examined the surface for any signs of foreign materials.

"Please." Cleena rolled her eyes. "I'm not that juvenile."

"You have acknowledged that you're incredibly young," Lourds pointed out.

Cleena rolled her eyes at him.

"We were discussing the possibility of you coming with us," Olympia stated bluntly.

"That isn't a *possibility,*" Cleena replied. "That's a *fact.*"

Olympia smiled sweetly, as if butter wouldn't melt in her mouth. "We weren't sure if you still wanted to go after everything that's happened."

Calmly, Cleena met the older woman's gaze full measure. "Are you thinking about of dropping out of this little treasure hunt?"

"It's not," Olympia insisted through gritted teeth, "a *treasure* hunt."

"Whatever." Cleena flicked her gaze to the book in front of Lourds. "But I'm betting you didn't invite the professor over for a little slap-and-tickle and a wild goose chase."

Crimson briefly colored the professor's cheeks before she regained her composure. But she was quick about it. "What Thomas and I have between us isn't so cavalier as you propose."

"Please," Cleena protested. "I'm trying to hold my drink down. What you and professor do in the *sanctity* of your borrowed hotel room isn't any business of mine."

"Yet you were a Peeping Tom."

"She has you there," Sevki said into Cleena's ear. Cleena's face burned for just a moment.

"Learn anything?" Olympia taunted.

"Only that wine and cheese are probably the only things that get better with age."

"Oh, that's cold," Sevki said.

Looking both irritated and discomforted, Lourds cleared his throat. "Ladies, perhaps we should stick to the agenda."

Olympia crossed her arms and glared at Cleena. "If you're looking for some sort of profit, you're going to be sadly mistaken."

Cleena sipped her water. "I know you and I don't hang in the same social circles, but one thing I can tell you that I've learned is that people don't kill each other for nothing. Whatever this thing is that you're looking for, somebody plans to profit from it. Money will be involved. Eventually."

That, she knew, was inarguable.

Lourds followed Olympia through the narrow streets that made up Istanbul's historic downtown section. Many of the older buildings hadn't changed over the years and still maintained architecture that dated back several centuries despite the times the city had been conquered. Street vendors occupied curbs and hawked their wares.

Galata had been colonized by the Republic of Genoa starting in 1273. According to legend, the name had been taken from Calata, which roughly translated into "downward slope." The city was also called Pera, taken from an old Greek name that meant "the fig field on the other side," referring to the Bosphorus between the city halves.

The walls of the medieval city had been torn down first during the Fourth Crusade, when Christians fought Christians and the line had been drawn between the Catholic Church and the Eastern Orthodox Church. The remaining walls had nearly all been destroyed under Muslim rule in the nineteenth century to allow further urban expansion.

Glancing over his shoulder, he checked on Cleena. The young woman trailed him by a couple strides and looked alert. She'd pulled her hair back into a ponytail.

"Have you been to Istanbul before?" he asked.

She glanced at him. "Making conversation?"

Lourds shrugged.

"Yes, I have," she acknowledged after a moment. "A few times."

"I love the older parts. This city has a lot of history written into it."

"Is that what this hunt is all about? History?"

"Yes."

Cleena smiled at him. "But you're not saying which history. The Greeks, the Romans, or the Ottoman Empire."

"Many other cultures have lived here," Lourds replied.

"But those are the big three."

"So they are."

They paused at the ruins of the Palace of the Genoese, which was called the Palazzo del Comune, the Palace of the Municipality behind Bankalar Caddesi, Banks Street, which featured several Ottoman-era finance structures.

"What have you learned from the book?"

Lourds stepped around a small group of children playing at the curb. "Maybe this isn't the time to talk about it."

"Really? Because I was thinking this was the perfect time. You know, before we get wherever we're going?"

Lourds resettled his hat on his head and shifted his backpack over his shoulders. He didn't say anything.

"You *do* know where we're going, don't you?" Cleena asked. "Your girlfriend *did* tell you, didn't she?"

"Somewhere safe," Lourds replied. "I'm also quite sure that Professor Adnan wouldn't appreciate being referred to as 'my girlfriend.' "

"I think 'main squeeze' would be less appreciated, don't you?" Cleena smiled sweetly.

Lourds chose not to respond.

"This place we're heading, is it somewhere *you* think is safe? Or somewhere *she* thinks is safe?" Cleena asked.

Lourds was certain that no matter what he answered, it was going to lead to an argument.

At that moment, six men gathered around a cart of melons turned toward the trio. Lourds caught sight of them from the corner of his eye. Cleena spotted the men as well and reached under the lightweight shirt she had hanging outside her jeans.

"Don't!" Olympia ordered. She walked back toward Lourds and Cleena.

Adrenaline cascaded through Lourds's bloodstream at the men's approach. He sought the quickest avenue of escape, but the street was packed.

Cleena had her pistol in hand and held the weapon out of sight beside her thigh.

"They're friends." Olympia stepped between the men and Cleena.

Personally, Lourds thought that was an extremely foolish move. Cleena probably wouldn't hesitate to shoot Olympia first. Before he could stop himself, Lourds stepped between Olympia and Cleena. *Now this*—this *is stupid.*

"Perhaps," he suggested while mentally chastising himself, "you could introduce us to your friends. . . ." His voice trailed off as he recognized one of the young men in front of them from the catacombs. It was the man that had been dressed in monk's robes and led him to safety.

Today there was no robe. Instead, he wore khaki cargo pants, white-and-navy Chuck Taylors, and a Coldplay concert T-shirt.

"Thomas," Olympia said almost brightly, "I suppose you've already met Joachim."

"Not formally, no." Lourds didn't know whether to extend a hand in greeting or take a step back. Only that would have made him an even bigger target for Cleena.

Joachim kept his face somber and nodded. "Good afternoon, Professor Lourds. You have been highly spoken of."

"Thank you. I wish I could say the same of you."

Olympia took the young man by the arm and smiled. For a brief instant, something close to jealousy flared through Lourds.

"I know you've never gotten to meet," Olympia said. "But I'm glad the two of you do have this chance. I just wish it had been under better circumstances."

"What does he have to do with this?" Lourds asked.

"Joachim is going to help us," Olympia explained.

"How do you know that you can trust him?" Cleena asked.

"Because Joachim is my brother."

Now that he was given more time and wasn't as stressed out, Lourds could see the family resemblance between Olympia and Joachim. Her brother was younger, older than Lourds had first thought in the catacombs, but surely no more than his late thirties.

After meeting in the street, Joachim had guided them to an apartment building. He had rooms set up on the third floor. In addition to sleeping quarters for Lourds, Olympia, Cleena, and the men, there was a sizable kitchen and dining room, as well as a large room equipped with a conference table and computer hardware, including a satellite uplink.

"Have you eaten, Professor Lourds?" Joachim asked politely.

"Not since breakfast with your sister," Lourds answered. "I had planned to take her to dinner before we were interrupted at the university." He put his backpack on the floor next to one of the chairs at the conference table.

"The gunmen," Joachim said.

"That would be the reason." Lourds sat at the table and took out the book from his backpack.

Joachim set across from Lourds. "Olympia said you had no idea who the men were."

Lourds shook his head. "No."

"Nor whom they might be working for?"

"They were Americans. Is there any reason why the American government would be interested in this manuscript?"

"If they knew what it represented, perhaps."

"If someone there ascribed to the same beliefs you and Olympia have." When no further explanation was forthcoming, Lourds said, "Because the fate of the world depends on what's in these pages." He raked the ball of his thumb along the book's pages.

Olympia sat across the table near her brother. She frowned slightly. "Thomas is having a little trouble believing that."

Cleena sat with a chair between herself and Lourds. She sipped from a bottle of water, remaining quiet and watchful.

Joachim rubbed his hands together, and for the first time Lourds realized how heavily calloused they were. "Let me assure you, Professor, you don't need to be a believer to help us. If you can translate that manuscript that's all the assistance we need."

"You expect this to tell you where the Scroll of Joy is?"

"It will." Joachim's voice carried conviction. "You will see." He took a minute to ask one of the men to prepare a meal, then turned back to Lourds. "We can't very well work on empty stomachs."

Within minutes, the smell of spices and cooking lamb filled the rooms. Lourds's stomach growled in anticipation. He nursed a cold beer as the conversation continued.

Joachim was attentive, like a student preparing for a final.

"You can't read this book?" Lourds asked.

"No," Joachim answered.

"Can any of your people decipher it?"

Polite impatience flickered across Joachim's face. "I assure you, if anyone among us could read that book, Olympia would not have involved you in this matter."

"How long has the knowledge in the book been lost?"

"Since the time of Constantine."

"How did it become lost?"

"You're familiar with the history of this city."

Lourds nodded.

"In addition to the wars that have been fought over and throughout this city, there have also been many natural disasters. Earthquakes. Fires. Even the passage of time has served to hide the scroll as the city fell and was raised up again and again by succeeding generations."

"If the scroll was written on Patmos—"

"It was. Our histories are very clear about that."

"Then how did the scroll come to be here?"

"During Constantinople's reign, he sent out many search parties to locate and take into custody relics of Jesus Christ's life as well as early Christianity. As you know, the Roman Empire tried to kill our religion during its infancy. They failed, but many precious things were scattered or destroyed or lost to us."

"Those were turbulent times," Lourds agreed. "Constantinople, the king, wanted to safeguard Christianity."

"One of the people searching for Christian artifacts was Helena,

Constantinople's mother," Joachim said. "She also had a strong belief and a strong desire to protect holy things. During her travels, she discovered the Brotherhood of the Scroll and went to the island of Patmos to negotiate on behalf of her son. Constantinople only wanted the documents protected."

"As strong as his rule looked, and as deeply entrenched as he was in Eastern Orthodox Christianity, it would've made sense." Lourds constructed a time line on a page of his personal journal. "So the Scroll of Joy remained at the Island of Patmos for almost four hundred years after it was authored."

Joachim nodded.

Helena had been a powerful figure in Emperor Constantine I's courts. Historians attributed the discovery of the relics of the True Cross to her and her efforts to find them. The Chapel of Saint Helen, constructed to identify the Burning Bush of Sinai, had been erected at her orders. During a dig under the temple to Venus built near Calvary over the site of Jesus Christ's tomb, her people had found three crosses. One of them was supposed to be the cross that Jesus was crucified on, while the others held thieves.

According to the stories, Helena had taken a diseased woman from Jerusalem to touch the crosses. Upon touching the third cross, the woman had recovered from her ailment. The Church of the Holy Sepulchre was built on that site, and more churches on holy sites followed thereafter.

Legend had it that she'd discovered the nails from the cross as well. Back home, she had tasked a blacksmith to put one in Constantine's helmet, and another in his horse's bridle.

"How did Helena persuade the Brotherhood to give up the scroll?" Lourds asked.

"Her presence there alone told them that the scroll was no longer safe. In those days, the Brotherhood was trained only in the ways of peace. If they had tried to defend the scroll, they would have died."

Lourds glanced at Joachim's callused hands. "Now the Brotherhood is different?"

Sadness flickered across the other man's face. "Over the years, the Brotherhood has become forced to become more than it was ever intended to be. We hang on to our peaceful nature, but we're unafraid of violence."

"So you're killers?" Cleena asked. "That doesn't make you sound much better than Qayin and his people."

"No!" Joachim slapped the tabletop with his open palm hard enough to jar their drinks. "We do not kill. The Brotherhood has never taken a human life."

Lourds noticed the modifier but decided not to ask.

"If you don't kill," Cleena pointed out, "it's going to be hard to put up a fight."

Joachim looked at her. "An incapacitated foe can't fight any better than a dead one. We have trained ourselves to incapacitate those that threaten the scroll. We don't have to kill to achieve our goals."

"Altruism aside," Cleena said, "not killing the people that are after us is going to put you at a decided disadvantage."

"Don't you mean 'put us'?" Olympia asked.

"No, I don't." Cleena's voice was perfectly neutral, but the threat was naked in her words.

Lourds sought safer conversational ground. "Helena convinced the Brotherhood to move the scroll."

"It looked like a win–win situation for the Brotherhood and Constantinople," Olympia stated. "At the time of the scroll's arrival, along with the Brotherhood, Constantinople was building the Megale Ekklesia."

"What's that?" Cleena asked.

"The literal translation is 'Great Church,' " Lourds answered. "Constantinople started building it during the fourth century. He didn't live long enough to see it completed."

"But he did live long enough to hide the scroll," Joachim said.

"In the church?" Distress filled Lourds. "The original church was destroyed a little over forty years later."

"Forty-four years. The church was built in A.D. 360 and destroyed in A.D. 404."

Lourds waved a hand in acknowledgment. If he had known where he was supposed to be looking, he would have known the dates, too. Scholars didn't have to know everything. All they had to know was where to find everything.

"John Chrysostom was appointed archbishop of the Church of the Holy Wisdom, as the Great Church was named in those days by Constantinople—"

"In A.D. 398," Joachim interrupted.

Lourds sipped his beer. "I suppose there's a lot of rote work in the Brotherhood."

Joachim smiled.

"While holding his office," Lourds went on, "John Chrysostom ran afoul of Theophilus, who was Patriarch of Alexandria at the time, and Emperor Arcadius's wife—"

"Aelia Eudoxia," Joachim supplied.

"Thank you. With the Patriarch, John Chrysostom refused to bow down, and with the Empress, John Chrysostom took to task women that chose to flaunt their wealth in clothing. The patriarch and the empress arranged the Synod of the Oak in A.D. 403 and banished John Chrysostom. The people became enraged and demanded that he be returned to his position."

"There was more to it than that," Joachim said. "On the very night that John Chrysostom was arrested, an earthquake happened. Many, including the empress, believed it was a sign from God."

Lourds thought he remembered something like that, but wasn't certain. "During that confrontation, the first Church of the Holy Wisdom was destroyed." He studied Joachim. "How are you sure that the Scroll of Joy wasn't incinerated in the fire that claimed the church?"

"Because the Scroll of Joy was hidden in the maze of tunnels beneath the church."

"Beneath the church?" Lourds rubbed at the stubble that covered his jaw. "Not in the church?"

"Exactly."

"Then why haven't you found the Scroll of Joy before now? Your Brotherhood has had sixteen hundred years to accomplish that."

"Because for many years we weren't supposed to find it. King Constantinople and a few members of the Brotherhood knew the hiding place where the scroll was kept. Despite being in a land where everyone felt the scroll was protected, the king and the elder brothers knew that many enemies remained outside the city walls. The choice was made to keep the number of people who knew where the scroll was to a handful. Each generation in turn handed down the knowledge of the scroll to only a few people. That number was cut further after the Nika Riots."

"The War between the Blue and the Green," Lourds said.

"Yes."

"What is the War between the Blue and the Green?" Cleena asked.

"During this time, the early 530s, I believe," Lourds said.

"532," Joachim supplied, then smiled. "It is as you say. A *lot* of rote work."

"There were a lot of social associations called *demes.* They supported the different teams that competed in chariot racing and other contests."

"You mean like bookies?" Cleena asked.

"Nothing so small," Olympia said. "Think of the demes like long lines of political parties and street gangs. It wasn't just about the sporting events. They actively pursued social issues of the times and fought against those they didn't like. Battles often broke out in the streets between the different groups and the emperor's soldiers."

"To make matters worse," Lourds said, "many of those demes were patronized by Roman aristocrats. Several of them believed they deserved the throne more than Emperor Justinian I, who currently held the throne. There was a riot in 531 that resulted in murder. Members of the Blues and Greens were arrested and held accountable. Most of them were hanged. However, early in 532—" He looked at Joachim.

"On January tenth, to be exact," Joachim said.

"One of the Blues and one of the Greens managed to thwart their guards and flee into the crowd that had already formed to protest the hangings. Already stretched thin between internal strife and negotiations with Persia, Justinian elected to negate the death sentences and give the men life in prison."

"I assume they didn't take it," Cleena said.

"No," Lourds agreed. "The chariot races took place at the Hippodrome next to the palace and the Church of the Holy Wisdom. During the course of the day, violence broke out and swelled into a riot that lasted five days and left the second church burned to the ground."

"And still the Scroll of Joy remained hidden," Joachim said.

"Hidden or lost?" Lourds countered.

"Hidden only. But, as I said, the Brotherhood decided to limit the number of people who knew the Scroll of Joy's hiding place."

"Why?"

"Because the city seemed to be in chaos. There were enemies outside the gates and unrest throughout the streets. It was feared that if anyone

knew the power of the scroll and its whereabouts, there would be no stopping those who came after it. The Elders locked themselves away in the underground tunnels. Those that were chosen never again saw the light of day."

"That's insane," Cleena whispered.

Lourds didn't disagree, but he knew that the practice wasn't unique.

"Ultimately that proved their undoing, didn't it?" Lourds asked. "Too few people with the knowledge, and all of them grouped in one place."

"They did the best that they were able," Joachim said. "They thought what they were doing was the best and safest thing to do."

"The Brotherhood just hadn't counted on the Fourth Crusade," Lourds said.

"Maybe I'm misunderstanding here," Cleena said, "but weren't the Crusades fought between the Muslims and the Christians?"

"Yes," Lourds said, "and no. At the outset, the Fourth Crusade was supposed to be an invasion of Muslim Jerusalem by way of Egypt. Instead, The Roman Catholic Church chose to invade and sack Constantinople. The siege and battles lasted five years. At the end of that time, much of Constantinople lay in ruins. Thousands of citizens were dead in the street or displaced from their homes. Everything of value that the crusaders could find was taken."

"But they didn't get the scroll," Joachim said quietly.

Lourds look at the man. "You're sure about that?"

"The world still stands and spins in her orbit, Professor Lourds. That's how I know. Once that scroll reaches the wrong hands, all we know will be lost. I promise you that."

"What happened to the elder brothers?"

"They stayed in the tunnels below the church. Their guards were slain, but they managed to lock themselves into a small sanctuary. The elder brothers starved or thirsted to death before anyone could reach them. Much treasure was found, or I should say lost, in those tunnels where the king's soldiers tried to hide it, but the Scroll of Joy remains."

For a moment, Lourds thought about everything Joachim had revealed. Then he tapped the book in front of him with a forefinger.

"Where'd you get this?" he asked.

"Most of the documents in that book were written after the Elders

were known to be dead. Some of the papers were copied from notes they had managed to write and leave in a crack in the ceiling of the room where they died."

Images of the abandoned monks filled Lourds's mind. What must it have been like to be closed up in a tomb while thirsting and starving to death?

And all you had to do to be free was share one secret.

Lourds didn't think he could have done it. Then again, he didn't think he would be able to steal the book from Qayin and his followers either.

Yet he had.

"I've been patient so far, Professor Lourds, out of respect for what you have done and gone through, as well as for my sister because she believes in you," Joachim said.

"I told you if anyone can do this, Thomas would be the one," Olympia said in Turkish.

"English," Cleena stated. "Speak English for the slow kids."

Olympia repeated her comment in English, which only drew a snort from Cleena.

"I need you to prove to me that you can help us." Joachim's dark gaze held Lourds. "Can you do that?"

Lourds nodded. "I can, but first I need you to do one more thing for me."

Joachim leaned back in his chair and folded his arms across his chest, obviously displeased.

Ignoring the man, Lourds opened the book to the page with the rubbing. He indicated the image.

"This. I need to know where you got this."

Joachim shook his head. "There's nothing there."

"*You've* found nothing there." Lourds leaned back in his own chair. "I will."

"What makes you so sure?"

"This rubbing was taken from a stone in the room where the older monks gave their lives to protect the secret of the Scroll of Joy."

Olympia turned to her brother. "Is that true?"

Holding his gaze steadily on Lourds, Joachim didn't answer.

"Joachim?"

Finally, Joachim nodded. "That was where it was found. But you could only be guessing that."

Lourds turned back a few pages and tapped again. "This is one of the pages that were also found in that room. Or am I still just guessing?"

Joachim stared at the page, then back at Lourds. "How do you know this?"

"Because I can read this page now." Lourds couldn't help smiling at his obvious success, especially when Joachim's eyes widened still further. "Would you like to know what it says?"

CHAPTER

18

CENTRAL BUSINESS DISTRICT
KING ABDULLAH ECONOMIC CITY, SAUDI ARABIA
MARCH 19, 2010

The hotel suite was nothing more than an overly comfortable prison cell. Webster knew that and barely tolerated the situation. He wanted to leave the room just to prove that he could. And maybe, he wanted to push Prince Khalid to see how far the young man would go.

Although there were no armed guards outside Webster's door, they were posted at all the entrances to the building. He didn't doubt that the room was bugged as well. If he had been in charge as Prince Khalid was, he would've had the room wired for sound and video.

But that was why he was using one of the CIA's white noise generators to cover his phone call.

For the last few hours, he had plied himself with liquor to take the edge off, and consoled himself with Vicky DeAngelo's carnal attentions. For an older woman, she was a demanding and generous lover. Webster had been surprised, but his mind had focused on the promise brewing in Saudi Arabia and the threat building in Istanbul.

In the end, though, Vicky proved to be as much like

him as he had believed. Once the fighting had broken out in the streets, she had deserted his bed and returned to her room and her computer to take control of the reporters still loyal to her within the country. News streamed from those reporters on the ground, but Prince Khalid's soldiers worked hurriedly to find them and shut them down. Some of them had already been killed, but Prince Khalid hadn't approached Vicky about the matter.

Webster stood to one side of the polarized balcony window and let the loose folds of the drapes conceal him. Beyond the glass, under the night sky, the city spread in neat squares, some of them lighted and some of them not. Power hadn't been connected to all of the new areas.

Webster kept the lights out behind him and was more comfortable in the darkness. He held the sat phone close to his ear as he spoke. Out in the streets, armed forces patrolled in heavy numbers. Tanks as well as soldiers moved constantly.

On the other side of the room, the muted television continued rolling smuggled footage from Saudi Arabia on WNN News. FOX, CNN, and MSNBC also carried much of the same footage. A lot of it came from Vicky's people.

Prince Khalid had made good on his promise to remove the enemies of his country. Within minutes after speaking to Webster, special teams had hit the streets and begun sweeping Shia, suspected Shia, and Shia sympathizers from the cities. That also meant routing many American and European businessmen. It also meant that anyone who had a taint of Shia about them got the boot.

A religious purge had started and the repercussions were only now building strength. Webster felt the power of it around him, like roaring dark tide. It wouldn't be calmed and he looked forward to watching it feed.

Many of those persecuted people fought, not wanting to relinquish their businesses or their wealth. Several of those people, in fact—Webster suspected—most of those people, were killed outright. Others received rough handling or worse as they were loaded on to trucks and taken to train stations where they were herded like cattle onto boxcars. From there they were taken to India and Pakistan to be deported.

Already having dealt with problems of displaced people before, neither

India nor Pakistan welcomed the Shia refugees. Those displaced would create a huge drain on the economies of both countries, as well as tying up manpower to keep the inevitable refugee camps manageable.

Webster knew that Prince Khalid counted on both of those facts. The drain on finances and workload of the military would leave the borders of both those countries weak. If the arrivals hadn't been Shia, or presumably Shia, neither Pakistan nor India would have tolerated the forced expulsion flooding into their countries.

And the refugees would continue to come like locust plagues. Those countries would be torn apart by Shia within their own borders who wanted to protect the new arrivals, as well as Sunni predators that would see the refugee camps as easy targets to hunt their enemies. Some attacks there had already started.

"If you're looking at the same thing I am," President Michael Waggoner growled, "then I think we're looking at the seeds of a Middle Eastern war the like of which we've never seen."

Although most people wouldn't have recognized the tension in the president's voice, Webster had known the man for years. Waggoner was as close to losing his cool as Webster had ever seen.

"I'm looking at it," Webster said. "On the television and in the streets here."

Waggoner cursed, another thing he rarely did. "I hadn't forgotten you were there in the middle of it, Elliott. Sending you there might not have been the best idea after all. I'm worried about you, too."

"I know, Mike. It's a tough time for all of us."

"Are you all right? If you think you or your people are in danger, just say the word. I've got a marine special OPS HRT waiting on board an aircraft carrier nearby. The colonel says he and his teams can be there in twenty minutes or less to get you out."

"There's no need to do that yet," Webster said. "We're safe enough here at the moment. If we do pull out, it could be taken as a sign of weakness. We don't want that hanging over us."

"I know. I keep telling myself that." The president sighed tiredly. "I just don't know how this situation went south so quickly."

"Our presence here didn't have anything to do with that," Webster lied. "Prince Khalid already had an agenda. This whole time, the Middle East was only two heartbeats away from this kind of madness. Those two heartbeats have been silenced."

"Does Khalid really think he can get away with this without any repercussions?"

"Prince Khalid's in a powerful position. He's not addicted to wealth and power, like his father and brother. He's looking to avenge his father and his brother who were lost. He doesn't care about repercussions. He wants to prove his manhood to the world. And he doesn't think anyone can stop him. More than that, no one will stop him. Not everyone, perhaps no one, can afford to stop buying the oil Saudi Arabia has to sell."

"He's insane is what he is."

"Crazy like a fox, maybe."

Below in the street, a few quick flurries of flashing lights drew Webster's attention. He recognized the muzzle flashes at once and knew then that another battle or massacre had begun.

"I thought you had a handle on this guy," Waggoner said.

"With his father in place, I did. I'd hoped some of that goodwill might rub off on the son eventually. But he's young and convinced of his own rightness in the world. We can both remember being that young, Mike."

"I know."

"His brother was much more manageable."

"Just our luck that we end up with the wrong son in power."

It wasn't luck, Webster thought. *Everything is going according to plan.*

At least, everything was going almost according to plan. The situation in Istanbul was more than a little troublesome. Webster had expected Eckert to report success there. They hadn't, and things were still loose regarding the whereabouts of the scroll. That was troubling, but Webster had full confidence that the scroll would soon be his.

On the television, Saudi Arabian tanks rolled through the streets and scattered pedestrians in all directions. A man darted out in front of a tank. He held a Molotov cocktail in one hand. Hardly pausing, he lobbed the bottle and it shattered against the tank's armored skirt.

Flames licked over the metal and drove the commanding officer back inside. Then a machine gun opened up on deck and .50-caliber rounds hammered the man to the ground. Before the body stopped twitching, the tank ran him down. When the tank passed, nothing recognizable as human remained.

"I'm getting a lot of pressure here at home," Waggoner said. "A lot of American corporations are concerned about having their assets nationalized over there. They're thinking that the Saudis are going to be drilling wells with their equipment, then selling the oil to China or India. Needless to say, that doesn't make anyone here happy."

"That's going to happen," Webster said. "There's nothing we can do about it if Khalid wants to do that. Unless they're willing to pay the oil prices here, which I'm betting will be raised in the near future."

"They're going to be less enthusiastic about paying inflated oil prices there when it's been pumped through equipment they financed or built and claims they've located."

"I've been thinking about that. Maybe it's time to let Prince Khalid know that we can play hardball, too."

"What are you talking about?"

"As you pointed out, we've got a marine expeditionary force and the U.S. Navy not far from here. It could be time for us to flex a little muscle."

Waggoner was silent for a short time. "I'm not entirely satisfied that we're there yet."

"I understand, but the longer we wait, the harder this is going to be to get control of."

"I know, I know." Waggoner sucked in a deep breath and expelled it. "Do we know if a Shia assassination team is even behind the attack?"

"No. The prince insists that it was a Shia cell."

"No one had eyes on those people?"

"No. Prince Khalid has found a trail that leads back to Shia extremists."

"Are they extremists?"

Webster approached the desk where his laptop lay open. "According to the CIA, they are." He glanced at the faces displayed on the screen.

Eckart and his men had found the "Shia terrorists" nearly a month ago. They had actually been Shia businessmen operating in Economic City. During their surveillance, Eckart had sent pictures on to Webster, who in turn had paid a computer cracker to insert the images and files at Langley.

Overnight, they had become terrorists, but that hadn't been revealed until the night they had "killed" the Saudi king and his firstborn son.

"We knew about these people?" Waggoner demanded.

"We did, Mike, but we didn't know they were going to do this."

"Or do it so well."

"No, we didn't." Webster sipped his whiskey. It was bourbon mash from Tennessee and he took it straight. The fiery liquid burned the back of his throat.

"If we could find these guys, prove it was them, do you think the prince would be satisfied with his pound of flesh?"

Webster watched the fighting scroll across the television. More news, much of it directly linked to the violence in Saudi Arabia, scrolled across the bottom in ticker tape fashion.

The death toll mounted almost every minute.

Back on one of the new stations, a reporter at ground zero for an armed conflict was shot down. The cameraman got it all, then took off running for cover. Judging from the tumultuous way the camera flipped through the air and landed so suddenly, Webster didn't think the cameraman made it.

"It's not just about Prince Khalid and his father," Webster said. "Not anymore. Even if we could calm down the prince, do you think the Shia would back down at this point?"

"No. But maybe we could open up peace talks."

"Because those have worked so well the past." Webster let the sarcasm sound in his voice.

"We've got to do something. If the situation in the Middle East gets torn completely to shreds, the United States might not be able to withstand the economic repercussions."

"I know. You're forgetting who wrote most of the Middle East diplomacy scenarios we've been working with while you've been in office."

"I hadn't forgotten, Elliott. I just hoped it would never come to this."

An excited smile spread across Webster's face. He felt it stretch his lips. He hadn't thought things were going to be so easy, or that President Waggoner would ever concede to the desperate measures they had concocted.

"We're not ready—our country isn't ready—to give up our dependency on oil," Webster said calmly. "Steven Napier is close to a solution. But even when he has an alternate fuel source that works as well as we need it to, converting the United States over to that alternate fuel source is going to take time. We need time. That time was one thing you and I both agreed on."

"I know. I do know. And I still agree. I just don't like where this leaves us."

"We didn't leave us here, Mike. We didn't leave the American people without recourse. Khalid did. If you'll keep that in mind, that will turn everything around for you."

"Not entirely, Elliott. If we do this, a lot of lives are going to be affected."

"If we do nothing, a lot of lives are going to be affected. There's no getting around that."

Waggoner didn't speak.

"The American people—our people—are depending on us to do the right thing," Webster said. "And the right thing isn't letting Prince Khalid hang us out to dry or start a religious war that may leave the whole Middle East disrupted for years, if not generations."

Waggoner didn't say anything at the other end of the connection.

"Let them fight over whatever they want to out here," Webster said. "They've been doing that ever since the first one of them picked up a rock. No matter how much we try to civilize these people, they're never going to tolerate someone who isn't them."

"If we do this, if we—God help me—invade that country—"

"Not invade, Mike. We're only going to make sure the whole world isn't disrupted. Someone has to. Otherwise, we won't have heat in the winter. Our elderly and our children will freeze. Our industries will lapse into recession. And these people won't care. They don't have to because we've always handled them with kid gloves." Webster set his empty glass down on the windowsill. "The world is always divided into *us* and *them.* Only civilization allows for one *us.* If these people can't be civilized, then they have set themselves up against us."

"This is still a big step." Hesitancy vibrated in Waggoner's voice.

"Genocide isn't an acceptable retribution," Webster said. "And that's what Prince Khalid intends. That's what all of these countries intend over here. Retribution. Destruction. Winner take all."

"We can't live like that."

"No, Mike, we can't. Our people can't live like that. Do you want your children growing up in a country without hope, without a future?"

"Of course not. I just keep hoping there is some other way."

"If there was another way, I'd let you know. You know that, don't you?"

"Yes."

"Do you trust me?"

"I always have, haven't I?"

"Then trust me now."

Gazing into the window, Webster saw his reflection highlighted by fires burning aboard luxury vessels moored in the marinas. Webster didn't know if the fires had been started by Shia resistance or by Sunni military units seeking to do as much damage to Shia property as possible.

In the end, it didn't really matter. The flames just needed to be fanned.

Webster licked his middle finger and thumb and smoothed his eyebrows into place. "Mike? Are you still there?"

"Yes."

"Then let's get this done. Let's set the hounds loose and let them hunt. We don't have to get our hands dirty, and we'll come out of this looking like heroes."

Around the world, the President of the United States took a deep breath and let it out. Webster listened to the sound and knew he had the man right where he wanted him.

In fact, nearly everything was right where he wanted it.

"All right," Waggoner said. "Make your calls."

"I will." Webster smiled at his reflection. "Everything will turn out okay, Mike. I'll make a believer of you yet."

"Call me as soon as you know something," Waggoner told him.

"All right, but this will take some time. Keep your chin up. We're going to win this one." Webster broke the connection then started calling numbers he knew by heart.

CATACOMBS
HAGIA SOPHIA UNDERGROUND
ISTANBUL, TURKEY
MARCH 19, 2010

The tunnel was only wide enough for them to walk comfortably in single file. Lourds's head kept knocking against the low stone ceiling. Only the sound of shoes scuffing the stones beneath their feet and their breathing echoed within the tunnel.

All else was silent as a crypt—a crypt like the room where the elder monks of the Brotherhood of the Scroll had willingly paid the final price to protect John of Patmos's secret.

Sometimes, my friend, you are far too imaginative for this profession, Lourds told himself.

Imagination was a necessary component of his work, though. Translating and deciphering ancient and dead languages required someone who could navigate between creative thinking and logic, between fantasy and fact. Either one of those two disciplines could bring him to a manuscript and begin a basic understanding, but it wasn't until he was able to combine both that he was at his best.

He flicked his flashlight beam around the tunnel. Shadows shifted like oily ghosts, plunging into the voids left by the lights. The halogen beam easily cut through the darkness and revealed the rough walls. Pickax scars showed in the strata, softened over the years by the passage of bodies.

He wondered what stories those old scars could tell if they could only speak. The Hagia Sophia had enjoyed—or suffered, depending on one's point of view—a vigorous history. It had been built on the site of a former pagan temple, a common practice in those days. It had stood for forty-four years before getting burned to the ground by Empress Aelia Eudoxia.

The empress been at odds with John Chrysostom, the Patriarch of Constantinople at the time. Chrysostom had denounced extravagance regarding women's clothing choices, and the empress had taken the matter personally.

The second church had lasted one hundred twenty-eight years before getting burned down during the Nika Revolt. It had immediately been rebuilt.

But the tunnels beneath the structure had been maintained and grown more labyrinthine over the succeeding generations. Lourds would have loved to have time to thoroughly explore the tunnels. Even after all these years, there were treasures yet to find for someone who was looking.

"Are there tunnels underneath this whole city?" Cleena asked. She followed Lourds.

"Yes," he answered. "And cisterns."

"What's a cistern?"

"A cistern catches and holds rainwater, maybe groundwater if it's available," Lourds replied. "The word comes from Latin. *Cisterna,* and the root of that is *cista,* meaning 'box.' Of course, that came from the Greek language, as most Latin did. The original word was *kiste,* meaning 'basket.' "

"Container for water would have done nicely."

"You're welcome. If you get the chance, before you leave Istanbul, you should go see the Yerebatan Sarayi. It's also known as the Basilica Cistern and Yerebatan Sarnici."

"Not exactly here on a sightseeing tour," Olympia said from in front of Lourds.

"Of course," Lourds responded. They hadn't talked much the last hour as Joachim had led them through the underground network of tunnels.

The prolonged lack of conversation bothered Lourds more than walking around in the dark. Admittedly, tensions ran high. Although Lourds had proved himself, Joachim and the other monks weren't happy about revealing their secrets to an outsider. Part of it was a pride issue, but Lourds felt some of it was fear.

He couldn't bring himself to believe that the fate of the world could depend on a two-thousand-year-old scroll that might not be translatable.

Or are the final blitherings of a madman, he told himself.

Still, a part of him was—perhaps—a bit afraid. He had never been superstitious. Not exactly. However, he had seen things that had given him pause over the years. He had never expected lost Atlantis to be found again, and especially not to have walked through part of those fabled lands himself.

But he had.

"So tell me about the cistern," Cleena invited.

Ahead of Lourds, Olympia blew out an angry breath and cursed.

Lourds didn't mind.

"Today, the cistern is more commonly known as the Basilica Cistern, which was the name first given to it." He spoke quietly but his voice still echoed. "The Turks called it Yerebatan Sarayi, which means 'Sunken Palace,' and Yerebatan Sarnici, which means 'Sunken Cistern.' In fact, we shouldn't be far from it. The cistern was constructed near the Hagia Sophia."

"Since the Cistern's sunken, I suppose that means it's underground."

Lourds negotiated a particularly narrow passage and continued. "Exactly. And it ties back to the construction of the church. It was built underneath the Stoa Basilica, a public square everyone used. The emperor still allotted the water usage during times of drought, but people were free to come and go and use as much as they needed."

"I guess during times of drought though, the emperor wasn't so generous."

"No, he wasn't."

"Having the cistern so close to the castle meant the emperor's guards could easily defend it."

"Yes."

"Constantine sold the idea of the cistern to the people by saying it was for the common good, then took it back if he needed it. Close placement to the castle just made it easier."

"I suppose so," Lourds said. "But it also made the cistern more defensible when the city was under siege. I think that was the original concept. I don't know that Constantine ever kept citizens from the water, but the city was sacked and besieged on more than one occasion." He did, however, think the comment was indicative of her particular mind-set.

"How big is the cistern?"

"It's the largest in Istanbul. As I said, Constantine started the cistern, but Justinian I had it enlarged after the Nika Riots of A.D. 532. It's almost five hundred feet long, a little over two hundred feet wide, and thirty feet deep."

"Big swimming pool," Cleena commented.

"When it was full, the cistern held almost three million cubic feet of water. There are also over three hundred marble columns that support the cistern's ceiling. It looks like rows of picket fencing. Interestingly, there are two Medusa heads in the cistern."

"Medusa heads? As in the snake-haired woman whose glance turns people to stone?"

"Yes," Lourds allowed. "That Medusa."

"Sounds kind of strange for a Christian emperor to put in his cistern, don't you think?"

"There is some conjecture regarding the placement of the Medusa heads. One stands upside down, and the other lies on its side. Both support pillars. Some historians believe that Constantine simply availed himself of whatever materials there were to build the cistern. The heads were thought to have been salvaged from a Roman building."

Olympia stopped so suddenly that Lourds ran into her.

"If you'd been paying attention," Olympia said, "that wouldn't have happened."

"My humblest apologies." Lourds didn't put his heart into the effort. He knew she was primarily irritated by the attention he was paying to Cleena. "Why did we stop?"

"Because we're here." Joachim shone his flashlight over the wall to his right. Ahead of him, the passageway split into a *Y* and continued into double-barreled darkness.

Lourds played his light over both tunnels but saw no discernible difference between them. "Which way?"

"Here." Joachim leaned into the wall and pressed a series of stones.

Faint clicks barely reached Lourds's ears. He placed his hand against the wall and felt the vibrations as Joachim shoved back a section large enough for them to pass through.

"Come on." Joachim disappeared into the hole in the wall.

On the other side of the wall, Lourds pointed the flashlight ahead of him, then behind. There was only one way to go: forward. The tunnel dead-ended behind them. This tunnel was also narrower than the first tunnel. He had to turn sideways to go along now.

"This way was made for smaller men," Joachim said.

"Obviously." Lourds held his hat in one hand over his heart. His backpack slid along the rough stone, catching every now and again. Against his forearm, the stones were worn smooth. He couldn't help wondering how many people had traversed this tunnel since its construction. He also imagined the stories they would've had to tell.

"No one has been here in a long time," Joachim said. "I've been here only three times my whole life."

"Why?"

"Because this is a holy place, and because the scroll is not here."

Lourds knew the last was intended as a goad but he ignored it. He hadn't told any of them that the Scroll of Joy was within the room. He just hoped he was right concerning his other suspicion.

"Who knows about this place?"

The grade in the tunnel angled more downward. Lourds stepped carefully now as he descended. He thought he felt impressions that might once have been steps carved into the solid stone. The center of the passageway was bowed slightly, more worn in the middle.

"Everyone in the Brotherhood."

"Do they come here?"

"No one is allowed here. Until today, no woman has ever been in this passageway."

"Not even Olympia?"

"Not even my sister."

"Joachim was even better at keeping secrets than I expected," Olympia said. "I didn't know he was part of the Brotherhood until a couple months ago."

"How are the brothers chosen for the order?" Lourds asked.

"Usually it passes from father to son," Joachim answered. "Occasionally a nephew must be brought in, or an older monk may pass his knowledge on to a grandson."

"Your father?"

"Yes."

"Another big secret-keeper," Olympia said.

"Our father began telling me about the Brotherhood when I was just a child," Joachim said. "I loved the stories and the idea of being part of something so secret and so important. As I grew older, I also grew more serious about my responsibilities." He paused. "The hardest part was occasionally losing faith and thinking that the scroll I had sworn to protect was already gone."

"What if we find out it is?"

Joachim halted in front of a bare wall. His flashlight beam bounced off the stones and highlighted his features. He looked grim.

"As I told you before, Professor Lourds, as long as the world is safe, we are not too late. The Scroll of Joy still exists. It is out there and we have to find it."

Lourds shone his beam over the blank wall. He searched for signs of crevices or cracks, but there were none that he could see.

"Another door, I suppose?" he asked.

"Not exactly." Joachim knelt and pressed against certain stones set into the floor.

In the next moment, a section of the floor receded a few inches. Joachim hooked his fingers into the gap and pulled. Stone ground as the hidden door slid out of the way.

The glare of the gathered flashlights revealed stone steps that led downward. Joachim led the way.

CHAPTER

19

CRYPT OF THE ELDERS
HAGIA SOPHIA UNDERGROUND
İSTANBUL, TURKEY
MARCH 19, 2010

The stone steps had the same grooved wear as the passageway earlier. In this case, though, the steps were steeper and shorter. Lourds struggled to keep his balance as he went down. The staircase also corkscrewed and filled his head with thoughts of premature burial. He forced himself to focus on the curiosity and certainty that had brought him to this place.

"Is it getting hard to breathe?" Cleena asked.

"The air contains more moisture," Lourds told her. "Just take normal breaths and you'll be fine." But the confined space was getting to him as well.

Finally, they came to the end of the tortuous corkscrew staircase and stepped into a square room. The discomfort Lourds felt was extinguished as soon as he laid his eyes upon the library shelves that covered one wall. Dusty journals filled the shelves in neat rows.

Unbidden, drawn by his excitement, Lourds approached the shelves. He shone the flashlight along the spines and saw names and dates handsomely lettered there. They went back hundreds of years.

"Those are the journals of the Elders who occupied this room all their lives," Joachim said.

"How far back do they go?" Lourds asked hoarsely.

Joachim came to stand beside him. "To the beginning."

"Of the church?" If that was the case, the shelves contained at least sixteen hundred years of history.

"To the time of John on Patmos Island."

That knowledge halted Lourds for a moment as he realized how much information lay practically at his fingertips.

"May I?" He gestured to the shelves.

"Those books don't tell us anything of the whereabouts of the Scroll of Joy."

Without a word, Olympia stepped close and took down one of the books. She handled it gently, as if it might disintegrate.

"You had these down here all this time, Joachim?" Her voice was hushed and tight with awe. "Do you know what I would have given to have been able to study these? Do you know the information that is probably contained within these books?"

"The brothers only wrote benedictions to God," Joachim replied. "Father didn't ask me to be a librarian. He asked me to keep the Scroll of Joy safe. The monks didn't bother themselves with the secular world."

"That doesn't matter." Carefully, Olympia leafed through the book. "Any contact they had with the world outside of this place would have rubbed off on them. No matter what you think, there will be artifacts of everyday life reflected in passages in these books."

"That's why archaeologists are now studying the literature of the past." Lourds crossed over to stand behind Olympia. "Until the last few years, the study of novels and poetry and the like for historical detail hadn't been recognized as a hard science."

"Look at this, Thomas." Olympia kept turning pages and her fascination grew.

Lourds felt the same way, and his mind was totally captivated by the neat lines of script that crawled across the pages. The volume Olympia held was written in Ancient Greek and detailed a day trip around Patmos Island by a new monk.

"Can you imagine the wealth of knowledge contained within these pages?" Olympia asked in hushed tones.

"I can." Lourds glanced over his shoulder at Joachim. "Are there any journals here written by John of Patmos?"

"No." Joachim's voice was short. "Professor Lourds, I have to remind you, we came here to find the Scroll of Joy. We cannot afford to waste time. You already know others are searching for it as well."

Frustrated, Lourds swallowed his curiosity. "Perhaps there's something in these books that you have missed. If we could find the volumes that were written by the monks during the time of Constantine, maybe we could learn more about the scroll's location."

Joachim's eyes narrowed. "Only a short time ago, you told me you could find the scroll's hiding place by seeing the stone where the rubbing was taken. Was that the truth?"

Reluctantly, Lourds nodded.

"The stone is over here." Joachim directed his flashlight to a corner of the room.

Despite the bright halogen beam, Lourds had a hard time spotting the engraving that had been done on the stone. The work was skilled and delicate, something done by a true craftsman. If Joachim had not pointed out the stone, if the light had not fallen just so, he would never have noticed it.

The curiosity about his hypothesis grew strong enough to draw him from the library shelves, filled with the thoughts of the men who had followed John of Patmos's final instructions.

The fate of the world, Lourds reminded himself, steeling himself to walk away. In the end, he didn't think the situation would be anything so weighty, but the possibility of finding a document written by one of Christ's twelve Apostles was a magical elixir that made his blood sing. He crossed the room, took off his backpack and stored it next to the wall, then knelt in front of the stone.

He ran his fingers across the engraving. The depth was no more than a fraction of an inch, hardly noticeable. He reached into his backpack and took out a pad of paper and writing utensils.

A skilled stonecutter had built the wall. The stones were uneven sizes, but they'd been carefully mortared together. Lourds ran his hand along the wall and felt the smoothness, noting that the man must have polished the stone. No rough surfaces remained.

"A lot of time went into the construction of this place," Lourds commented.

"After the brothers took their vows to protect the Scroll of Joy, they didn't leave this place." Joachim knelt next to Lourds.

"That's a hefty price to pay."

"I know."

"Have you given any thought to what you're going to do if—*when*—we find the Scroll of Joy?"

"Protect it."

"Even if it means spending the rest of your life locked away from the world in a room like this?"

Joachim didn't hesitate. "Even if that were so."

Lourds fitted a blank piece of paper over the stone.

"What are you doing?" Joachim asked.

"Taking a rubbing." Lourds selected a piece of charcoal from his kit and began gently rubbing it over the paper. The engraving on the stone started coming to life immediately.

"Why?"

"To match it against the one in the book. Have you done that?"

Joachim was silent for a moment, then shook his head. "I haven't. We already have a copy of the rubbing and it told us nothing."

"Does Qayin know where this stone is?"

"No, he doesn't. And if he did, what would it matter?"

Lourds took his fresh rubbing and matched it against the one in the book he'd gotten from Qayin. "Can you hold the book for me?"

Joachim took the book.

"Hold the book so the page with the rubbing hangs down by itself," Lourds instructed. Joachim did so. By that time the others had all come around to watch what he was doing.

Lourds folded the new rubbing so that it fit over the one in the book. Then he held his flashlight behind the papers so that both were illuminated. When he had them lined up, they matched exactly.

He grinned. "Looks like the same stone to me."

"That wasn't necessary."

Lourds rummaged in his backpack for a digital camera. "Of course it was. Empirical evidence is always important. Especially when you're saving the world."

"You still don't believe."

"Have you stopped to think that maybe I'm able to read that language because I'm *not* a believer? I'm not looking for the same things you are. I don't have preconceived notions about what we're supposed to find and how we're supposed to find it. I've got a more open mind about what we're looking for."

Joachim didn't say anything.

"One thing I do believe is that I'm going to get you the answers that you haven't had in over eight hundred years. Now hold that flashlight on this stone for me."

"More empirical evidence?"

"No," Olympia said with a knowing grin. "Thomas likes his souvenirs."

Finished with the camera, Lourds replaced it in the backpack. "Now I'm going to need you to use some of that faith you so readily claim to have." He took a small pry bar from an outside pocket of the backpack.

"What are you going to do?" Joachim demanded.

Lourds pointed with the pry bar. "I'm going to take that stone out of the wall." Hardly had the words left his mouth than Joachim hit him in the face with a balled fist. Pain exploded in Lourds's face as he sailed backwards.

Deep in the passageway now, Colonel Anthony Eckart stood still and studied the terrain through the night vision goggles he wore. So far there was still no sign of Lourds or the others.

Eckart's gut clenched and ached in anticipation. He couldn't wait to meet the redheaded woman close up and personal. The men he had lost at the university were good men, in no way friends, but good soldiers were hard to come by.

"Mayfield, do you have a reading on our position?" Eckart asked.

"Affirmative, sir. I've rerouted the overland support teams to you. They're almost directly overhead."

"Near the church?"

"That's affirmative. I'm reading your position under the church now."

Eckart gazed at the blank walls. "What's under here?"

"Tunnels. Lots and lots of tunnels. From the maps I've been able to download from the geological survey services in the city, it looks like a regular rat's warren down there."

"It is. Do you have any idea where our target is headed?"

"Negative. Like I said, there are a lot of tunnels down there. On multiple levels as well. Some of them cross over or under without touching any other tunnels."

Eckart thought about that. Back in the early days of war, tunnels had been important defensive and offensive measures. Tunnels enabled large groups of warriors to either vanish or appear somewhere else on a battlefield. Sappers were specially trained troops that dug under castle walls and other fortifications to tunnel in or bring down the walls. Ammo and supply routes ran underground as well, as did retreats.

"It's got to be something to do with the church," Mayfield said. "That church has had treasures in the past. Maybe there's something like that hidden down there."

"All right," Eckart said, "the GPS reads us five by five?"

"Affirmative. And I'm keeping an eye on your back door."

Eckart waved his point man back into motion. The group moved out like a well-oiled machine.

Only a few minutes later, they came to a fork in the tunnel. Eckart waved one of his men forward. The man used a latent thermographic scanner to pick up the heat signature left by the man they followed. The body temperature of the group had soaked into the rock enough to leave a ghost trail that was just strong enough. If they got too far behind them, and the trail was allowed to cool, they would lose them.

A short distance farther on, they came to another fork. This time the scanner didn't pick up the trail.

"What's wrong?" Eckart asked as the soldier turned around and checked the readings again.

"I'm not getting the readings anymore, sir."

"You said we were practically on top of them."

"Yes, sir. We were. Actually, we still are." The soldier looked at the wall next to them. "The readings show that they walked right into this wall."

"Or through it." Eckart pushed on the wall, but it felt solid. "Mayfield."

"Yes, sir."

"Do you still have our position?"

"Affirmative."

"Do you see a tunnel along the north wall?"

Only the popping crackle of the stressed signal sounded for a moment. "No, sir. According to the maps I'm looking at, nothing is there."

"Well, the maps are evidently wrong because these people didn't just vanish into thin air." Eckart shone his light on the floor.

There were no scrapes or scuff marks on the floor, nothing to indicate the presence of a door that opened outward.

If not outward, then inward, he reasoned. He reached into his chest pack med kit and took out a pair of aspirin. He crushed the tablets between his fingers and dropped the fine white powder into his other palm. Lying on the floor, he dusted the area in front of the wall, then gently blew the powder toward it.

Some of the white powder slid gracefully through a carefully mortised crack that hadn't been visible to his naked eye. In bright sunlight he might have seen it, but not in the eternal darkness of the passageway. He studied the wall again. There was nothing there to indicate the presence of the hidden door.

He got to his feet and called for his demolitions expert. Maybe Eckart didn't know all the tricks or the secret word to get through the door, but there was always another way to make an entrance.

"Joachim! What are you doing?"

Stunned and hurting, Lourds watched Olympia grab hold of her brother's arm and haul him backward before he could strike again.

"I'm protecting this place," Joachim snarled, his angry features looming out of the darkness. "As I promised our father I would do."

"You can't just hit him like that!" Olympia protested.

Actually, Lourds thought that Joachim could hit him like that anytime he chose to. Lourds wasn't eager to repeat the encounter. He sat up gingerly and worked his jaw. He tasted blood.

"I guess you're not very big on the trust part," Lourds said.

Olympia wheeled on Lourds. "And you! What did you think you were doing telling him you were going to pry that stone out of the wall?"

"Well," Lourds replied, "with all of us crammed in here like sardines, it didn't seem very likely that I was going to be able to get the stone out of the wall without him seeing me do it. I thought it would be better to tell him what I was going to do."

"Why would you want to take the stone of the wall?"

"This can't be allowed," Joachim protested. "This is the crypt of the Elders. This is where those men gave their lives to protect the secret that John of Patmos entrusted to our order."

"To ensure the safety of the world," Lourds said in a bored tone. Joachim took a step toward him. Lourds took a step back and bounced off the wall behind him.

"Nonbeliever!" Joachim accused.

"You're the one with belief problems, not me. I believe the answer to the location of the Scroll of Joy is behind that rock."

Silence filled the chamber.

For the first time, Lourds noticed that Cleena had moved toward him. Her hand rested on her hip, but he knew it was only inches away from the pistol she carried.

"Joachim," one of the other monks said. "Perhaps we should listen to the professor. After all, he was able to decipher the text that we could not."

"It could all be a trick," Joachim said. "Don't you see? We don't know that anything he is telling us is true."

His pride stung, Lourds responded, "I read about the Scroll of Joy. I deciphered that language."

"Qayin knows about the Scroll of Joy as well. For all we know, Qayin told you about it when he had you captive."

"That didn't happen," Cleena said. "I was there with him every minute. Qayin didn't mention the Scroll of Joy."

"You were also his kidnapper," Joachim said angrily.

Cleena shrugged without concern. "I was just one of many that day. And, as I recall, you were awfully quick to reach us after Qayin had us."

"This room should remain undefiled," Joachim said. "Those Elders need to have their final resting places respected."

"Their final resting places?" Lourds repeated.

Joachim pointed to the floor. For the first time, Lourds noticed the nine rectangles made of different colored stone set into the floor.

"After their deaths," Joachim said, "when it was once more safe to return to this place, the Brotherhood returned and buried the Elders."

"In the floor?"

"Yes. Saints are buried in churches. This is hallowed ground."

"Where were the other monks buried?"

"In cemeteries. But these men were special. Their passing could not go unmarked."

Lourds blotted his bloody lips on a shirtsleeve. "I'm not going to defile this room. I'm going to simply remove that stone and look behind it. When I'm done, I'll put the stone back."

"You said nothing about removing the stone earlier."

Nodding, Lourds agreed. "I didn't. Because I figured you would have this kind of reaction." He touched his bruised face gingerly.

"Why do you think there's something behind that stone?" the other monk asked.

"According to all of you, the Elders were the only ones who knew where the Scroll of Joy was kept," Lourds said.

The monk nodded.

"During the sack of Constantinople in 1204, the monks knew they could be found out and their secret stolen," Lourds said. "They were aware no one else knew where the Scroll of Joy was. So they had to leave behind a message. In this room."

"The stone," Olympia said.

"Exactly." Lourds wiped more blood from his mouth. "One of the monks inscribed that stone with the message you couldn't read while they were in here slowly dying."

"Your translation was, 'A stranger shall be required to read the message we have left behind,' " Olympia said.

"That's right. Now what do you make of that?" Lourds stared at them.

"It doesn't make any sense, just as I told you," Joachim said.

"That's because you don't have any faith," Lourds replied. He hurried on before Joachim could choose to take umbrage with his accusation. "Why a stranger? Why someone outside the Brotherhood? Why did they write the message in a language they created instead of one that would be easily understood?"

"The last thing we seem to need is a lot more questions," Cleena said.

Despite the pain in his mouth, Lourds couldn't help grinning. "It's a logic problem. Not a faith problem. This place is hidden." He waved his arms to take in the room. "Strangers don't come here. Strangers aren't allowed." He paused. "So why bring a stranger here?"

"To see something someone familiar with the place wouldn't see," Olympia said.

"Close," Lourds told her. "But you're already off on a tangent."

"Make sense," Joachim ordered impatiently.

"Sure, but it seems as plain as the nose on your face." Lourds looked at them. "What do you have to fear from strangers?"

No one answered.

"That a stranger won't revere those things that you hold precious." Lourds pointed at the wall. "Like that stone. You see a precious relic that ties to a very sad, very terrible story. Maybe even to the nine men that gave their lives to protect it. But do you know what I see?"

Only silence greeted his question.

"What I see," Lourds said in one of his more dramatic voices, "is merely the *first* message. Or maybe the second. It depends on whether you believe the artificial language was the first or second message the Elders left."

"You're saying that you believe the Elders took that stone from the wall and put the Scroll of Joy behind it?" Cleena asked.

"No, I'm not."

Exasperation tightened Olympia's face. She wrapped her arms around herself and stared at him. "Thomas, I'm lost."

"Once more for the slow kids," Lourds said. He ticked off points on his fingers. "One, the Elders had to work with what was inside this room and needed something that would be left alone, but hopefully noticed. They had to leave a message indicating where the Scroll of Joy could be found. So they chose the stone. The message about the stranger was because none of you would dare desecrate this place."

"That makes sense," the other monk said.

"Two, the artificial language probably ties into the Scroll of Joy. Maybe the whole thing is written in an artificial language that John of Patmos created or caused to be created. Possibly, the writing on that stone is a Rosetta of some sort. A key to help with the translation."

"It's a stretch," Olympia said.

"Remember, they were desperate, and they could only work with what they had in this room. They left two clues wrapped in one, and both of those were to lead to the third."

"Thomas is right, Joachim," Olympia said quietly. "None of you would have touched that stone. Without him, or someone else, that stone would never be removed."

"Why wouldn't they use another stone?" Joachim asked. "What makes you so sure that your foolishness won't have us dismantling this whole room?"

"Because they wouldn't have wanted to dismantle this room either," Lourds answered. "And they didn't want to have the clue too far removed from the Brotherhood. I'm sure they didn't intend for the Scroll of Joy to be lost for so long."

Joachim gazed at the stone and the wall and tapped the pry bar against his thigh. Finally, he handed the tool over to Lourds.

"When this is over, after you have discovered the error you have made, you will put the stone back."

Lourds met the other man's gaze full measure. "When this is over, and you discover I am right, I will put stone back and it will be as good as new."

Joachim stepped across the room and jammed his hands into his pants pockets. He looked like the next man in line to visit the headsman's axe.

Showing as much confidence as he dared, Lourds focused on the stone in the wall. He knelt and set the edge of the pry bar against the mortar.

Cleena watched with growing interest as Lourds managed to break up the mortar around the inscribed stone. Piles of chips gathered steadily on the floor in front of the professor.

"Can you talk?" Sevki whispered in her ear.

Masking her mouth with her hand, Cleena whispered, "No."

"I've been picking up the conversation through your earwig. I wish I had a video link to you. This is really cool stuff."

If you like old things and dark places, Cleena mused. She was barely keeping the claustrophobic feeling at bay. Every nerve in her body screamed at her to get out of the room.

"Did you know about any of this?" Sevki asked.

"No."

One of the nearby monks must have heard her talking, because the man turned to look at her. Cleena coughed delicately and patted her chest.

"Dust," she said.

The monk nodded and turned away.

"Ooops," Sevki said. "Sorry. I got carried away."

Most of the mortar lay on the floor at Lourds's feet. A pool of light from the flashlight collective played over the action. Lourds paused and reached into the gaps he'd created to seize the stone.

"I don't hear the hammer anymore," Sevki said. "Is the scroll there?"

Cleena ignored him, but she felt the same mixture of excitement and curiosity that coursed through Sevki. For the moment it gave her an edge over being in the enclosed space.

Lourds strained to free the stone but it didn't budge. He returned to work with the pry bar for a few minutes. The only sound that could be heard in the room was the sound of the pry bar meeting stone and Lourds's heavy breathing. Everyone else seemed to be holding theirs. The professor put the pry bar against the stone above the inscribed stone and used leverage.

The resulting crack sounded like a pistol shot inside the room.

"You know," Sevki said, "this is the part in a horror movie where the dead would rise up to defend their treasure."

Cleena glanced at the nine graves set under the room's floor. Nothing moved there. *Thanks for that thought, Sevki. As if being chased by flesh and blood killers isn't threat enough.*

Lourds put the pry bar aside, raised one knee to brace against the wall, and grabbed the stone with both hands.

"Did you get it?" Olympia asked.

"I think so. I wasn't able to reach all the mortar at the back. The stone is longer than I'd thought." The muscles in Lourds's forearms corded with effort.

Then, rasping, the stone came away from the wall. No one spoke. Carefully, Lourds laid the stone aside and peered into the dark cavity. "I need a flashlight, please."

Olympia handed him hers.

On his stomach, Lourds trained the flashlight beam into the hole in the wall.

"What are you doing?" Joachim asked.

"Making sure the Elders didn't leave any nasty surprises behind." Lourds moved the beam from side to side, up and down.

"They wouldn't do that."

"Perhaps not, but if someone beat us to the scroll, they might have. It's better to be safe than sorry." Satisfied, he reached into the hole, but Cleena still saw the tension and wariness tightening his body. His arm sank into the wall much deeper than the area filled by the stone.

"Did he find it?" Sevki asked.

Cleena watched Lourds, but she didn't respond.

"I guess maybe there would be a cheer or something," Sevki said. The disappointment weighed his words down.

Then, inexorably, Lourds withdrew his arm from the hole. His hand held a leather tube with a dull gray glob at one end.

Joachim stepped forward immediately. The suddenness of the man's movement made Cleena reach for the pistol at her back.

"Did Lourds find the scroll?" Sevki asked.

As Cleena's fingers closed around the pistol butt, Joachim extended his hand.

"May I?" Joachim asked.

Lourds hesitated.

"Of course." With obvious reluctance, Lourds placed the tube in Joachim's hand. "Please be careful with it."

Without a word, Joachim took a small pocketknife from his pocket and pushed the tip into the glob.

"Carefully," Lourds said. "We don't know how it's packed. The scroll could actually be touching the wax seal."

Once Joachim had cut around the wax seal, he gently pried it from its moorings. Upending the tube, Joachim poured the contents into his palm.

A single roll of what looked like paper slid into his hand. He caught it, then tucked the tube into his back pocket.

Lourds moved closer and Cleena saw by his anxious behavior that it was everything he could do to keep his hands off the scroll. He took pictures of the scroll, and the sudden flashes from the digital camera made Cleena's eyes ache.

"Do you recognize the seal?" Lourds asked.

"Yes," Joachim whispered. "The impression is from one of the signet rings that belongs to the Brotherhood of the Scroll of John."

"Do you still have the ring?"

"Yes."

"And this is a match?"

Joachim nodded.

"What is the device?" Lourds asked. "Four Horsemen?"

"Yes. Signifying the end of the world."

The other members of the Brotherhood closed in and started whispering among themselves. Cleena got the impression that many of them were surprised that the scroll had actually been found, and that it was what they had expected it to be.

"Let me get a picture of the seal." Lourds gestured with his camera.

Joachim presented the scroll while the professor took pictures.

Then everyone took a collective deep breath.

Gently, Joachim slid a thumbnail under the curve of the paper and sliced through the red wax drop that closed the scroll. When he was finished, he unfurled the parchment. He stared at the writing for a long time.

Stepping closer, Cleena peered at the page as well. She didn't recognize the words, but it was handwritten in beautiful, flowing script. Nine names lined the bottom of the page.

"What does it say?" Olympia asked.

Reluctantly, Joachim shook his head. "I don't know. I can't read it." His shoulders sagged a little.

Lourds started to say something immediately, then caught himself and stopped. He licked his lips, eyes never leaving the scroll, and said, "May I?"

Joachim let out a frustrated breath. "Of course." He handed the scroll to Lourds.

Cleena moved closer to the professor, drawn by the inexorable mystery of the scroll. She wondered what everyone was going to do if Lourds said he couldn't read the document either.

Sevki's voice sounded tense when he spoke. "You've got problems."

"What problems?" Cleena asked.

"I don't think you're down there alone anymore."

STONE GOOSE APARTMENTS
ZEYTİNBURNU DİSTRİCT
İSTANBUL, TURKEY
MARCH 19, 2010

"What do you mean, we're not alone?"

Sevki's adrenaline spiked as he stared at the computer monitor before him. He had hacked into the security cameras around the Hagia Sophia once he had found out that was where Cleena and the others were headed. It was a reflex move on his part.

Hacking the camera system served two purposes. One, it would give him a visual presence over the area. Two, it was possible he might catch someone else hacking into the system. Either way would provide an early warning system.

On the screen, three sport-utility vehicles sat along the main road. Though the cameras weren't of top-shelf quality, they were good enough for him to see the man's movements. Those movements were deliberate, and the man walked a grid, returning over the same area again and again.

It was obviously something they had been trained for.

"I think the guys you ran into at the university are back," Sevki told her.

"Where are they?"

"On the grounds around the church."

"Then they're not down here," Cleena said.

Sevki watched as light flickered from a device one of the men held.

"I wouldn't want to bet on that," he replied. "They're carrying devices around and walking a set pattern. It appears to mean that they're tracking something."

"Us?"

"Or another team that's gone underground." Sevki watched the figures for a moment and the sense of unease within him grew. "You've got the scroll. If you ask me, it's time for you guys to get out of there."

Before Cleena could answer, the sound of a deep, powerful explosion rocketed along the earwig transmission frequency.

CHAPTER

20

CRYPT OF THE ELDERS
HAGİA SOPHİA UNDERGROUND
İSTANBUL, TURKEY
MARCH 19, 2010

Lourds stared at the open scroll in his hands. The handwriting looked familiar, and he felt certain that it had belonged to one of the scribes that had written in the book Qayin had shown him. When working with written documents rather than inscribed, the writer's handiwork often showed itself in stylization, size, and placement on documents.

Knowing that the writer might be the same was worth something. It helped place the timeline of the document. But the bottom line was that Lourds couldn't read it. Some of the words looked familiar, but the context was wrong and he couldn't make sense of too many of the words on the vellum.

Resigning himself to defeat, Lourds looked up at the anxious faces surrounding him. Before he could say anything, Cleena freed her pistol and the monks nearest her stepped back and spread out.

Then a deafening blast crashed through the room. Immediately, a fusillade of broken rock tumbled down the corkscrew stairway, followed by a dust cloud that pooled into the room.

With the *booooom* of the explosives echoing around him, Eckart took a fresh grip on his pistol and the small flashlight he held. Dust coated his tongue and caked his nostrils. His breath seized at the back of his throat.

When he played his flashlight over the wall, he saw the charges had destroyed the secret door and fractured the walls on either side. Farther down the exposed passage, a jumble of rock half closed the hidden entrance.

Eckart peered over his gun sight but saw nothing moving. He waved to his point man and indicated the doorway. At once, the man crouched and followed the steps down. Eckart trailed behind him with his pistol gripped in both hands. The other men fell in behind him.

Only a few steps later, the debris rose enough to close the stairway. Broken rock had tumbled down and gotten caught to form a dam against forward progress.

Eckart cursed the bad luck, then holstered his weapon and snugged his gloves. "Form a line. We've got to clear debris."

The point man slung his weapon over his shoulder and reached for the first rock. He swung around and handed the rock to Eckart, who swung around and handed it to the next man in line. By the time he turned back, the point man had another rock ready. He listened for noise on the other side of the barrier and wondered if his quarry had gotten away again, or if the blast had killed them.

When the force of the blast filled the room, Lourds grabbed Olympia and pulled her down with him into a protective embrace. She clung to him as rocks ricocheted from walls. Several of them slammed against Lourds's back and shoulders and stung sharply.

Choking on the dust, Lourds looked up. Grit stung his eyes and brought tears. For a moment, he sat frozen and wondered what he was supposed to do. He thought about how the Elders had perished in that room all those years ago. Primitive fear screamed through his brain at the thought of being buried alive. He had to force himself to be calm. Even with his arms wrapped around Olympia, he hadn't dropped the scroll.

"Is everyone all right?" Joachim asked. Blood leaked from a shallow wound by his left eye.

The other monks answered affirmatively. Behind them, Cleena shoved herself to her feet. She still held the pistol in one hand.

A few loose rocks bounded down the staircase and bounced into the room. Scrabbling noises followed.

"They're still up there," Lourds said. More rocks tumbled into the room.

"They'll dig down to us as soon as they can." Joachim turned to Lourds and held out a hand. "The scroll, please, Professor."

Reluctantly, Lourds passed the scroll over to Joachim. The monk dropped the scroll into the leather tube and blocked it once more with the wax seal.

"Quickly. We haven't much time." Joachim crossed the floor to the gravesite in the corner opposite the one that had held the scroll. "Professor, your pry bar, if you don't mind."

Lourds picked the pry bar from the floor and joined Joachim. The monk hunkered down over the grave and took the pry bar in one hand.

"What are you doing?" Olympia asked. She stood behind her brother.

More rocks shifted in the stairway. Men's harsh voices pealed into the room. Occasional shafts of light from flashlight beams splintered through the debris. Lourds knew it wouldn't take much longer for the men to break through. Then they wouldn't have a chance.

"Lessons were learned after the deaths of the Elders." Joachim shoved the pry bar into a gap between the stones. He leaned on the bar and mortar cracked. One of the polished stones lifted from the floor. "An escape route was added from this room when there had not been one before. No longer has the Brotherhood depended solely on secrecy."

Thank God for that, Lourds thought.

He and two of the monks helped clear stones as Joachim freed them. They clacked and skidded across the floor. Some of them ricocheted against the loose stones clattering down the stairway. Cleena and Olympia held flashlights on the enlarging hole taking shape in the floor.

In seconds they had cleared enough of the stones to reveal the plain wooden coffin beneath the floor. The stench of mold and mildew invaded the room and warred against the encroaching dust cloud.

"Brother, forgive me for disturbing your rest," Joachim said quietly. Then he reached for the first of the rope handles attached to the coffin.

Lourds grasped another and set himself while the other two monks grabbed handles as well.

"Together," Joachim said. "Set—and lift."

The weight surprised Lourds. He knew the body within hadn't been preserved and probably only desiccated skin and bones remained. But his position was awkward and he wasn't able to properly set himself. His back and shoulder muscles burned with effort.

The coffin came free of the hole awkwardly and slammed against the sides on its way up. It was only a foot deep under the stone floor. Nothing marked the coffin, no name and no indication of what happened to the man within.

Once the coffin reached the level of the floor, Joachim pulled it toward him and set it down. At his direction, they shoved the coffin against the wall. He asked Olympia for her flashlight, then shined it down into the hole.

The tunnel opening looked incredibly small. There wasn't room to stand and Lourds wondered if there was even room to crawl.

"That doesn't look big enough," he said.

A fresh cascade of rock tumbled down the stairway and drew all their attention to the threat of the men coming from above.

"We don't have a choice," Olympia said.

Joachim helped his sister down into the hole. He returned the flashlight to her. She hesitated, then lay on her stomach and slithered into the hole.

"The tunnel wasn't made for comfort," Joachim said. "There's room enough but it will be tight."

"You do realize that the average size for a person has increased," Lourds said.

"We don't exactly have time to enlarge the tunnel," Cleena said.

"Someone could get stuck."

"That's why you're going to go last."

"Me?" Lourds looked around.

"You're the biggest person here," Cleena said. "If anyone's going to get stuck, it's going to be you."

Lourds quickly realized what she said was true. He was the tallest and the broadest across. He looked at the others for support or least sympathy. None was forthcoming.

"Absolutely delightful," he muttered.

Cleena followed Olympia into the tunnel. At Joachim's instruction, the other monks quickly dropped into place and began the journey.

"How long is the tunnel?" Lourds asked.

"About five hundred yards," Joachim answered.

"I don't suppose anyone has used this tunnel the last eight centuries?"

Joachim dropped into the grave. "No. We haven't had cause to flee from this room before."

And knowing the way is clear is too much to ask, Lourds thought sourly. "You realize, of course, that earthquakes could have collapsed the tunnel anywhere along the way."

"I certainly hope that isn't the case." Joachim looked at the staircase as more rock tumbled into the room. "Professor, my sister has always maintained that you're an intelligent man. If you think your chances here are greater, you may stay." He dropped to his stomach and crawled into the tunnel.

"They could seal the tunnel after us," Lourds pointed out. "If it's blocked ahead, we'll be entombed."

Evidently Joachim was saving his breath for crawling.

Cursing, realizing he was more afraid of losing touch with the puzzle than he was of getting trapped underground, Lourds dropped into the grave, fell to his stomach, and entered the tunnel.

STONE GOOSE APARTMENTS
ZEYTİNBURNU DİSTRİCT
İSTANBUL, TURKEY
MARCH 19, 2010

Sevki sat on the edge of his chair and captured images of the men waiting around the Hagia Sophia. When he had them all, he turned to another monitor and cropped the images into head shots of the individuals, choosing full frontal and profile shots where he could find them.

His software was exotic, a blend of high-tech government imaging programs equipped with special code he added. When he didn't have a full frontal or profile shot, he resampled the image, corrected the angle, and had the program fill in the blank spots. It wasn't perfect, but he'd found over the years that it was good enough.

Often, employers hired him to cover payoffs and exchanges so they wouldn't be surprised who was there. Or to get a record of who was there so they could exact revenge if necessary.

Once he had the images in the shape that he wanted, he ran them through international identification systems he had hacked into. He knew he was probably going to burn one of the back doors he'd built into the system because he was dumping eight faces in at one time.

Someone was going to catch him this time. He only hoped he could get in and out with the information he needed before that happened.

While the programs ran, and he surveyed the connections to know when a protective firewall discovered his false identification, he stared at the church grounds. His thoughts ran rampant.

A scroll. Buried and lost for hundreds of years. How much is something like that worth? The question buzzed inside Sevki's mind, but he already knew the answer: enough to get killed over.

The communication he had with Cleena over the earwig was intermittent, interrupted by the surrounding rock and the other shielded communications within the area used by the men chasing her. The rasp of her breathing and the infrequent curses and yelps of pain let Sevki know she was still alive and still running.

The first face froze on the monitor as identification was made.

In neat lines of script beneath the face, Sevki learned that the man was Corliss Baker, a marine sergeant killed in action in Iraq six years ago. Baker was recognized for several acts of bravery.

Then the second man was identified. His name was Zachary Stillson. He'd also died in Iraq six years ago. Strangely enough, he had been killed in the same engagement that had taken the life of Corliss Baker.

A third man, Henry Marstars, also a marine, died in that same battle.

A warning icon flashed onto the screen and let Sevki know he had alerted the gatekeepers at the other end of the hacked connection. He dumped a potpourri of foolies and false trails into the mix in case they had managed to tag him—which he considered doubtful—and fled the site.

When he settled back into his chair, he wasn't surprised to learn he was drenched in sweat. Digging around in American military or corporate databases always left him like that. Those entities had a habit of hiring people as gifted as he was.

No matter how curious or financially rewarding a cyberscore could be, Sevki didn't want to lose his home. He had worked hard to buy the building and he was happy there.

But he was also a game player. And the gauntlet had been thrown by the "ghosts" currently haunting the Hagia Sophia.

He continued monitoring the situation on the ground at the church, but he opened up a new window on another screen and began tracking down what he could of the military engagement in Iraq. He did love a conspiracy.

CRYPT OF THE ELDERS
HAGİA SOPHİA UNDERGROUND
İSTANBUL, TURKEY
MARCH 19, 2010

Sharp stone bit into Lourds's knees and elbows as he crawled through the narrow tunnel. He held his hat in one hand because he couldn't crawl while wearing it. He banged his head several times on the low roof. That chill clinging to the earth leached into his bones and tightened his muscles.

He couldn't see past those in front of him and that worried him considerably. The tunnel wasn't straight. Occasionally it dipped or rose, probably to avoid harder strata above or below. Scars of tools used by those who had dug the tunnel lined the passageway.

He was certain he was bleeding from a score of small wounds but couldn't be sure in the darkness. His strained breathing rasped in his ears and he wondered if the oxygen level was enough to sustain them all.

Perhaps the efforts of so many people all at one time were charging the air with carbon dioxide and they would all suffocate before they reached the other end.

That's the problem with being over educated, he chided himself. *You can always find something with which to scare yourself.*

He kept crawling, forcing away the pain in his elbows and knees that felt like tiny teeth tearing into his flesh. Then, he thought he heard the sounds of pursuit. The idea of the gunmen slithering through the tunnel behind him in the darkness filled him with fear that was even colder than the earth around him.

"I think I can get through, sir."

Eckart looked at the soldier nearest the stairway blockage. Through the hole they'd created, he saw only darkness. Either the people they were after had extinguished the lights or they'd abandoned their positions.

"Do it," Eckart ordered. "Kill anything that moves."

The man nodded and drew his pistol. "Including the professor?"

"It's dark down there. You don't have time to separate who's who."

"Yes, sir." With a pistol in one hand and a halogen flashlight in the other, the soldier dived headfirst through the opening in the fallen rock. He slid, feet spread wide to help control his descent, but he went in a rush and an avalanche of small stones trailed him.

Tense and annoyed, Eckart waited and peered into the darkness.

"The locals are coming up to speed," Mayfield warned over the headset. "Someone has called in an alert and claimed that shots have been fired in your twenty."

"Roger that," Eckart replied. "Topside and support, clear out. We'll stay with this in an attempt to flush the professor." Webster wouldn't be happy unless they came away with the scroll or Lourds.

At the bottom of the rock slide, the point man got to his feet and shined his light around. The illumination shifted and changed, but no shots were fired.

That was a bad sign.

"Clear," the point man called up. "They're not here."

Eckart cursed and slid down feet first. At the bottom, he stood and moved to the other side of the room from the point man in case a trap had been laid. Desperate men did desperate things, and they still weren't sure who the men were that had accompanied Lourds.

The room looked like living quarters of some kind, but there was no electricity and no sign of running water. Eckart flicked his flashlight beam across the ceiling out of habit. Most people didn't look up. Soldiers were trained to for urban assault.

All he saw was the stone ceiling.

The rest of his unit slid into the room as well. They spread out without being told.

"Any other exits?" Eckart asked.

"Negative, sir. None that I see."

"Check for those you don't see. Those people didn't just vanish."

"Affirmative, sir."

The point man halted beside a large rectangle in the floor. His flashlight illuminated a wooden coffin.

"Sir," the point man called.

Eckart joined him, gazing briefly at the coffin, then into the open grave in the floor. "A rat hole?"

"Yes, sir." The point man nodded. "That's what it looks like."

"Find out." Eckart played his flashlight beam around the room but didn't see any other ways for the professor and his companions to get out. The soldiers were already checking for hidden doors.

The point man squatted at the bottom of the grave. "Sir, there is a tunnel here. It's not very big, looks like crawlspace only, but it's big enough."

"All right. Let's see where it takes us. Drop your pack. It'll only slow you down. Take your flashlight, pistol, and extra magazines. We'll bring your gear." Eckart looked around the room and chose another small man. "Carter, you strip down and go with him."

Carter dropped his pack immediately and kept only his pistol and flashlight. He crawled into the hole behind the point man and they disappeared in the space of a drawn breath.

Eckart slid free of his pack and tied it to his left ankle. He dropped his pack into the hole then slid into the tunnel. As he crawled, the line kept his pack tethered to him.

Lourds and his people couldn't be far ahead. They didn't have that big of a lead. Eckart scrambled like he'd been taught back in basic, elbows and knees, eating up the distance.

Joachim stopped crawling unexpectedly. Sharp pain exploded through Lourds's cheek as his face skidded over the monk's hiking shoe.

"What's wrong? Why have you stopped?"

"I don't know. Everyone else has stopped."

Lourds twisted painfully in the tunnel and looked back the way they'd come. Bright yellow light flashed through the darkness.

"We're about to have company," Lourds said.

"I see them." Joachim raised his voice. "Olympia."

"The way is sealed," she responded.

Lourds's spirits sank. He had known from the beginning it might end up like this, but dealing with it in the darkness was much different. He didn't think he could take another five hundred yards of crawling on his elbows and knees. He was certain he'd rather be shot.

"How is it sealed?" Lourds asked.

Behind them, the flashlight beams closed the distance.

"It looks like a solid wall."

"It's not debris? Something caused by a cave-in?"

"No."

"Is it man-made?"

Olympia sounded irritated. "I don't see a toolmark."

"That's not what I mean. It's not a hidden door?"

"I already checked for that, Thomas. I'm not totally witless."

"This doesn't make sense. They wouldn't build a tunnel that went nowhere." Lourds thought desperately, trying to imagine what the Brotherhood might have done to fool potential enemies. "The entrance was located in a grave. The tunnel was meant as an escape. Joachim, you don't know anything about this, do you?"

"No. The knowledge about the escape tunnel was passed down, but nothing more," Joachim answered.

"How do you get rescued from the grave?" Lourds asked himself.

"If you're dead, you have to wait till the Second Coming," Joachim said. "When Jesus Christ returns, the dead will be lifted from their graves and—"

"I'm familiar with the theology," Lourds interrupted. Then a thought struck him. "Olympia, look up. What do you see?"

There was a pause, during which Lourds noted that the flashlights were coming closer, then Olympia called back, "Nothing. Just a stone surface."

"Smooth or unfinished?"

"Smooth."

"Any markings?"

"I don't see—wait. There's a fish symbol here."

"Push against the ceiling," Lourds said. "That should be a door." *Now if only it works.*

Stone grated in the darkness and Lourds held his breath as he watched the approaching flashlight beams. They couldn't be too far off now, but in the darkness it was hard to judge distance.

"It's a door!" Olympia called back.

"Go!" Lourds said. "Hurry!"

One by one, they went, and the flashlight beams crept up on them. Lourds was certain he wasn't going to make it. He sat on his haunches and passed his backpack and hat up to Joachim. His heart gladdened at the realization that the next section of the escape route was larger than the first. Once the way was clear, he stood up through the narrow passage, gripped the edges, and hauled himself up with the aid of Joachim and another monk.

Light seeped around the edges of the door from below. The men pursuing them gathered there. Lourds was certain they wouldn't be stymied for long.

He glanced up at Joachim and whispered, "Do you know where we are?"

Joachim shook his head.

"We need something to jam this door shut," Lourds said.

"Will this do?" Joachim pulled the crowbar that had caused all the commotion from under his jacket.

"Just the thing," Lourds said. He took the crowbar and inserted one end into the mortise of the stone door and kicked it hard, wedging the heavy door shut.

"That should slow them down," he said.

The hidden door had let out against a wall at the end of the passageway. There was only one way to go.

Only a little farther on, the new passageway dead-ended as well. Olympia immediately searched the wall while everyone else searched the ceiling.

"Here," Olympia said. She signed her flashlight on a fish symbol near the top of the dead end. "This has to be a door."

Hammering and banging came from the other end of the passageway. Lourds hated thinking about the abuse his sacrificed books were going through.

"Permit me," Lourds suggested.

They made way for him and he stood up at the door. He ran his flashlight beam around it, but didn't see any crevices or anything that gave any indication that the wall was indeed a door.

"I found something," Cleena said. She held her flashlight beam on a small square at eye level on the right hand wall. "It looks like a picture, but it was covered over with dust." She brushed at the thick layers of grime to reveal the image.

"It's not a picture," Joachim said. "It's a mosaic."

Upon closer inspection, Lourds realized that it was a mosaic. Created of tiny colored stones, the image showed thirteen people seated at a table.

"The Mystical Supper," Joachim said in awe.

"I take it you haven't been in this particular passageway before," Lourds said.

"Never."

"It would really have helped if you had." Lourds pressed the mosaic but nothing happened. He trained his beam on the walls. "Check the walls. There has to be something else here." Then he stopped and went back to the mosaic. "The Mystical Supper. That's what it was called by Eastern Orthodox Christianity. Paul was the first apostle to describe it."

"In First Corinthians chapter eleven, verses twenty-three to twenty-six," Joachim agreed.

"Yes." Lourds knelt below the mosaic. "That supper provided a lot of material for legends and mythology. The jug used to serve the wine has been purported by some to be the Holy Grail, sought after by King Arthur and his Knights of the Round Table. It's also supposed to be the beginning of the Eucharist, the sharing of Jesus' blood and body."

"Yes, but what does that have to do with opening this door?" Olympia asked.

Lourds smiled confidently. "In Orthodox churches, where do you expect to find a picture of The Mystical Supper?"

Joachim knelt beside him and began feeling the wall as well. "Above the Holy Doors."

"Yes. They're also called the Royal Doors and the Beautiful Gates." Lourds trailed his fingers along the stone. A moment later, he felt a raised pattern. He shined his light on it and wiped at the accumulated dust.

His efforts quickly revealed three more small mosaics. One was of a man with a nimbus around his head.

"The sainted deacon," Lourds said. "Usually it's Saint Stephen or Saint Lawrence or one of the others."

The second mosaic presented an engraved door that looked like it had been rendered in gold.

"The Beautiful Gates," Joachim said. "That is the door Christ enters through."

"The Russian Orthodox call them the Red Gates," Lourds said. "But the meaning is relatively the same."

A winged angel filled the third mosaic.

"Archangel Michael?" Joachim asked.

"Or Archangel Gabriel," Lourds said. Then he shrugged. "Unless it's another archangel."

"What does it mean?" Cleena asked.

"The Beautiful Gates," one of the monks said, "is a symbol of penitence that worshipers shouldn't forget. It reminds them that sin separates man from God."

"The last thing we need right now is a church lesson," Cleena said. "Unless we can find a quick way out of here, you're about to be ungraciously ushered into the presence of the Almighty."

“Please don’t make light of God’s works,” the monk said.

“I think we’ve been presented with a way out,” Lourds said. “The Mystical Supper is above the door. I’d wager my life on that.”

“You’re going to be,” Olympia said.

“Apparently we’re given three choices,” Lourds went on, unperturbed. “As much as I’m willing to bet one of these mosaics opens the doors, I’m also willing to bet the other two may lock it forever.”

“Why?” Joachim asked.

“In order to protect whatever lies beyond.”

“What do you think that is?”

“Another clue to the location of the Scroll of Joy.” Lourds reached for the three mosaics.

Joachim grabbed his hand and stopped it. “What are you doing?”

“Opening the door.”

“You’ve got one chance in three.”

“Not if you have faith and a little knowledge of the church,” Lourds said with a smile. “Which door would you pick?”

The hammering back at the jammed entrance took on a different timbre. Instead of trying to figure out the puzzle logically, the men had decided to use brute force. The stone door wouldn’t stand up to much of that.

Joachim hesitated only moment. “Two chances in three. The sainted deacon’s door or the angel door.”

“Why?” Lourds asked.

“Because those are the doors used by the clergy.” Joachim released Lourds’s hand.

Lourds pressed the mosaic with the sainted deacon. The mosaic sank into the stone a few inches, gliding effortlessly. Sharp clicks sounded within the stone wall as primitive tumblers fell into place.

A section of the wall slid backward to reveal another passageway. Lourds took the lead and entered. Once everyone was inside the passageway, he tripped a lever and the wall section slid smoothly back into place.

Long moments later, Lourds found yet another door. This one held no puzzle and, when opened, revealed only a small cave. To the left, Lourds spotted an opening that showed the star-studded sky.

Less than a minute later, he crouched at the mouth of a vine-covered cave and looked down over the Hagia Sophia. Several police cars surrounded the church.

"It's nice to see that not all of that went unnoticed," Lourds said. "But I hate to think of all those books, all that knowledge, that may be lost now."

"The police may not know how to find the tunnel," Joachim said. "They may only be responding to the threat aboveground."

"I hope so." Lourds removed his hat and squatted down to rest for a moment. The air in the cave was warmer than the dankness that had permeated the tunnels. He gazed around the cave.

Numerous beer cans and secondhand camping paraphernalia revealed that the local teens favored the cave as well.

"Local lovers' lane?" Cleena asked.

"One of the many," Olympia replied. "There are a number of caves around the city."

"I take it you have personal experience?" Cleena said.

Olympia frowned at the other woman and started to say something.

"Maybe we could concentrate on surviving tonight," Lourds interrupted. "Evidently there are a lot of people who know about the Scroll of Joy and want it. Until we have our hands on it, it's in danger of becoming lost to us."

Without a word, Joachim took out the leather tube and handed it over to Lourds.

Lourds looked at the other man.

"You saved us back there," Joachim said. "All of that, the Cave of the Elders, the passageways, all of that was new to you. My sister trusted you to find the Scroll of Joy, even though she didn't know what we were looking for. Now, after everything I've seen you do, I would be a fool—more than that, I would be remiss—if I didn't show you the same trust."

Lourds recognized the cost of Joachim's concession. He took the scroll in his left hand and offered the monk his right. "This is what I do, Joachim. If there's anyone better at this, I haven't met them. If there's a way to get an answer to this, I'll get you an answer. I promise."

CHAPTER

21

CENTRAL BUSINESS DISTRICT
KING ABDULLAH ECONOMIC CITY, SAUDI ARABIA
MARCH 24, 2010

Webster stood in the early morning darkness of the hotel high-rise and looked out across the city in the sea. Dawn was less than an hour away, but he knew the violence waiting to sweep over the land would arrive before the sun.

And he was just where he wanted to be: in the eye of the approaching storm.

The last five days hadn't been without their frustrations, though. Lourds and the Brotherhood of the Scroll of Joy had vanished in Istanbul. Despite Eckart's best efforts, no trace remained of them.

Webster knew the professor and his new allies remained within the city proper. If they had their hands on the Scroll of Joy, the vice president remained certain that he would know it. He would feel that threat as surely as he felt the promise of the impending violence about to engulf Saudi Arabia.

He sipped his scotch and water and glanced at the television in the corner the room. He maintained his own satellite dish that linked him to western world news and not just the propaganda Prince Khalid allowed to air on local stations.

The American networks and the BBC all covered the mounting military presence along the Middle Eastern borders. In the last few days, the area had become a powder keg. One spark would set them all off, and the world would march toward a fiery conflagration.

He intended to provide the spark.

Exhilarated, he used the television remote control to switch through the news channels. Video footage, some of it old and some of it new, showed armored ground units, aircraft, and soldiers preparing for full-on military engagements. Israel was curiously silent, but no less industrious. India and Pakistan, as well as China, had also upped their border defenses and patrols.

In Iraq and Turkey, American forces prepared as well. In the Gulf, navy ships ran strict grids and maintained constant contact.

Webster was inordinately pleased. All he needed was the Scroll to complete things and ensure his ultimate victory.

"Are you still awake?" Vicky DeAngelo stared at Webster from the tangled sheets of his bed.

"I napped briefly," Webster admitted. "But I can't sleep very well. Too many things to do."

Vicky sat up in bed and pulled the sheets up after her. Only the full, heavy roundness of her left breast was visible, and Webster felt certain she knew exactly what she revealed as well as what she hid. Her slim, tanned legs crossed but the sheet covered her lap.

She smiled. "I thought I had exhausted you."

"You did your best."

Vicky arched a salacious eyebrow. "Is that an assessment, or challenge?"

"Perhaps a little of both."

"Are you going to come over here? Or do I have to come after you?"

Webster didn't reply.

Vicky tossed the sheets away and stood revealed in her full glory. She was beautiful, with alabaster skin and a body molded by relentless exercise designed by a personal trainer and the narcissistic expertise of a gifted plastic surgeon. Not a blemish remained on her.

She crossed the floor like royalty, claiming every inch of space with undeniable carnality. She was a temptress from the Old Testament, a siren who could topple kings and heroes, and Webster couldn't help but be moved by the sight and promise of her.

When she reached him, she wrapped her left arm around his neck and took his drink in her right hand. She tossed back the rest of the scotch and water, then molded her fiery lips against his. He lifted her in his arms, stepped between her thighs, joined them, and turned so that her back was to the wall.

Arching his body fiercely, he drove himself into her again and again. She cradled his head and covered his face in kisses. She surged against him and screamed in completion again and again, till there was almost nothing left of her. With one final thrust, they both fell silent.

Slowly, Vicky regained control of her body. Tears ran down her cheeks, a mixture of pleasure and pain. Despite the adrenaline and lust that filled her eyes, Webster saw fear in there as well.

"I've never felt anything like that before," Vicky gasped.

"I know," Webster told her.

"Awfully confident of yourself, aren't you?"

"Do I have any reason not to be?" he taunted.

"No, not at all." Vicky kissed him. "I have to admit, I expected you to turn me away after we arrived here."

"I don't have to play the grieving widower anymore." Webster kissed her again.

"You were playing?"

"No. I loved my wife." Webster was certain that was why she had been taken from him. Her loss had been one of the few setbacks in his relentlessly successful life. But now his plans were at last nearing fruition. He could afford a bit of amusement. He turned to her again and took her in his arms.

She opened herself willingly.

Nothing could stop him. He wouldn't allow it.

OCEANVIEW OFFICES
EMINONU DISTRICT
ISTANBUL, TURKEY
MARCH 24, 2010

"Would you like tea?"

Lourds looked up from the notes he had taken the previous night, still groggily struggling to make sense of them. He'd had a plan of attack, more likely a conjecture he'd realized at this point, but it had been starting to make sense before he'd laid his head down and gone to sleep.

Olympia stood in front of his borrowed desk and looked as tired as he felt. She and the monks had been busy searching through books they'd borrowed from local libraries, the university, and bought along Cagaloglu, the street filled with a collection of booksellers and printers.

Their efforts had gleaned a few facts no one else had known, not even the monks, but it hadn't helped with the translation Lourds struggled with. Cleena had stayed with him as his bodyguard, but she hadn't seemed happy about it. Lourds wondered again what kept her with them when she'd seen firsthand how dangerous it was to do so.

"I'd love a cup of tea," Lourds answered.

"What about breakfast?"

"We have breakfast?"

"I went to the market this morning," Olympia explained. "It's nothing fancy, but it will help hold body and soul together."

"I'd be very interested in breakfast."

"Good. Why don't you go grab a shower and we'll take breakfast out on the balcony. The sun has only just risen, and the weather's perfect for early morning dining."

"I really don't have time to—"

"Thomas," Olympia said gently and reached out to hold his face between her hands as if he were a child. "For the last four days, you've done nothing but sleep, eat, and breathe that scroll. If you ask me, you've exceeded all expectations of human endurance. All you're doing at this point is locking yourself into tunnel vision." She smiled at him. "Take a shower. Eat breakfast with a beautiful woman. Catch your breath. Take a nap. Then look at the scroll with fresh eyes."

"You do make sense."

"Of course I make sense." She leaned in to kiss him. In that tender touch, he realized that he had missed sharing her bed the last four days.

Some vacation, he thought ruefully.

Olympia glanced down at him, and smiled. "Maybe you should make that a *cold* shower."

"Or," Lourds prompted, taking her hand in his and kissing her fingers, "you could shower with me."

"And who would get your breakfast ready?"

"When we get back, all scrubbed clean and satiated, I'll help you get both our breakfasts ready."

"You do realize that if we get caught, it could mortify my brother."

"I suspect it would take rather more than that to mortify your brother."

Olympia hesitated only a moment; then she nodded and took Lourds by the hand.

Oceanview Offices had at one time been the workspace for an import/export business. Lourds hadn't gotten the whole story from Joachim, but the gist seemed that the business had ended suddenly.

A few bullet holes and suspicious looking stains decorated the walls and floor of two of the rear offices. Lourds had pointedly stayed out of those rooms. He didn't believe in ghosts, but he didn't want to chance negative energy that might be left over there.

Whatever business had actually taken place in the offices, the enterprise had been well accoutered. In addition to the conference room where Lourds worked that had a view of the coastline and of the Hagia Sophia, there were five other smaller offices, two bathrooms—one with a small shower and a kitchen. The monks had brought in simple sleeping bags and kitchen utensils.

At the moment, the offices were between leases. Lourds didn't know if Joachim had made arrangements with the owners or if they were simply squatting there. In the end, it didn't really matter. They wouldn't—couldn't—be there long.

Still feeling refreshed from the shower, Lourds helped Olympia make breakfast from the breads, fresh fruit, cheeses, and sausages she'd brought back from market. When they finished assembling their plates, they retreated to the balcony with a pot of dark Turkish coffee.

Sometime over the last few days, someone—and Lourds suspected it was Olympia—had brought a stray table and five mismatched chairs out onto the small balcony overlooking the waterfront.

"I'm surprised your watchdog hasn't made it up yet," Olympia said, referring to Cleena.

Lourds looked out over the water and the line of restaurants that stood at its edge. "Don't you think you're being a little unfair to her?"

"She did force her way into our group."

"Perhaps."

"And that's only because she bungled the original kidnapping for Qayin and his people."

"As I recall, she rescued me from Qayin."

"Only after bringing you to him."

Lourds couldn't argue the point there.

He buttered a roll and ate it thoughtfully. His mind still churned through all the symbols he had been studying for the last few days. A few times, he had thought they were starting to make sense, then they would just slip away like minnows through his fingers.

"And the little friend she keeps in her ear is another problem," Olympia said. "How do we know we can trust him?"

"How do you know it's a him?"

Olympia gave him a look. "Please. It shows in the way she acts. The friend is a man. You can trust me on this one."

"Okay, I trust you."

A look of frustrated disbelief filled Olympia's face. "You'll trust me that her friend is a man, but you won't trust me that having her with us is a bad idea?"

Olympia picked up her tray, silverware, and cup and departed without another word.

Lourds sighed tiredly. Obviously there were *two* languages he presently didn't understand. He sipped his coffee and caught movement from the corner of his eye. At first he thought it might be Olympia returning. Instead, it was Cleena.

The young woman only had a couple of pieces of buttered toast, grapes, and melon wedges on her plate. She wore her red hair pulled back.

"Are you planning on going anywhere for the next hour so?" Cleena asked.

Suspicion darkened Lourds's thoughts. "I hadn't planned to. Why?"

"I've got an errand I have to run."

Cleena smiled at him and lifted an eyebrow. "You don't trust me?"

"I do," Lourds assured her. "As much as I can."

"Do you trust me as much as you trust your girlfriend?"

"She's not my—"

"Maybe no one else noticed you slip off to the shower together a few minutes ago, but I did." Cleena bit into a melon wedge. Juice trickled down her chin.

"I trust you a lot, as it happens. In fact, I think I'm the only one who trusts you."

"Probably." Cleena glanced at the notes he had at the side of his plate. "Still haven't figured out that scroll?"

"Not yet, no."

"I have faith in you," Cleena said simply.

"What's your errand?" Lourds took a bite of melon and found it sweet.

"I've got to go somewhere."

"Where?"

Cleena gave him a wan smile. "Running out of trust, Professor?"

"It appears to be a scarce commodity these days."

"Old Mother Hubbard and her cupboard, eh?"

"Something like that," Lourds replied. "You've been around our group for four days, and you've talked less than anyone."

"I'm a private person."

"Private people don't force their friendship on others at gunpoint."

Cleena smiled. "You have to admit, it's a lot more effective and it gets quicker results."

"There's something to be said for people who take the long way to do things."

"There's not always time for that."

"You're asking for a lot, and are giving only a little."

"Maybe I'm giving you more than you suspect."

Lourds took a breath and let it out. "We're coming to a critical juncture in our partnership. Trust is getting to be a hard thing to come by, so maybe it's time you started trusting me."

"Are you forgetting who you're up against, Professor?" Cleena pinned him with her gaze. "You've got a phantom army on your tail, judging from those 'ghosts' that have wandered out of Iraq. You've got Qayin and his people on another side. Then there are the monks."

"They're on my side."

"For the moment. But you have to remember: They didn't tell you everything at the beginning. Neither did your girlfriend. The church I was brought up in? Omission was still considered a lie. If you're not going to trust me, do yourself a favor and don't trust them either."

Before Lourds could respond, Cleena picked up her plate and coffee cup and departed. He sat in the chill morning shade and watched her walk away, and he didn't know whether to be more afraid of her or for her.

"Where would you like, miss?"

Cleena pulled her attention from the ocean and peered along the line of shops and bars on the left side of the street. Cruise ships lined the docks and tourists were out in force. Hawkers called out their wares from doorways and carts. Small bazaars had opened beneath cargo tents in alleyways.

The masses of people would make it difficult to keep an eye on her surroundings, but she hoped they would also provide an easy way to disappear if it came to that.

"There." Cleena pointed to a cybercafé that advertised battling robots rendered in neon tubing. Popular game names and posters littered the windows.

"Of course, miss. At once." The driver cut across two lanes of traffic, narrowly avoided locking bumpers with another taxi trailing too close, and skidded against the curb.

Cleena paid the man and tipped him well enough, but not so well that he would remember her, and got out. She stepped into the flow of human traffic and looked around.

"Sevki," she said.

"I haven't seen anyone yet." Sevki sounded frazzled and she felt badly about asking him for so much.

"None of the monks?"

"Not a one."

"I don't think they let me go alone because they trusted me."

"They probably thought you were going to lead them into a trap."

Cleena grinned at that. The thought of the monks being afraid of her rocked her world a little. They were smug with their holier-than-thou attitudes.

But they weren't the ones she was intent on trapping.

"You'll see someone soon. Just keep a close watch over me."

"Always. But you know, I really have to protest this course of action."

"Again?" Cleena pulled open the cybercafé door and entered the darkness. She slipped her sunglasses off and surveyed the large room.

Patrons occupied most of the three or four dozen computers scattered around the room. Nearly all of them were involved in online gaming or surfing porn sites. Sometimes they did both.

"Yes, again," Sevki said. "You didn't listen the first few times."

"It wasn't a few." Cleena went to the front desk and negotiated a computer. She showed one of the fake identifications Sevki had arranged for her and paid cash, English pounds.

"It wasn't enough," Sevki countered. "These guys you're playing with, they're out of your league."

"I got drafted into this." Cleena sat at the table and swiped the card she'd been given through the data reader. The computer powered up and allowed her access. "If it had been up to me, I'd still be playing in the minor leagues."

"I know."

"These aren't the kind of guys that will simply let you fade once everything is said and done. You know that."

Sevki sighed. "I know."

"All I can do is increase their cost to play. The same way we did when you stepped wrong around the Russian Mafiya." Cleena felt badly about bringing that up, but she also felt that she didn't have a choice.

"I know. I still owe you for that."

"No, you don't." Cleena took a deep breath. "But I could use help now. I can't do this by myself. If I can't be safe, I want my sister to be."

"She will be. Are you at the computer?"

"I am."

"Then go to this IP address."

Cleena did, and once she was there, she downloaded all the programs and applications Sevki had waiting there. The computer protested just for a moment, then the warning screen for the firewalls quieted and went away. Within seconds, Sevki had the machine slaved to his own.

"We're set up," Sevki said a short time later.

Tension knotted Cleena's stomach. She forced herself to pick up the phone handset on the table and slot it into the USB port. In seconds, the Internet phone connection linked up.

She dialed the number she'd been given, then settled back to watch the front and back doors. If she was right, and she felt certain that she was, things would happen very quickly.

She just had to make certain they didn't happen to her.

The phone rang.

When CIA Special Agent in Charge James Dawson heard the strident ring of the phone on the nightstand beside the bed in his hotel room, he held up a hand to the young woman straddling him. She stopped her wild gyrations but continued a gentle rocking that held him right at the brink.

He checked the number and saw that he didn't recognize it. There was only one person who could possibly be calling him from a phone he wouldn't have the number for. He flipped the phone open confidently and ran his free hand over the sweat-slick body of the young woman atop him.

"Ah, Miss MacKenna," Dawson greeted. "Just when I had almost given up on you."

"Your goons at the Hagia Sophia nearly did their job too well," she said.

Genuine puzzlement nagged at Dawson. "I wouldn't know what you're talking about."

"I didn't think that you would. But their attack created a problem."

Some of Dawson's confidence oozed away. "Is the professor all right?"

"He is. But only just. And not for the lack of trying on the part of your hired help."

"I must protest, Miss MacKenna. I don't know what you're talking about." Dawson didn't know what she was talking about, but she seemed awfully sure of herself.

"Did they tell you that the professor found a scroll?"

That caught Dawson's attention. "What scroll?"

"I don't think it's the main one," she continued. "Everyone here seems a bit disconcerted that it hasn't turned up yet. But they also seem convinced that the professor will find it soon enough."

"Good. When he does, you'll be out of this situation. So will your sister."

"My sister's already out of it."

Dawson grinned at that. "I'm aware that your sister has dropped from sight, but I have a great many people at my disposal that are really good at finding people that try to lose themselves."

Her voice hardened. "I wouldn't try to do that if I were you."

"You do pose a challenge," Dawson said, "but you'll never be in any position to carry out any of your threats." He paused. "Why are you calling me now?"

"To negotiate."

"You have nothing to negotiate with."

"I know where the professor and the first scroll are."

"But you don't know where the main scroll is."

"Once you have the professor and the scroll he has now, you should be able to find it."

"What do you want?"

"A cease-fire. Between you and me. The deal is this: I give you the professor and the first scroll, and you forget about my sister and me."

Dawson glanced at his watch. Enough time had passed that the electronics teams tracing calls into this phone should have a location.

"I'm in the middle of something here," Dawson said, smiling up at young woman. "Can I call you back?"

"I'd rather be the one doing the calling."

"Fine. Then call me back in an hour." Calmly, Dawson closed the phone. It rang immediately. "Tell me you got a location."

"We did. She's at a cybercafé in the harbor. We've got a team en route."

"Have them stay back. I don't want her to see them until it's too late. No one makes a move until I clear it. Understood?"

"Yes, sir."

Dawson folded the phone and placed it once more on the nightstand. He reached for the young woman astride him. Rather than proving distracting, the phone call reinvigorated his sex drive. He looked forward to proving to Cleena MacKenna that he was the most dangerous man she'd ever crossed paths with.

Cleena stared at the computer monitor. "Did I keep him on long enough?"

"You did," Sevki said in her ear. "I managed to trace the signal back to the United States. It was tricky, because they used a lot of satellite cutouts. Government issue, heavily encrypted."

"I get it. I'm supposed to be impressed."

"Unfortunately, you're not informed enough to be duly impressed with what I've just done." Sevki sighed as if stricken.

"So who is it?"

"The Central Intelligence Agency, if I had to guess."

A wave of fear vibrated through Cleena. Even though she'd suspected CIA, hearing it spoken out loud was frightening. In her arms deals, she had sometimes brushed up against intelligence operatives. Always before, she'd cut her losses and run.

"Not people we want to be trifling with," Sevki pointed out.

"I know."

Sevki whispered a curse. "But you're going to anyway."

"This guy threatened my sister. If it's the same guy, he hurt her. I'm not going to allow that." Icy calm thrummed inside Cleena.

Sevki cursed again, this time with more passion. "Well, you're going to get your chance. I just finished chasing down all the connections. This guy, whoever he is, is here in the city."

Paranoia bloomed within Cleena, spicing up the fear already coursing through her. "In Istanbul?"

"Yes. His communications people were cute about it, and if I hadn't been as good as I am and had enough time, I might not have found him. But I did. He's in the city. My bet is that you'll have company soon."

"Everything here is set?"

"Of course."

Cleena pushed up from the chair and headed for the back door. Sevki had already briefed her on how to get out of the building without being seen.

"We own the perimeter."

"Affirmative. If possible, I want the target alive. Damage at this juncture is a moot point. But I want the target able to answer questions."

"Then you'll get it."

Settled into the passenger seat of the SUV across the street from the cybercafé, Dawson held his pistol in his lap and watched the takedown team in action.

Dawson lifted his sat phone and called another number. When it was answered, he said, "Sir, we are at go."

Vice President Webster didn't hesitate. "Secure your target. I want to talk to Professor Lourds."

"Yes, sir. I'll call you when we have the secondary target."

"Do that. And good luck. We're in very dangerous times at present. All of us."

The gravity in Webster's voice was unmistakable, and Dawson had never before heard that tone so strongly. Dawson couldn't help thinking about the vice president more or less marooned behind enemy lines in Saudi Arabia. Tensions in that part of the world continued to escalate as skirmish wars and civil unrest broke out like grass fires.

"Are you all right, sir?" Dawson asked. If the vice president had asked, he would have abandoned the mission in Istanbul at once and charged to his rescue.

"Don't worry about me," Webster replied. "I'll be fine." His voice grew stronger. "Glory is about to rain down on us. Trust me on that."

Dawson hesitated, not at all certain what the vice president was talking about. But he heard the conviction in the man's words. The stakes, whatever they turned out to be, were huge. Dawson just wished he could see the connection between what was taking place in Saudi Arabia and Istanbul. As far as he knew, no other American intelligence community was interested in Professor Thomas Lourds.

"I do trust you, sir," Dawson replied.

"Good, because we're going to have to trust each other a lot over the next few days," Webster told him.

"What do you mean, sir?"

"Soon, Jimmy. Everything will happen in due time. I've planned this for a long, long time. Get Lourds and bring him to me."

"Yes, sir."

The vice president hung up the phone, but not before Dawson heard explosions in the background. He knew from the news reports coming out of the area that hostile aggression had increased within Saudi Arabia.

The Saudi army had mobilized and begun spreading out across the major cities. But their efforts weren't enough to keep Shia terrorists, or rebels as some of the local news stations were calling them, from striking back. The Shia targeted American and European businesses as well as Saudi government buildings. Several oil fields were burning, and international investors complained bitterly and threatened to take action.

Dawson's headset buzzed for attention.

"The clerk has made a positive ID on our target," the agent inside the cybercafé said.

Dawson glanced at the cybercafé. "Do you see her?"

"No, sir. She's not at one of the computer terminals."

"But she was?"

"Definitely. The clerk IDed her."

"Then where is she?" Anger and frustration welled up in Dawson.

"I don't know, sir. We're looking."

Dawson cursed. "Don't just look. Find her." He slipped the restraining loop from the hammer of his pistol and pushed the door open.

Across the street, the rest of the team flooded into the building.

Dawson's driver got out and stood beside him. He was a young, intense man with black sunglasses that made him look like a spy. He whirled around and lifted his pistol from hiding beneath his jacket. Dawson didn't know what had caught the man's attention, but he turned with him.

Cleena MacKenna was on them with the speed of a stalking predator. She fired a Taser at the driver. Both darts struck the man in the chest and unleashed their voltage. The driver shook and shivered for a moment, then dropped to the ground.

By that time the woman had already closed on Dawson. A stun baton extended with a meaty *chukk!* sound. Instinctively, Dawson pulled his pistol up to fire. He never had the chance. The woman whipped the baton across Dawson's right wrist.

Incredible pain exploded through Dawson's right arm, but his hand went numb immediately. The pistol dropped from his nerveless fingers.

Dawson grabbed at the woman with his other hand. She smiled at him cruelly and hit that hand with her baton as well. Before he could react to the new pain, she swept the baton up into his crotch. As he dropped to his knees, she hit him again, this time on the side of the neck.

Agony swarmed inside Dawson's head. He almost passed out. Vomit burned up his throat then shot through his lips to splatter against the sidewalk. He was almost too weakened to hold himself up out of the mess on his arms.

Coolly, as if she had all day and there weren't a dozen specially trained men tearing through the building across the street, Cleena MacKenna popped the car's passenger door open. She pulled the baton up under Dawson's throat, into a chokehold, and forced him into the passenger seat.

She knelt beside the driver for just a moment, then plucked the car keys from his pants pocket without hesitation. That she knew which pocket the man had kept the keys in told Dawson that she had been watching them get out of the car.

The whole meeting was a setup.

Dawson thought he'd been outfoxing her and he had only put himself into a box. He tried to flex his hands, tried to move, but it only doubled the pain and nearly made him pass out. He was helpless.

Cleena MacKenna slid into the driver seat, started the engine, and buckled up.

She looked at him and there was no emotion in her eyes. "If you try anything, if you lie to me, I'm going to kill you. I already owe you that for hurting my sister."

Dawson cleared his throat with effort as she pulled out into traffic. "But I didn't—"

She backhanded him in the mouth without looking. His lips split and his mouth filled with the taste of salt. "Don't," she snarled. She grabbed his numbed right hand and held it up to him. "See this bruising?"

Dawson did, and he remembered his trip to Boston.

"That tells me you hit someone not long ago. If you try to sell me that the someone you hit wasn't my sister, you're going to be wasting breath. And I meant what I said. Killing you isn't going to get me into any more trouble than I'm already in."

Believing her, Dawson sat back in his seat and hoped that he passed out. The woman was good. But stealing the car was a mistake. She was going to find that out. Soon.

And then Dawson fully intended to kill her.

CHAPTER

22

OCEANVIEW OFFICES
EMINONU DISTRICT
İSTANBUL, TURKEY
MARCH 24, 2010

Lourds nursed a beer as he sat on the office balcony and stared out at the green-blue sea that filled the harbor as he tried to order his thoughts. Though his body was at rest, his mind spun like a dervish, bouncing off the various tangents he'd had to consider. He had the scroll deciphered. He even felt certain he had the hiding place for the Scroll of Joy figured out.

What he found immensely distracting was the purpose of the Scroll of Joy.

After finding lost Atlantis, Lourds hadn't thought anything would ever shock or surprise him again. He was both disturbed and relieved to find that was not true. However, the potential cost of that joy of discovery—could be devastating.

The fate of the world, he mused. *That used to have a much more dramatic sound to it, and it wasn't all that frightening.*

That was no longer true. Lourds was frightened. At least when he didn't force himself to totally disbelieve the story the scroll had revealed.

His beer finished and his intestinal fortitude screwed up as tightly as possible, he picked up the bottle, stood, and reentered the office.

Joachim and Olympia sat in the kitchen area and talked over cups of tea. Although both of them tried to look like they were at ease, Lourds spotted the tension in both.

They looked at him expectantly.

Olympia's eyes gleamed. "You solved it." Her voice was quiet. "I know that look."

"Yes," Lourds replied. "I broke the language."

"You know where the Scroll of Joy is?" Joachim asked.

"I believe I do."

Olympia searched Lourds's face, then shook her head and looked troubled. "You didn't break it just now, Thomas. You've had it broken for some time, haven't you?"

Lourds opened the refrigerator and took out another bottle of beer. He leaned a hip against the counter and cracked the beer, then took a sip.

"I finished the translation almost an hour ago," he said.

Joachim's face darkened in anger. "Why have you waited till now to tell us?"

"I wanted some time to think about things. Alone. Without preconceptions."

"Qayin and his followers might have—"

"Do you really think they can find the Scroll of Joy?" Lourds interrupted. "Do you think they're any better informed than you are? And you certainly didn't find that scroll."

Joachim restrained himself from making further comment and the effort turned his lips white.

"We can't get the scroll now anyway," Lourds said. "We're going to have to wait till tonight."

"Why?"

"Where it's at will be filled with too many people during the day. Going at night will be risky enough."

"Where is it?" Joachim's voice was so hard that the question might as well have been a demand.

"We'll get to that in a moment." Lourds stood ready to move. He didn't think Joachim would attack him, but there was a lot on the line. "For now, we need to talk about a couple of other things."

The fate of the world.

"Do you know what the Scroll of Joy is supposed to do?" Lourds asked Olympia. "Besides save the world, I mean?"

Olympia shook her head.

"For you, it was just that something that old, an historic artifact of incredible importance, existed. You loved the idea of that. Something written by someone two thousand years ago. The fact that it was reportedly written by a disciple of Jesus was just a bonus."

"Yes."

Lourds locked eyes with Joachim. "But you know what the scroll's true purpose is, don't you?"

Joachim said nothing.

"Someone," Olympia said in a tight voice, "had better tell me something. My life has been put on the line, and I know that police officers will have plenty of questions as well. They're going to need answers. *I* need answers."

"Not to mention the international incident that I'll have to deal with." Lourds fixed his gaze on Joachim. "And for what? Childish fear of the dark?"

"Is that what you think this is about, Professor Lourds?" Joachim spoke softly, but there was an undercurrent of aggression. "Childish fear of a nonexistent threat? I assure you, that threat the Scroll of Joy speaks of is very real. And it's here among us."

"For God's sakes, man." Lourds voiced some of the frustration he now felt. He had been shot at, nearly killed, was in more trouble than he'd ever previously been in, and had spent days working on a scroll that had only proven to be an exercise in futility. "At best, that scroll and the Scroll of Joy are ineffectual but well meaning humbug. At worst, both are just superstitious strikes at shadows."

"You're not a believer, are you?" Joachim challenged.

"A believer in what?"

"Of God and his works."

Lourds thought back to his hunt for Atlantis and his discovery of the Tree of Knowledge and the First Son. He remembered the story of the First Flood and the Words that would remake the world. Did he believe in God? Yes. Whether or not God was still taking an active part in the world was a different matter.

"The Scroll of Joy isn't about God," Lourds said.

"Everything is about God," Joachim corrected.

"Not this document. This is about Lucifer."

"Yes." Joachim nodded. "It is about Lucifer, or any of the other names he's known by. But Lucifer, before and after his fall, was created by God."

"What are you talking about?" Olympia asked.

"This document," Lourds said, turning to face her, "if it exists and isn't just a glorified goose chase, is supposed to rid the world of the Devil, by all of his names."

"Not get rid of Lucifer," Joachim corrected. "John of Patmos knew that Lucifer was loose in the world. He knew from Jesus' own blessed lips how the Devil had heaped temptation upon Jesus while he wandered in the wilderness. Since Lucifer was cast down from the heavens and Adam and Eve were driven from the Garden of Eden by God's angels, the Devil has been loose the world. For thousands of years he has gathered his strength in hopes of conquering this world and tilting the odds in his coming war with God. The Scroll of Joy was written to break the hold John of Patmos had envisioned Lucifer would one day have on the world. That time is now."

"That's insane," Lourds said.

"Believing in Lucifer?"

"Yes."

"But you said you believe in God."

"God's existence doesn't depend on Lucifer's. Just because you have a Great Savior doesn't mean that a Great Enemy also exists."

"No," Joachim agreed. "God never planned on one of his angels falling from grace. Nor the other angels that fell after the first, all of them drawn by fascination to God's greatest creation: man. But it happened. And the Scroll of Joy will correct some of the evil that is loose in the world."

"You're saying that if we find this scroll that it has the power to create world peace." Lourds tried to keep the sarcasm from his voice but he was certain he failed.

"Again, no. All the Scroll of Joy is supposed to do is drive Lucifer from his fortress and the power he has built in this world. These are perilous times for us all. Wars threaten globally. The economy is in disarray. Many people feel we're only one short step from the end of the world."

"And Lucifer is to blame for all of this?"

"No. That has always been man's choice. But Lucifer has taken advantage of the confusion and fear that's going on. That's always been the Great Deceiver's greatest strength."

"You talk like Lucifer is real, a person. Not a fallen angel."

"He is real."

"As a divine force, you mean."

"No. He has manifested in this world as Jesus did. At this point, he is flesh and blood."

"Just showed up one day?"

"He was born to a mortal woman and took his place among men."

Lourds made himself calm down. His head spun with the implications, but he couldn't bring himself to believe. It was all too incredible to believe. "Do you know who Lucifer is?"

"In his present mortal guise?" Joachim shook his head. "Doesn't the scroll you translated mention something about Lucifer revealing himself at the time the Scroll of Joy is found?"

"Yes. But it didn't say how."

"Think about it, Professor Lourds. Since you first arrived, since you began searching for the Scroll of Joy—even though you didn't know that's what you were doing—you've been beset by opposing forces."

"Coincidence." Even as he said it, Lourds realized how weak the answer sounded.

Joachim smiled. "Do you really think so? After all these years, my sister tells me of you. You met her some time ago, but I hadn't yet told her my secrets. Then when I did, she suggested you could help. You are asked to come here. Suddenly, a search for the Scroll of Joy is escalated by everyone, including the United States CIA and a military force we haven't yet identified and weren't known to even be involved. And you are the only person that has managed to translate a scroll that even its protectors could not translate for the last eight hundred years."

As incredible as it all sounded, Lourds knew he didn't have an answer or a rebuttal. The only true break in the link would have been if he had failed to translate the language.

But he hadn't failed. And now he knew what Joachim and his predecessors had been trying to know the last eight centuries.

Still, even with everything he knew, Lourds didn't know what the eventual prize would be. The Scroll of Joy had to be more than just some kind of document to ward off the devil. If nothing else, he knew his own curiosity would be much too strong to resist.

Taking a deep breath, Lourds took the beer bottle from the counter and rubbed the chill, sweaty side across his forehead. The coolness felt welcome to the throbbing headache he felt was only just now beginning.

"You do realize what you're saying, don't you?" Lourds asked after a bit. "If we get caught by any of the law enforcement agencies looking for us, our only excuse for doing everything we have done is simply: the Devil made us do it."

"Maybe we should plan on not getting caught," Joachim suggested.

"Given where we have to go, what we have to do, as well as who's looking for us, that's not very bloody likely, now is it?" Lourds snorted in frustration, took another beer from the refrigerator, and returned to the balcony.

Cleena trapped her pistol between her thigh and the car seat as she sped through traffic. "If you do anything stupid," she advised the man she'd taken prisoner, "I'll kill you."

He said nothing but continued trying to work feeling back into his numbed hands by squeezing them into fists. His gaze was hot and defiant, but fear lurked in there as well.

"You're going to have to lose the car," Sevki advised. "They'll have a GPS locater on it. That's standard operating procedure."

Cleena hadn't thought about that, but she hadn't planned to stay with the car for long anyway. "What is your name?"

"Kidnapping me is going to get you a life without parole sentence," he told her viciously. "I guarantee that."

She glanced at him. "Then shooting you isn't going to make my situation any worse." Lifting her pistol, she shot him through the meaty part of his left thigh. Trapped inside the car, the harsh *crack* of the pistol rolled like thunder.

The man howled in pain and surprise and gripped his wounded leg. Blood spread through his fingers but there was no arterial bleeding.

"I left you the use of your leg," Cleena said. "The next shot will require reconstructive surgery on your knee. Maybe you'll be a cripple."

The man cursed her.

"Any signs of pursuit?" Cleena asked Sevki.

"Yes."

Her stomach clenched and she smelled the hot, fresh iron of the man's blood.

"Ten blocks back and closing fast," Sevki advised.

Cleena estimated with traffic conditions that she had at best a couple minutes before her pursuers caught up to her. She swerved into the first alley and felt the seatbelt squeeze into her flesh as she bumped over the curb.

She parked the car in the middle of the alley, got out, then walked to the passenger side of the car and yanked her prisoner out. He feigned helplessness that wasn't entirely faked.

"Walk," Cleena said, "or I'll make sure you never can again."

The man walked and favored his wounded leg. He left a blood trail on the cracked stone.

At the end of the alley, when the pursuers were still two blocks away, Cleena turned right and walked into a parking lot just off the alley. A young attendant came out of the kiosk to greet them.

"May I help you?" he asked.

Cleena pointed to the nearest sedan. "I want the keys to that car."

"Do you have your ticket?"

She showed him the pistol. His eyes widened and he reached inside the kiosk to retrieve the keys. Cleena reached inside as well and yanked the phone cord from the wall.

"There will be men after me," Cleena said. "American. They'll be hard men and you won't want to talk to them because they're not going to be friendly. Understand?"

The young man nodded and looked panicked. "Sometimes my English isn't so good."

"They'll probably beat good English into you if they have the chance." Cleena indicated the blood trail her prisoner had left. "Maybe they won't follow me here, but I think they will."

She opened the sedan's passenger door and shoved her captive inside. The man groaned and slumped into the seat. Cleena walked around the car and slid behind the steering wheel. The engine caught immediately. She backed out of the parking space, then headed back out into the alley.

She continued away from the vehicle she'd left behind. In her rearview mirror, she saw a car arrive and stop behind the abandoned vehicle. Before she cleared the alley mouth, a second car had arrived.

"They're going to find you," the man said weakly. He'd gone pallid.

Cleena worried that the man would go into shock and pass out. "It'll be too late to help you."

"You don't know who you're messing with."

"The CIA. How's that for starters?"

The man tried to control the surprise on his face.

Cleena drove smoothly, keeping with the flow of the traffic. "Now give me your name or I'm going to do the knee." She kept her voice cold and distant, like this was everyday conversation.

Shifting slightly, the man leaned against the door.

Cleena pointed the pistol at his knee. "Go on. Jump out of the car. And when you do, I'm going to back over you."

The man wilted, obviously resigned to his fate. "Trust me. You do not want to hurt me any more."

"Actually, I do. But right now that's negotiable."

Stubbornly, the man failed to respond.

"Three, two—"

"Dawson," the man said. "James Dawson."

"And you're with the CIA?"

"Yes."

"What are you doing in Istanbul?"

"Investigating a possible terrorist cell."

That, she knew, was a lie, but she led it ride. "Why is Thomas Lourds involved in your investigation?"

"Our information leads us to believe that Lourds is designing an artificial language for terrorists."

"That's a load of crap," Sevki said over the earwig connection. "He thinks he's dealing with idiots. It would actually be a great plan if used, but terrorist cells are set up to function independently. There is no communication between terrorist cells. That's part of why they're so dangerous."

Cleena knew that as well.

"That isn't what Lourds is doing," she said.

"I leaned on you, and your sister, to get information concerning Lourds's whereabouts," the man said. "We had to have it."

Cleena stopped the car at a red light in a busy intersection. "One last question, and you get to walk."

Dawson started to say something, then thought better of it and didn't.

"Who are you working for?"

"The CIA. You know that."

"The scroll Lourds is looking for isn't something the CIA would be interested in."

"The artificial language—"

"No," Cleena said. She leveled pistol at his knee. "Who sent you after Lourds?" She glanced up at the traffic light. "You have until the light changes colors."

"Webster," Dawson whispered.

"Webster?"

"I was here under orders from Vice President Webster."

The light changed to green and the car behind Cleena honked impatiently.

"The American vice president?" Sevki sounded in total disbelief.

Cleena knew how he felt. Another honk sounded from the car behind her. She gestured to Dawson.

"Get out of the car," she said. "And whatever you do, don't ever come near my sister or me again."

"Don't worry about that. You won't see me next time. By the time you realize I'm there, it will already be too late." Dawson closed the door and stood at the open window as he pulled his courage together. "The only question will be whether I kill your sister before or after I kill you."

Sevki cursed.

Dawson turned began to walk away.

"Agent Dawson," she said.

He turned to face her, a confident smile twitching his lips. He started to open his mouth to say something, then he saw Cleena point the pistol at him.

She squeezed the trigger smoothly and felt the pistol buck in her fist.

The bullet caught Dawson below his left eye next to his nostril. Several people near the car recognized the sound of the shot and dove for cover.

"Oh my God," Sevki said. "Did you just shoot him?"

"Yes." Cleena dropped her foot on the accelerator and sped through the intersection as Dawson sprawled into the street. "I couldn't let him live. He would've done what he said he would do."

"Lourds is the target. You should have just stayed low and gotten out of this. They couldn't come after you and the professor."

Cleena made a right turn. Paranoia still thrummed within her as she checked for pursuit. "Do you think I can just run?"

"You can. I can create false identities for you and your sister."

"To live where?"

"Here, for starters."

Tears burned at the back of Cleena's eyes as she realized everything that was now at stake. "I can't do that to my sister," she whispered. "You don't realize what she's been through. The home she has now in college? That's the only home she's truly known. I can't take her away from that. Not when she's so close getting out and starting her life her way."

"Then what are you going to do?"

"I'm going to ride this thing out. See where it goes." Cleena made a few sharp turns and parked the car at the side of a shop. She left the keys in the ignition and got out.

"You've seen what you're up against. What you're talking about is suicide."

Cleena strode forcefully, putting as much distance as she could between the car and herself. "We've come this far."

"You don't even know if there's anything to this," Sevki protested. "Long lost secrets don't just fall out of the closet."

"Sometimes they do. You know that. Part of your business is based on that."

"Two thousand years is a long time to keep a secret."

"People say the Egyptian pyramids were buried longer than that."

Sevki sighed.

"You can have out," Cleena said. "There's nothing holding you to this. I needed you to help me find whoever hurt my sister. You did."

"Neither one of us has any sense. You know that, don't you?"

Cleena smiled and her steps felt a little lighter. “I didn’t know, but I’d hoped.”

“Let’s just cross our fingers that the professor is as good as everyone thinks he is.”

“When the Hagia Sofia was built at the direction of Constantinople,” Lourds said as he smoothed out the maps Joachim had brought him of the temple, “several mosaics were built into the walls. They remained there for hundreds of years until the Muslims conquered the city and took over the church.”

Joachim and Olympia crowded in for a closer look. The other monks followed suit until there was scarcely standing room around the conference table.

“Many of those mosaics were also stolen during the Fourth Crusade,” Joachim said. “They were kept in private collections or sold to collectors later.”

Lourds placed his half-empty bottle of beer on one corner of the map to hold down the curling paper. Sweat beads slid down the bottle and stained the map.

“They were,” he agreed. “More were damaged during the Muslim renovations. But there are four that were hidden under the church in passageways. According to the scroll I read, the Scroll of Joy can be found using the information in those mosaics.”

“That’s impossible,” Joachim said.

“Why?” Lourds asked.

“Because we have been over every inch of those passageways. There are no more hidden passageways that we don’t know about.”

“If that’s true, then I don’t have a clue where the Scroll of Joy will be.” Lourds returned the monk’s gaze full measure. “So how do you want to do this? Either I know what I’m talking about, or I don’t. This is what I translated.”

“If this passageway was there, we’d have found it.”

“Not if God didn’t want you to.”

“That’s sacrilege.”

“Is it? Either you believe everything is coming together for a reason now—or you don't. That's what the Scroll of Joy is all about, isn't it? The omens? The rise of Lucifer in this world."

"You're an outsider. This shouldn't fall to you."

"It wasn't exactly my choice either," Lourds agreed. "I had a rather leisurely working vacation planned." He tapped the map. "But I'm telling you now, that scroll I read details how to find this passageway. If we go and look, and it's not there, then I don't know what to tell you." He paused. "I'm going there. If for nothing more than to satisfy my curiosity. But I'm also going in hopes of ending this. I don't have a choice at this point. We've nothing to lose."

"We'll go," Joachim said, but he clearly wasn't happy about it.

"We'll need supplies." Lourds rolled the maps and stuffed them back into a protective cylinder.

"You're going to have to forgive my brother, Thomas."

Lourds stood beside his bed and laced up his hiking boots. Outside the bedroom window, the sun was going down. Golden sunlight filtered into the room but it was on the wane.

"Joachim is used to doing things his way," Olympia went on.

"I got that." Lourds stamped in his boots, making sure that the fit was good. "But he can be a tad insufferable when he puts his mind to it."

"The biggest problem is that you and he," Olympia told him with a smile, "are so much alike."

"Me and your brother?" Lourds couldn't believe it. "I hardly think so."

"Both of you are willful, prideful, and full of self-importance. Neither of you plays well with others. In short—insufferable."

"Is of any of this supposed to make me feel better?"

Olympia grinned at him. "You're both also intelligent and decisive. And stubborn."

"As some of my college students would say, not getting the warm fuzzy out of this."

Olympia crossed the room and folded Lourds's collar down. "What I'm trying to get at is that the two of you would be better off working together than being at loggerheads. You both need to listen to each other. You know more than he does about where the scroll could possibly be and that bothers him. And he has access to those wonderful monastic accounts that he won't let us see. Not only that, no one has gotten to see them." She paused. "Feel free to stop me when I start making sense."

"If he weren't so insufferable and cocksure of himself we'd probably get along better."

"Funny. He said something similar about you."

Lourds closed his notebook computer and put it away inside his backpack. "At least we can agree on that."

Olympia's smile faded as seriousness tightened her features. "If you're right, and I think that you are, tonight is going to be very dangerous."

"I thought things had already been very dangerous."

"They have, but you've been consumed by the scroll these last few days. You haven't seen what's going on out in the world."

Lourds knew that was true.

"When John of Patmos wrote the scroll, he made a prediction."

"That the scroll would be revealed during perilous times?" Lourds smiled at that. "A statement like that has to accompany every document that prophesizes the end of the world. It's to be expected."

"Come with me."

Curious at Olympia's serious demeanor, Lourds slung his backpack over a shoulder and trailed after her. In the common room she walked to the television that had been brought in to monitor local news.

When she switched it on, the screen filled with a local news station. The dateline showed Riyadh, Saudi Arabia, and showed troops mobilizing. Tanks sped through streets and across deserts while fighter jets blasted off airfields and streaked through blue skies as well as night skies.

"What's going on?" Lourds asked.

"The king of Saudi Arabia was assassinated a few days ago."

Lourds vaguely remembered something about that but it hadn't caught his full attention.

"His youngest son, Prince Khalid, has ascended to the throne. No one thought that would happen," Olympia said. "Prince Khalid has, more or less, taken a genocidal approach to politics within his country." She nodded at the television. "Apparently that view is currently quite popular."

Lourds was quite familiar with the young prince. He'd been in the news several times despite his father's remonstrations.

"It's the hand of the Lucifer," Joachim stated quietly.

"It's tension in the Middle East," Lourds responded. "Those problems have always been there. Sadly, they'll probably always remain. I wouldn't read any more into this than you see."

"Yet you advised me to trust you. It's time that you returned that trust."

Feeling slightly flummoxed, Lourds tugged at his goatee, then caught himself doing that and stopped.

"The destiny of our world lies in those lands," Joachim said. "And in this one. It's always been that way."

A knock sounded at the front door.

The monks gathered around.

"It's me," Cleena called from the other side of the door. "I'm alone and I'm coming in." The door opened and she stepped through.

Olympia frowned in distaste. Lourds knew she had hoped they'd seen the last of Cleena MacKenna when she'd left earlier.

"Is that blood on your sleeve?" Joachim pointed toward Cleena's right sleeve.

Lourds noticed the speckles Joachim pointed at. They were only now starting to turn to a crusty brown.

"Nothing to worry about," Cleena shot back.

"What have you done?" Olympia demanded.

"Nothing. If anything, I've bought us some time. But not much." Cleena stood her ground. Her hand wasn't far from her pistol and Lourds knew she didn't trust any of them too much. He couldn't help wondering what had brought her back. "This isn't even my problem. But I came back to help."

"Out of the goodness of your heart?"

Cleena shot the other woman a hard look but didn't respond. "You people don't realize what we're really up against. Or who."

"Lucifer," Joachim said without hesitation.

Cleena cursed. "Save your devils and demons. For whatever reason, the United States has declared an interest in this scroll."

"What do you mean?" Joachim said.

"The men back at the university," Lourds said. "The ones that followed us down into the tunnels."

"Yes," Cleena said. "Elliott Webster sent another team of CIA agents into Istanbul. I'd be willing to wager that he's also the one behind the military team that's been hot on our heels."

"Elliott Webster?" Olympia said. "The Vice President of the United States?"

"Unless you know another Elliott Webster that could give the CIA orders, yes. That's the one."

"Vice President Webster is there," one of the monks said.

"Where?" Lourds asked.

The man nodded toward the television. "There. In Saudi Arabia. He went over on a peacekeeping mission. Although everyone knows it's only to speak for the American and European business interests that have holdings there. At present, he's more or less a hostage in that country."

CHAPTER 23

KING ABDULLAH ECONOMIC CITY, SAUDI ARABIA
MARCH 24, 2010

"My God," Vicky DeAngeleo said as she stood at Webster's side and watched a row of buildings out on Financial Island suddenly blossom into surging infernos. Light erupted out over the dark water in the harbor and reflected on the rolling waves. "They've gone insane."

Webster couldn't help thinking that God had nothing to do with what was taking place in Saudi Arabia at the moment. In fact, Webster was positive of that. He almost laughed aloud at the thought.

"You know, boss," Tristan Hamilton said with a trace of nervousness clogging his baritone, "it might be an idea to step away from those windows. Even if no one decides to shoot up in here because they know you're here, a blast might come too close. If those windows explode, flying glass could chop you up into hamburger."

"We're going to be all right," Webster said. "This won't touch us."

"I don't know about you," Hamilton said, "but I got compadres plenty worried about the way the rebels have been lighting up oil fields like Roman candles. You get nervous people like that, something's gotta give. The United States can't run without oil. Our country will grind down to dust without it."

"That's one of the reasons I've been pushing to develop my technology," Stephen Napier said.

"Yeah, but you've been salting the mine, buddy," Hamilton said. "I know a lot of your heavy investors are oil people, and you're holding a few blue chip shares in corporations over here as well. If this cash cow dries up, you're gonna be hurting, too."

Another explosion, this one even larger, seared the night sky. This time the detonation rattled through Webster's flesh a few seconds later.

Hamilton cursed.

Vicky's phone rang. She answered it and stepped away, talking hurriedly.

Retreating to the bar, Webster poured himself another drink.

"You don't mind me saying," Napier told Webster when he joined him, "you seem to be awfully calm about this."

"I am," Webster said as he turned back toward the window. "The American navy is sitting out there as we speak. All it will take is one word from me and marines will be in here to get us out."

"That's good to know."

"It is, isn't it?" Webster drained his glass and made another.

"Why don't you call them in now?"

"Because the time isn't right. You know about timing, Stephen. How close are you on that alternative fuel source?"

Napier hesitated only a moment. "I don't suppose it would be too much telling you that we're closer than anyone knows."

"No, it wouldn't."

"But the timing of the new energy source is going to be tricky."

"Because if you wait too long, you're going to be playing catch-up in a deflated market that's not going to be able to pay top dollar. And if you break it too fast and people refuse to change over, you're going to be forced to sell it more cheaply than you otherwise could just so you can stay in business."

Napier nodded. "You understand."

"I do. When most of Japan's heavy industry sites were destroyed in World War Two, they had to start over from scratch. As a result, they used better equipment and created a much better product than American industry."

"Just like that. Except they were outside the American economy. The U.S. just pushed the import taxes up enough to help American car manufacturers stay in business."

"Until 1987 when the Japanese rescued the American dollar. After that, new arrangements were made to allow part of Japanese import manufacture to take place here, getting around the import tax."

"Then over the next twenty years, Japanese car sales started outstripping domestic products," Napier said. "And look at the state of the car industry today." He sipped his drink. "We can sell my product to America."

"But that's not the only market you want."

"No."

"You want it all. The world market. Or it's not worth having."

"Or at least as much of it as I can get."

"I can understand that." Webster glanced at the television where Vicky was watching with keen interest. "And I don't blame you."

"It'll be better for all of us if the alternative fuel is launched big," Napier said. "More profits means we can back up the changeover, create a cushion for the economy. As people get laid off from the petroleum industry, we should be able to absorb them. Most of them. But only if we capture a world share."

"I know."

"This situation, though, it's going to change the dynamic of everything."

Webster nodded. He knew that, too. He was counting on it.

PASSAGE OF OMENS
HAGİA SOPHİA UNDERGROUND
İSTANBUL, TURKEY
MARCH 24, 2010

"There's nothing here, Professor Lourds."

Ignoring the fierce vindication in Joachim's voice, Lourds shone his light over the passageway. He ran his hand over the wall and felt only the cold, *solid* stone. He took out his pocketknife and used it to tap against the wall.

"You're wasting our time," Joachim insisted.

"Can you cut him some slack?" Cleena asked.

The young woman's defense surprised Lourds. For a moment he forgot to tap. Evidently it had the same effect on Joachim because he just stared at her silently.

"He's trying to do something here," Cleena continued. "You're expecting him to do in days what you people couldn't do in eight hundred years. You might want to chill out a little and think about that."

Lourds smiled at that. Cleena joined him at the wall. She took out a knife and began tapping the stone surface as well.

"You're listening for hollow noises, right?" Cleena asked.

"I am," Lourds agreed. "When did you become a believer?"

"Me?" Cleena shook her head. "I'm a lapsed Catholic. Way lapsed."

"Not in God." Lourds moved out a few inches and tapped again. The stone still sounded solid. "In me."

"I wouldn't let it go to your head if I were you. It's a choice between you and the sourpuss over there. I'd rather believe in you. Otherwise we're going to be back at that hidey-hole they've carved out for themselves watching you read books. Personally, I'm up to my eyeballs with watching you read."

"I wasn't just reading," Lourds said defensively.

"I understand that, but you know what I mean." Cleena moved down a little bit and started tapping again.

Olympia picked up a loose stone from the ground and used it to tap on the wall as well. "You're sure it's this side of the passageway?"

"Yes. This is where it has to be according to the scroll I deciphered." Despite his own insistence, though, Lourds felt his confidence waning. He had stepped off the distance himself, then stepped it off two more times. According to everything he had figured out, the entrance to the Passage of Omens had to be within this general vicinity. He didn't know how they could have missed it.

Only solid stone met his efforts.

"You're sure about the distance?" Cleena asked.

"Yes."

"Did they use different measurements back in those days?"

"Now why didn't I think of that?" Olympia asked sarcastically.

"Careful," Cleena said. "You keep up with that ill-tempered attitude and somebody may just drop a house on you."

"Really?" Olympia said. "You did not just say that. We're here, following up in the footsteps of a man who gave us the most intriguing and important book in the Bible, and you're talking about *The Wizard of Oz?*"

"Actually it wasn't the wizard. That was an allusion to one of the wicked Witches."

"I knew what the allusion was to. I just think maybe—"

"Ladies," Lourds interrupted.

They looked at him, faces lifted out of the darkness by the flashlights everyone carried.

"I can't hear the sound of the tapping," Lourds pointed out. "If I can't hear the tapping, I can't hear the hollow sounds."

Both the women turned their attention back to the search. In both directions down the hallway, Joachim and the other monks were busy tapping as well.

Lourds brushed the sweat from his forehead with his sleeve. Then he resumed his task. He was right about the translation. The door had to be here. Somewhere.

KING ABDULLAH ECONOMIC CITY, SAUDI ARABIA
MARCH 24, 2010

"My God," Vicky whispered. Her eyes never left the television. She held a sat phone to her ear. "Keep them in there. This footage is amazing."

Crossing the room, Webster joined her. The camera angle was sketchy at best, bouncing around crazily. On the screen, Saudi tanks rolled through the street. From the angle and the geography, Webster guessed the tanks were somewhere near the row of buildings that had just blown up.

A wave of gunmen backed away from the approaching tanks. The men took cover behind buildings, but it ultimately did no good. The tank crews fired into them, blasting through stone walls with main guns and .50-cal machine guns. Dead men and broken buildings littered the street amid an ocean of blood. Like mechanical predators, the tanks rolled over the corpses and debris, grinding them into dust and organic pulp.

The cameraman was shooting from only a few steps behind the wave of rebels. Obviously in fear for his life, judging from the quick, awkward movements the man made, he dodged and scampered.

Another man trailed him and mixed in with the line of rebels. The second man had a microphone clenched in his fist. Tension knotted his face.

"—can see that Prince Khalid's shock troops aren't holding any—," the man with the microphone said.

"Stay in line with that camera, Jernigan," Vicky ordered in a hard voice. "These shots are money. I'll make sure your name is known in every household in the United States. Just calm down and stay with—"

At that moment, a round from one of the heavy machine guns caught the man in the back of the head. Blood, bone, and brain matter exploded in a liquid rush. Some of it caught the camera lens and put a scarlet film over the view.

Vicky cursed. "Harrison! Listen to me! I know he's dead. I saw it happen. Stay with the shot. This is the kind of footage that makes cameramen legends."

It's also the kind of footage that will be played on YouTube for years, Webster knew. And he knew that Vicky DeAngelo was more interested in that aspect. All that footage would be watermarked with her media logo.

The tanks advanced over the bodies that had dropped into the street. One of them belonged to the reporter.

The camera wavered hard to the right. Webster knew from the angle the man was considering diving into the nearest shop.

"Harrison," Vicky stated coolly, "stay on task. Stay on the tanks. We need—"

The camera view suddenly swung away and up. It focused on the leaping flames overhead for a moment, then whirled to the ground in a kaleidoscope of spinning landscapes.

Vicky swore and punched another button on her sat phone. "Harrison, you'd better be dead or missing a body part!"

Webster smiled as he listened to Vicky directing the news producer to move to the next hot spot in the city. As the view shifted, Webster's sat phone rang. The caller ID confirmed it was coming from the White House. He thumbed the button and answered.

"Hello," President Waggoner said. *"Elliott?* Elliott, is that you?"

"Yes. I'm here, Mike." Crackles echoed along the connection.

"Thank God," Waggoner said. "We'd lost touch with you."

Actually, Webster deliberately hadn't answered the last call and he knew that the Secret Service agents' effort to remain in contact with their primary handler had been blocked. Spider had seen to that. The man sat in the corner of the room and stayed hooked into his computer.

Webster knew Spider was in his element, weaving tactical forays through the domestic internet and the international one. He was also the one responsible for making certain Vicky DeAngelo's broadcasts got out to the communications satellites. Spider was the man behind the curtain, the wizard who made the whole experience work around the globe.

"We're still here," Webster said.

"Is there any way you can get clear of that place?" Waggoner asked.

"Not without considerable risk."

"You're already in considerable risk. I just watched a reporter get killed on national television."

When Webster glanced at the television, he saw that Vicky had already looped the action on the broadcast. It spun again and again in a screen-in-screen presentation. By tomorrow morning, that would be one of the images most remembered from tonight. As Webster watched, the reporter died again, and the camera view turned red. Then it began once more.

"I have Prince Khalid's promise that nothing will happen to us," Webster said.

"Even if the king's army doesn't lay a finger on you, the rebels are gunning for you. The CIA has intercepted encrypted communications in that area between the Shia terrorists."

That was also courtesy of Spider. Of course, the idea for that had come from Webster. Humans thrived on drama. Nothing divided them more quickly and "breaking" television news had become the drug of choice. That was one of the weaknesses of giving humans free will. They had to be constantly stimulated in order to use it. When the stimulation didn't occur naturally, they artificially created it.

"That surprises me," Webster said, though it didn't.

"They think the United States is in league with the Sunnis and the king."

"We've always given that impression. We've had a long history of agreeing to terms with these people. Until our presence in Iraq to shore up the Shias."

"I know, but now there's some rumors flying around that the United States plans to take advantage of all the confusion going on there to make a land grab."

"We both know that's not true." But it was exactly what Webster had intended.

"Not entirely," the president said.

"What do you mean?"

"I've heard rumors that some of the domestic corporations are planning to use mercenary units to protect their assets over there."

"You could hardly blame them." Webster watched as a large freighter blew up out in the harbor. "Neither Prince Khalid nor his opponents care about collateral losses. Those corporations are going to lose millions by morning. Those losses won't mean much to the Saudis. Their economy will still be stable. They have what everyone wants, and nearly all of that is safely underground. After the fires go out and the dust settles on this, corporations will line up again to pay for rights to drill."

"Only for the moment," Waggoner said. "That will change as soon as we no longer need their oil."

"Things always change."

"But until that time, we need to salvage as much of this situation as we can."

A military helicopter flew uncomfortably close to the building. Hamilton and Napier drew back from the floor-to-ceiling glass. In the next moment, the helicopter fired a series of rockets that reduced the street in front of the hotel into piles of flaming rubble. The cannonade vibrated through the building under Webster's feet. Smoke drifted up and momentarily obscured the battlefield outside the glass.

Waggoner swore. "Is that your hotel?"

Webster glanced at the television screen and saw that the view was indeed of the hotel. He wondered if Vicky DeAngelo's people had followed a group of Shia there or if they'd returned in hopes of being granted asylum.

In the next second, a wave of fire washed over the front of the building. The heat immediately killed the landscaped grounds in front of the hotel. Only a moment later the expensive façade scorched and carbon covered the glass for a short time before the windows cracked and fell apart.

"Yes," Webster said. "That's our hotel."

"Elliott, you can't take chances like this. You need to get yourself and those people out of there now."

"And where would we go?"

"I've got a fleet standing by. They've got people on board that can get you out of there."

"I'm not convinced we're through here yet."

"The borders of that country are becoming free fire zones."

"I know, but if the United States sends a military force into this country—even to rescue the vice president—those free-fire zones are going to turn into a conflagration that will sweep across the Middle East. Our actions will be interpreted by the Sunnis as supporting the Shia. The Shia will interpret those actions as a lack of faith and weakness in the Sunnis." Webster paused. "We're stuck between a rock and a hard place, Mike. I don't want to have to make any decisions prematurely."

"Your hotel is on fire," Waggoner said. "If anything, you're making decisions too late."

"A lot of American people work in this country," Webster said. "*Our* people, Mike. People that you and I swore to defend when we took office. I can't bail on them." He paused, knowing he was hitting every narcissistic patriotic button Waggoner had. "If we decide to get me out of here, I want to get all of the American people out of this city. When we finish our terms, I want to go out with a bang, not a frightened whimper. I don't want to be remembered as the vice president that tucked his tail between his legs and ran out of Saudi Arabia to leave all his fellow countrymen to die."

Waggoner was silent for a time.

On the television, the lower story was suddenly filled with a snowstorm. Webster knew that the fire-suppression system had been triggered. Saudi military units rolled two fire trucks toward the hotel. Within seconds, the teams had offloaded hoses and sprayed water over the fire.

"Do you know what you're asking for, Elliott?" Waggoner asked.

"A way to keep our people safe. Just like we promised."

"To do that, we'd have to create an American beachhead somewhere near your location. We'd have to control real estate over there. The Saudis—Prince Khalid—won't like that because it'll look like we're undercutting his authority and that we don't have faith in him."

"I know. But that may be what's called for. As far as the prince's authority, there are a lot of people flaunting it right now." Webster didn't intend to settle for anything less than what he wanted.

"And you don't think that's going to cause an international incident?"

"On the contrary. I know it will. I don't want to do that unless we have to. And if it should come to that, we need to make a statement. We may be buying the oil from this country, but that also counts as a huge investment." They would have to make that statement. Webster was going to see to that. Spider would make certain of it. "If the Saudis can make any headway in this, if they can contain the violence—soon, then it's not going to matter. I feel certain Prince Khalid will honor his promise to take care of our people. But if he can't, we need to be ready to take care of our people ourselves."

"You're talking about an invasion force."

"No. An invasion force comes to stay or to plunder. I just want to get our people out with as few casualties as possible." *That sounds positively noble, doesn't it?* Webster knew the president wouldn't be able to resist the bait to outgrandstand him.

Outside, another series of explosions made the window tremble and rolled echoes through the building. Vicky wrapped her arms more tightly around herself and shivered, but she never stopped giving orders.

Hamilton and Napier were also engaged on their sat phones.

"You know what I'm saying is right, Mike," Webster said gently, "and I know this is all scary." He basted his words in conviction. "We didn't ask for the situation. If Prince Khalid hadn't risen to power, we wouldn't be here now. But he did, and he started this mess that's currently threatening to swallow this country and has endangered our people."

"He has the army on his side. This engagement shouldn't take long."

"That was said about Iraq. Both times."

Behind the hotel, toward the heart of the city, more explosives ripped a naked skeleton of a building in progress to shreds. The steel girders collapsed and spilled into the street like a child's game.

"Look at the big picture over here," Webster said, "If we don't step in, the Chinese will. They need the oil as badly as we do. In fact, if we don't do something soon, they may view this as the perfect time to advance and grab a stranglehold. And once they're in, Mike, you know they're not going to be easy to dissuade. They have their own needs."

The president sighed tiredly. "This is getting to be a bed of snakes, Elliott."

"It's always been a bed of snakes. The snakes are just more prevalent at the moment."

Vicky turned to Webster with a look of surprise. "There are unidentified aircraft flying into the oil fields. Do you know anything about that?"

Webster shook his head.

"What was that?" the president asked. "Something about aircraft?"

"Do you have anyone out there?" Webster asked Vicky.

The woman shook her head. "So far, Prince Khalid's forces have managed to keep the fighting from reaching the oil fields. I didn't think we needed anyone in the area. I've got a team en route that way now."

"Never mind," the president said. "Evidently World News Network has picked up the story."

"WNN already has someone there," Webster told Vicky.

"I know. How do you think I'm getting my information?"

Webster pulled out his TV remote control handset and changed the channel to the WNN Channel. The ante had obviously just been increased. He wanted to see the results.

PASSAGE OF OMENS

HAGİA SOPHİA UNDERGROUND

İSTANBUL, TURKEY
MARCH 24, 2010

"You're refusing to admit defeat, Professor Lourds," Joachim accused. "That passageway, if it was ever here, isn't here now." His frustration echoed along the hallway.

A few of the monks continued checking the wall, as did Cleena and Olympia.

Lourds refused to be distracted. He took a bottle of water from his backpack and reviewed his mental notes regarding his translation. He'd gotten the directions right. This was the tunnel. He was certain of that.

But where was the hidden door?

"We need to try somewhere else," Joachim said.

"No," Lourds said. "It's here."

"Then where is it?"

"Obviously, it's hidden." Lourds put away the water bottle. "The scroll said that the Passage of Omens wouldn't be found until the time was right."

"Then maybe the time isn't right?" Olympia joined them. Perspiration gleamed on her skin.

"That would be an easy answer for failure," Joachim said.

"Don't," Olympia told him. "We wouldn't be this far if it weren't for Thomas."

"We don't know how far we are, do we?" Joachim walked away to join the other monks and once more begin the assault on the wall.

"For a monk, he doesn't have a lot of faith, does he?" Lourds asked.

Olympia sipped from a water bottle. "I can understand his frustration. Can you imagine having the kind of knowledge he's had all these years and not being able to find the Scroll of Joy?"

Lourds thought of the lost library of Alexandria and how he had spent the last twenty-something years chasing scraps of information, myths, and rumors in an effort to locate whatever books might have survived that fire all those years ago.

"Actually, I can imagine. And it is frustrating."

Olympia looked down the passageway. "Is it possible that another tunnel was dug? That the one we're actually looking for is on either side of us?"

"We didn't see another tunnel."

"That doesn't mean there isn't one. This area is honeycombed with tunnels. It's worse than a rabbit's warren."

"Reminds me a lot of London's underground," Lourds admitted. "The underground beneath New York pales by comparison. At least the tunnels there are larger."

"That's because they were made for subways and utility lines. These were only made for refugees."

"You would think it would be easier to find a hidden passageway in this restricted space." Fatigue ate at Lourds as he stared into the darkness.

"There were no other clues about the location?"

Lourds shook his head. "The scroll said the location of the Passage of Omens wouldn't be revealed until the time was right."

"And what time would that be?"

An ungracious smile pulled at Lourds's mouth. "It's amazing how oblique things like this scroll can be when it comes to the concrete details."

"Surely there was something."

Lourds quoted. " 'Only a fearful and penitent man will find the doorway to the Passage of Omens. The righteous will never know the way.' "

"That's all it said?"

"That's all. Other than the directions of how to get here." A thought suddenly struck Lourds and he wondered why he had not realized it before. He strode forward, back to his original location in the tunnel. "A fearful and penitent man. Not a righteous one."

"Thomas?" Olympia trailed after him and her movement attracted the attention of everyone else in the passageway.

Lourds silently cursed himself. At the spot he had marked, he dropped to his knees and looked at the floor. Carefully, he used his free hand to brush away the accumulated debris that had gathered for hundreds of years. Gradually, the stones became clear.

Without a word, Olympia and Joachim joined him in his endeavor. The cleared space grew larger and larger.

Joachim paused. "I found something." He shined his light on one of the stones. "There's writing here. I can't read it."

Lourds walked over and squatted down beside him. The writing was there, but it was almost illegible, almost worn away by the passage of feet and time. He took his water bottle from his backpack, unscrewed the cap, and poured some of the contents onto the engraved stone.

The water further washed out the inscription and made it easier to read, but the shadows were deceptive even after Lourds dried the area with a shirtsleeve.

Taking his journal from his backpack, Lourds laid a page over the inscription and made a rubbing. The result was even clearer. He held up the page and Joachim trained his flashlight on it.

"You can read this?" Joachim asked.

"I can," Lourds replied. "It's the same language that was in the scroll." He worked the translation in his head, then said it out loud. " 'Look to God for the answers that you seek.' "

Joachim trained his beam on the ceiling. Spiderwebs obscured the roof over the passageway.

Lourds put his journal away and stood. He took his shirt off, stripping down to his undershirt, then he waved the shirt overhead and knocked the cobwebs away.

On one of the stones overhead, Lourds barely made out the inscription, but he knew what it was.

The Passage of Omens.

CHAPTER 24

PASSAGE OF OMENS
HAGİA SOPHİA UNDERGROUND
İSTANBUL, TURKEY
MARCH 24, 2010

Joachim and another of the monks held Lourds's feet and boosted him toward the ceiling. He swayed drunkenly at first, then caught his balance and easily made the ascent. He braced himself with one hand against the ceiling while he inspected the inscribed stone with the other.

"Perhaps you could hurry, Professor Lourds," the monk suggested.

"Oh. Sorry." Lourds wanted to get a rubbing of the stone but that didn't seem feasible at the moment. He turned his attention to finding a locking release mechanism.

The entrance was defined by the small cracks around it. The doorway looked scarcely large enough for a grown man to crawl through. Joachim and the monk were straining in their efforts to hold him when he found the release.

Something clicked within the stone door.

Lourds had figured that the door would open outward and had prepared himself for that eventuality. Instead, the door remained in place.

Tentatively, Lourds pushed against the door. It was heavy,

but it swung backward on hinges and crashed against the upper floor. The resounding boom echoed and let Lourds know the room beyond was fairly sizable.

"Come on down," Joachim said. "Let's regroup and think about our next—"

Overcome by his curious nature, Lourds tossed his flashlight through the opening and caught the edges in both hands. He flexed his knees and pushed against Joachim and the other monk, knocking them off balance and sending them toppling to the floor.

Joachim protested at once, scrambling to his feet.

Lourds barely even considered apologizing. He didn't get enough spring from his jump to get him through the opening, but it brought him closer. He hoisted himself up, then through, and into the hidden passageway.

Panting from the exertion, almost vibrating from the excitement, Lourds picked up his flashlight and played the beam around the room. The passageway was narrow and ran between two short walls that held a succession of beautiful mosaics.

"Lourds," Joachim bellowed from below. "Come back."

Lourds couldn't have come back. His fascination was too complete. He played his beam over the mosaics and saw images ripped from the Old Testament. In one mosaic, God created man. In another, God cast an angel from heaven. A third showed an angel with a flaming sword driving Adam and Eve from the Garden of Eden.

Another flashlight beam joined Lourds's as he walked along the passageway. He barely took notice of Joachim behind him. The monk was overcome by everything that he saw around him.

Olympia came next, followed by Cleena, then the other monks. There was scarcely room for all of them within the passageway.

"Oh my God," Olympia whispered. Her voice, trapped in the small enclosure, sounded loud. "These are beautiful."

"More than that," Lourds told her, "they're history." He reached out and touched a mosaic depicting Noah's ark surging across a storm-tossed sea.

"These are from God's Holy Word," Joachim said. "Not just history."

Lourds didn't bother to argue the point. He was consumed by everything he saw.

"You could spend years studying everything that's in this passageway," Olympia said. "The subject matter. The artists involved. The media and techniques used."

"Not exactly what we're here for," Cleena said. She didn't seem to be awed by the history surrounding her.

"She's right," Joachim said. "Where's the Scroll of Joy?"

Lourds pressed on. "The scroll didn't mention the actual location, but it did say the answers were here."

The tunnel ended only a short distance ahead. Lourds shined his light over the small room and saw more mosaics on the walls.

"There are candles." Olympia picked out the iron sconces on either side of the entrance with her flashlight beam.

Forcibly, Lourds tore his attention from the mosaics on the other side of the room and pulled out his lighter. The conditions inside the passageway had remained relatively constant for the hundreds and possibly thousands of years the candles had sat in the sconces.

For a moment, as Lourds held the flame to the wick, he didn't think it would light. Then slowly, the twisted fibers accepted the flames and swelled into a golden nimbus that chased darkness from the room. Olympia lit the candle on the other side of the entranceway. Joachim and the monks entered the room and lit still more candles.

When they were finished, the mosaics gleamed on the wall and the scent of burning animal fat tickled Lourds's nostrils.

The four mosaics showed different images but were framed in similar white borders that stood out starkly against the stone walls.

The first mosaic showed a cistern where an upside-down Medusa head sat submerged in blue water.

"That's the Basilica Cistern," Olympia said.

Lourds nodded in agreement. With the Medusa head in the mosaic, it could be no other place. An inscription, done in tiny bright stones, threaded through the bottom of the mosaic.

"What does it say?" Joachim asked.

" 'When the monster's head rights itself, you will see the first sign of the approaching apocalypse. Only the Scroll of Joy may prevent the Great Deceiver's lies. Your journey begins here.' "

Lourds opened his backpack and took out his digital camera. He quickly shot several images of all the mosaics, each in turn. He also wrote the information down in his journal. Then he moved on to the second mosaic.

The second mosaic showed a picture of a church with a dome top. Inside the building, the unmistakable figure of Jesus, his head surrounded by a halo, lay at rest.

"What place is that?" Cleena asked.

"Golgotha," Lourds answered.

"Where Jesus was crucified and laid to rest," Joachim explained. "It's in Jerusalem's Old City."

"It's also where the True Cross was kept for a time," Olympia added. "Constantine's mother Helen ordered the Bishop of Jerusalem to build the church there. As soon as it was built, Christian pilgrimages there began. Unfortunately the church was a center of unrest for a long time. The fragments of the True Cross were lost to Muslim invaders at the end of the tenth century. Tariqu al-Hakim, one of the caliphs, destroyed the church all the way down to the bedrock as a protest against Easter pilgrimages."

"The downside of tourism," Lourds commented. "Al-Hakim's son, Ali az-Zahir, agreed to let Constantine the Eighth rebuild the church, but it wasn't until the arrival of the Crusaders that the church was once more made whole. Since that time, it's been damaged on a number of occasions."

"This inscription looks different from the first," Olympia observed.

"It is." Lourds wrote in his journal as he translated. " 'Two Brothers will make war on each other, believers both in a new prophet yet to be born of the word, and they will fight over the return of my son.' "

"The only new prophet born after Jesus is Mohammad," Olympia said.

"If you choose to believe the Qur'an," Joachim said sourly.

"Also a valuable document of history," Lourds said. "But if I had to guess, I'd guess that the prophet this is referring to was Mohammad." He nodded at the mosaic. "There's more. It says, 'When the shadow of the True Cross returns to the temple of our savior, you'll know that the End of Days is near.' "

"How is the shadow of the True Cross supposed to return to the Church of the Holy Sepulchre?" Olympia asked. "The True Cross was destroyed and lost forever."

"I don't know," Lourds answered. "I'm only reading what's here." He moved on to a third mosaic.

"This looks like another picture of the Church of the Holy Sepulchre," Cleena said. "Except this one has a weeping woman."

"Not a woman," Joachim said. "Mary, the mother of Jesus." As with Jesus, Mary's head was also surrounded by a glowing halo.

"New Jerusalem Church," Lourds said. "I've been there. They have a fantastic collection of Greek and Slavonic manuscripts. Patriarch Nikon, Nikita Minin, belonged to the Russian Orthodox Church. As its seventh patriarch, he headed up a number of reforms. Unfortunately, those reforms ended up splitting the church and gaining him eventual disfavor with Tsar Alexius, who until that point had been his best friend and a source of financing."

"New Jerusalem Church has been returned to a monastery," Joachim said.

Lourds nodded. "That happened back in 1990. For a while it was completely shut down. Many of the church's treasures and icons were lost, but they retain the statue of the Virgin Mary."

"What does this inscription say?" Olympia asked.

" 'A great friend of the church will fall, but not before he rises up an echo of the final resting place of our blessed Savior. When the statue of his blessed Mother weeps, you will know the end of the world is near.' "

"Doesn't exactly sound hopeful, does it?" Cleena asked.

"We wouldn't have been sent here if there was nothing we could do," Joachim stated. "We all have a purpose in this place."

The fourth mosaic showed orange trees around a fountain. A church was in the background, but had Islamic architecture instead of Byzantine or Gothic. Lourds knew the church's long and interesting history because he'd studied there for a time.

"This church, I'm supposing it's a church, doesn't look like the other two," Cleena commented.

"It's a church," Olympia replied. "This is the Great Mosque of Córdoba. Also known as the Mezquita of Córdoba."

"A mosque isn't a place where I'd expect to find Christian artifacts."

"The two cultures have regularly tramped the same grounds," Olympia said. "Just as the Hagia Sophia, for a time, became an Islamic church, so did the Great Mosque of Córdoba in Spain."

"It looks like it's always been a mosque."

"No, it began as a Visigothic Church."

"I'm not going to pretend I know what that is."

"They were the East Germanic tribe of the Goths. Not the vampire wannabes."

"That, I had figured."

"Just checking. I don't want to go too fast for you."

"I'll let you know if you do."

"Anyway," Olympia continued, "the Visigoths began the church there in A.D. 600. Then the Muslims arrived. Emir Abd ar-Rahman I annexed it and named it in honor of his wife. He began the reconstruction, and that lasted for two hundred years."

"So who owns it now?"

"King Ferdinand the Third of Castile took the church back in 1236 and it eventually became called the Cathedral of the Assumption of the Virgin."

"What does the inscription on this one have to say?"

Lourds leaned in for a better look. Then he translated, " 'At the church that is a crossroads where the east meets the west and both of those revere the Holy Mother, there will be made a pool. When the waters of the pool run red with blood, the end of the world will be near.' "

"And this is supposed to help us?" Cleena asked. "This isn't even a good pep talk."

"Don't blaspheme," Joachim admonished.

"You don't realize how astonishing this is," Lourds said. "John of Patmos died hundreds of years before the Great Mosque of Córdoba was constructed. Any of the times it was constructed. That he was able to predict it, and even guide the mosaic artists in these renderings so that we can tell what these things are now is incredible."

Lourds's mind worried at the information. Nothing in his education had prepared him for something like this. Of course, he hadn't been prepared for Atlantis either.

"Figuring out how that guy knew all this stuff isn't going to help us now," Cleena said.

Joachim said, "Now you are the one who should be patient."

Cleena ignored him. "So where is the Scroll of Joy?"

Lourds stepped back from the wall and tried to take in the room.

"If the scroll isn't here, shouldn't there be another clue?"

Staring at the mosaics, Lourds felt as though there were something he was missing. He was also certain that it was right in front of him, as plain as the nose on his face.

Something about the mosaics. Something in the background. But it wasn't visible to the casual eye. He took a deep breath and let it out, letting his mind soak up everything in the room. The candle flames wavered only slightly and caused brief shadows to scamper across the mosaic surfaces.

Just as he almost had it, he reached for it—and it disappeared, eluded his grasp like fog. The mosaics all had amazing perspectives. They looked three dimensional, just like someone could—

Lourds focused, hardly daring to believe what he was thinking. He strode forward and ran his hands over the mosaics.

"Thomas, what are you doing?" Olympia asked.

"It's got to be here. There's no reason to hide the scroll anymore. This room, this passageway, that was the secret. The scroll was hidden here. It still is."

As his body shifted in front of the mosaics, his shadow drifted across them. And a momentary flicker on the second mosaic caught his eye. It had only been a subtle shifting of shadows.

When he tried to touch that spot, his fingers seemed to pass through the mosaic. Once the illusion was broken, he saw how clever the artist had truly been. There in the final resting place of Jesus, Lourds found the hole that contained a cylindrical shape. He smiled both at his own cleverness as well as that of the designer.

He drew it from within the depths. The cylinder was carved wood and held only a few words in the language that Lourds had only just learned. When translated, they read: *The Joy*.

Lourds's hands trembled with excitement as he opened the cylinder.

KING ABDULLAH ECONOMIC CITY, SAUDI ARABIA
MARCH 24, 2010

Anticipation filled Webster as he watched the helicopters descend on the oil field. The private security team had to have been staged on a freighter somewhere offshore to get this close.

Saudi forces battled what Webster assumed were Shia forces. The helicopter pilots opened fire with heavy machine guns and killed them all indiscriminately.

"Do we have someone there?" Vicky DeAngelo demanded as she watched the attack. "You've got an international incident taking shape out there right now and I'm having to watch on WNN News! That is not what I pay you for!"

Webster walked back to Spider. "Who's in the helicopters?"

Spider smiled slyly. "Them cowboys belong to Carnahan Oil. They're the same bunch that settled the labor dispute in those West African companies a few years back."

Webster remembered the story. Carnahan Oil was known for riding roughshod over third world countries they did business with.

In Africa, the way the oil business generally worked was cutthroat. Once oil was discovered, the politicians—or king—struggled to keep as much money as possible. All the while, they promised to spread the wealth. When the average citizen noticed that the wealth wasn't being spread, they usually went on strike. Then the king, or politicians, called in the military to break up the strike and get the oil pumping again. Problems started when the military started thinking they were taking all the risks and not getting paid nearly enough. Then a coup took place, and the king, or politicians, were replaced by a military dictator who spread the wealth around to his troops.

During the West African debacle, Carnahan Oil had sent in their shock troops, regretfully weren't able to save the king, and shot the oppressive dictator dead in the throne room. They put their own person in charge, spread a little more wealth around to the citizens, and cut out the middleman.

Almost overnight, the paradigm for doing oil business in West Africa changed. No longer did the bulk of the profits go to the country that owned the oil. Now it went to those able to extract the oil.

Across the room, Tristan Hamilton cheered on the arriving helicopters.

"Elliott," the president called over the phone.

"I'm here, Mike. As you can tell, the problems over here are multiplying."

"You need to get out of there," Waggoner said. "Once everyone knows Americans are over there pulling this kind of crap, the Saudis and the Shia are going to retaliate."

"Not just me, Mike. We've got to find a way to get us all home."

"All right," Waggoner said. "Let me get with the Pentagon and see what they can put together. You stay healthy till I get back to you, do you hear me?"

"I do. I will." Webster looked at the television then at the wall of glass, catching his own flickering reflection in the fires that burned around the city. "We'll come through this okay, Mike. You'll see."

The president broke the connection and Webster pocketed the satphone.

Vicky used the remote control to change channels on the television. Once she had it back on her network, she seemed more relaxed. Her people were more deeply entrenched in the oil field confrontation than the reporters from WNN News. Webster wouldn't be surprised if there was another fatality. He was certain Vicky DeAngelo was counting on that.

"That was the president?" Vicky asked. She didn't miss much, especially when she was in hyper mode.

"It was."

"He wants to get you out of here."

"Yes, he does."

"But you are not going to go?" Vicky looked up at him.

"You're in the news business. You want to tell me how you would present a story about the Vice President of United States deserting a country where hundreds of his fellow citizens were left in danger?"

Her smile was cold enough to adorn a morgue. "Truth to tell, Mr. Vice President, I'd crucify you."

"Now there's a particularly gruesome death." Webster smiled in remembrance.

"So you're staying here."

"How would you feel if I left you behind?"

"I'd crucify you twice."

Webster smiled.

"I have to admit that I'm somewhat irked at your lack of willingness to be rescued."

"Why?"

"Because if you get rescued, I would get rescued, too. Seems pretty selfish of you to decide we can all die here."

"We're not going to die here."

"How would you know?"

"Because I would."

Vicky looked at him, new understanding and suspicion dawning in her eyes. "Waggoner's going to do it, isn't he? He's going to try to get us out of here."

"Are you going to quote me on this?"

"No."

"Then yes. He is going to try to get us out of here."

"When?"

"Soon."

Vicky looked back through the window at the burning city. "Well, he'd better not be late."

Webster threw an arm around her and pulled her close. No matter how much Vicky DeAngelo liked to pretend she was captain of her own fate, she lived with fear. Everyone on the planet did.

Of course, they didn't know what real fear was. Yet. But when the time came, if they didn't align themselves with Webster, he intended to show them.

At that moment, a bolt of pure cold lanced Webster's heart. He swayed for a moment and nearly fell. He forced himself to remain on his feet and the feeling went away.

Vicky looked at him with concern. "Are you all right?"

"Of course." Webster smiled at her reassuringly. "Why wouldn't I be?"

"You would be. You always are." Vicky patted his chest.

But he knew what had happened. Someone had found that cursed scroll that John of Patmos had written. He left Vicky and retreated to the corner. He took his sat phone out of his pocket and called Eckart's number.

"You haven't found them."

"Not yet," Eckart replied. "We will. It's just a matter of time."

"They found the scroll."

"Where?"

"I don't know. If I did, I would've sent you there first." Webster made himself relax and take the edge out of his voice. If they had found the scroll, it meant that Lourds had broken the language the Brotherhood of the Scroll had developed.

One of the languages anyway.

For thousands of years, the plan had been in effect. Even the Brotherhood of the Scroll had been breached in the end. Constantinople, the king, had been but the beginning. He had helped foster the paranoia inside the brotherhood, making them aware of how vulnerable their knowledge was. God had created man to be open, to have no secrets.

God didn't have secrets, though. That was one thing man had not understood. And that was why the serpent was so successful in the Garden of Eden. The serpent had encouraged Adam and Eve to know the things that not even God would have been able to explain to them. The serpent had known, but not even the serpent could have explained God's ways.

They just were.

All it had taken was the suggestion that there were things that God did not want man to know. The rift had started then and had not ended.

"Find them," Webster ordered. "And when you do, kill them."

"What about professor?"

"Kill him, too. I no longer care to know what he knows. Kill him and bring the scroll to me." Webster put the phone back in his pocket.

In all of his plans, he had never factored in someone as gifted—or, in reality, as lucky—as Professor Thomas Lourds. Now the man's skills were going to earn him nothing more than an early grave.

PASSAGE OF OMENS
HAGİA SOPHİA UNDERGROUND
İSTANBUL, TURKEY
MARCH 25, 2010

In the steady, golden candlelight, Lourds translated the scroll and read it aloud.

> *Let it be known that this is the last writing of John, also known as John of Patmos. I am an old man, and I am come*

willingly to the end of my days. I write now under no threat of coercion only what the Lord my God would have me write.

I came to this island to spend my final days in peace, but I did not find peace. I found only the end of the world. I have seen him, I have seen the Beast, the Devil by all his names, and I have seen his efforts to take the world down before Jesus comes again.

I was there when Jesus returned to us the first time, and I saw myself the holes in his blessed hands and his blessed feet. We were not all believers. It changed me to admit this, but we were not. Even after everything we had seen him do, after we had seen him walk on stormy waters, after we had seen him raise the dead, we could not easily believe he had risen after dying so painfully.

As hard as it had been to watch him die, it was harder still to watch him take his leave of us. And more difficult again to take our leave from each other.

Many of us are dead now. In fact, I believe myself to be the last of his chosen alive, and that won't last much longer.

You have read my visions of what is to come, of the seven years that will plague those who do not truly believe. But I have not revealed everything that will pass.

There will come a day when the Great Deceiver will rise to power among men. He will pass among you as one of your own and you will know him not. He will have practiced to be one of you. He will be born unto woman, but he will be darkly evil. In those End Times you will not recognize evil as surely as you may think. But when you know the Devil, know also that no weapon made by human hands will truly destroy him.

Only one thing is capable of that, and I will soon give it to you. It is called the Scroll of Joy and it has the power to strip away the Great Deceiver's might that he will have accumulated by the time you read this.

The Scroll of Joy has, like the writing that has led you here and given you these secrets, been written in another language. Four keys to this language have been hidden in the places in the mosaics. Together, they will give you enough information to decipher the Scroll of Joy.

Now, please forgive me for I am very weary and wish only to see my Master in all His Glory. God be with you and reward you with his mercies.

Lourds looked up from the scroll. "That's all there is. Except for the second scroll."

The second scroll had been wrapped in the first. True to John of Patmos's words, Lourds hadn't been able to read the second scroll.

Joachim looked at the wall behind Lourds. "These places then."

Lourds looked at the mosaics as well. "These places. And with everyone pursuing us."

With a smile, Joachim turned to him. "Now you will find your faith, Professor Lourds. With all that is arrayed against us, I think we can agree that we will not get through this alone."

I don't know if we're going to get through this alive, much less alone, Lourds thought.

BASİLİCA CİSTERN
HAGİA SOPHİA UNDERGROUND
İSTANBUL, TURKEY
MARCH 25, 2010

"How are we supposed to get the Medusa head to turn over?" Cleena asked.

They stood in the huge room filled with stone columns. Every sound they made echoed throughout the building.

"With this," Lourds said. He held up the first scroll and showed them the end. He had been puzzling over it since he'd first seen it. Now he felt certain that it was a key. But where was the keyhole?

"Here," Olympia called. She'd evidently deduced what the rod was going to be used for as well.

Lourds walked around to her on the other side of the Medusa head. She aimed her flashlight at a crevice between a pair of snakes that sprouted from the Medusa's head.

Sliding the rod into the crevice, Lourds felt the channel bottom out. He turned the rod and heard tumblers click.

Then the Medusa head vibrated as mechanisms inside slid into place. Four snakes elongated and became a pedestal. Stone ground against stone as the snake legs took the weight of the head and allowed it to flip right side up.

Lourds watched in amazement. A moment later, what had been a seamless forehead split open and revealed a gap that held a gold ring with a four-inch span. As the noise died away, Lourds reached for the ring and removed it from its hiding place.

He felt the inscriptions on the inside of the ring before he saw them. They were etched fine and sharp, looking as though it had been only days instead of two thousand years since they'd been made.

"What is it?" Joachim asked as he joined Lourds.

Lourds fingered the notches cut into the side of the ring. "Part of a device that, hopefully, will prove to be a Rosetta Stone."

"Are you certain?" Olympia asked.

"I am," Lourds said, "unless John of Patmos intended to have a final joke at the expense of this world." He put the ring carefully in a protective pouch inside his backpack. Then he took the rod from the Medusa head.

Another series of grinding noises took place in the Medusa head as it once more turned upside down and locked into place beneath the stone column above it.

"Do you think Constantine knew about the Medusa's head?" Olympia asked.

"I do," Lourds answered. "His hand has been in everything we've touched so far."

"He kept his secrets very well."

Lourds silently agreed. Then he shouldered his backpack and headed out.

"Getting across the borders while we're being hunted isn't going to be easy," Joachim said.

"Really?" Lourds acted surprised. "Then isn't it lucky that we have a professional smuggler with a network of travel coordinators for contraband along with us?"

Cleena didn't turn around and didn't say anything, but Lourds could tell the young woman smiled.

Olympia scowled. “Don’t act like you planned this, Thomas,” she said quietly. “I know very well why you allowed that young woman to come with us.”

“Well, she is quite handy with weapons.”

Olympia said something completely unladylike.

CHAPTER 25

ARCH OF THE FOUR WINDS
VILLA DORIA PAMPHILI
ROME, ITALY
APRIL 3, 2010

"Thomas! Over here!"

Feeling beat up from the last few days of travel and all the stress he'd been under since they'd left Istanbul, Lourds didn't see his old friend and mentor for a moment. He stopped and stood still, looking for any unfriendly movement around him.

"You're clear, Professor." Cleena's voice echoed in Lourds's ear canal.

Although he'd worn the earwig for the last week or so, he still hadn't gotten used to the device or the need for it.

Father Gabriel Madeiro sat on a bench in the shade of a copse of trees. He was a short man, but filled with boundless energy. He was almost as wide as he was tall and his hair and beard had gone snow white so that it stood out against his dark skin.

He closed the fat book he was reading and used a thick forefinger to mark his place. Lourds knew without seeing the cover that it would be a thriller. Father Gabriel had introduced Lourds to James Bond and Jason Bourne at the same time he was instructing him in the intricacies of Latin. It had been Father Gabriel's love of language, of old dead books as well as potboilers, that had ignited the passion within Lourds.

When he got close enough, Father Gabriel grabbed Lourds in a powerful bear hug for a moment and lifted him clear off his feet. In his sixties, Father Gabriel remained a powerful man.

"It's so good to see you," Father Gabriel said when he released Lourds. "I miss having you underfoot."

"Hopefully these days I wouldn't be underfoot so much," Lourds said.

"I don't think you would." Father Gabriel waved Lourds to the bench. "You're having quite the career these days. Atlantis?" He raised his eyebrows. "Now that must have been exciting."

"It was."

"I read your book. Very enjoyable."

"I'm glad you thought so. I would have much rather told you the story in person."

"I would have much rather heard it in person." Father Gabriel lifted his shoulders and let them drop. "Unfortunately, I was doing some work in Rio de Janeiro."

"And avoiding the winter, as I recall." Lourds smiled, and for a moment the visit almost seemed casual. Except that he had the four rings he'd collected from Córdoba, outside Moscow, Jerusalem, and Istanbul.

"I missed winter, but not too terribly much." Father Gabriel's dark eyes regarded Lourds speculatively. "I wouldn't have figured you to turn out to be a criminal, though. I thought I'd mentored you better than that."

"A criminal?" That surprised Lourds.

Father Gabriel nodded. "The word I've gotten is that you absconded from Istanbul with some very important religious artifacts."

"Do you believe that?"

"Not for a minute."

Lourds grinned. "Well, actually that part is true."

"Really?" Father Gabriel gave him a look of mock shock.

"I seem to recall a certain Roman Catholic priest—"

"Who shall remain nameless."

"—who might *prefer* to remain nameless," Lourds went on, "that wasn't above a bit of skullduggery now and again."

"Perhaps a toe over the line here and there." Father Gabriel grinned in delight.

"You shouldn't have taken me along. You corrupted me."

"I didn't corrupt you. You were sixteen—"

"I was *twelve,*" Lourds objected.

"—and your babysitter—"

"Au pair."

"—had already corrupted you." Father Gabriel tugged at his beard. "Or perhaps you corrupted her. I forget how that went exactly."

"It was mutual corruption," Lourds said. "She was experienced, but I was better read."

"Another fault of mine, I suppose."

"You're the one that left those trashy spy novels lying around."

Father Gabriel grinned. "So I did."

Lourds was silent for a moment. "I've missed you."

"I know," the old man said solemnly. "I've missed you, too. The years grow shorter—"

"—and they move ever faster," Lourds finished. "I think I'm finally understanding what you were talking about."

"Good. My efforts weren't wasted after all. I'm relieved." Father Gabriel focused on Lourds. "How much trouble are you in?"

"A stone's throw away from the yawning mouth of Hell."

Father Gabriel rubbed his hands together. "It's been a long time since I could make any such claim. Tell me about it."

Seated there in the shade, with the whisper of the wind around them, knowing that Cleena MacKenna guarded him with her pistol only a short distance away and that her friend had a spy satellite watching over them, Lourds did.

He told Father Gabriel about the rapid trips to Russia where the statue of the Virgin Mary wept, and how they'd found the second golden ring within one of the foundations of the church that Patriarch Nikon had purposefully placed there when he built the church.

He told his friend of the journey to Jerusalem to the Church of the Holy Sepulchre where they'd discovered the third ring inside one of the walls near the ladder that no one had moved on the second story for over a hundred years. That ladder had marked the spot where the True Cross's shadow had fallen at the time of the Crucifixion.

And finally, Lourds told Father Gabriel of the pool at the Grand Mosque of Córdoba and how the waters had turned red as blood only a few days before their arrival there.

When he finished, Lourds sat back and waited to see what Father Gabriel's reaction would be.

"You think the Vice President of the United States is Lucifer?"

Lourds hated the way that sounded when said naked like that. "It's not just me," he answered defensively. "Several other people think that, too."

"Tell me, Professor, what do you think your colleagues at Harvard would think if you told them this?"

"Honestly, I shudder to think. My parking privileges would probably be revoked."

"You realize that they'd rather think you were a thief than a wild-eyed madman. Being a thief has a certain sexy cache."

"Do I look like a wild-eyed madman to you?"

"No, you don't. You look incredibly tired is how you look."

"I feel incredibly tired. These past few days, the last three weeks, have been a blur."

"And yet you found Lucifer."

"Truth be told," Lourds said, "I wasn't looking, and apparently it isn't that hard."

"Because he was looking for you."

A cold wind blew down the back of Lourds's shirt. "Not," he said, "a good thought."

Father Gabriel pulled at his beard. "The Vice President of the United States."

"Yes."

"That certainly takes some getting used to."

"It does."

Then Father Gabriel smiled. "But I'm not surprised to find out Lucifer decided to go into politics. Though it could have been worse."

"Worse?"

"He could have become a televangelist. If I'd had to guess, that's what I would have put my money on."

In spite of the situation, Lourds laughed.

Father Gabriel joined him, and then asked, "How can I help you, Thomas?"

"I need a place to stay where I can work," Lourds said. "Somewhere safe."

Father Gabriel nodded. "Of course."

"Enough room for my road companions."

"One of them is a woman?"

"Two, actually."

"Including the young redhead over there by that tree looking like she's innocently hanging about?"

Cleena cursed, eliciting a smile from Lourds. She made an obnoxious gesture at the priest.

"Ah, a young woman of genteel breeding, I see." Father Gabriel chuckled. "I take it you're in constant communication with her."

"Yes."

"Two women are harder to manage than one," Father Gabriel said. Lourds knew the double entendre was intentional.

"You said this man was like a father to you?" Cleena asked.

"Yes," Lourds answered.

"No wonder you have the morals of an alley cat."

"I meant *father* as in 'priest.' "

Across the distance, Cleena came to a halt and looked shocked. "You just let me flip off a priest?"

"It's not like you asked my permission or gave me any advance warning about what you were going to do."

"You are an *idiot*!"

"I'm not the one that flipped off the priest."

Father Gabriel waved to Cleena. Embarrassed, the young redhead waved back at him.

"She doesn't look like a linguist," the priest said.

"Thankfully she doesn't look like a gunrunner either," Lourds replied.

"I *so* hate you right now," Cleena said.

"She probably hasn't been to confession in a long time either," Lourds said.

Cleena poured pure invective into his ear.

"Besides sleeping quarters and a safe place where you can work," Father Gabriel asked, "is there anything else you need?"

"Books," Lourds said. "I'm going to need some of those special books the Vatican keeps locked away. I've got to break this language, and it's going to be even more difficult because it's been broken into four parts."

"Done." Father Gabriel stood. "Did you drive?"

"We took a cab."

"You *are* putting your life in God's hands." Father Gabriel started walking away. "Come along, Thomas. You can ride with me. I'll make a few phone calls and everything should be arranged by the time we get where we're going." He looked over his shoulder where Cleena trailed after them. "Your impertinent little friend can ride along as well, as long as she promises not to make a spectacle of herself."

Cleena waited tuntil Father Gabriel was looking away, then flipped Lourds off.

"God saw that," the priest said.

Tired and frustrated, Lourds entered the large kitchen where Father Gabriel managed several pots on the stove. Lourds knew from earlier inspection that the pots contained a selection of pastas and vegetables. The priest had even managed to bake bread and the warm, yeasty smell pervaded the large loft he had secured for them.

The loft had six bedrooms, three bathrooms, a massive kitchen and dining room, and a large common area. Lourds couldn't imagine the size of the family that lived there. He also couldn't imagine where they could've gone. When he'd asked Father Gabriel about it, the old priest had simply waved the question away.

"Some people have old sins that just won't go away," Father Gabriel said. "Every now and again, I'll give those people a chance to do something good. This is simply one of those times."

Maybe the accommodations were simple, but Lourds struggled with the puzzle of the final language.

Lourds filched one of the rolls that had just come out of the oven, then had to juggle it in both hands because it was so hot. When it had finally cooled down enough, he broke it open and slathered it with honey-wheat cream cheese.

Father Gabriel mopped at his sweaty brow with a shirtsleeve. "Progress?"

"A little, maybe. I can't tell. I've been at this so long that I can't tell up from down anymore."

"Of course you can. You're the finest student I've ever had. I'll take your failure personally."

"You could help, you know."

Father Gabriel stirred one of the pots, then reached for the next spoon. "No, I don't think so. You surpassed my meager abilities a long time ago. If I tried to help you, I'd just embarrass me and distract you."

Lourds ate part of the roll. The bread was delicious. "I can't help feeling I need a fresh pair of eyes on this."

"It'll come. Just give it time."

"We don't have time." Lourds glanced at the television over in the corner the kitchen.

The unrest in Saudi Arabia continued as Prince Khalid made war along his borders. Shia warriors had started slipping across the borders to shore up the rebellions spread throughout the country. To make matters worse, private security services hired by the United States and European corporations also continued to filter into the country to secure valuable assets.

The images on the television showed death and disaster, smoke and machine-gun fire and explosions. Helicopters and planes dropped from the sky when they were hit by enemy fire. Tanks exploded on the streets. Along the borders, soldiers fought with and taunted one another. Several times that broke out into violence.

"Even if you hadn't told me Lucifer was involved with this," Father Gabriel said softly, "I would have seen his hand in it."

"Where's the vice president?" Lourds asked.

"Still there in King Abdullah Economic City. It looks like Webster is going to get the troops he's been asking for."

"What troops?"

"Webster has asked for a military operation into the country."

"On Saudi Arabian soil?"

"Yes."

"There's not much chance of that starting an international incident, is there?" Lourds asked sarcastically.

"Surely not."

"Oh. Sarcasm."

"Yes. However the comment isn't without merit and truth. As it turns out, Webster's quite the organizer. He's already got several European and American corporations backing everything he's doing over there."

"They're all afraid of losing their money," Lourds said.

"Given all the recent economic frustrations, I can see where people who want to hold on to what they have are willing to take the extralegal step to maintain it."

"This isn't just extralegal. The Saudis won't tolerate it. The Middle East will be up in arms for generations to come."

"If we last that long," Father Gabriel agreed. "And by that, I mean the world."

"And no one sees this?"

"Of course someone sees this. But the people who have the muscle to make these things happen—politicians, big businessmen, and even religious figures—all believe what Webster has to say: If a stand isn't taken in the Middle East, a Western world stand, then they're going to lose everything they know."

"That's foolish."

"Do you really think so?"

Lourds didn't reply.

Father Gabriel looked at Lourds. "These are frightening times, Thomas. Money isn't what it used to be. Jobs aren't always there. Security is a half-remembered memory. This—this is something that's been building for a long time." He glanced at the television. "And it's coming home to roost."

Lourds woke at the desk where he'd been working nonstop for three days. He barely managed to halt a teetering stack of books before they fell over and scattered across the floor.

You've got to get some sleep, he told himself. But he knew that trying would be worthless. As soon as he went to sleep, he'd be awake again. Just like now.

He was so close to solving the puzzle of the rings. He'd worked with them so much that he could effortlessly picture them in his mind. They spun constantly, one over the other. It didn't seem to matter how many times he shifted their rotation or in what order he put them.

None of it made sense.

The words on the Scroll of Joy remained elusive, just out of his grasp.

It was maddening.

He crossed to the shopping bag that held his toiletries and spare changes of clothing. Joachim and his friends ended up not being as poor as church mice, and Cleena had money hidden in a variety of locations, though she seemed much more reluctant to part with it than Joachim and his brothers.

He padded quietly to the nearest bathroom, vaguely aware that it was the middle of the night and no one else was awake. He also failed to be aware that the tub was occupied until he was pulling his shirt over his head.

"What are you doing?"

Recognizing Cleena's voice, Lourds froze. "Sorry," he apologized hastily. "I didn't realize you were in here." Even though he knew he shouldn't, he couldn't resist peeking in the mirror in the hopes of catching her reflection there.

Fog blurred the image, though, and he cursed the luck.

"Don't get out," he quipped. "I'll see myself to the door."

Water shifted behind him as he grabbed his things.

"You don't have to go," Cleena told him.

Slowly, Lourds turned around, still half out of his shirt, and looked at her.

She lounged in the tub and the soapy water scarcely hid her breasts. She had her hair pulled back in a ponytail. Her freckled shoulders looked soft and rounded, but Lourds knew they would be corded with muscle.

"I don't have to go?" Lourds asked hoarsely.

"You don't. It's a big tub."

"Yes. Yes, it is."

"Well? What are you waiting for? Suddenly shy?"

"No." Lourds divested himself of his clothing and joined her. The water was freshly drawn, still so hot that he could barely ease into it. But his mind was on other things. The heaving water pushed at Cleena's breasts, revealing the strawberry-tipped nipples.

"What are you doing up?" she asked.

"Couldn't sleep."

"You seemed to be doing quite well when I checked on you earlier."

"I can't sleep now."

"Neither can I."

Lourds inhaled the fresh fragrance of the soap. He felt like he'd died and gone to heaven. She shifted and pushed her legs over his, allowing them each more room.

"I'll scrub your back if you'll scrub mine," Lourds offered.

Without a word, Cleena scooted toward him and wrapped her arms around his neck. He reciprocated.

"When I first saw you, I told myself this would never happen," she told him, staring into his eyes.

"When I first saw you, I'd hoped," Lourds said honestly.

She rolled her eyes at him. "That doesn't exactly make me feel special. If a woman walks by, you notice her."

"I'm very attentive." Lourds stroked the back of her neck and caused her to shiver.

"I know this isn't going to mean anything more than it does right now."

"Right now means a lot."

She cupped his face in her hands. "Right now does mean a lot."

Lourds filled his hands with her willing and pliant flesh. Her hot kisses boiled his blood and made his head spin, but he knew part of that was just the hot water and lack of sleep.

She reached into her purse and took out a condom, then she reached down for him. He was instantly ready as she put it on him. Positioning herself above him, she joined them, gripped the sides of the tub, and began a steady rocking motion that pushed them both away from fear and stress.

Lourds felt eyes staring at him. He also felt a slender, naked body pressed against him from behind. The lingering fragrance of perfume told him who was in the room, and—if memory served right and he believed it did—the lissome body behind him belonged to someone else.

This is not a good time to wake up, he told himself. *Just go back to—*

"I know you're awake," Olympia said. "I've slept beside you enough to know when you're actually sleeping."

Lourds opened his eyes, blinked away his bleary vision, and looked at her. "I suppose you have." He didn't try to apologize for Cleena's presence.

Olympia sat at his desk, arms folded and clearly not happy. "It's not like I was foolish enough to believe you would be faithful, Thomas, but I would have thought you'd have the decency to wait until we'd gone our separate ways."

"This wasn't exactly planned." Lourds sat up and draped the blanket across his thighs.

"Oh, and now you're going to be modest?"

Or protective, Lourds thought. He'd never been around Olympia when he'd had another lover. He didn't know what to expect from her, but if this was any indication, it wasn't going to be good.

"This—" Lourds searched for the right words. All those languages he knew, and he didn't know what to say. "This just sort of—"

"Oh my god," Cleena groaned. "Are you two going to just sit here and talk?" She sat up in bed, unmindful of her nudity in front of Olympia.

"This doesn't concern you," Olympia said. "This is between Thomas and me."

"Not when I'm the one you're going to talk about." Cleena pulled her hair back, used a rubber band from her wrist to put it in a ponytail, and got out of bed. "You know what? I don't need this. I need sleep. You two can figure out whatever it is you need to figure out. But I'm going to get a few more hours of sleep."

Even though he knew it probably wasn't in his best interests to, Lourds couldn't help watching Cleena. She was sleek and tawny like a cat, and her muscles bunched and rolled as she moved.

She scooped up his T-shirt from the floor and pulled it on, added her panties, then grabbed a pillow and a blanket and headed out of the room.

"She isn't much of a morning person," Lourds said.

Olympia arched an eyebrow. "I came in this morning to offer breakfast."

"Breakfast would be good," Lourds said, wanting desperately to be amenable.

"At this point, you can fix your own breakfast."

"Oh. Right. I can do that."

"How are you coming with the work you're supposed to be doing?"

"I don't know." Lourds sat up with his back to the headboard. "Every time I think I'm about to make a breakthrough, nothing works."

"Look, we'll talk about the relationship stuff at another time. Clearly, I'm not happy."

That was particularly clear.

"But I can be grown up about this. We're two adults."

Three, actually, Lourds thought, and barely managed to restrain himself from pointing that out. It would not have been good to mention.

"The main thing is translating the Scroll of Joy. You've been keeping up with the news coming out of Saudi Arabia?"

"Yes. Somewhat. Father Gabriel keeps me apprised."

"Things are getting worse there. American forces are massing in the Gulf. Many people are just waiting for the vice president to send in the troops."

"If they do that," Lourds said, "the Middle East is going to be torn up for years to come."

"I know, and when it is, it may well sweep into Istanbul and Turkey. I want my family safe, Thomas."

"I understand. I'm doing everything I can, Olympia."

"I know. I wasn't going to say anything to you. Then I saw you there with her—" Olympia shook her head.

At that moment, Lourds's sat phone rang. He was grateful for the reprieve.

Until he heard the voice.

"Professor Lourds?"

Lourds had heard the voice on a number of occasions. Usually on talk shows and dealing with the news people. The voice was an orator's dream.

"Yes," Lourds answered.

"I suppose you know who this is?"

"I do."

"What you don't know is that I have Cleena's younger sister in my custody. Not here in Saudi, but in the United States. Either you come meet me, or I'll kill her sister."

Lourds took a slow, cautious breath. "All right. Where do you want to meet?"

Fear chafed Lourds as he stood in the boarding gate at the airport. Late-night travelers filled the terminal. With everything going on in the Middle East, air travel had backed up and become problematic.

Olympia stood at his side. He felt the tension rolling off her in waves.

"You don't have to do this, you know?"

Lourds glanced at Olympia but didn't allow himself to be totally distracted from the people milling around them. After everything that had gone on these past few weeks, he was totally paranoid about the men and women surrounding him.

"I do." Lourds kept his voice quiet, barely audible above the air terminal noise and PA announcements.

"We don't know that Webster has Cleena's sister."

"Cleena says her sister is no longer where she left her in New York."

"How did Webster's people find her so fast?"

"He is the Vice President of the United States." *And a fallen angel.* Lourds didn't give voice to the last.

Olympia stared into his eyes. "This isn't what I brought you here for, Thomas."

Recognizing the guilt in her, Lourds made himself smile in spite of the fear and the doubt. "I know that."

"You weren't supposed to get hurt. You weren't supposed to be at risk." Tears glinted in her eyes.

"I don't think any of us had any right to expect safety and security under these conditions. I mean, look at who we've been chasing."

"I know."

"John of Patmos foresaw this." Lourds gripped her shoulders. "He gave us the weapon we need to defeat our enemy."

"I'd feel better if you'd translated the Scroll of Joy."

"I would, too."

"I don't mean any recrimination."

Lourds kissed her forehead and inhaled the scent of her. "I know."

"And I can't help feeling upset with you over Cleena."

Wrapping her in a hug, Lourds nodded. "I understand."

"I swear, you're like a kid in a candy store at times." Olympia turned her head up to his. "So juvenile and so selfish. But I think that's what makes you so passionate and so good at what you do."

"Maybe. And it could just be a flaw."

"I just want you to be safe."

"Me, too." For a moment, Lourds clung to her and thought about the situation he was about to walk into. Everything in him screamed at him to run. He wasn't a hero.

But the secret of the Scroll of Joy tantalized him. The symbols kept floating through his mind, constantly in motion and making different connections. Unfortunately, none of those connections was the right one. Fear might seek to drive him away, but curiosity kept him circling the flame even more strongly than saving Cleena's sister.

Darkness filled the airfield on the other side of the terminal glass. Jets moved, a stream of flashing lights as some took off and some landed. A fresh surge of passengers deplaned across the terminal.

Lourds caught movement in the glass and saw the reflection of the big man bearing down on him as he held Olympia. Lourds recognized the man instantly as one of those that had pursued them in Istanbul.

Even though the man wore civilian clothing, it didn't hide the military bearing. Lourds was pretty certain that the man didn't have a weapon in the airport, but that didn't make him any less dangerous.

"Professor Lourds." The man's voice was tight and controlled, carrying just enough to reach Lourds.

Lourds pushed Olympia back and inserted himself in front of her. His knees quivered and he tried to ignore it. "I'm Lourds."

"Of course you are." The man nodded toward one of the doors. "We've got a private plane waiting."

Lourds looked at the e-ticket in his hand. It had been waiting in his name at the front desk. "I guess this isn't any good."

"No."

Lourds took a deep breath.

"Do you have the scroll, Professor?" The man remained calm.

"Yes."

The hard eyes searched Lourds's. "I'm not going to ask for it here, Professor. My employer is going to ask for it himself. At that time, you will give it to him."

Lourds tried to speak and couldn't.

"If you don't," the man continued just as pleasantly as he had been speaking, "I'm going to kill you. If that's what my employer wishes. He's not one to trifle with."

Unable to say anything, Lourds nodded.

"Good. I'm glad we could clear that up. Now, kiss your lady friend good-bye and let's get going."

Olympia stepped in and hugged Lourds. Her voice when she spoke was a whisper meant only for his ears. "Be careful, Thomas."

Lourds hugged her tightly, then released her, picked up his rucksack, and proceeded the man out of the airport. When he stepped out of the terminal, the humid night closed in around him.

He controlled the fear running rampant in him only by concentrating on the permutations of the mysterious fifth language he felt certain would unlock the message contained in the Scroll of Joy.

CHAPTER

26

STONE GOOSE APARTMENTS
ZEYTİNBURNU DİSTRİCT
İSTANBUL, TURKEY
APRİL 7, 2010

Sevki sat at his computers and watched the monitors. One of them was dedicated to the news coverage coming out of Saudi Arabia. American and British news anchors and reporters focused on the massing of ships and military hardware. Reports continued to stream from Vice President Webster. The man didn't miss a photo op.

"Are you there?"

Cleena's voice drew Sevki back to the communications links he'd set up.

"Yes." Sevki's hands flew over the keyboards as his various snooper programs sought to break in through the Saudi Arabian cybernetic defenses. "Where are you?"

"Closing in on the coastline."

Sevki triangulated her transponder signal and tracked it back to the Saudi Arabian coast north of King Abdullah Economic City. "I see you."

"Let's hope you're the only one."

Tension knotted Sevki's guts. He felt certain several things—several lives—hung in the balance in Saudi Arabia at the moment even though he didn't comprehend everything that was going on. And one of those lives belonged to Cleena. She'd trusted him to help the ship she'd hired steer clear of Saudi Arabian and American protection.

"I am." Sevki scanned the surrounding terrain. "All the action is south of you." He stretched his fingers to relax and rejuvenate them. "For the moment, you're safe. But I don't understand how you hope to get around inside the city."

"Once you're in-country, getting around is easier."

Sevki stared at the images of the battles filtering across the news presentations. "It looks like a war zone over there."

"It is a war zone."

The calm acceptance in her voice surprised him. Then he thought about the fact that her sister had been taken. Sevki knew there was going to be hell to pay for the people responsible.

Cleena's voice drew him back into focus. "Do you know where Lourds is?"

Turning his attention back to the computers, Sevki tapped the keyboard. A map of King Abdullah Economic City filled one of the monitors. A blue light pulsed on the screen.

"He's still an hour or so out of the city." Sevki ran a GPS route and confirmed his estimate. "As long as Eckart stays with Lourds, we'll have him. If they separate, I can't guarantee anything."

"They won't separate. Eckart's one of Webster's top people."

Webster. Sevki still couldn't get over the fact that the United States vice president was behind the current unrest in the Middle East. Growing up in Turkey, where the American military had maintained a presence for so long, he'd gotten used to American politics and thinking. He'd never agreed with most of it, but he'd always believed the United States government was behind everything that went on.

Not one man.

"Our best guess is that Eckart is one of Webster's best men."

"I trust us."

And there's nothing else we have at this time, is there? Even as he thought that, Sevki felt guilty. He knew he should have faith. That was what this was all about, wasn't it? He pushed away the immensity of the task, limiting it to the part he had to play with the computers.

"We also have to hope that the GPS locator Eckart was tagged with wasn't given to someone else to lay down a false trail."

"So far that tracer is headed in the right direction. Let's play this one out."

"All right." Sevki judged the distance again. "You've got maybe fifty minutes before Professor Lourds lands there."

"Then we'll have to make the most of it, won't we?"

Silently, Sevki watched the pulsing blip slowly cross the computer monitor.

KING ABDULLAH ECONOMIC CITY

Webster stared at the screens depicting the street-to-street violence breaking out throughout the city. More battles erupted along the borders and the bloodshed was mounting.

"My, my, it does look like your war is getting off to a grand start, Mr. Vice President." Vicky joined Webster. Her eyes burned with intensity. Her headset ran along her jawline and she made notes one-handed on a PDA.

"Not big enough." Webster paced the floor and felt the excitement roaring within him. He had waited for a long time for this. "Not yet. But soon. How long will it be before your people are ready to go live with a broadcast?"

"Eighty or ninety minutes."

"You're certain I can get the broadcast attention I'm wanting?"

Vicky smiled at him and patted his cheek. "You are the man of the hour, Mr. Vice President. Stuck here in enemy territory, the world hovering on the brink of disaster. *Everyone* wants to talk to you. The hardest part of this is deciding who will be allowed their fifteen seconds of fame with you."

"Only fifteen seconds." Webster was firm about that. This was his show, his play, and he was going to run things.

"Of course, Mr. Vice President. You will be the man with all the answers. We're lining up the celebrity news and religious leaders now."

"Limiting the number of politicians?"

"No politicians. You're going to be talking to people the public of any country can recognize. Academy Award–winning actors. Several televangelists."

"All people who know how to work the limelight."

Vicky smiled. "Of course. And all people that support views of the Middle East as a hotbed of danger." She looked at him. "You're certain when you deliver your plea for help that we will get out of here? If Prince Khalid hasn't thought of holding us hostage before then, he will at that time."

"I'm counting on our young prince doing exactly that." Webster paused to watch a Saudi Arabian tank run over a mass of people. "That's why I asked you to have a live-camera crew ready to film our 'escape.' And that's why Eckart will be taking care of us at that time."

"Where is Eckart?"

Webster consulted his watch. "Eckart's plane should be touching down momentarily. He'll call me as soon as he's on the ground."

"And he'll have Professor Lourds?"

"Yes." Webster couldn't wait. Once the Scroll of Joy was in his hands, there would be no turning back. Everything would be his to control.

"You've never said what part the professor will play in this?"

Webster smiled. "A small one at best. And one that's very tragic."

"Will he be in the 'escape'?"

Webster shook his head. "No. I'm afraid Professor Lourds will have outlived any potential interest he might have in things before we get that far." In fact, the vice president was going to make certain of that.

After he took possession of that cursed Scroll.

Lourds rode in the cargo area of the big Chinook helicopter and tried to keep his thoughts ordered. He sat under guard, watched over by a half dozen armed men, including Eckart. All of them looked positively fearsome. Lourds honestly didn't believe he could have taken the weakest among them in a fair fight. Having six of them watch over him was merely adding insult to injury.

Even worse, they'd handcuffed him in the disposable plastic cuffs that he'd seen in the movies. At least they'd had the mercy to tie them in front of him, rather than behind his back. He could scratch his nose, which was itching furiously. He swayed and jerked to the Chinook's gallop as they approached the city.

Antiaircraft missiles exploded hot and bright against the night sky. Lourds drew his extremities in, as if being sprawled out too far might incite the antiaircraft gunners to aim better.

"Isn't there a chance we could get shot down?" Lourds asked nervously.

"Maybe," Eckart replied. "But this baby is armored up pretty good. Anything less than a direct hit isn't even gonna leave a scratch."

Lourds wished he could have emulated the man's simple faith, but Eckart knew his tools best. Lourds just gritted his teeth and prayed that he survived.

Several minutes later, the Chinook's approach altered. Then it heeled over at an angle and started descending. More antiaircraft bursts filled the air around them. A couple of them seemed to bounce off the helicopter.

"They're getting better, sir," one of the other soldiers said.

Eckart grinned. "For all the good it will do them. Wait until they're face-to-face with American special ops guys. You ask me, I wouldn't care for the locals' chances."

The men laughed, and the harsh barking noise sounded alien to Lourds's ears.

Not for the first time, he wondered if his decision to answer to Webster's demands had been his wisest course of action.

Don't worry, Cleena had told him when he prepared to meet. *I'll be there.*

Lourds hadn't asked how. He hadn't wanted to know because he'd been afraid all he would do is pick apart any plan she and Joachim presented. Joachim and the other monks were coming with her in a small strike force.

The Chinook settled down with a harsh bounce. More antiaircraft fire lit up the sky overhead. Lourds squirmed in his seat and tried to free the restraining belt.

"Hurry up," Eckart said. "We're sitting ducks up here." He reached across and flicked Lourds's belt free.

"Thanks," Lourds said automatically, forgetting just for an instant that he was a prisoner and not a guest.

"Don't mention it," Eckart said. Then he grabbed Lourds by the shoulder and propelled him through the cargo doors. "Get him into the building."

One of the soldiers grabbed Lourds by the handcuffs and hauled him across the rooftop. The man moved so quickly that Lourds almost fell. He envisioned himself getting dragged bodily across the rooftop.

"Incoming!" someone yelled.

The soldier pulling at Lourds whirled suddenly and clapped a big hand on top of Lourds's head. He shoved Lourds face first onto the rooftop. Lourds hit the ground hard and his breath exploded from his lungs. As he tried to recover, he spotted the Chinook rising from the rooftop like a fat goose.

A Saudi helicopter gunship settled into the airspace over the street. Then it opened fire with some kind of weapon. In the next instant, the Chinook turned into a whirling mass of fireballs and broken debris.

Razor-sharp pieces of metal sliced into the rooftop around Lourds but thankfully none of it touched him. Sour bile erupted against the back of his throat.

"I'm hit! I'm hit!" someone yelled.

"Get up!" The soldier accompanying Lourds got to his feet and yanked roughly on the plastic cuffs.

The hard material sliced into Lourds's hands. A slight trickle of blood flowed as he forced himself to his feet and followed the soldier.

Eckart and his men turned their weapons on the offending helicopter. Bullets chopped into the helicopter's body and Plexiglas nose. The pilot tried to get away, but he reacted too late.

Out of control, the helicopter veered away and slammed into a nearby building. For a moment it looked like a bug crushed up against a windshield. Only bugs didn't explode into thousands of fiery pieces.

The soldier guided Lourds into a rooftop access door and they entered.

Cleena stared through her binoculars as the Chinook exploded. The flare of the explosion made it look like the whole rooftop had caught fire. A half dozen men scattered across the building with fire extinguishers in hand as they fought the dozens of fires that spread out from the destroyed helicopter.

"Lourds?" Joachim stood at Cleena's side. His voice was quiet and controlled, but there was no mistaking the anxiousness in his words.

"He's all right." Cleena watched Lourds as he was hustled across the rooftop and shoved into the building's access hatch. Eckart trailed them and she let out a sigh of relief. "Sevki, do you mark the location?"

"Yes. The building that currently houses the vice president."

"Webster's still there?" Cleena and Joachim had been cut off from the news services while they'd made their way across the city. Thankfully the fighting had been so blatant that they'd managed to arrive at their destination with only a few skirmishes that left them bloody but without losing anyone.

"Yes. He's overdue for a response, though. Some of the news show anchors are starting to get fidgety."

"He's building the anticipation like a circus ringmaster." Joachim's disapproval was thick and angry.

Cleena silently agreed. "But he's not counting on us being here." However, she would have felt better if Lourds had been able to translate the Scroll. Without it, they wouldn't have a chance against their enemy.

Lourds tried to catch his breath as the soldiers forced him along an immaculate passageway. He couldn't take notice of the details around him. They passed the elevator by, which he couldn't believe given how far they evidently had to travel, and hurtled down six flights of stairs.

Just when he thought for certain he was going to collapse or throw up, the soldier pulled Lourds through a doorway instead of down another flight of stairs. They negotiated a maze of corridors and ended up at a suite of rooms.

Guards in black suits stood watch over the doors. They acknowledged Eckart and his men, then opened the doors and allowed them entrance.

United States Vice President Elliott Webster stood on the other side of the door. Other people, some of them with faces Lourds thought he recognized from the news, stood inside the room as well.

Webster smiled disingenuously. "Welcome, Professor Lourds. It's a pleasure to see you."

Cold dread filled Lourds. He wasn't sure if the feeling was a natural one at meeting Webster or if it was caused by the knowledge of who he was. For a moment, Lourds stood frozen.

Then the nearest soldier tripped Lourds and sent him sprawling. Hands bound in front of him, he landed in a heap before Webster, unable to keep his face from thudding into the floor. Groaning in pain, Lourds pushed himself to his knees before his enemy.

"I trust your trip wasn't too much of a hardship," Webster said, but his casual tone indicated that he didn't care.

"Not as bad as the last week or so has been," Lourds admitted. He was surprised that he spoke so casually.

"I would guess not. All those places, and all those treasures. It must have been exciting."

"Under better circumstances," Lourds said, "and if we'd had more time, I would have considered the time spent pleasant."

Webster smiled. "You haven't lost your sense of humor."

Lourds didn't respond.

"That's one of your traits that I really admire," Webster said. "I enjoyed your books immensely. Especially *Bedroom Pursuits.* Although it was a little tame for my taste."

"Glad I was able to provide a little diversion."

"You know, since your capture, I've even toyed with the idea of having you as my chronicler."

"Chronicler?"

"Of course. Once I begin my ascent into power, I'm going to be famous. People would love to read about me, and you've already got quite a legion of literary admirers." Webster paused and shrugged. "Admittedly, I'm already famous, but what happens here—and in the rest of the world shortly thereafter—will make me even more famous." He locked eyes with Lourds. "And you're going to be part of it."

"Anything I can do to help." Lourds looked at the men around him, wondering why they didn't react to what Webster was saying.

"They don't hear exactly what I'm saying to you," Webster said. "That's just one of my abilities. When I speak, I can make the listener hear whatever I want them to."

"Must have been a great trick back in junior high school."

"You have no idea. Truly." Webster held a hand out and gazed at it. "When I'd first decided on this route for my return to this world, the idea gave me pause. The idea of allowing myself to be born into a mortal body, to deal with the frailties and hardships of the flesh—not all of them, mind you—was anathema to me. But now I'm quite used to it. The serpent's body was more elegant, more sure, but the pleasures are enhanced dramatically in this form."

Lourds remained on his knees. He gazed around the room and spotted a woman and three men. One of them sat at a laptop and occasionally hit the keyboard.

"My brain trust," Webster said. "Without their networks and resources, I couldn't have come this far."

"It's good to have friends," Lourds said. "Especially when you're planning on taking over the world."

"It's a big job."

"One supposes."

"Indeed. You wouldn't have gotten this far without your friends. Then again, the Scroll of Joy might have been left lingering out there as well. So we both succeeded in our pursuits."

"Too bad they weren't mutually exclusive and mutually beneficial."

"You'll have to take that up with God," Webster said. "I'm not the one that plays by the rules. If it were me, I wouldn't have created a weapon that my enemy could have used against me."

"And maybe he was a little too understanding when it came to letting his greatest enemy live."

Webster grinned. "Oh, he didn't have a choice about that after he'd created the light and the dark. You simply can't have one without the other. And he did try to keep you humans from knowing such things as good and evil existed."

Lourds's stomach turned and threatened to empty. Even though he knew who he was talking to, part of him wanted to deny that was what was really going on.

"Exactly." Webster walked over to Lourds and almost interrupted his personal space. "You can see me, hear me, know who I am, and your first impulse is to deny my identity. You people grasp at a God you can't touch and struggle to believe in, but you deny me." He smiled. "Of course, that doesn't stop you from blaming me and my influence for everything that goes wrong in your lives."

"I think most people blame God for that."

Webster backhanded Lourds without warning, so fast that Lourds didn't register the blow until his head had popped back and pain filled his right cheek and temple. He worked his jaw, not certain at first if it hadn't been broken.

None of the people in the room reacted to the blow.

"Your insolence won't be tolerated," Webster stated in a low, dangerous voice. "Neither will your continued existence if you insist on being unpleasant."

Lourds hoped that Cleena and Joachim had found entrance to the building. Their plan had been desperate, but there'd been no other way that allowed Lourds to get in close to Webster. Things would have been better if he'd already had the Scroll translated. Stubbornly, though, the manuscript's secrets continued to elude him. But he felt certain it was right there. Symbols swam through his head. All he needed was the key to how they fit together.

"You people need me," Webster said. "The God you revere has left a void in your lives. He doesn't touch you every day. I will."

"Control, you mean?"

"Guide."

"Slavery by another name."

Webster exhaled. "Do you know how many people are lost out there? How many that are uncertain how they're supposed to proceed in their daily lives?"

Lourds didn't reply.

"All of them," Webster said. He closed a fist in front of Lourds's face. "They want a god that will be in their daily lives. One that will provide meaning and establish goals. One that will validate them in immediate response. That's why people will turn to me."

"I'm not turning to you." The words were out of Lourds's mouth before he realized it. "Not all of them will."

"Then the ones that don't will die. I will crush them and leave their rotting corpses in the street."

"You may be gifted, but that doesn't mean everyone will follow you. There are others who know you for who you truly are."

Webster shook his head. "They are the walking dead. They've already ceased living and don't know it yet."

"That's the whole problem of free will," Lourds said softly. "Such a small, seemingly insignificant thing. Yet so powerful."

"A fascinating thing. Mankind's greatest freedom and its greatest servitude. All rolled up into one package. If you ask me, I'm offering a much better deal."

"Doesn't matter. In the end, you're going to be defeated."

"Bah. Only if you believe the rhetoric."

"John of Patmos didn't see it as rhetoric."

"John of Patmos was a senile old man. Even the Roman Catholic Church agrees with me there."

"He foretold your coming."

"Of course he did. I've only been here since *what*? The beginning of the human race?"

"And you haven't managed to take over the human race yet." Lourds shook his head. "That must be very frustrating."

"Subjugate. Destroy." Webster shrugged. "It's all the same to me. I've already made a lasting mark in this world. People have talked about me, feared me, since time began." He smiled. "I can live with that."

Lourds felt the increased chill from the evil that clung to the man. It was like nothing Lourds had ever before experienced. It left him terrified and shaking.

Webster checked his watch. "I don't have a lot of time left." He waved at room next door. "I've got a television crew waiting to hear my impassioned plea for help from the president. I promise, it's going to be a barnburner. Then, of course, there's going to be the whole 'escape from Saudi Arabia and the evil Prince Khalid' thing I've got planned."

"A barnburner? I knew there'd be fire involved."

Webster chuckled. "It would be amusing to keep you around, Professor Lourds. But you're much too dangerous to me. After the Brotherhood of the Scroll never used John of Patmos's final document, especially after it was broken apart and hidden away—"

"You knew about that?"

"Of course I did. Who do you think engineered the whole affair?"

Lourds thought about that and couldn't believe it. But yet, it made sense.

"I persecuted those people," Webster bragged. "And, occasionally, I found a weak one and exploited him. Over the years, fewer and fewer of them knew what the Scroll was or how to read it." He paused. "I thought it had actually been lost forever during the Fourth Crusade when I managed to split the Church."

"You did that?"

Webster performed a small bow. "Of course. Playing to my strengths. Put any two people together, anywhere in the world, and I'll be there. I am the paranoia that chases after free will. I am the lingering doubt and the malice over betrayal." He paused. "Now, let's see the Scroll."

Eckart stepped forward and handed Webster the wooden cylinder. The vice president uncapped the cylinder and gently prised the contents into his waiting hand. The scroll inside slid free and he caught it deftly. For just a moment, he held it, then he cast it aside with an obscenity and stared at Lourds.

"I did warn you about playing games. Where is the Scroll of Joy, Professor Lourds?"

Holding her silenced pistol before her, Cleena half ran through the underground passage that led to the building where Lourds had been taken. The hallway ran longer than she'd expected.

"You're sure this is the way?"

"Yes." Sevki didn't hesitate. "Getting the blueprints of those buildings was a major undertaking. I can't begin to express how much you owe me."

"After I help save the world, maybe we can discuss how large that debt is."

"Yeah. That."

Sevki didn't sound like he believed everything that was going on. Cleena didn't blame him. Even after everything she'd seen, she had trouble believing it herself. *That's one of Webster's strengths,* she reminded herself. Joachim and the Brotherhood had warned them.

Abruptly the hallway ended in a foyer that contained a number of elevators.

"Here." Joachim went to the right and found the door to a stairwell. He started to pull it open.

"No," Sevki interrupted. "The door is alarmed."

Joachim drew his hand back.

"Can you bypass the alarm from there?" Cleena stepped closer and looked at the alarm system.

"No. I tried. If I hack in, I might set it off. Then you guys are screwed."

Cleena put her pistol away and pulled her toolkit from inside her jacket. She wore body armor, as did the monks. Tension filled her body as she concentrated on the lock.

"Is there anything I can do?" Joachim stood nearby.

"I'll get it." Perspiration dripped through Cleena's eyebrows. "Sevki, do you have access to the building's security cameras."

He sounded distant when he replied. "I will. Possibly before you're through that lock. They've got someone inside that has enhanced the cybersecurity already in place on-site." He paused, then sounded pleased. "This guy is good."

"Are you through?" Cleena popped the first round of locks and went after the second.

"I've never failed you yet."

"Maybe we could hold the self-congratulations until the post-mortem." As soon as the words were out of her mouth, Cleena realized how unfortunate the term was.

"Let's refer to that as a debrief, shall we?"

Cleena ignored him as the last of the electronic locks gave way. Holding her breath, she put her hand on the door and pulled.

The door opened and she led the way inside with her pistol. She went up the steps rapidly.

Fear rattled through Lourds as he realized the full extent of the danger he was in. He hadn't known for certain if Webster would know the difference in the scrolls, but evidently something tied them together.

"I will not be trifled with," Webster roared. "I will have that girl killed." He took his phone from his pocket.

"All right." Lourds took his hat off with his cuffed hands and reached inside it. He removed the protective plastic bag containing the Scroll of Joy from behind the liner. It had amazed him that a document supposed to be powerful enough to save the world could fit behind his hatband.

Webster approached and reached for the package. Something, Lourds wasn't sure what, stayed his hand. He gestured at Eckart. "Seize that Scroll."

Eckart plucked the Scroll from Lourds's zip-tied hands. "Do you want to check it?"

"No." Webster wiped his hands on his pants. "No. That's the Scroll. I'm convinced of that. Just keep it with you."

Eckart tucked the document inside his jacket.

"Now, Professor Lourds," Webster said, "welcome to the end of the world as you know it. Within the next few minutes, the course of human events will drastically change." He looked at Eckart. "Bring him along." Then he turned and headed for the next room.

With Eckart's rough hand gripping his neck, Lourds followed Webster.

The next room looked like a view of perdition. Blood smeared the walls and bullet holes had chopped into the fine paneling. A half dozen dead bodies littered the floor.

Webster waved theatrically. "Does it appear convincing enough to you?" He jostled one of the corpses with a foot. "There are a lot of bodies out in the streets waiting to be claimed."

Not believing what he was seeing, Lourds glanced at the rest of the people in the room. No one seemed surprised or appalled. Lourds didn't know if it was because of Lucifer's powers or because the others had invested so heavily in the outcome of Webster's machinations that they didn't care.

Reaching down, Webster daubed fresh blood from a dead man, then carefully streaked his face with it. He grinned like a child at Halloween. "Effective, yes? And everyone will believe this is my blood."

Lourds didn't say anything.

"Come now, Professor. In your profession, with all the lectures and the attention, you've developed a sense of the theatric."

"Not for this," Lourds said. "I'll never develop anything for this except revulsion."

Webster chuckled and applied blood to the back of one of his hands. "The devil is in the details, Professor. Haven't you ever heard that?"

Lourds remained silent.

"Now, I've got a plea to make. One that will bring American military forces into this country in a way that has never before been seen, and one that will not be tolerated by Prince Khalid or the rest of the Middle East." Webster nodded at a woman. "Let's do this."

A camera crew walked in front of Webster and the lights came on.

Silently, Lourds watched and hoped that Cleena and Joachim were somewhere near.

"I'm in."

Cleena stood outside the stairwell door and gazed down the hallway. Guards stood at posts. "Good. Now find Lourds for me." She held her pistol in both hands.

"Got him. Two rooms over. Hey, the television news stations just broke for a special news bulletin coming live from Vice President Webster."

That, Cleena thought, *can't be good.*

She went through the door, raising the pistol and shooting the first man in the face as he tried to bring up his rifle. Joachim and the monks followed.

"My fellow Americans." Webster spoke eloquently into the microphone. "I come to you in a moment of dire straits. As you know, I came to Saudi Arabia on a peacekeeping mission. Unfortunately, things have gone badly awry here and I haven't been so successful as I'd hoped."

Lourds gritted his teeth and bit back a scathing retort that he felt certain wouldn't be well received.

"Now I find myself in as much danger as I'd hoped to save you from," Webster continued. "I've attempted—several times—to negotiate some kind of cease-fire, but I believe I've reached an impasse." He waved his hands to include the dead bodies around him. "As you can see, several of the support crews here have given their lives trying to help me."

As Lourds gazed around the room, he was surprised to see that a few of the television crew were openly weeping. He was certain they'd known none of the dead people.

"At this point," Webster said, "I feel I have no recourse other than to ask the president to issue orders that—"

The door burst open as Cleena, Joachim, and the monks filled the room. Fully automatic gunfire filled the room. Lourds threw himself to the floor and noticed that Eckart did the same.

A trio of bullets thudded into Webster's chest. Surprised, he glanced down and saw blood seeping into his shirt.

Then the room became hell on earth as bullets tore through the air and the monks threw flash-bang grenades into the room. Several of the television cameras became instant casualties of live rounds. The camera crews scrambled for safety.

"Get Lourds!" Webster yelled. He was lost somewhere in the haze of fog and bright lights from the flash-bangs. "Get Lourds now!"

Eckart grabbed Lourds and yanked him to his feet. When Webster ran for a door on the other side of the room, Eckart dragged Lourds at Webster's heels.

More shots rang out.

Desperate, not wanting the Scroll to be lost, Lourds dropped and tangled Eckart's legs in his. Eckart stumbled and fell, falling on top of Lourds in a loose-limbed sprawl. Adrenaline raced through Lourds's body as he continued to kick Eckart in the face. Eckart fought back, but one of Lourds's kicks caught him in the temple and stretched him out prone.

Overcoming his surprise, Lourds grappled with the unconscious man and found the combat knife secured to the equipment vest. Holding the knife to cut the plastic cuffs was difficult, but Lourds managed.

Webster saw what was happening and rushed back toward Lourds. "No!" Webster sounded desperate and near hysterical.

Lourds took out the Scroll of Joy and prayed that it would work. As he surveyed the symbols, his mind chugged through the final permutations to the solution of the puzzle. The rings hadn't all revolved in a stack after all. They had fit together on an axis, forming a cross. Once he'd realized that, the translation—though still incredibly difficult—was at least doable.

As he read, the characters on the Scroll turned ice blue and the parchment felt freezing.

"I name you Lucifer," Lourds said. *"I name you defiler and destroyer."*

With an inarticulate cry of rage, Webster burst through the rolling scarlet fog from the flash-bangs and rushed at Lourds. Instinctively, Lourds took a step back, but he was too late. However, before the vice president could close on him, a wall of force shimmered into being and held him back. Screaming and frothing at the mouth, Webster battered at the invisible wall.

"Stop!" he roared. "Stop!"

Lourds ignored him and continued. *"I name you false and usurper. I name you deceiver and lord of lies. I name you tempter and vain pride."*

"Would you like to know where the lost library of Alexandria is?" Webster pleaded. His eyes looked hollow and yellow, like those of a rabid animal.

Lourds hesitated.

"I can get you your heart's desire," Webster promised. "All these years you've searched for the library? I can fix it so you can find those books. Everything you've ever wanted. It's yours just for the asking."

For a moment Lourds imagined what it might be like to walk the halls of that great library. He'd gotten a taste of that when he'd found lost Atlantis. He'd even saved a few books from that event. Some of them he hadn't yet translated.

"I can give Alexandria to you," Webster said in a crazed voice.

It was the most temptation Lourds had ever faced. He felt his resolve weakening, then he pushed his desires away. He didn't want someone to simply hand him the lost library of Alexandria. After all this time of searching for it, he wanted to find it. That was what the dream was all about: the search.

"I name you," Lourds continued, focusing on the task at hand, drawn by the solution he'd figured out, *"so that others may know your falseness, too. Let each man whom you have befriended recognize you as no friend from this moment on. Let those who think they know your love recognize only the manipulation you offer. In the name of the Almighty God, I banish you from this disguise you have woven for yourself."*

When he stopped reading, Lourds didn't know what to expect. Webster still stood before him, but the man looked hammered, totally defeated. Slackness drained the anger and fear from his face.

Then the smoke from the grenades swirled up around Webster and obscured him. Fearful, heart hammering in his chest, Lourds waited for Webster to come at him through the smoke. Then the scarlet haze cleared, and when it did—Webster had disappeared with it.

"Don't just stand there," Cleena said as she joined Lourds. "You're going to get shot."

Holding on to the Scroll, Lourds took cover behind a desk. Most of the gunfire had died away.

"Where is Webster?" Cleena reloaded her weapon.

"I don't know."

"Did he leave?"

"I read the Scroll to him."

Cleena glanced at him. "You translated it?"

"I did."

"And Webster?"

Lourds shook his head. "Disappeared."

Cleena shot a guard that closed on them, then got Lourds headed back for the door she'd come through.

Slowly at first, afraid that the men who hadn't gone down before Cleena's sharpshooting skills would keep on shooting, Lourds crept from the room. Joachim and the monks—all of them amazingly still alive and convinced that it had been an act of God—joined them. All of them seemed dazed and unsure of what had happened. No one else had seen Webster disappear.

In minutes, Lourds and the others reached the downstairs lobby. Together, they made their way out of the building.

No one followed and the American forces were put on standby.

EPILOGUE

VATICAN CITY
APRIL 8, 2010

Lourds sat in one of the great libraries in the underground network beneath the Vatican. Father Gabriel occupied a comfortable chair across from him. If it hadn't been for everything that had happened the last few weeks, it would have felt like the old days when Lourds had studied there.

They watched WNN together.

"The search for United States Vice President Elliott Webster continues," the news anchor reported. "No one knows how or when the vice president disappeared from the hotel where he'd been a virtual prisoner in Saudi Arabia for the last several weeks."

"Do you think they'll find him?" Lourds asked.

Father Gabriel shook his head. "Not in this world."

"What do you think the eventual conclusion will be?"

"I don't know. Are you going to write a book about this?"

"A story without an ending?" Lourds smiled. "Not likely."

"Oh, so you think you could sell prospective readers on

the possibility that Lucifer, at least temporarily, found a home in the office of the vice president?"

"Sure," Lourds said. "But it has to have an ending."

"What kind of ending?"

"If they'd found Webster's corpse."

"Do you realize that you still refer to him as Webster?"

Lourds had noticed that. "I feel more comfortable with that name. Maybe saying the other—" He hesitated.

"Gives him more strength in our world?"

"Maybe that."

"Superstitious nonsense."

Lourds chuckled at that. "After everything we've been through and seen, you can say that?"

"Definitely. Lucifer has as much power in this world as we choose to give him. No more, no less. We can't lead him to victory, nor can we push him into defeat."

"I have to say in my own defense, he looked pretty defeated the last time I saw him."

"No. His fate has already been ordained by God. Satan doesn't have free will. Just as God knew Lucifer would fall from the heavens, he also knows Lucifer will ultimately be defeated."

"That's a discussion that would take far too long to explore at this point, and I do have things to do."

Father Gabriel grinned. "You have a woman waiting for you?"

"I do," Lourds admitted.

"Which one?"

"Both, actually."

Father Gabriel's eyebrows shot up.

"Not at the same time," Lourds said.

"Thank God you've got some morality left."

"Though the possibility is certainly of merit and worth investigating."

Father Gabriel covered his ears. "Don't. I'm an old man and you've been like a son to me. A wayward son, perhaps, but a son nevertheless. I really can't bear any further disillusionment."

Lourds reached into his backpack and took out the Scroll of Joy in its wooden cylinder. "I've talked it over with Joachim. We're both of the opinion that you would be the best person to offer safekeeping for this."

"Should Lucifer rise again."

"Exactly."

Father Gabriel took the cylinder. "I shall do my very best."

"As I knew you would." Lourds plucked his hat from the table. "Now, if you'll excuse me, I've got a picnic lunch to get to. Perhaps a scenic boat ride and a walk in the park for later."

"I would think you would want to rest."

Lourds stood and clapped his hat on his head. Then he smiled. "The business you're in, I'd think you'd know there's no rest for the wicked."

"You're not wicked." Father Gabriel stood and hugged Lourds fiercely. "You're just restless. Now go. I'm sure there are a lot more adventures waiting out there for you."

"I'd like to think I'd had my fill of them."

"There's still the library of Alexandria waiting out there somewhere."

Lourds smiled. "I know. Maybe one day." He gathered his backpack, slung it over his shoulder, and took his leave.